VINDICATION

PUBLISHED BY

TOP COW PRODUCTIONS, INC.

LOS ANGELES

To find the comic
shop nearest you, call:
1-888-COMICBOOK

Want more info? Check out:
www.topcow.com
for news & exclusive Top Cow merchandise!

For Top Cow Productions, Inc.
For Top Cow Productions, Inc.
Marc Silvestri - CEO
Matt Hawkins - President & COO
Elena Salcedo - Vice President of Operations
Vincent Valentine - Lead Production Artist
Henry Barajas - Director of Operations
Dylan Gray - Marketing Director

IMAGE COMICS, INC.
Robert Kirkman—Chief Operating Officer
Erik Larsen—Chief Financial Officer
Todd McFarlane—President
Marc Silvestri—Chief Executive Officer
Jim Valentino—Vice President
Eric Stephenson—Publisher/Chief Creative Officer
Jeff Boison—Director of Publishing Planning
& Book Trade Sales
Chris Ross—Director of Digital Sales
Jeff Stang—Director of Direct Market Sales
Kat Salazar—Director of PR & Marketing
Drew Gill—Art Director
Heather Doornink—Production Director
Nicole Lapalme—Controller
IMAGECOMICS.COM

VINDICATION

CREATED BY **MATT HAWKINS & MD MARIE**

WRITTEN BY **MD MARIE**
PENCILS BY **CARLOS MIKO**
INKS BY **DEMA JR.**
COLORS BY **THIAGO GONCALVES**
LETTERS BY **TROY PETERI**

PRODUCTION BY **CAREY HALL**
EDITED BY **ELENA SALCEDO**
EDITOR IN CHIEF **MATT HAWKINS**

COVER BY **JONATHAN DAVIS**

CHAPTER 1

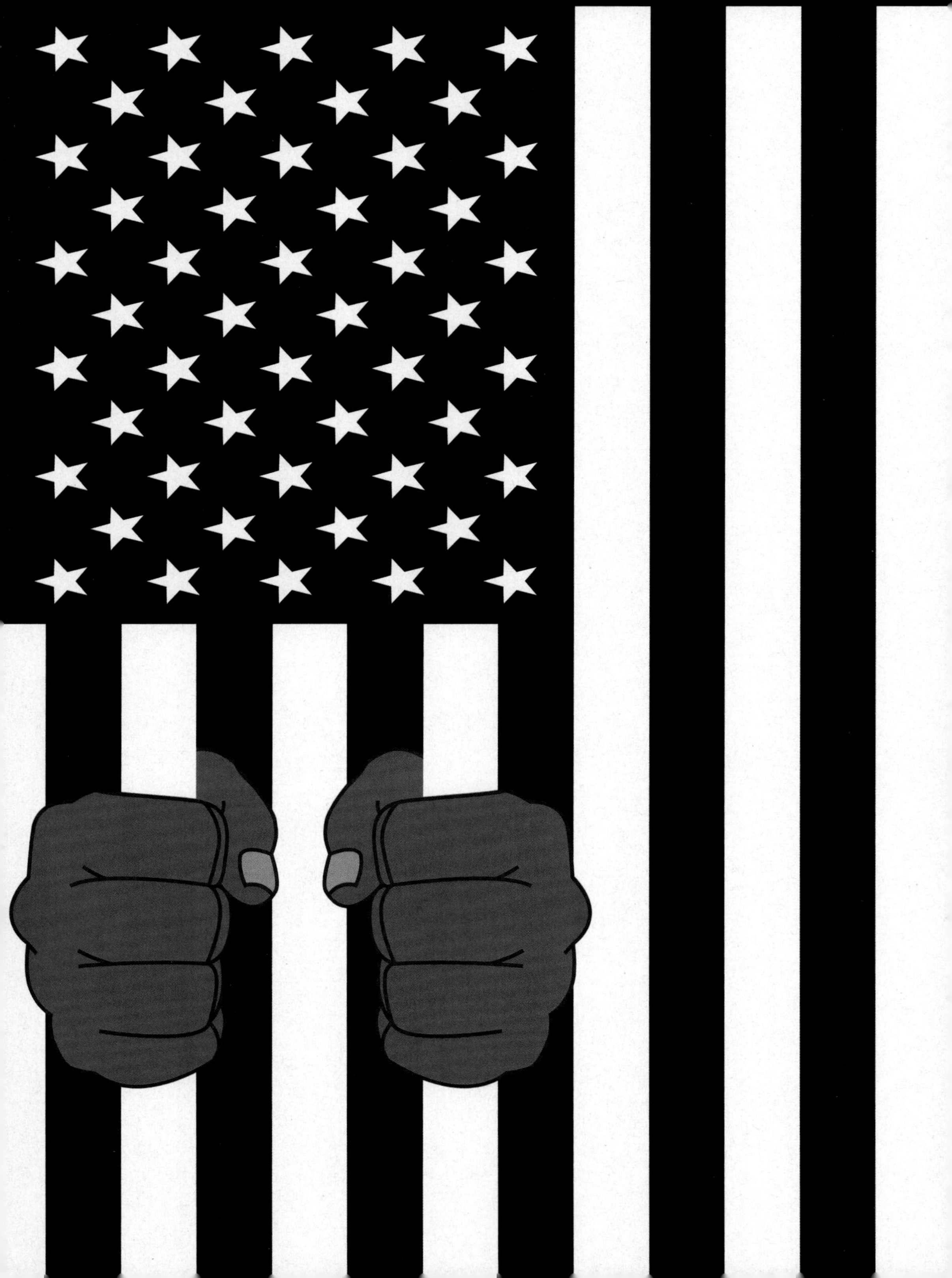

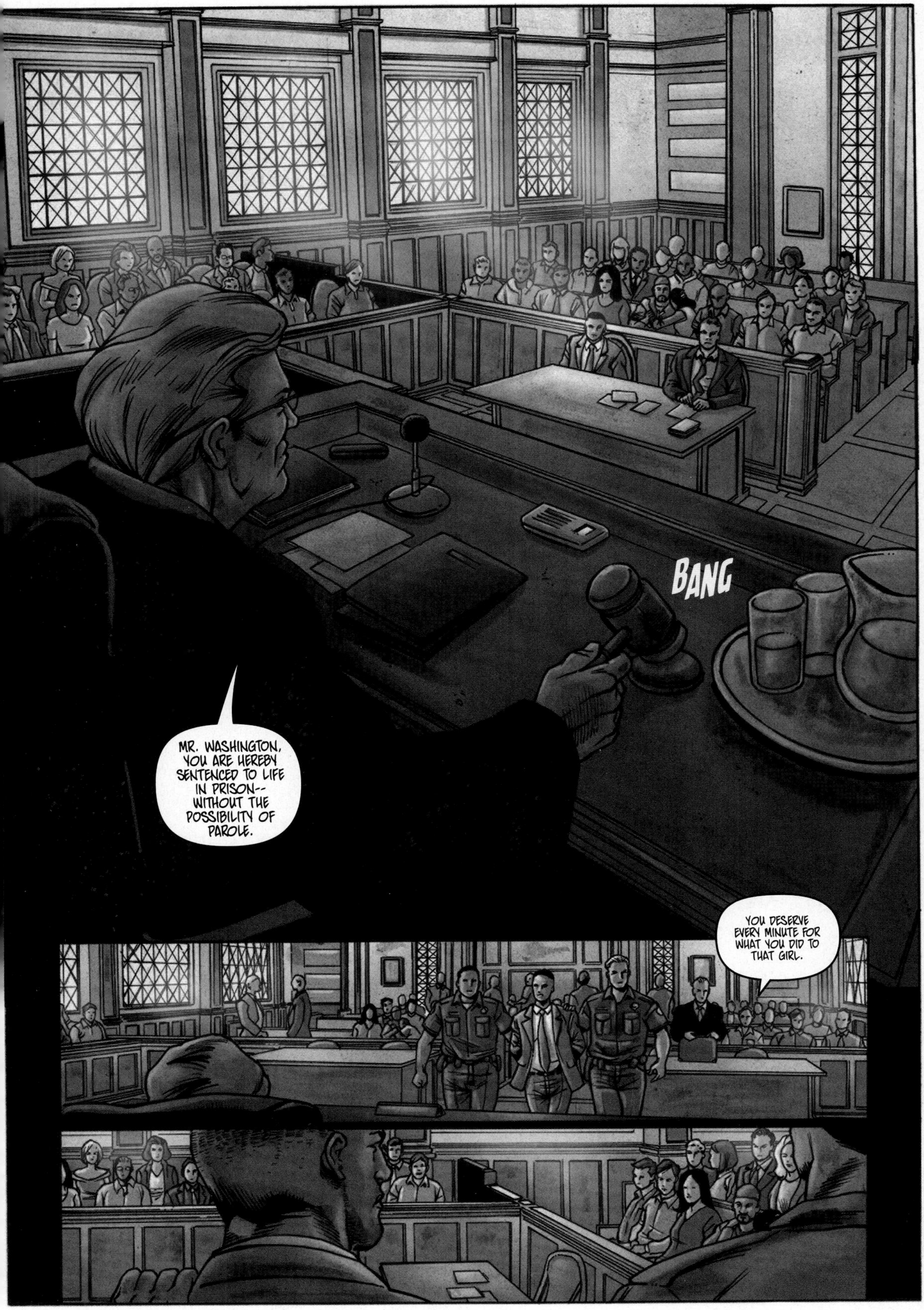
BANG
MR. WASHINGTON, YOU ARE HEREBY SENTENCED TO LIFE IN PRISON--WITHOUT THE POSSIBILITY OF PAROLE.
YOU DESERVE EVERY MINUTE FOR WHAT YOU DID TO THAT GIRL.

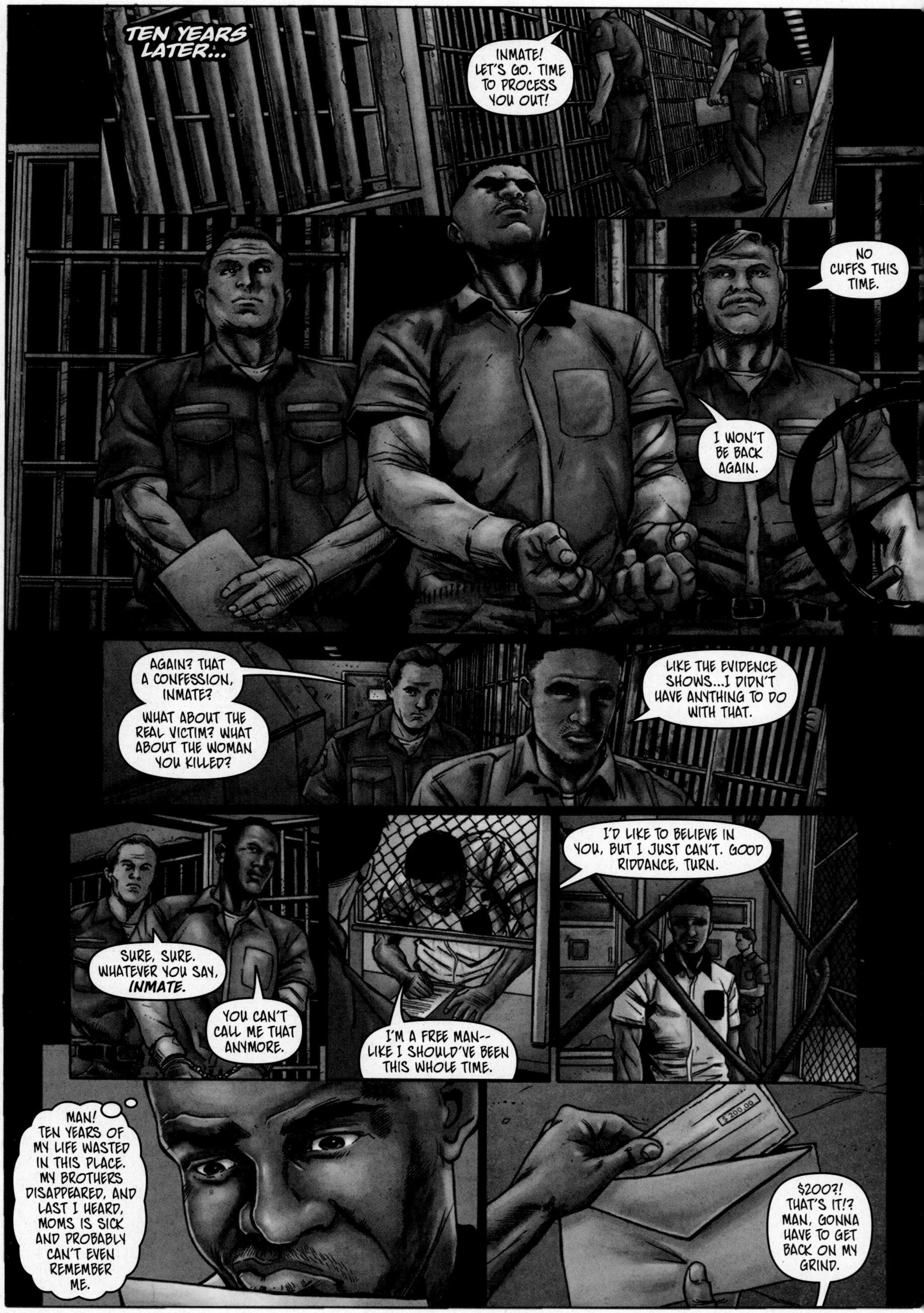
TEN YEARS LATER...
INMATE! LET'S GO. TIME TO PROCESS YOU OUT!
NO CUFFS THIS TIME.
I WON'T BE BACK AGAIN.
AGAIN? THAT A CONFESSION, INMATE?
WHAT ABOUT THE REAL VICTIM? WHAT ABOUT THE WOMAN YOU KILLED?
LIKE THE EVIDENCE SHOWS...I DIDN'T HAVE ANYTHING TO DO WITH THAT.
SURE, SURE. WHATEVER YOU SAY, INMATE.
YOU CAN'T CALL ME THAT ANYMORE.
I'M A FREE MAN-- LIKE I SHOULD'VE BEEN THIS WHOLE TIME.
I'D LIKE TO BELIEVE IN YOU, BUT I JUST CAN'T. GOOD RIDDANCE, TURN.
MAN! TEN YEARS OF MY LIFE WASTED IN THIS PLACE. MY BROTHERS DISAPPEARED, AND LAST I HEARD, MOMS IS SICK AND PROBABLY CAN'T EVEN REMEMBER ME.
$200?! THAT'S IT!? MAN, GONNA HAVE TO GET BACK ON MY GRIND.

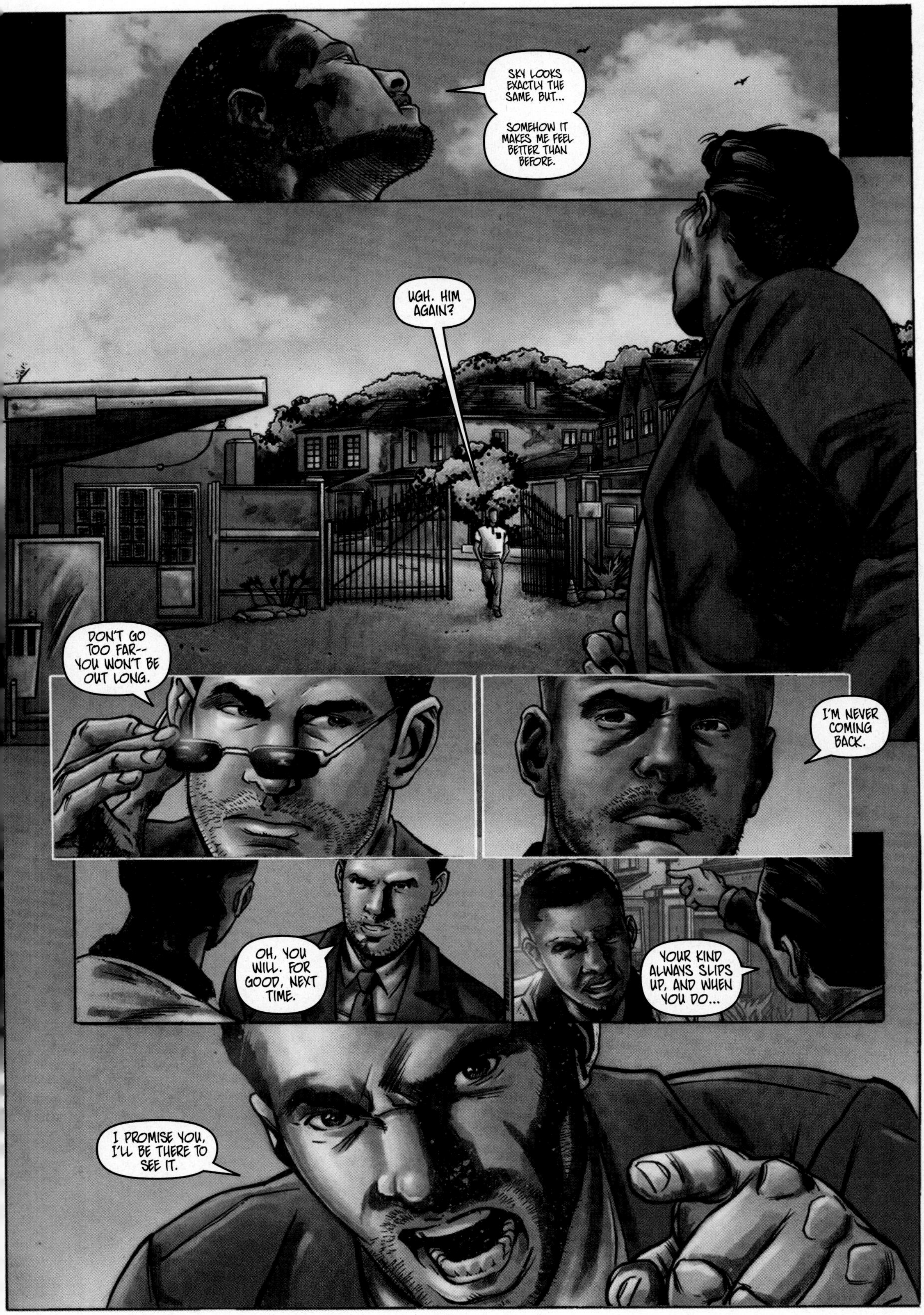
SKY LOOKS EXACTLY THE SAME, BUT...
SOMEHOW IT MAKES ME FEEL BETTER THAN BEFORE.
UGH. HIM AGAIN?
DON'T GO TOO FAR-- YOU WON'T BE OUT LONG.
I'M NEVER COMING BACK.
OH, YOU WILL. FOR GOOD, NEXT TIME.
YOUR KIND ALWAYS SLIPS UP, AND WHEN YOU DO...
I PROMISE YOU, I'LL BE THERE TO SEE IT.

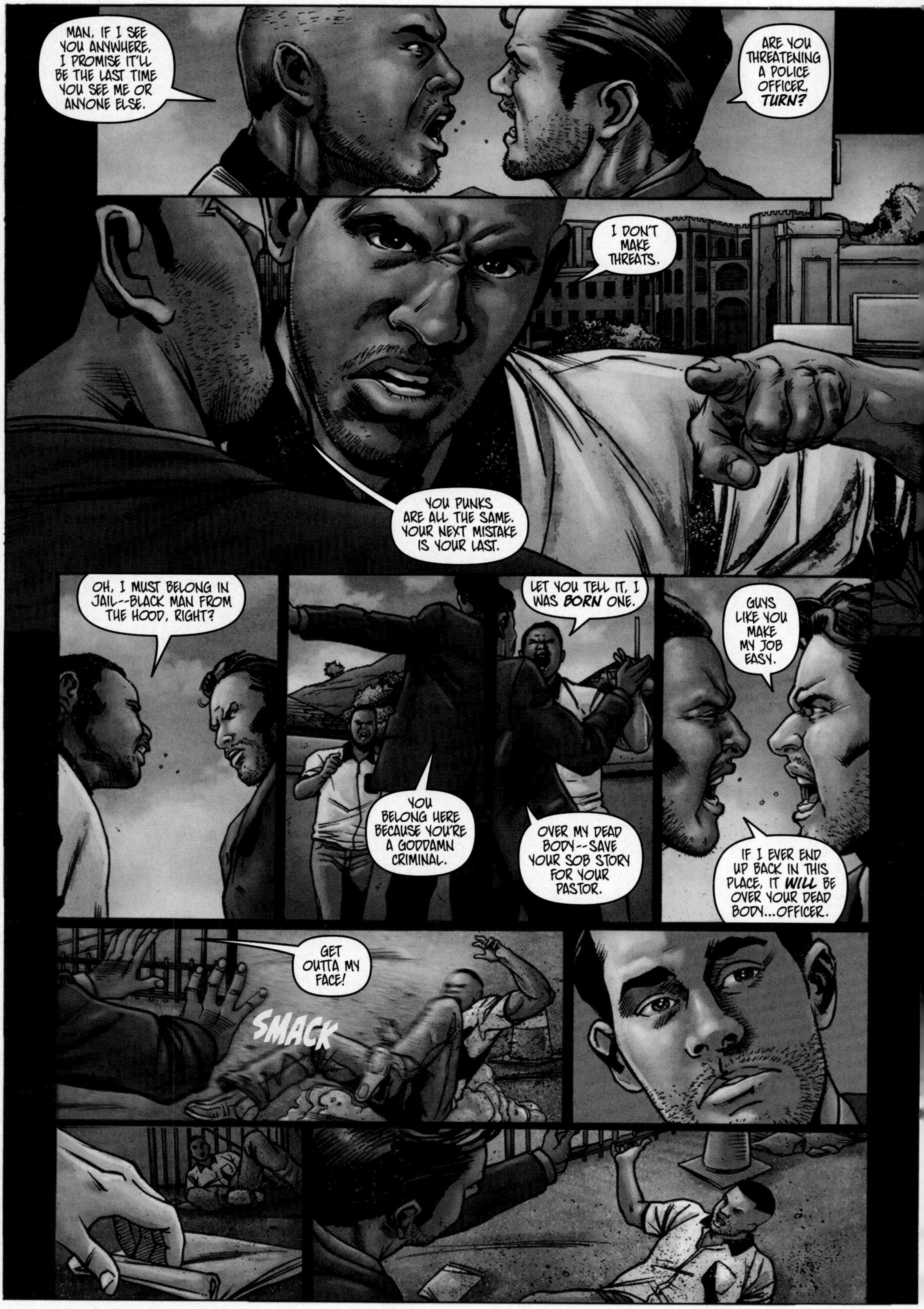
MAN, IF I SEE YOU ANYWHERE, I PROMISE IT'LL BE THE LAST TIME YOU SEE ME OR ANYONE ELSE.
ARE YOU THREATENING A POLICE OFFICER, TURN?
I DON'T MAKE THREATS.
YOU PUNKS ARE ALL THE SAME. YOUR NEXT MISTAKE IS YOUR LAST.
OH, I MUST BELONG IN JAIL--BLACK MAN FROM THE HOOD, RIGHT?
YOU BELONG HERE BECAUSE YOU'RE A GODDAMN CRIMINAL.
LET YOU TELL IT, I WAS BORN ONE.
OVER MY DEAD BODY--SAVE YOUR SOB STORY FOR YOUR PASTOR.
GUYS LIKE YOU MAKE MY JOB EASY.
IF I EVER END UP BACK IN THIS PLACE, IT WILL BE OVER YOUR DEAD BODY...OFFICER.
GET OUTTA MY FACE!
SMACK

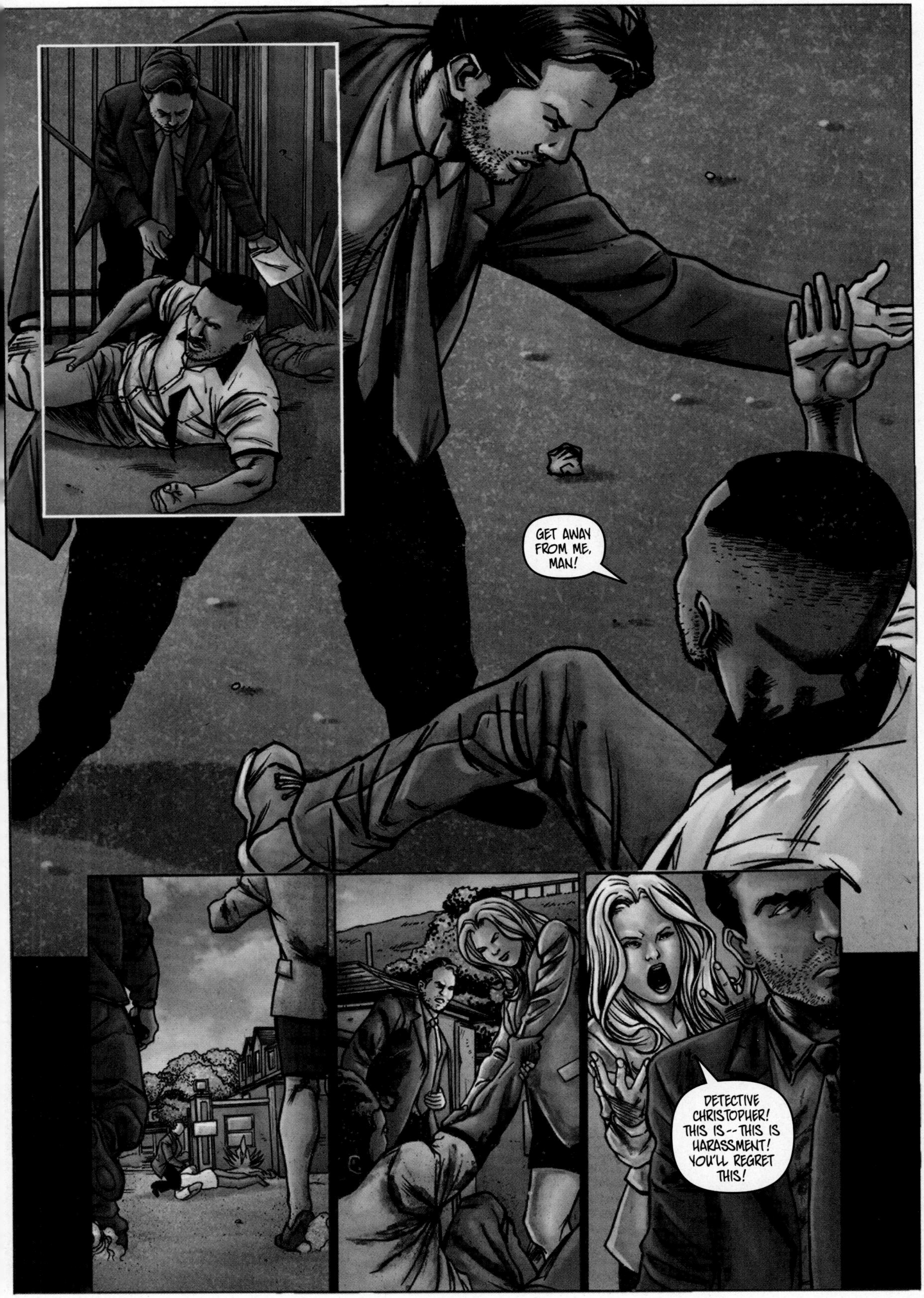
GET AWAY FROM ME, MAN!
DETECTIVE CHRISTOPHER! THIS IS--THIS IS HARASSMENT! YOU'LL REGRET THIS!

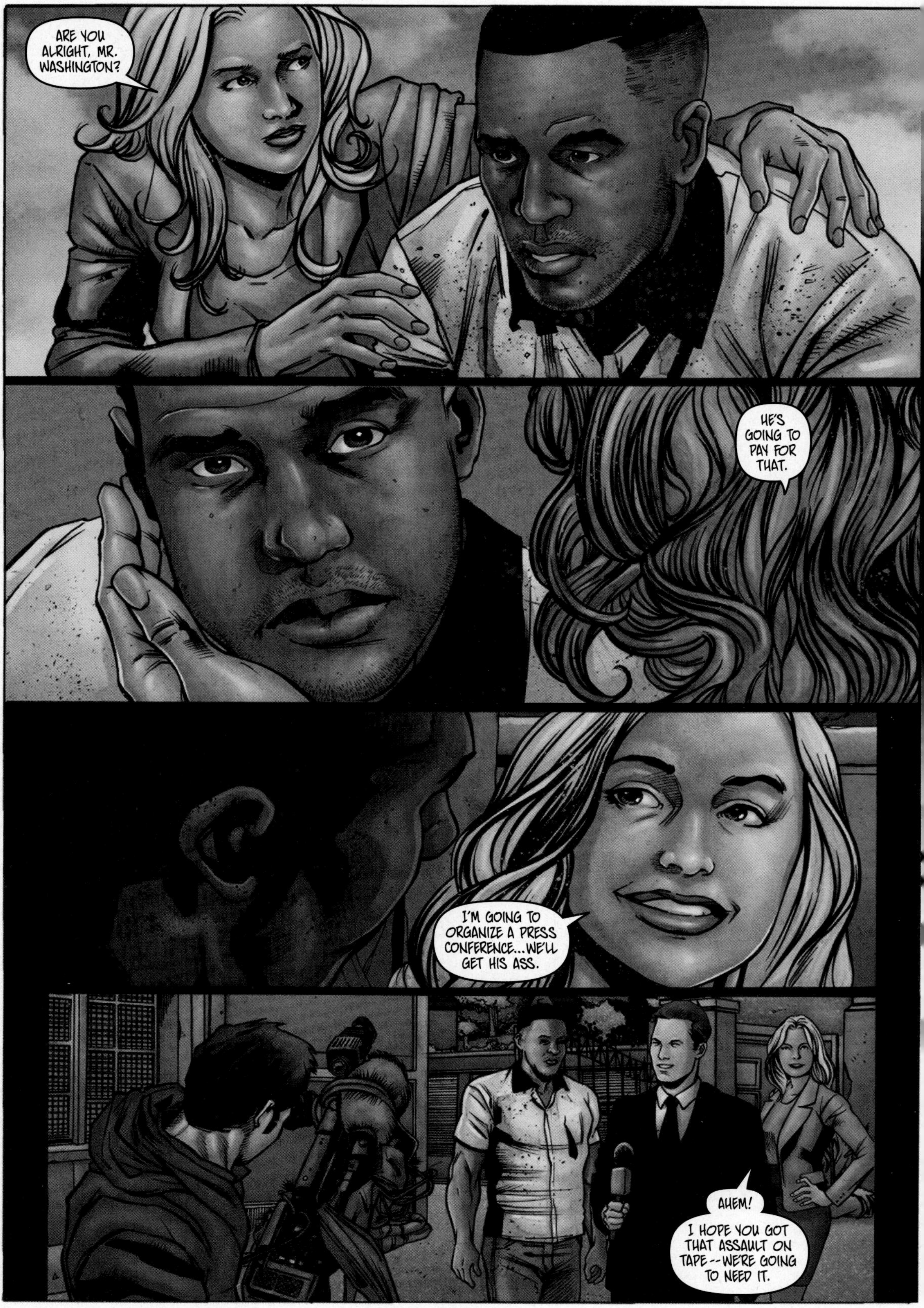
ARE YOU ALRIGHT, MR. WASHINGTON?
HE'S GOING TO PAY FOR THAT.
I'M GOING TO ORGANIZE A PRESS CONFERENCE...WE'LL GET HIS ASS.
AHEM!
I HOPE YOU GOT THAT ASSAULT ON TAPE--WE'RE GOING TO NEED IT.

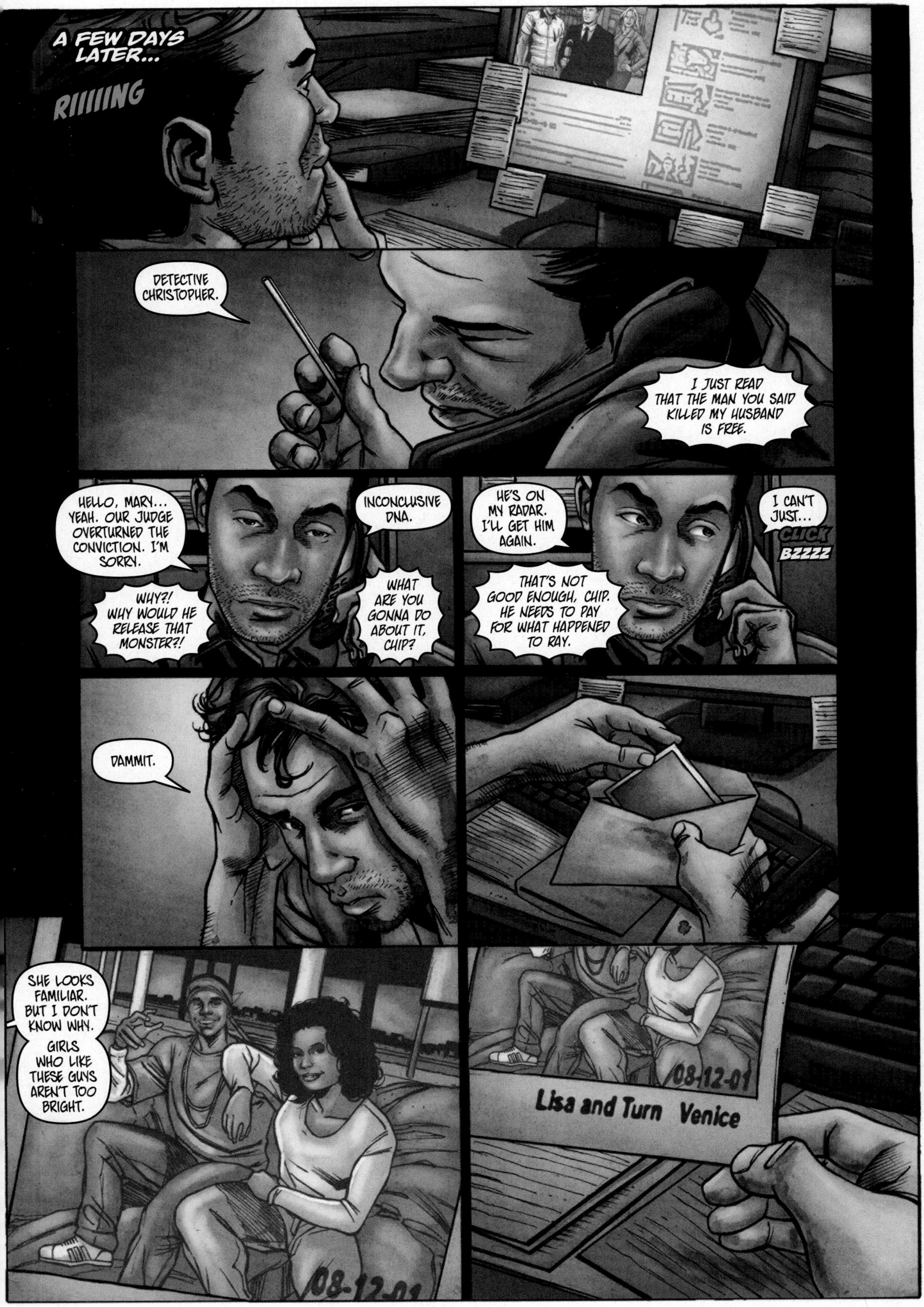

A FEW DAYS LATER...
RIIIIING
DETECTIVE CHRISTOPHER.
I JUST READ THAT THE MAN YOU SAID KILLED MY HUSBAND IS FREE.
HELLO, MARY... YEAH. OUR JUDGE OVERTURNED THE CONVICTION. I'M SORRY.
WHY?! WHY WOULD HE RELEASE THAT MONSTER?!
INCONCLUSIVE DNA.
WHAT ARE YOU GONNA DO ABOUT IT, CHIP?
HE'S ON MY RADAR. I'LL GET HIM AGAIN.
THAT'S NOT GOOD ENOUGH, CHIP. HE NEEDS TO PAY FOR WHAT HAPPENED TO RAY.
I CAN'T JUST...
CLICK
BZZZZ
DAMMIT.
SHE LOOKS FAMILIAR. BUT I DON'T KNOW WHY.
GIRLS WHO LIKE THESE GUYS AREN'T TOO BRIGHT.
08-12-01
08-12-01
Lisa and Turn Venice

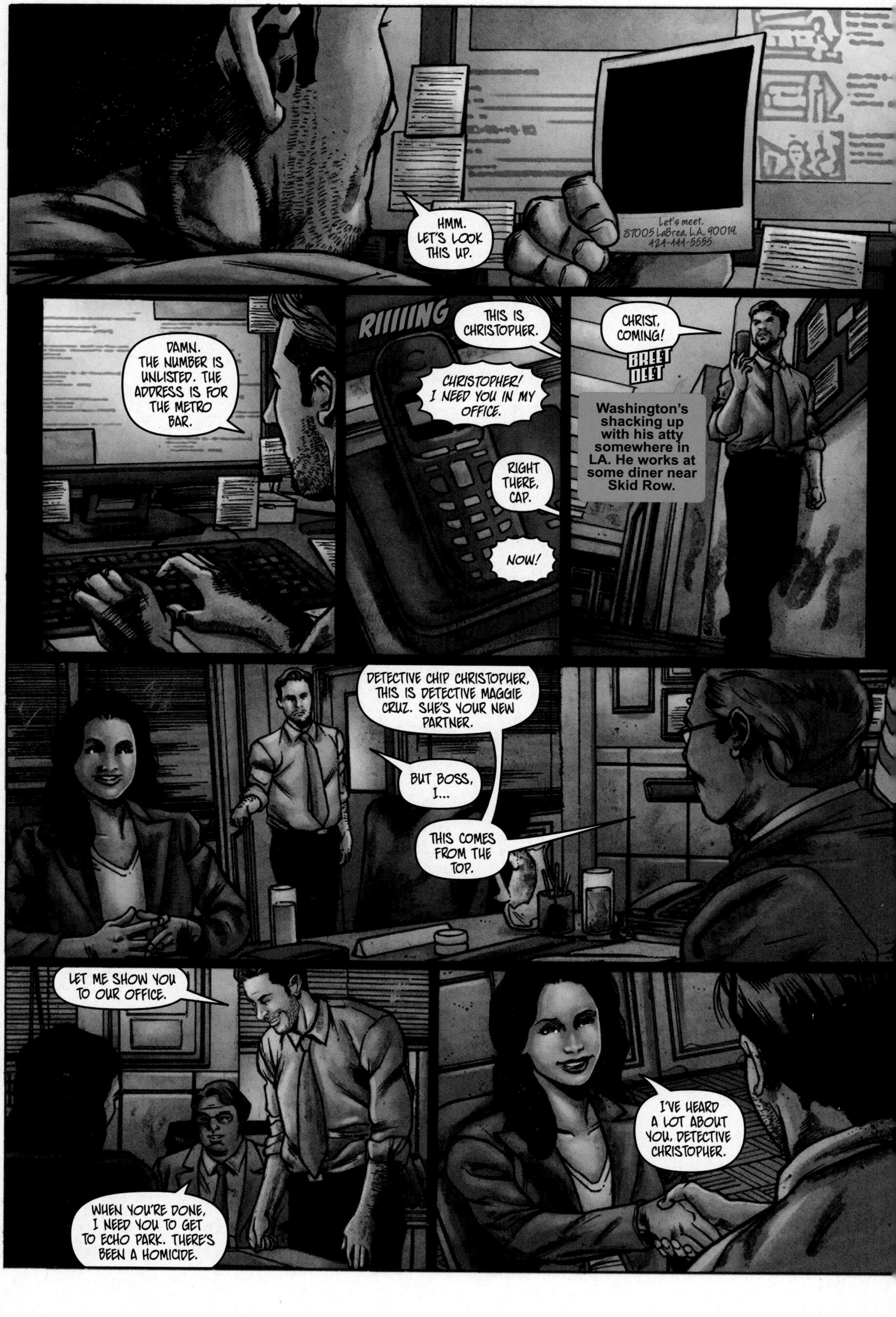
HMM. LET'S LOOK THIS UP.
Let's meet.
87005 LaBrea, L.A. 90019.
424-444-5555
DAMN. THE NUMBER IS UNLISTED. THE ADDRESS IS FOR THE METRO BAR.
RIIIIING
THIS IS CHRISTOPHER.
CHRISTOPHER! I NEED YOU IN MY OFFICE.
RIGHT THERE, CAP.
NOW!
CHRIST, COMING!
BREET DEET
Washington's shacking up with his atty somewhere in LA. He works at some diner near Skid Row.
DETECTIVE CHIP CHRISTOPHER, THIS IS DETECTIVE MAGGIE CRUZ. SHE'S YOUR NEW PARTNER.
BUT BOSS, I...
THIS COMES FROM THE TOP.
LET ME SHOW YOU TO OUR OFFICE.
WHEN YOU'RE DONE, I NEED YOU TO GET TO ECHO PARK. THERE'S BEEN A HOMICIDE.
I'VE HEARD A LOT ABOUT YOU, DETECTIVE CHRISTOPHER.

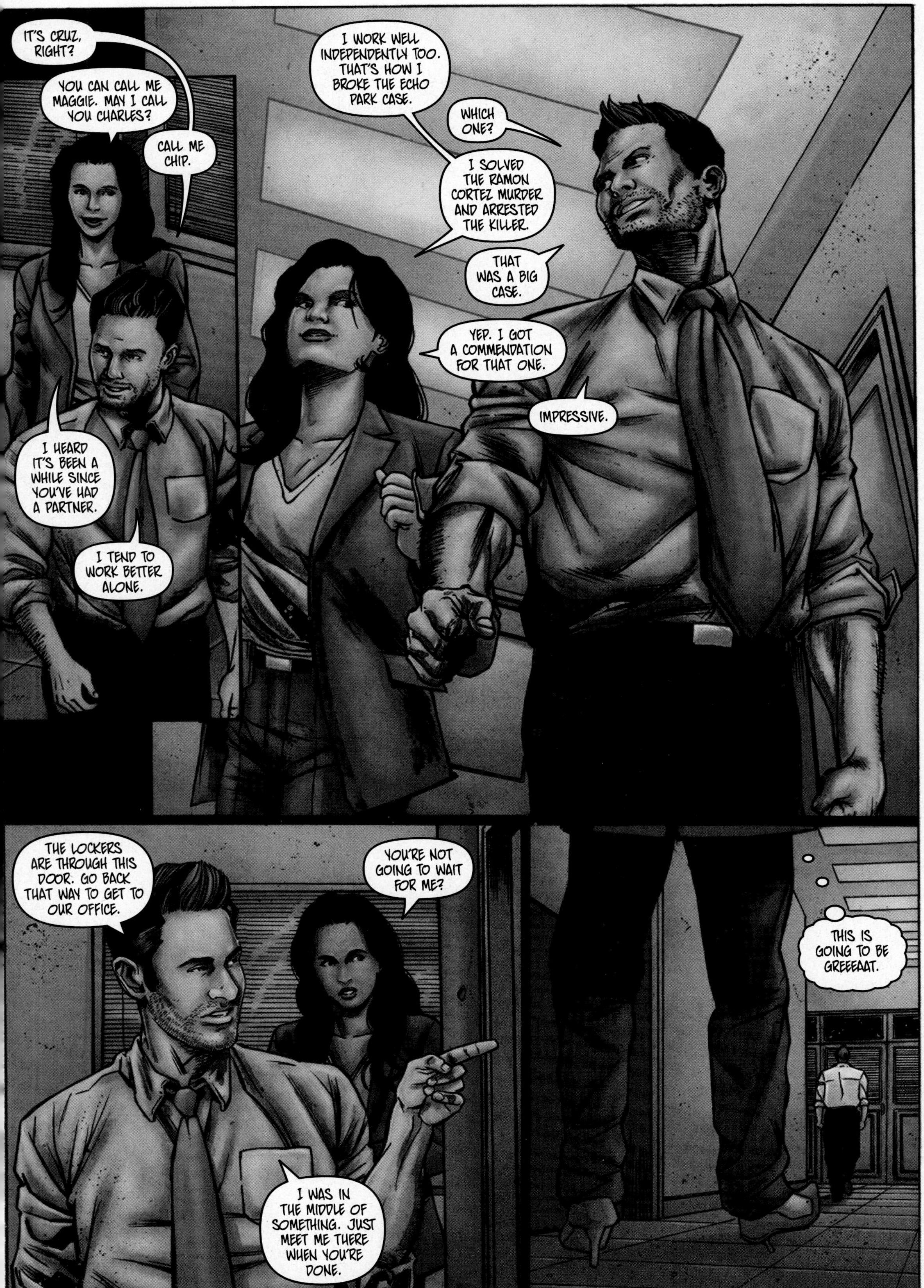
IT'S CRUZ, RIGHT?
YOU CAN CALL ME MAGGIE. MAY I CALL YOU CHARLES?
CALL ME CHIP.
I HEARD IT'S BEEN A WHILE SINCE YOU'VE HAD A PARTNER.
I TEND TO WORK BETTER ALONE.
I WORK WELL INDEPENDENTLY TOO. THAT'S HOW I BROKE THE ECHO PARK CASE.
WHICH ONE?
I SOLVED THE RAMON CORTEZ MURDER AND ARRESTED THE KILLER.
THAT WAS A BIG CASE.
YEP. I GOT A COMMENDATION FOR THAT ONE.
IMPRESSIVE.
THE LOCKERS ARE THROUGH THIS DOOR. GO BACK THAT WAY TO GET TO OUR OFFICE.
YOU'RE NOT GOING TO WAIT FOR ME?
I WAS IN THE MIDDLE OF SOMETHING. JUST MEET ME THERE WHEN YOU'RE DONE.
THIS IS GOING TO BE GREEEAAT.

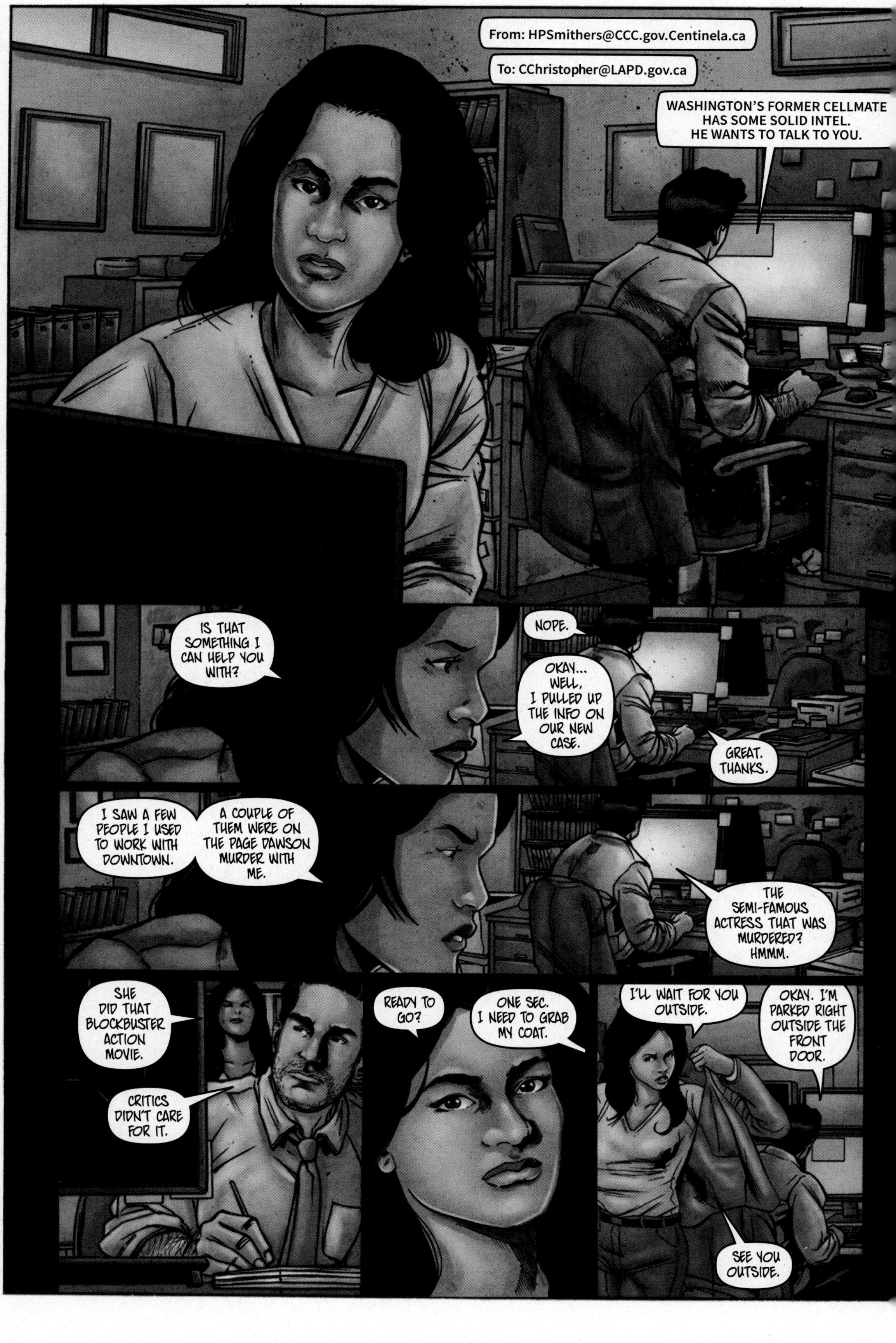
From: HPSmithers@CCC.gov.Centinela.ca
To: CChristopher@LAPD.gov.ca
WASHINGTON'S FORMER CELLMATE HAS SOME SOLID INTEL. HE WANTS TO TALK TO YOU.
IS THAT SOMETHING I CAN HELP YOU WITH?
NOPE.
OKAY... WELL, I PULLED UP THE INFO ON OUR NEW CASE.
GREAT. THANKS.
I SAW A FEW PEOPLE I USED TO WORK WITH DOWNTOWN.
A COUPLE OF THEM WERE ON THE PAGE DAWSON MURDER WITH ME.
THE SEMI-FAMOUS ACTRESS THAT WAS MURDERED? HMMM.
SHE DID THAT BLOCKBUSTER ACTION MOVIE.
CRITICS DIDN'T CARE FOR IT.
READY TO GO?
ONE SEC. I NEED TO GRAB MY COAT.
I'LL WAIT FOR YOU OUTSIDE.
OKAY. I'M PARKED RIGHT OUTSIDE THE FRONT DOOR.
SEE YOU OUTSIDE.

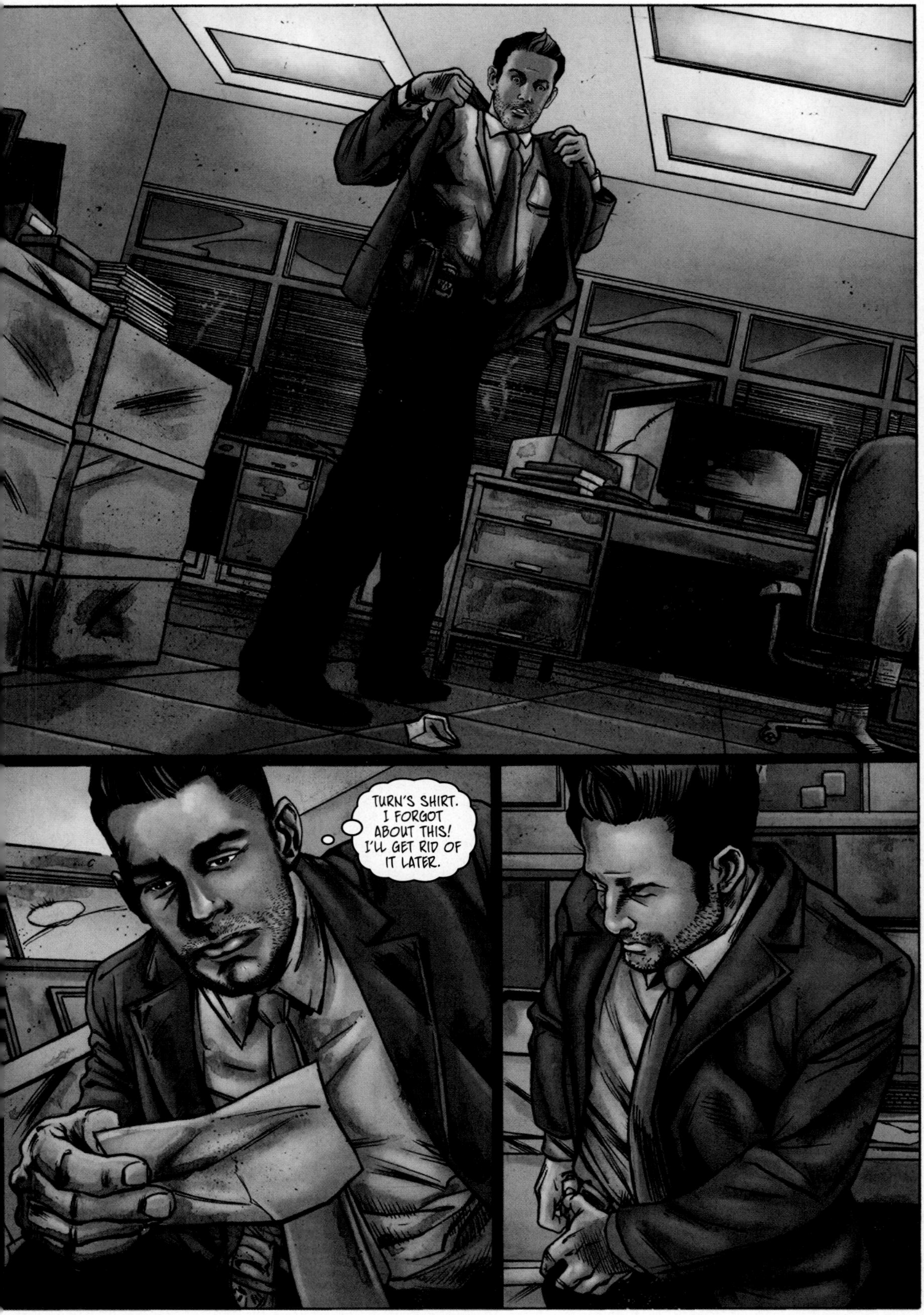
TURN'S SHIRT. I FORGOT ABOUT THIS! I'LL GET RID OF IT LATER.

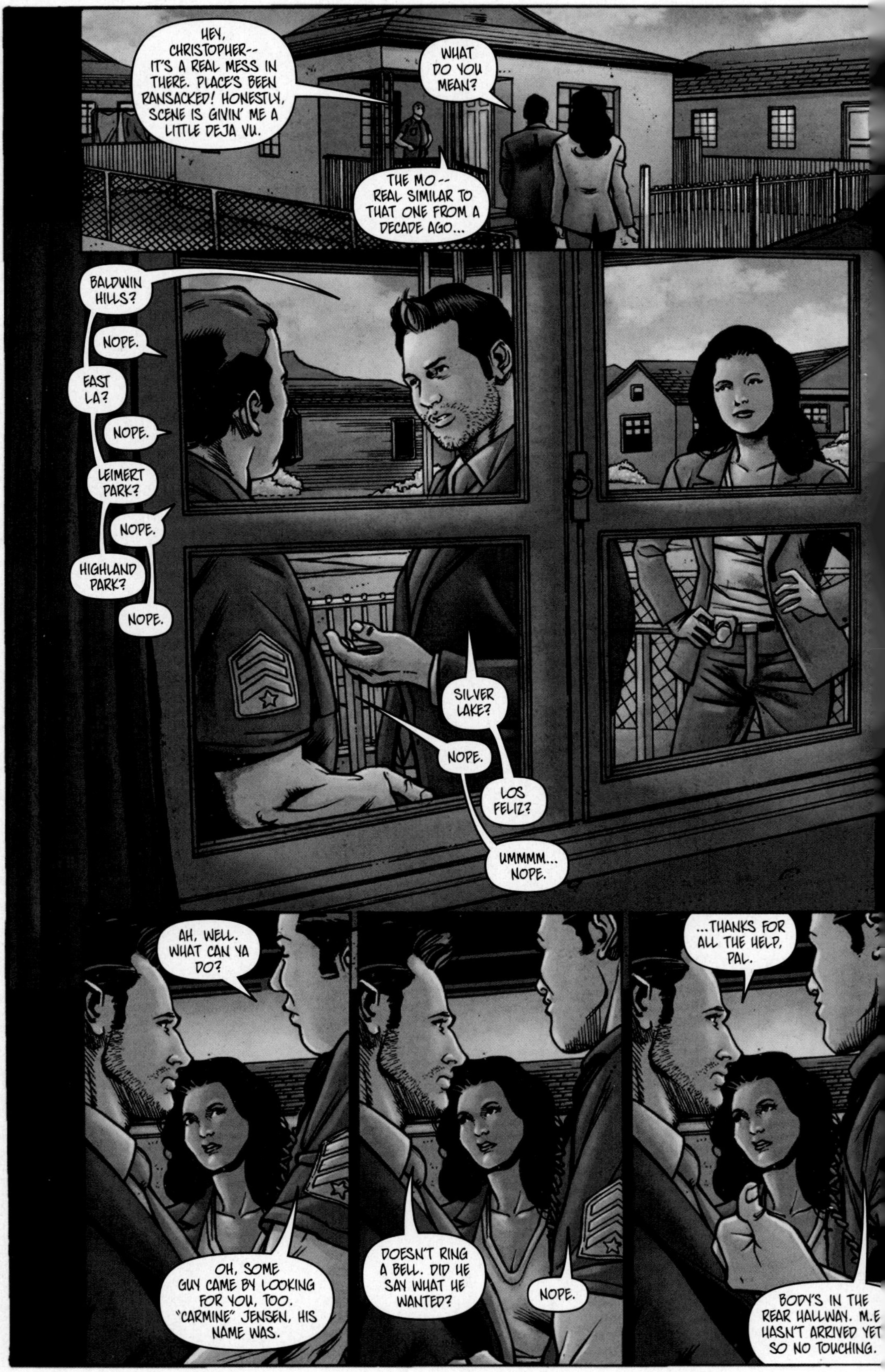
HEY, CHRISTOPHER-- IT'S A REAL MESS IN THERE. PLACE'S BEEN RANSACKED! HONESTLY, SCENE IS GIVIN' ME A LITTLE DEJA VU.
WHAT DO YOU MEAN?
THE MO-- REAL SIMILAR TO THAT ONE FROM A DECADE AGO...
BALDWIN HILLS?
NOPE.
EAST LA?
NOPE.
LEIMERT PARK?
NOPE.
HIGHLAND PARK?
NOPE.
SILVER LAKE?
NOPE.
LOS FELIZ?
UMMMM... NOPE.
AH, WELL. WHAT CAN YA DO?
OH, SOME GUY CAME BY LOOKING FOR YOU, TOO. "CARMINE" JENSEN, HIS NAME WAS.
DOESN'T RING A BELL. DID HE SAY WHAT HE WANTED?
NOPE.
...THANKS FOR ALL THE HELP, PAL.
BODY'S IN THE REAR HALLWAY. M.E. HASN'T ARRIVED YET SO NO TOUCHING.

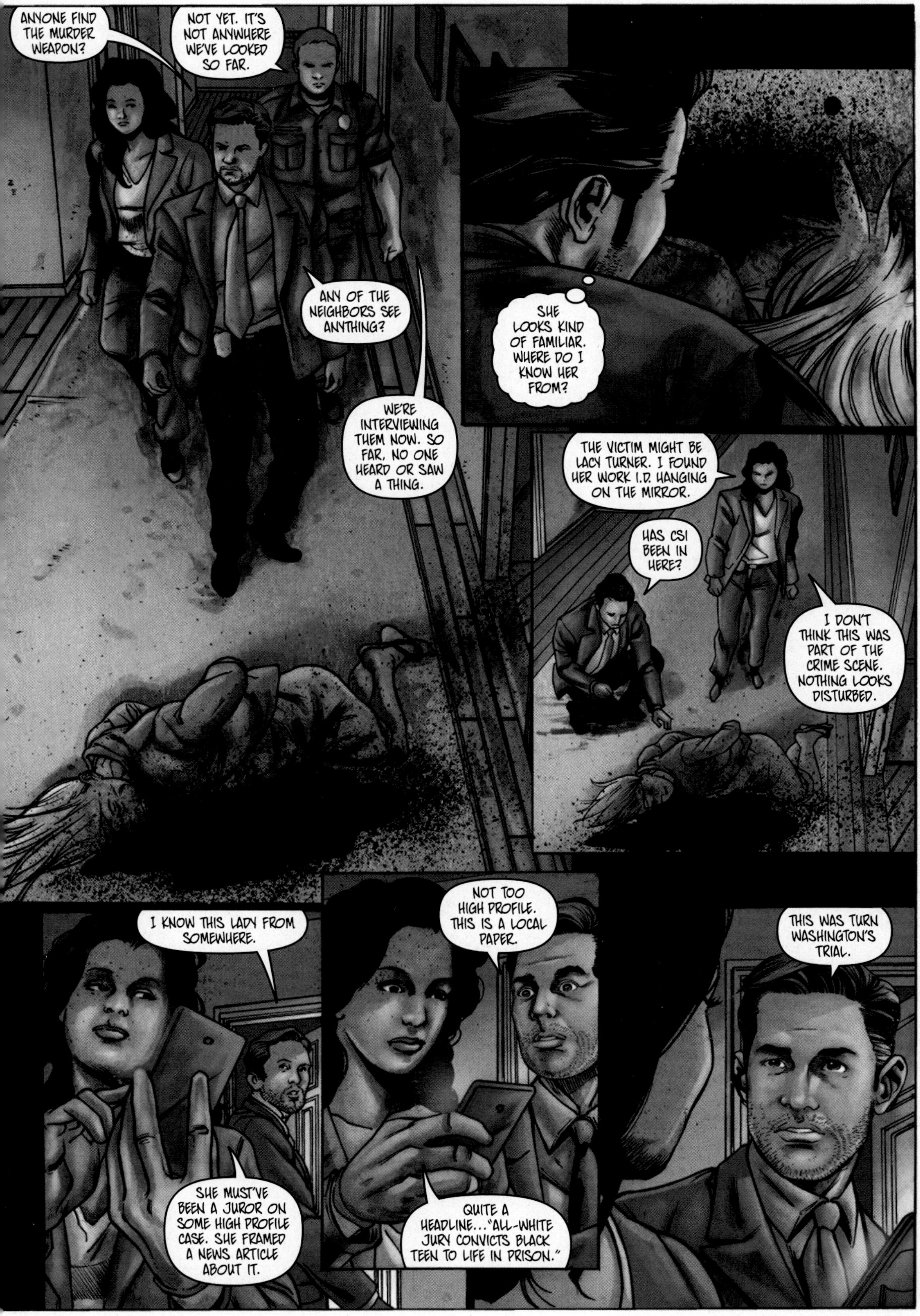
ANYONE FIND THE MURDER WEAPON?
NOT YET. IT'S NOT ANYWHERE WE'VE LOOKED SO FAR.
ANY OF THE NEIGHBORS SEE ANYTHING?
WE'RE INTERVIEWING THEM NOW. SO FAR, NO ONE HEARD OR SAW A THING.
SHE LOOKS KIND OF FAMILIAR. WHERE DO I KNOW HER FROM?
THE VICTIM MIGHT BE LACY TURNER. I FOUND HER WORK I.D. HANGING ON THE MIRROR.
HAS CSI BEEN IN HERE?
I DON'T THINK THIS WAS PART OF THE CRIME SCENE. NOTHING LOOKS DISTURBED.
I KNOW THIS LADY FROM SOMEWHERE.
SHE MUST'VE BEEN A JUROR ON SOME HIGH PROFILE CASE. SHE FRAMED A NEWS ARTICLE ABOUT IT.
NOT TOO HIGH PROFILE. THIS IS A LOCAL PAPER.
QUITE A HEADLINE... "ALL-WHITE JURY CONVICTS BLACK TEEN TO LIFE IN PRISON."
THIS WAS TURN WASHINGTON'S TRIAL.

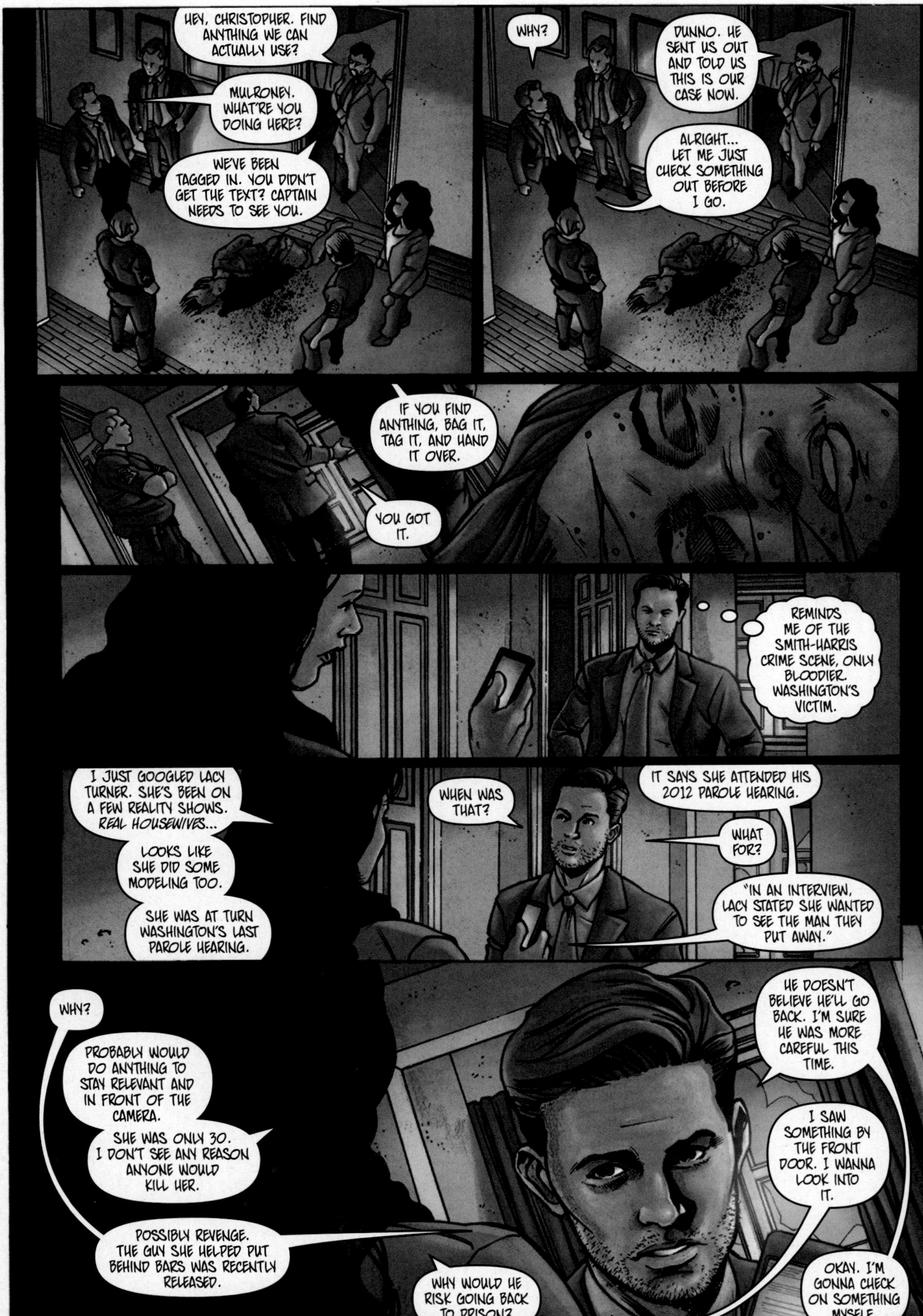
HEY, CHRISTOPHER. FIND ANYTHING WE CAN ACTUALLY USE?
MULRONEY. WHAT'RE YOU DOING HERE?
WE'VE BEEN TAGGED IN. YOU DIDN'T GET THE TEXT? CAPTAIN NEEDS TO SEE YOU.
WHY?
DUNNO. HE SENT US OUT AND TOLD US THIS IS OUR CASE NOW.
ALRIGHT... LET ME JUST CHECK SOMETHING OUT BEFORE I GO.
IF YOU FIND ANYTHING, BAG IT, TAG IT, AND HAND IT OVER.
YOU GOT IT.
REMINDS ME OF THE SMITH-HARRIS CRIME SCENE, ONLY BLOODIER. WASHINGTON'S VICTIM.
I JUST GOOGLED LACY TURNER. SHE'S BEEN ON A FEW REALITY SHOWS. REAL HOUSEWIVES...
LOOKS LIKE SHE DID SOME MODELING TOO.
SHE WAS AT TURN WASHINGTON'S LAST PAROLE HEARING.
WHEN WAS THAT?
IT SAYS SHE ATTENDED HIS 2012 PAROLE HEARING.
WHAT FOR?
"IN AN INTERVIEW, LACY STATED SHE WANTED TO SEE THE MAN THEY PUT AWAY."
WHY?
PROBABLY WOULD DO ANYTHING TO STAY RELEVANT AND IN FRONT OF THE CAMERA.
SHE WAS ONLY 30. I DON'T SEE ANY REASON ANYONE WOULD KILL HER.
POSSIBLY REVENGE. THE GUY SHE HELPED PUT BEHIND BARS WAS RECENTLY RELEASED.
WHY WOULD HE RISK GOING BACK TO PRISON?
HE DOESN'T BELIEVE HE'LL GO BACK. I'M SURE HE WAS MORE CAREFUL THIS TIME.
I SAW SOMETHING BY THE FRONT DOOR. I WANNA LOOK INTO IT.
OKAY. I'M GONNA CHECK ON SOMETHING MYSELF.

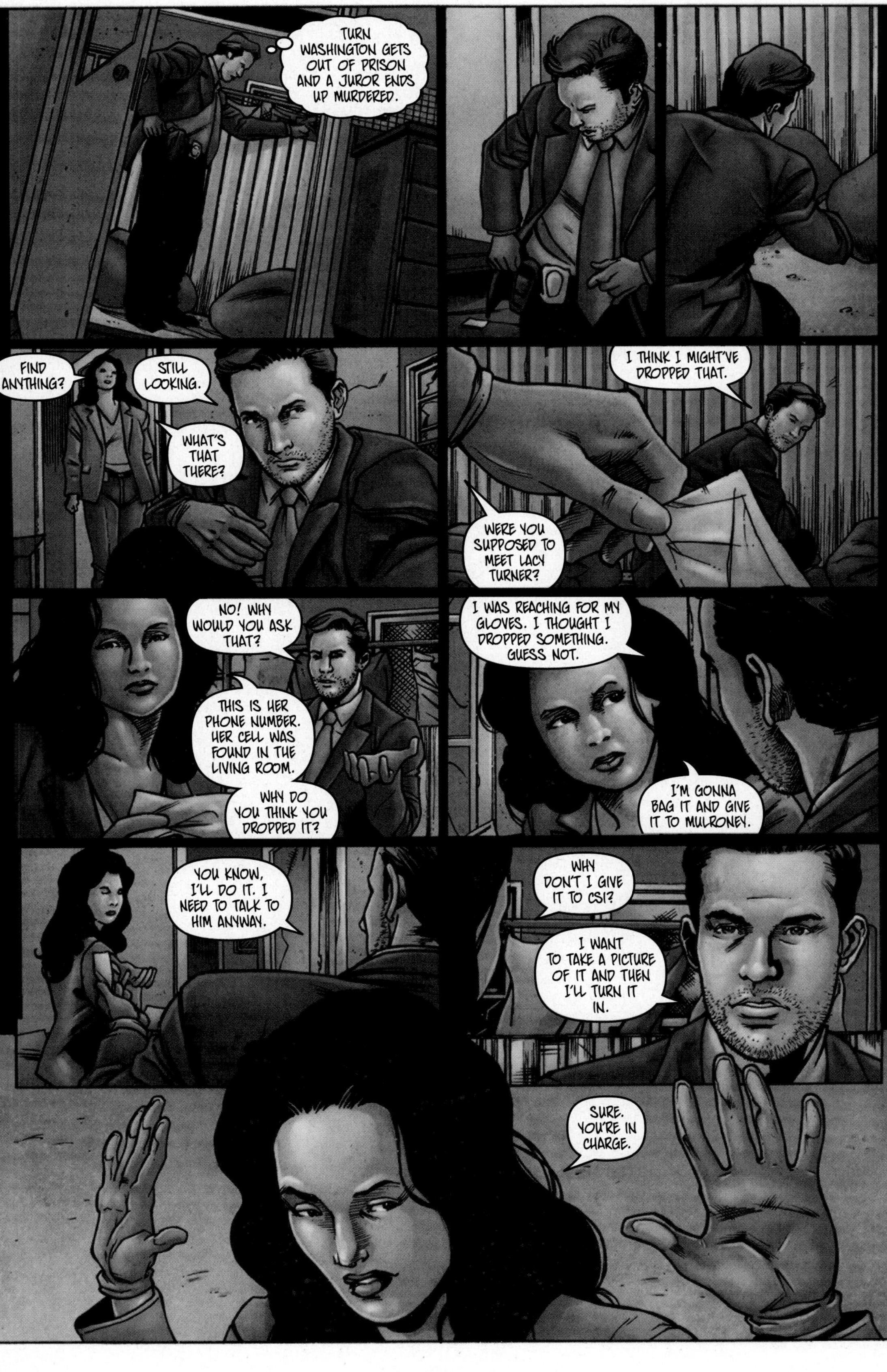
TURN WASHINGTON GETS OUT OF PRISON AND A JUROR ENDS UP MURDERED.
FIND ANYTHING?
STILL LOOKING.
WHAT'S THAT THERE?
I THINK I MIGHT'VE DROPPED THAT.
WERE YOU SUPPOSED TO MEET LACY TURNER?
NO! WHY WOULD YOU ASK THAT?
THIS IS HER PHONE NUMBER. HER CELL WAS FOUND IN THE LIVING ROOM.
WHY DO YOU THINK YOU DROPPED IT?
I WAS REACHING FOR MY GLOVES. I THOUGHT I DROPPED SOMETHING. GUESS NOT.
I'M GONNA BAG IT AND GIVE IT TO MULRONEY.
YOU KNOW, I'LL DO IT. I NEED TO TALK TO HIM ANYWAY.
WHY DON'T I GIVE IT TO CSI?
I WANT TO TAKE A PICTURE OF IT AND THEN I'LL TURN IT IN.
SURE. YOU'RE IN CHARGE.

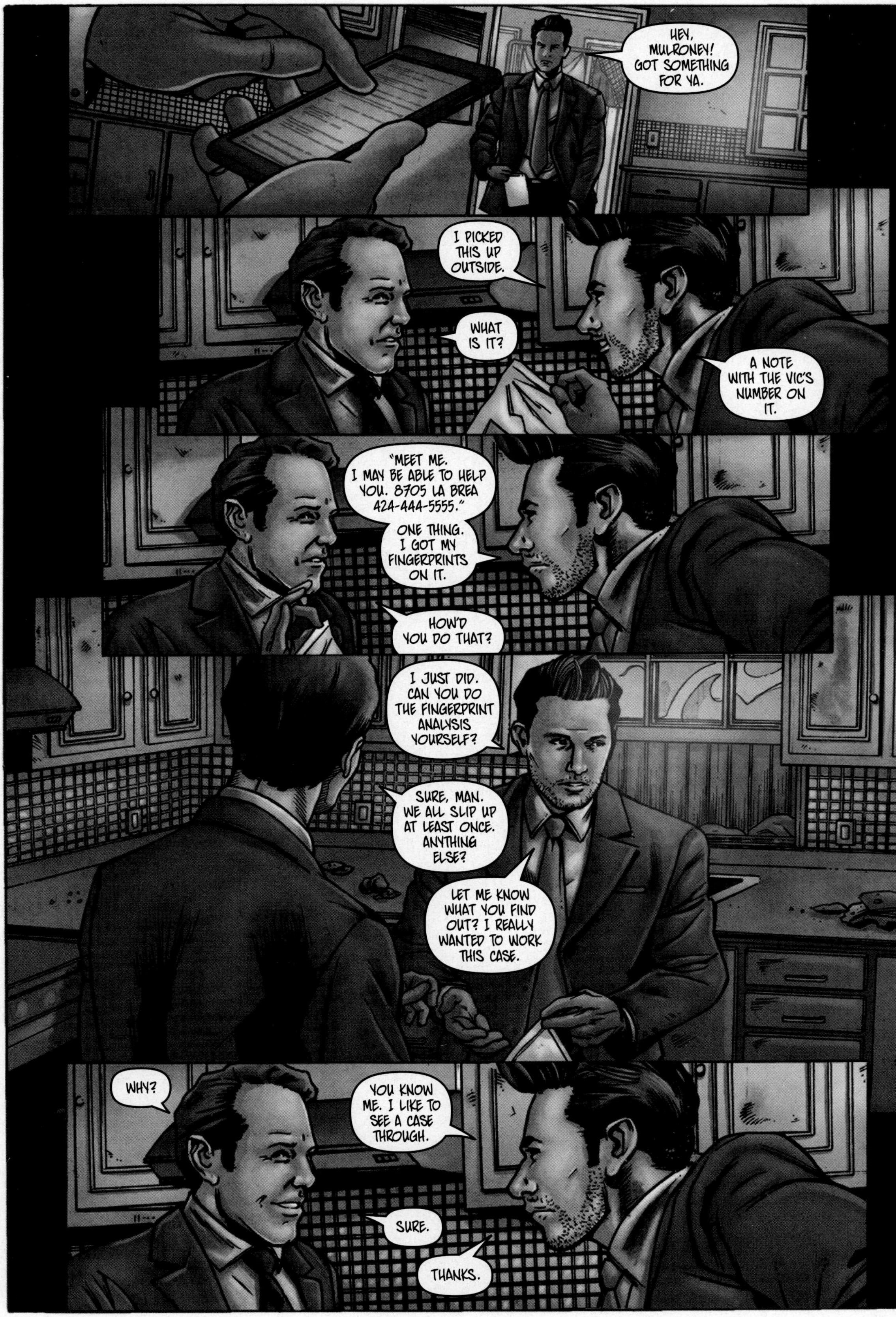
HEY, MULRONEY! GOT SOMETHING FOR YA.
I PICKED THIS UP OUTSIDE.
WHAT IS IT?
A NOTE WITH THE VIC'S NUMBER ON IT.
"MEET ME. I MAY BE ABLE TO HELP YOU. 8705 LA BREA 424-444-5555."
ONE THING. I GOT MY FINGERPRINTS ON IT.
HOW'D YOU DO THAT?
I JUST DID. CAN YOU DO THE FINGERPRINT ANALYSIS YOURSELF?
SURE, MAN. WE ALL SLIP UP AT LEAST ONCE. ANYTHING ELSE?
LET ME KNOW WHAT YOU FIND OUT? I REALLY WANTED TO WORK THIS CASE.
WHY?
YOU KNOW ME. I LIKE TO SEE A CASE THROUGH.
SURE.
THANKS.

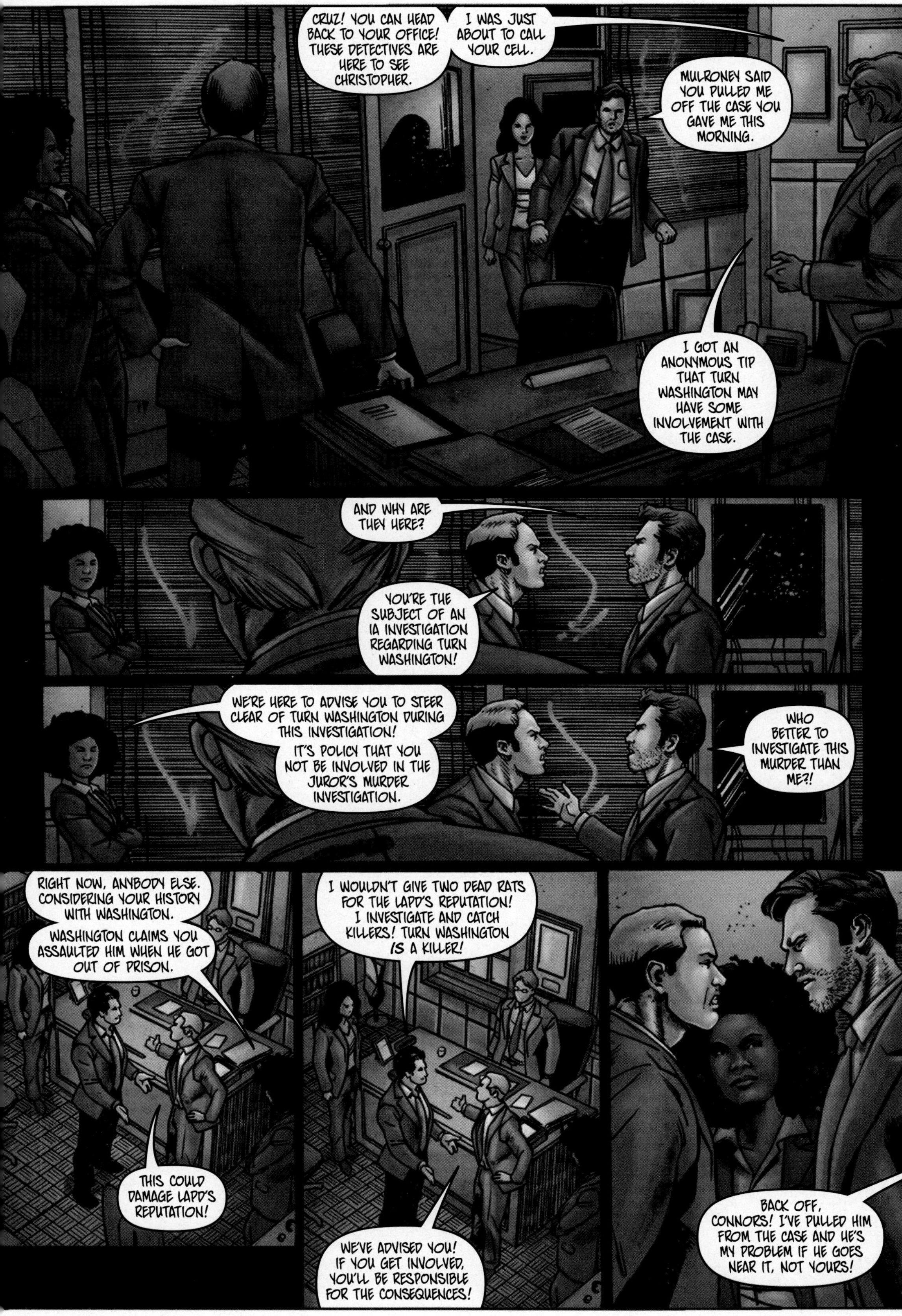

CRUZ! YOU CAN HEAD BACK TO YOUR OFFICE! THESE DETECTIVES ARE HERE TO SEE CHRISTOPHER.
I WAS JUST ABOUT TO CALL YOUR CELL.
MULRONEY SAID YOU PULLED ME OFF THE CASE YOU GAVE ME THIS MORNING.
I GOT AN ANONYMOUS TIP THAT TURN WASHINGTON MAY HAVE SOME INVOLVEMENT WITH THE CASE.
AND WHY ARE THEY HERE?
YOU'RE THE SUBJECT OF AN IA INVESTIGATION REGARDING TURN WASHINGTON!
WE'RE HERE TO ADVISE YOU TO STEER CLEAR OF TURN WASHINGTON DURING THIS INVESTIGATION!
IT'S POLICY THAT YOU NOT BE INVOLVED IN THE JUROR'S MURDER INVESTIGATION.
WHO BETTER TO INVESTIGATE THIS MURDER THAN ME?!
RIGHT NOW, ANYBODY ELSE. CONSIDERING YOUR HISTORY WITH WASHINGTON.
WASHINGTON CLAIMS YOU ASSAULTED HIM WHEN HE GOT OUT OF PRISON.
THIS COULD DAMAGE LAPD'S REPUTATION!
I WOULDN'T GIVE TWO DEAD RATS FOR THE LAPD'S REPUTATION! I INVESTIGATE AND CATCH KILLERS! TURN WASHINGTON *IS* A KILLER!
WE'VE ADVISED YOU! IF YOU GET INVOLVED, YOU'LL BE RESPONSIBLE FOR THE CONSEQUENCES!
BACK OFF, CONNORS! I'VE PULLED HIM FROM THE CASE AND HE'S MY PROBLEM IF HE GOES NEAR IT, NOT YOURS!

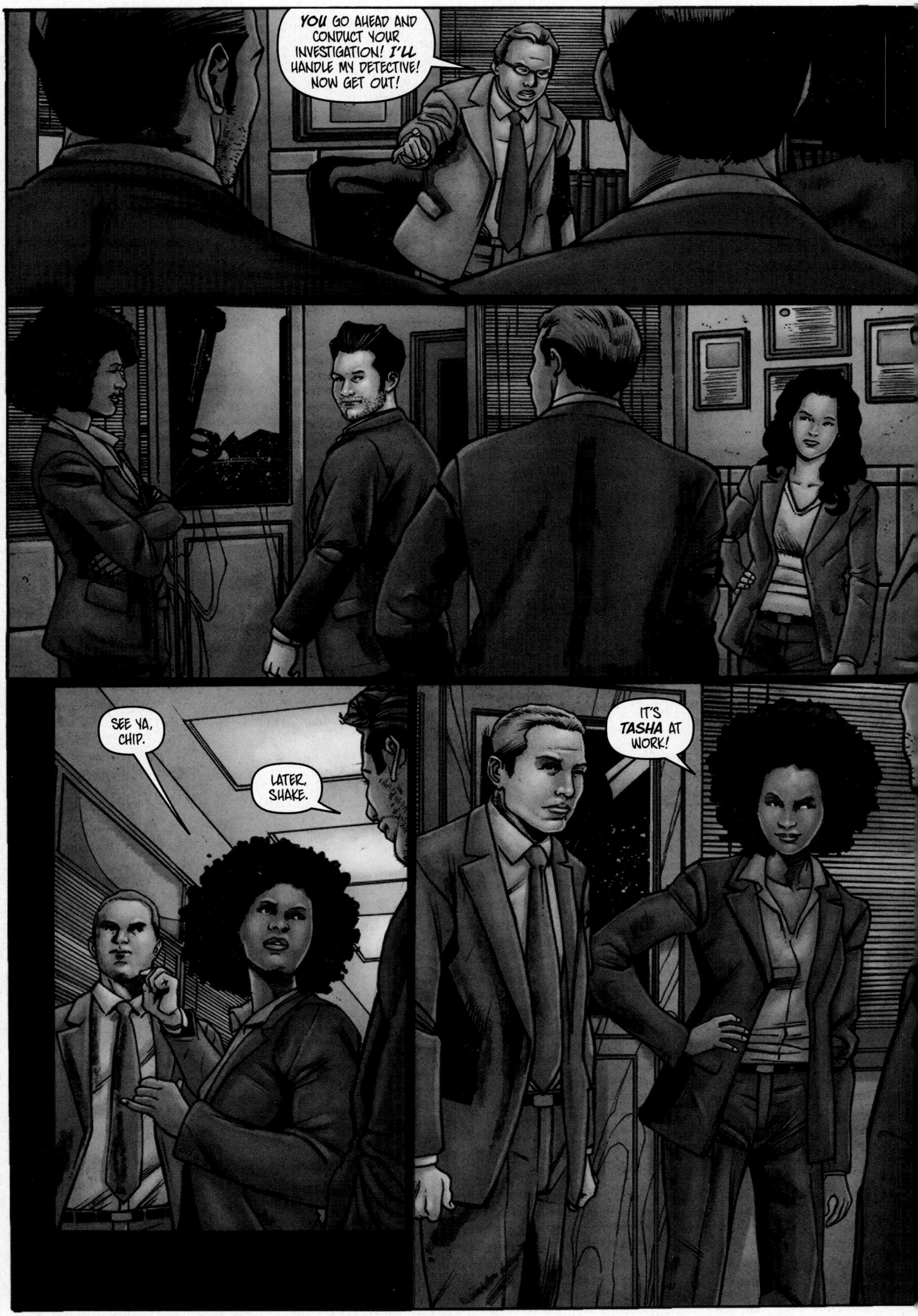
YOU GO AHEAD AND CONDUCT YOUR INVESTIGATION! I'LL HANDLE MY DETECTIVE! NOW GET OUT!
SEE YA, CHIP.
LATER, SHAKE.
IT'S TASHA AT WORK!

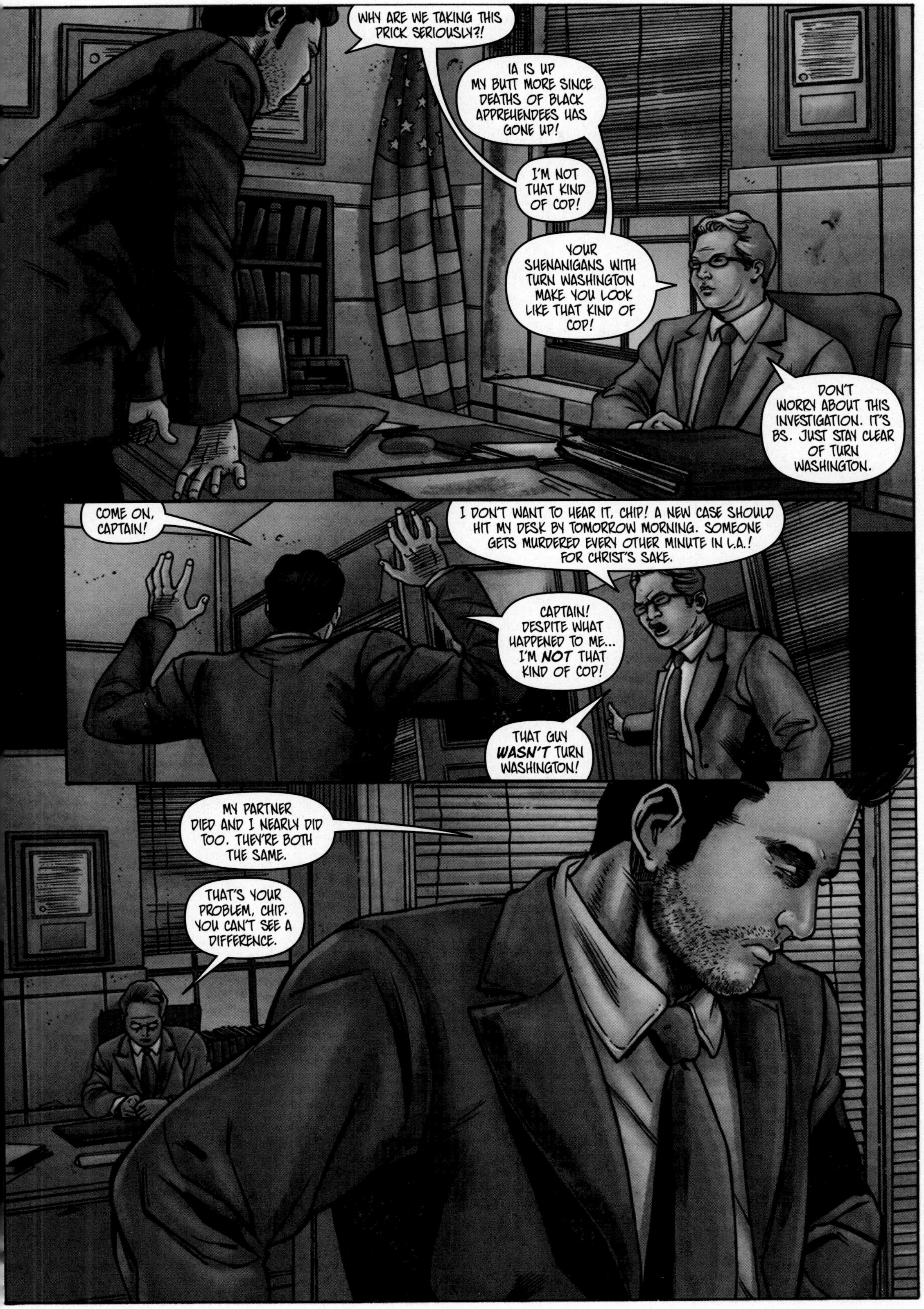
WHY ARE WE TAKING THIS PRICK SERIOUSLY?!
IA IS UP MY BUTT MORE SINCE DEATHS OF BLACK APPREHENDEES HAS GONE UP!
I'M NOT THAT KIND OF COP!
YOUR SHENANIGANS WITH TURN WASHINGTON MAKE YOU LOOK LIKE THAT KIND OF COP!
DON'T WORRY ABOUT THIS INVESTIGATION. IT'S BS. JUST STAY CLEAR OF TURN WASHINGTON.
COME ON, CAPTAIN!
I DON'T WANT TO HEAR IT, CHIP! A NEW CASE SHOULD HIT MY DESK BY TOMORROW MORNING. SOMEONE GETS MURDERED EVERY OTHER MINUTE IN L.A.! FOR CHRIST'S SAKE.
CAPTAIN! DESPITE WHAT HAPPENED TO ME... I'M **NOT** THAT KIND OF COP!
THAT GUY ***WASN'T*** TURN WASHINGTON!
MY PARTNER DIED AND I NEARLY DID TOO. THEY'RE BOTH THE SAME.
THAT'S YOUR PROBLEM, CHIP. YOU CAN'T SEE A DIFFERENCE.

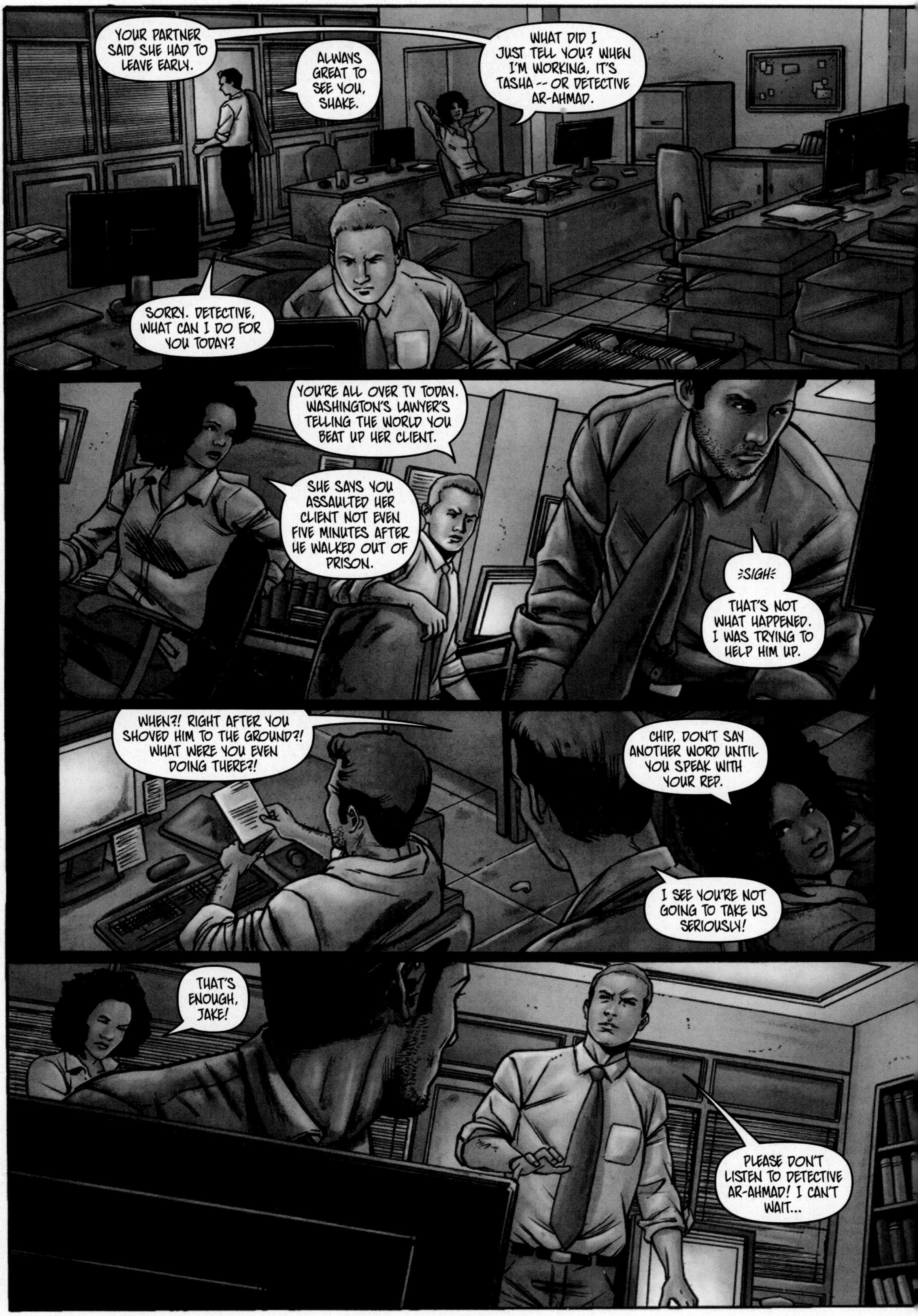
YOUR PARTNER SAID SHE HAD TO LEAVE EARLY.
ALWAYS GREAT TO SEE YOU, SHAKE.
WHAT DID I JUST TELL YOU? WHEN I'M WORKING, IT'S TASHA -- OR DETECTIVE AR-AHMAD.
SORRY. DETECTIVE, WHAT CAN I DO FOR YOU TODAY?
YOU'RE ALL OVER TV TODAY. WASHINGTON'S LAWYER'S TELLING THE WORLD YOU BEAT UP HER CLIENT.
SHE SAYS YOU ASSAULTED HER CLIENT NOT EVEN FIVE MINUTES AFTER HE WALKED OUT OF PRISON.
SIGH
THAT'S NOT WHAT HAPPENED. I WAS TRYING TO HELP HIM UP.
WHEN?! RIGHT AFTER YOU SHOVED HIM TO THE GROUND?! WHAT WERE YOU EVEN DOING THERE?!
CHIP, DON'T SAY ANOTHER WORD UNTIL YOU SPEAK WITH YOUR REP.
I SEE YOU'RE NOT GOING TO TAKE US SERIOUSLY!
THAT'S ENOUGH, JAKE!
PLEASE DON'T LISTEN TO DETECTIVE AR-AHMAD! I CAN'T WAIT...

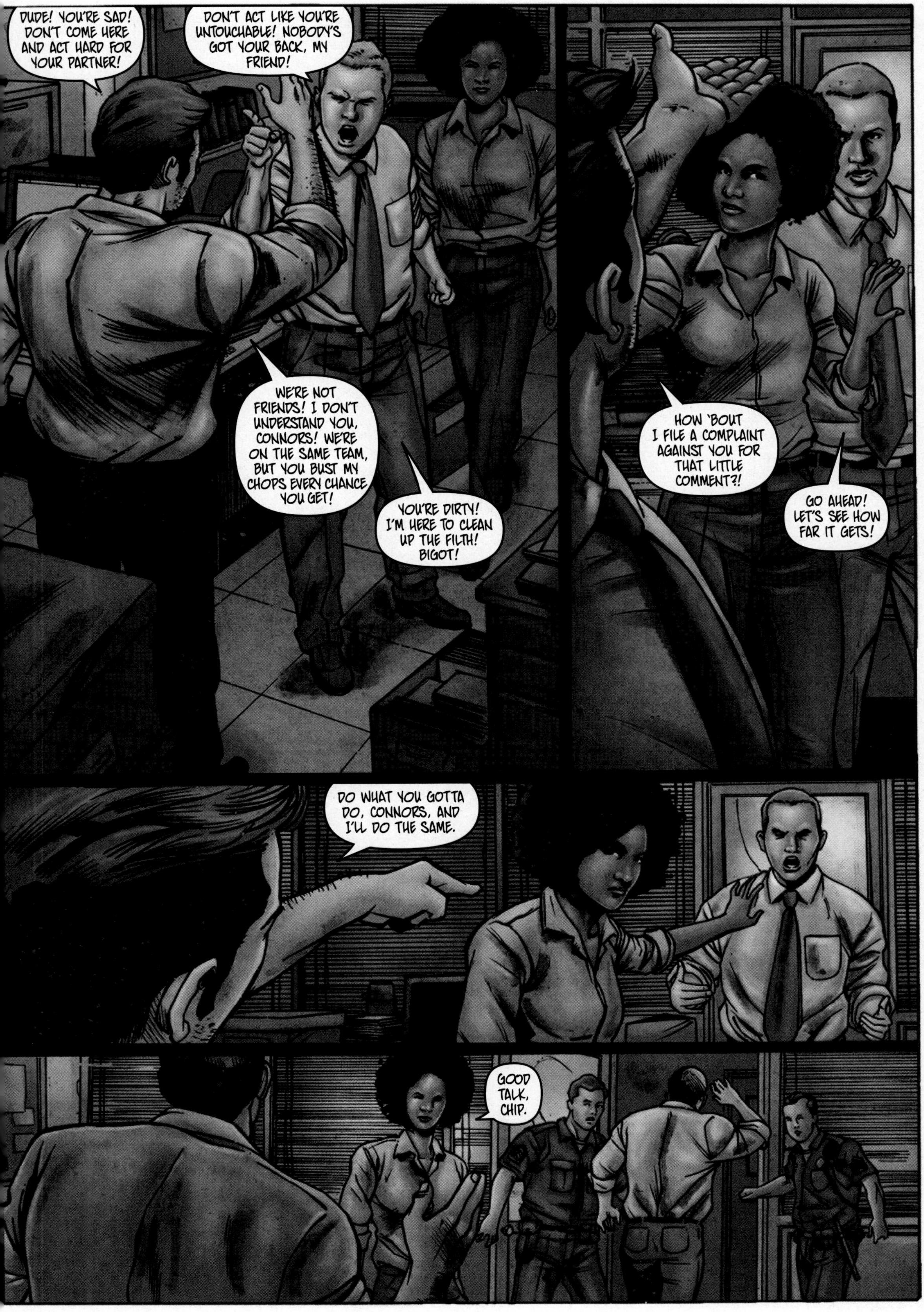
DUDE! YOU'RE SAD! DON'T COME HERE AND ACT HARD FOR YOUR PARTNER!
DON'T ACT LIKE YOU'RE UNTOUCHABLE! NOBODY'S GOT YOUR BACK, MY FRIEND!
WE'RE NOT FRIENDS! I DON'T UNDERSTAND YOU, CONNORS! WE'RE ON THE SAME TEAM, BUT YOU BUST MY CHOPS EVERY CHANCE YOU GET!
YOU'RE DIRTY! I'M HERE TO CLEAN UP THE FILTH! BIGOT!
HOW 'BOUT I FILE A COMPLAINT AGAINST YOU FOR THAT LITTLE COMMENT?!
GO AHEAD! LET'S SEE HOW FAR IT GETS!
DO WHAT YOU GOTTA DO, CONNORS, AND I'LL DO THE SAME.
GOOD TALK, CHIP.

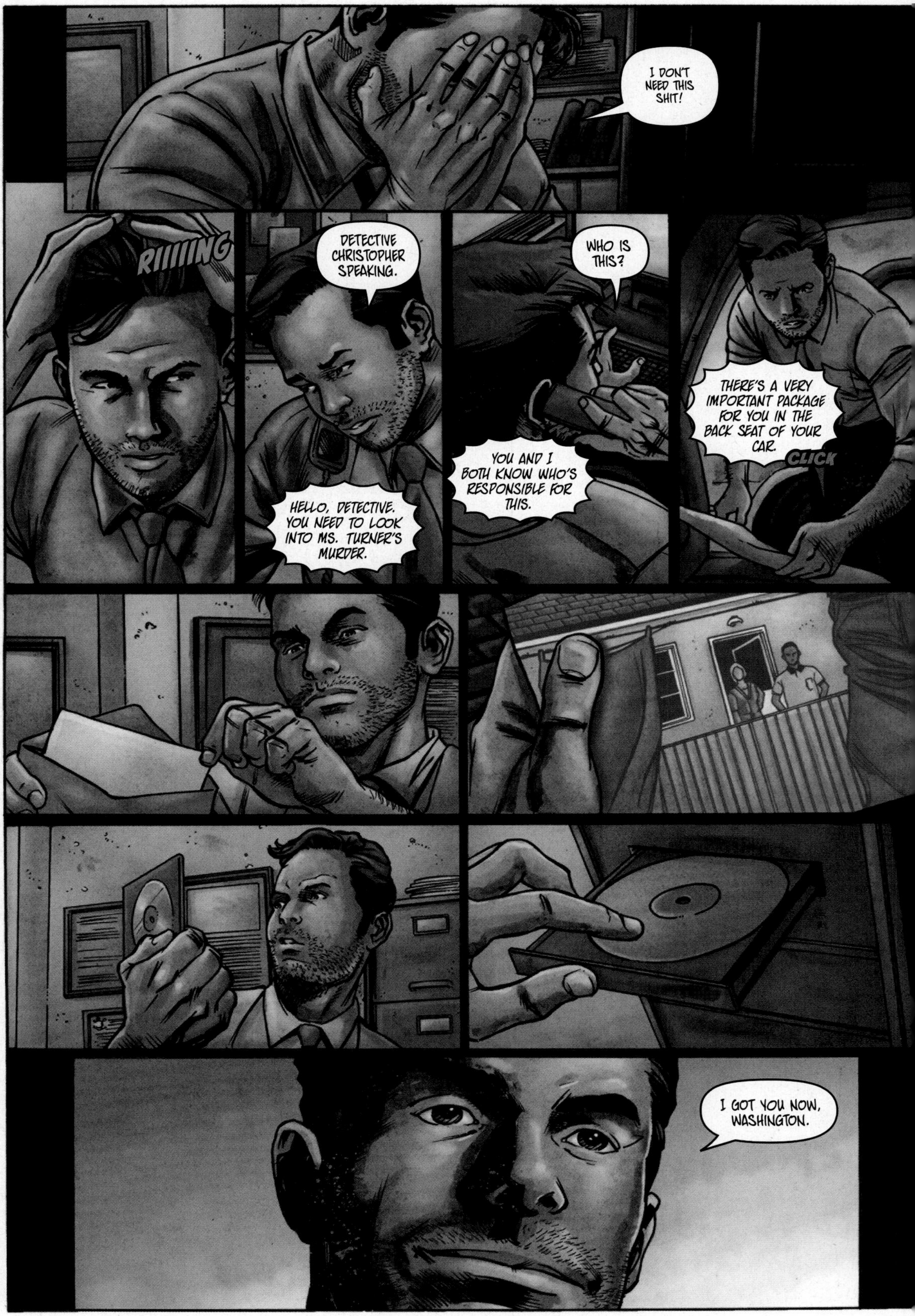
I DON'T NEED THIS SHIT!
RIIIIING
DETECTIVE CHRISTOPHER SPEAKING.
HELLO, DETECTIVE. YOU NEED TO LOOK INTO MS. TURNER'S MURDER.
WHO IS THIS?
YOU AND I BOTH KNOW WHO'S RESPONSIBLE FOR THIS.
THERE'S A VERY IMPORTANT PACKAGE FOR YOU IN THE BACK SEAT OF YOUR CAR.
CLICK
I GOT YOU NOW, WASHINGTON.

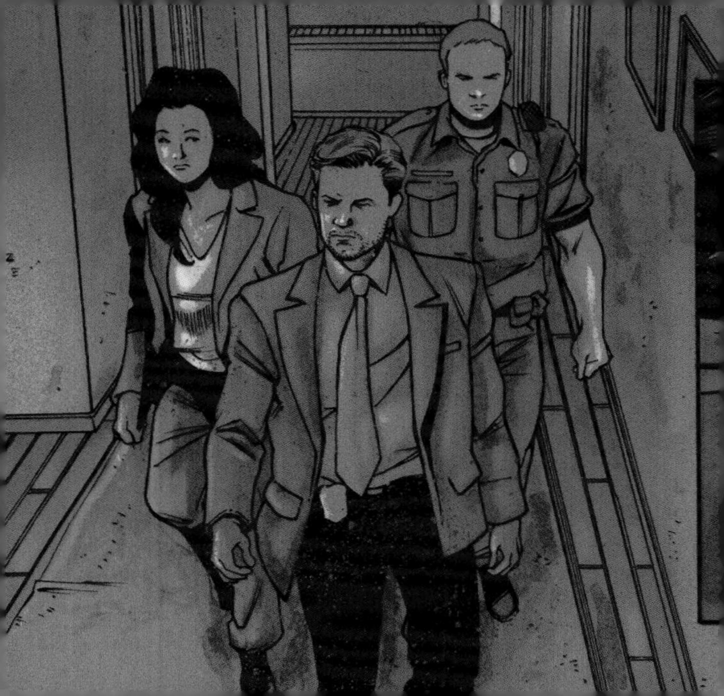

CHAPTER 2

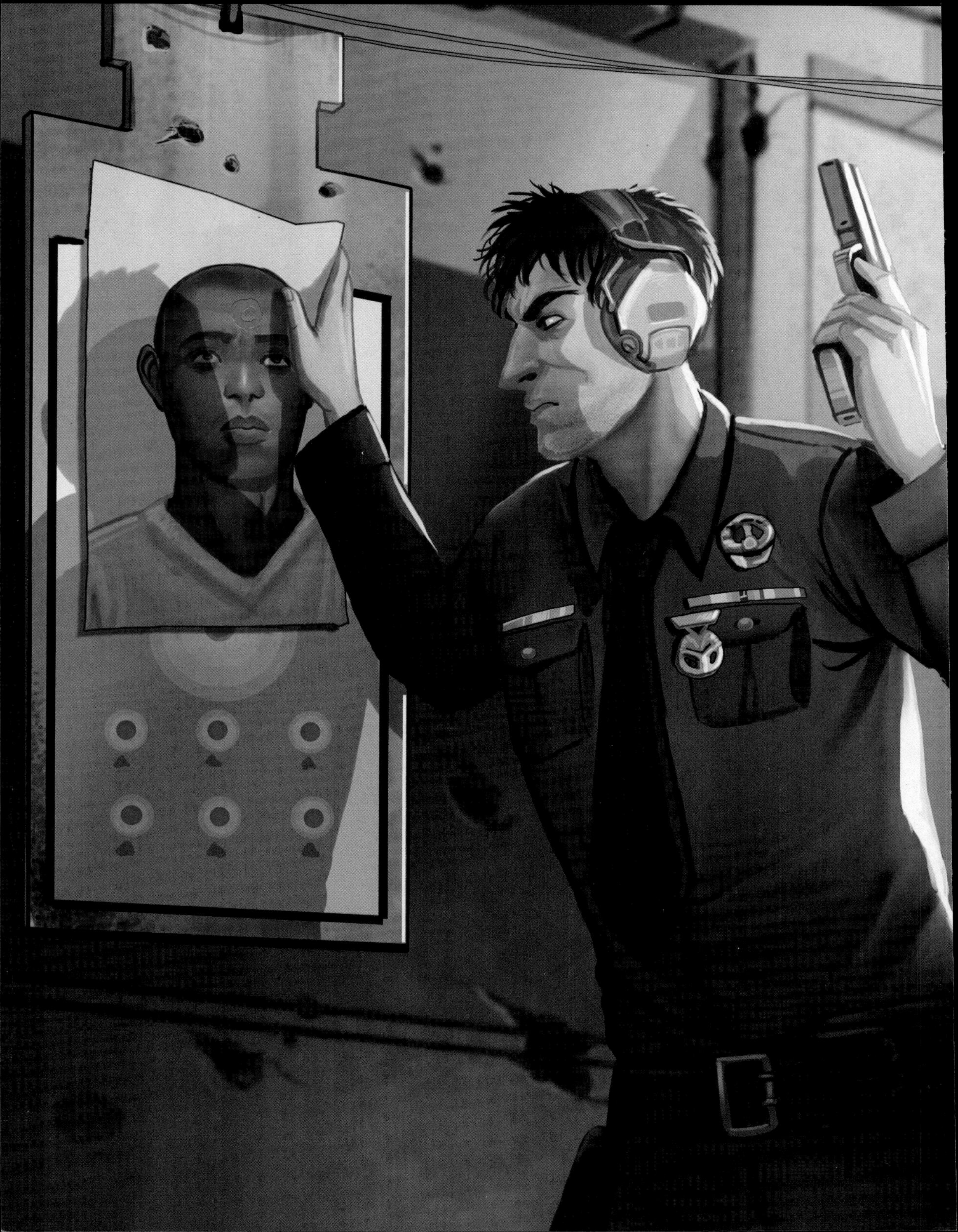

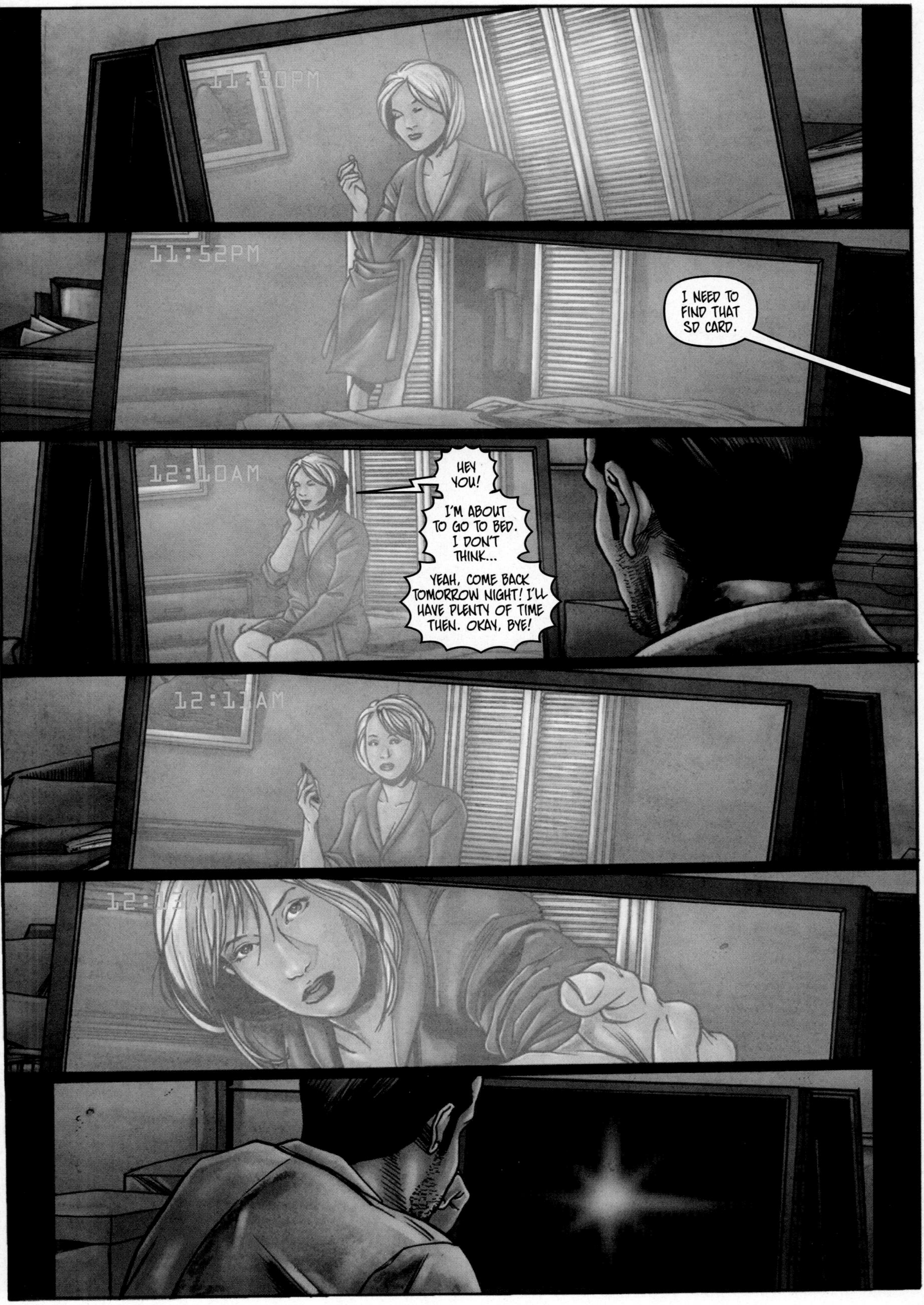
11:30PM
11:52PM
I NEED TO FIND THAT SD CARD.
12:10AM
HEY YOU!
I'M ABOUT TO GO TO BED. I DON'T THINK...
YEAH, COME BACK TOMORROW NIGHT! I'LL HAVE PLENTY OF TIME THEN. OKAY, BYE!
12:11AM

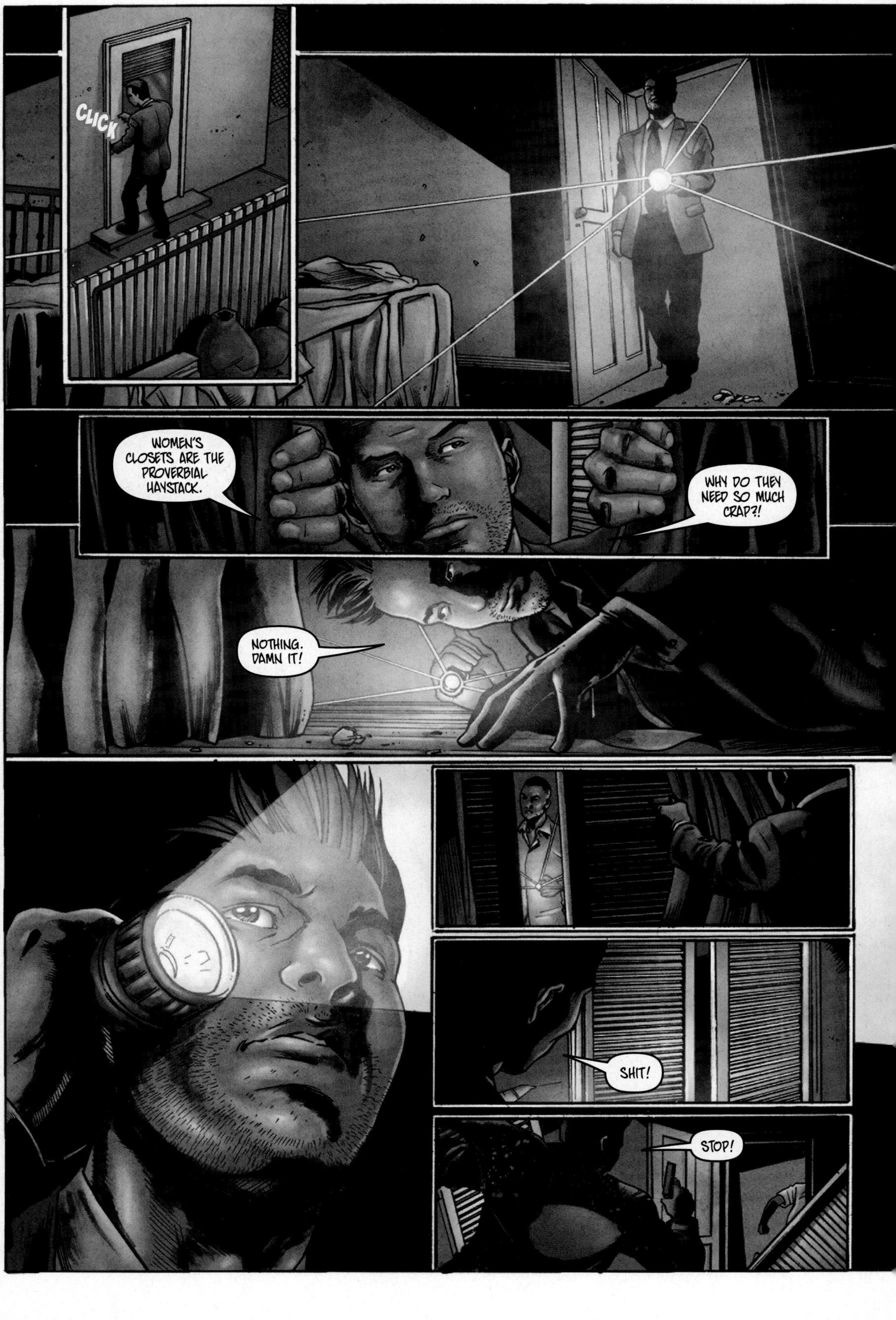
CLICK
WOMEN'S CLOSETS ARE THE PROVERBIAL HAYSTACK.
WHY DO THEY NEED SO MUCH CRAP?!
NOTHING. DAMN IT!
SHIT!
STOP!

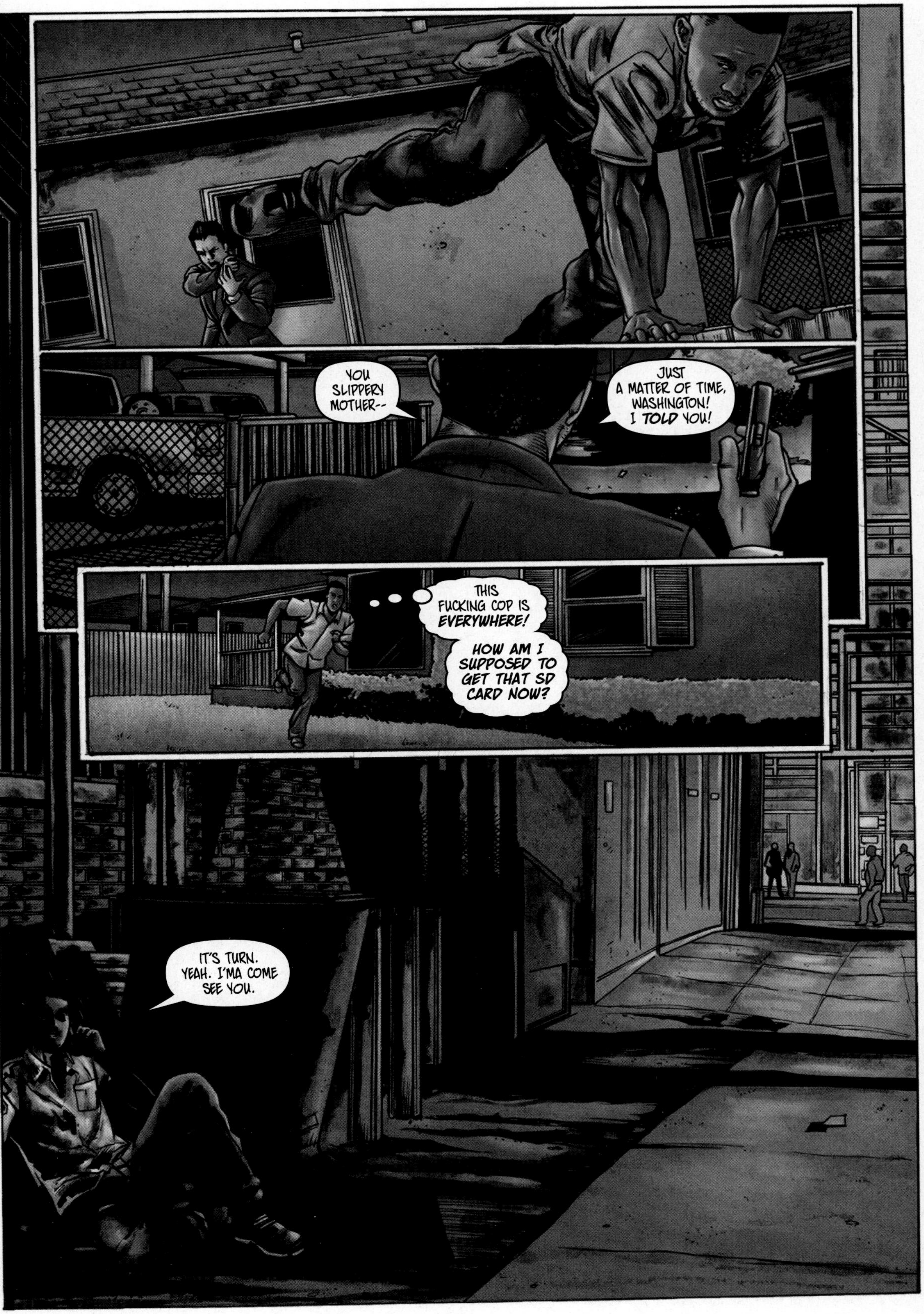
YOU SLIPPERY MOTHER--
JUST A MATTER OF TIME, WASHINGTON! I TOLD YOU!
THIS FUCKING COP IS EVERYWHERE!
HOW AM I SUPPOSED TO GET THAT SD CARD NOW?
IT'S TURN. YEAH. I'MA COME SEE YOU.

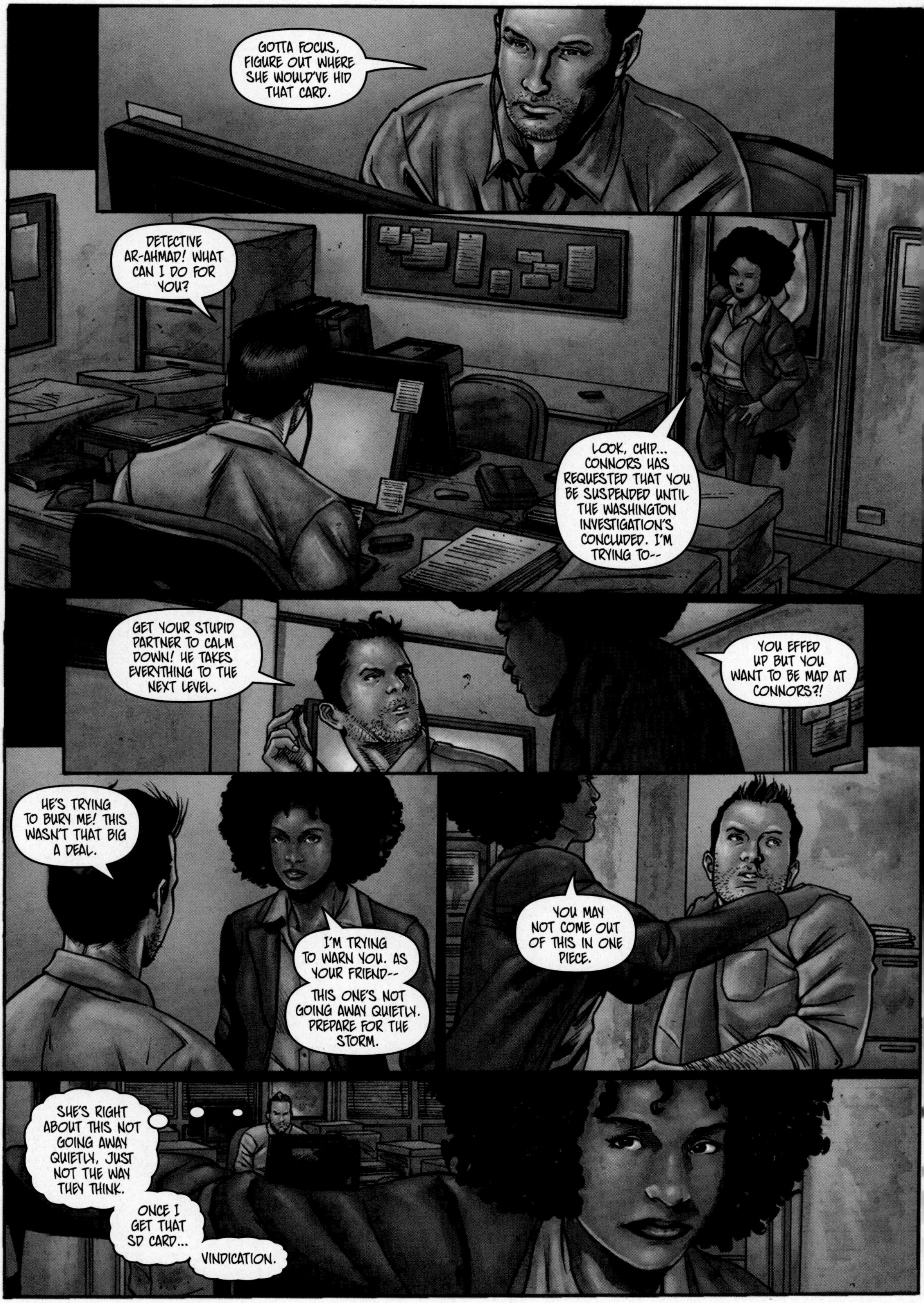
GOTTA FOCUS, FIGURE OUT WHERE SHE WOULD'VE HID THAT CARD.
DETECTIVE AR-AHMAD! WHAT CAN I DO FOR YOU?
LOOK, CHIP... CONNORS HAS REQUESTED THAT YOU BE SUSPENDED UNTIL THE WASHINGTON INVESTIGATION'S CONCLUDED. I'M TRYING TO--
GET YOUR STUPID PARTNER TO CALM DOWN! HE TAKES EVERYTHING TO THE NEXT LEVEL.
YOU EFFED UP BUT YOU WANT TO BE MAD AT CONNORS?!
HE'S TRYING TO BURY ME! THIS WASN'T THAT BIG A DEAL.
I'M TRYING TO WARN YOU. AS YOUR FRIEND--
THIS ONE'S NOT GOING AWAY QUIETLY. PREPARE FOR THE STORM.
YOU MAY NOT COME OUT OF THIS IN ONE PIECE.
SHE'S RIGHT ABOUT THIS NOT GOING AWAY QUIETLY, JUST NOT THE WAY THEY THINK.
ONCE I GET THAT SD CARD...
VINDICATION.

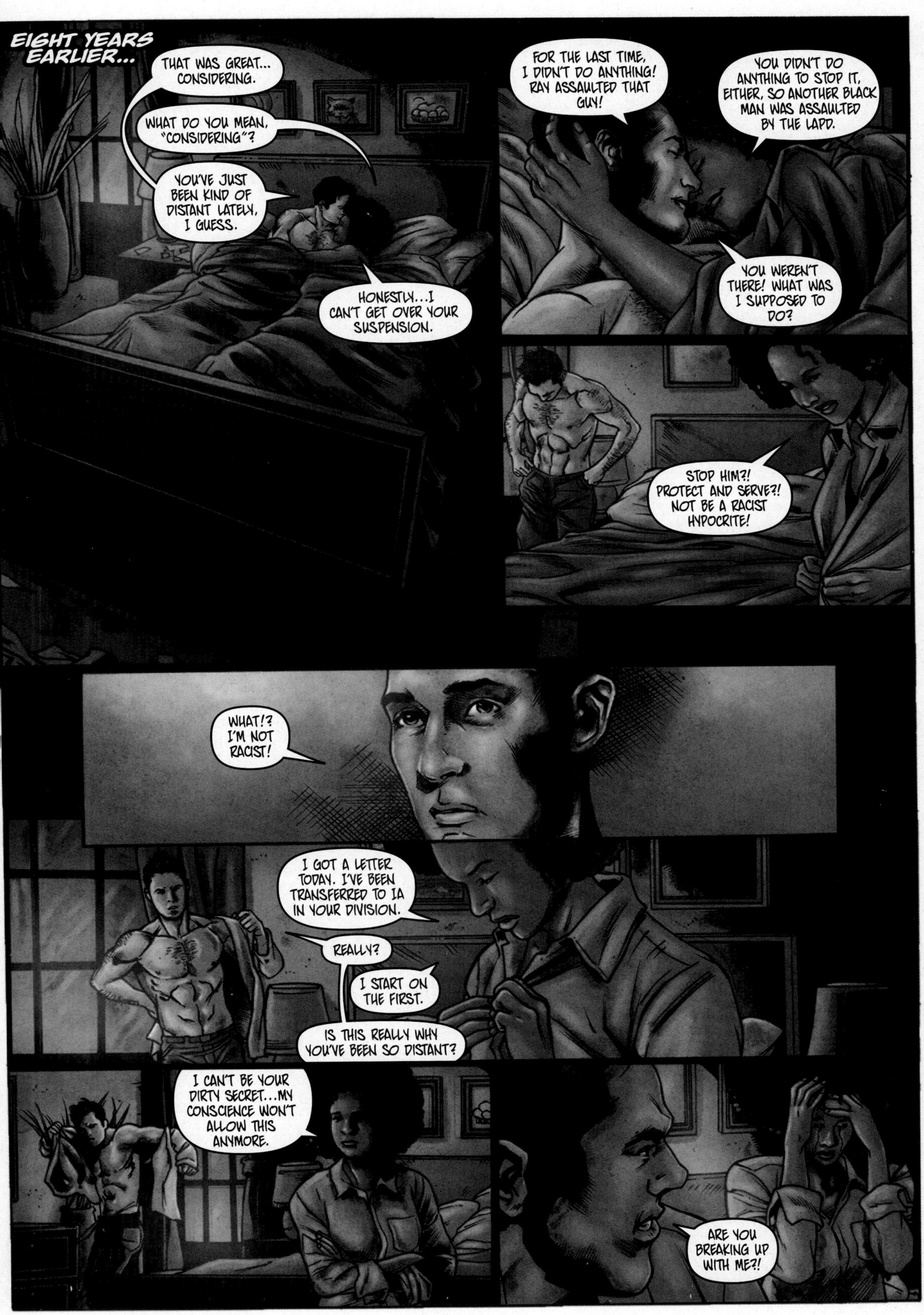
EIGHT YEARS EARLIER...
THAT WAS GREAT... CONSIDERING.
WHAT DO YOU MEAN, "CONSIDERING"?
YOU'VE JUST BEEN KIND OF DISTANT LATELY, I GUESS.
HONESTLY...I CAN'T GET OVER YOUR SUSPENSION.
FOR THE LAST TIME, I DIDN'T DO ANYTHING! RAY ASSAULTED THAT GUY!
YOU DIDN'T DO ANYTHING TO STOP IT, EITHER, SO ANOTHER BLACK MAN WAS ASSAULTED BY THE LAPD.
YOU WEREN'T THERE! WHAT WAS I SUPPOSED TO DO?
STOP HIM?! PROTECT AND SERVE?! NOT BE A RACIST HYPOCRITE!
WHAT!? I'M NOT RACIST!
I GOT A LETTER TODAY. I'VE BEEN TRANSFERRED TO IA IN YOUR DIVISION.
REALLY?
I START ON THE FIRST.
IS THIS REALLY WHY YOU'VE BEEN SO DISTANT?
I CAN'T BE YOUR DIRTY SECRET...MY CONSCIENCE WON'T ALLOW THIS ANYMORE.
ARE YOU BREAKING UP WITH ME?!

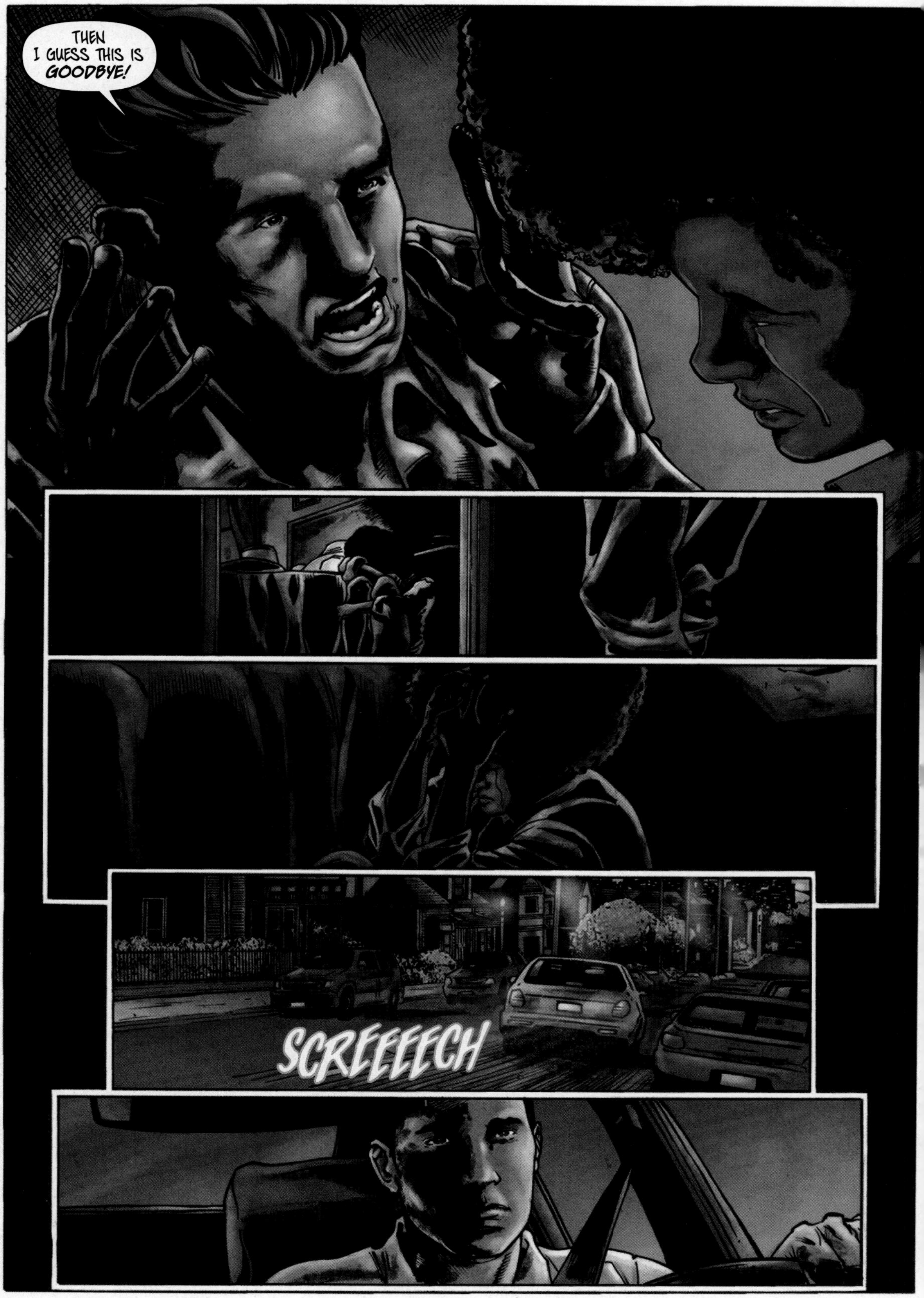
THEN I GUESS THIS IS GOODBYE!
SCREEEECH

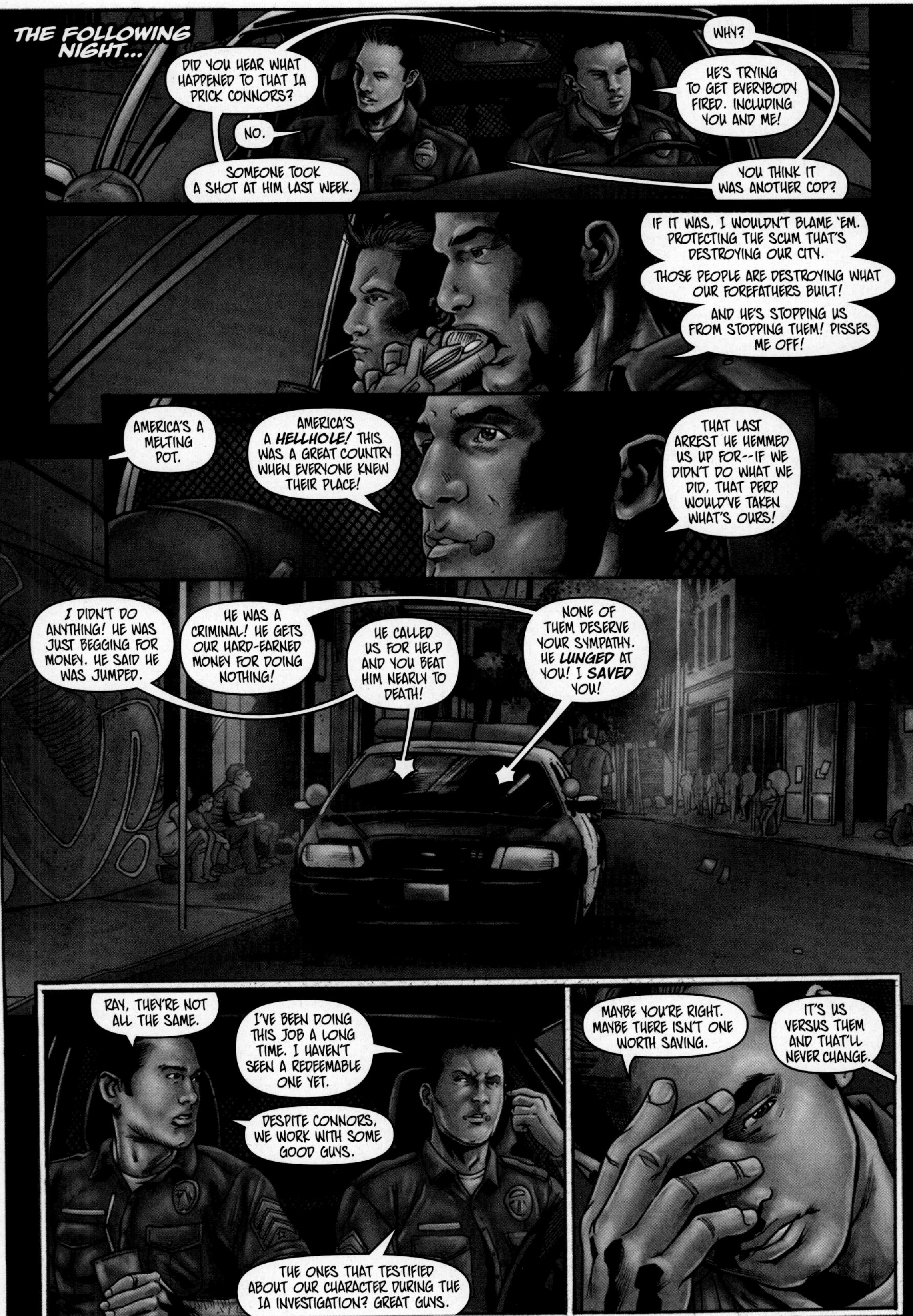
THE FOLLOWING NIGHT...
DID YOU HEAR WHAT HAPPENED TO THAT IA PRICK CONNORS?
NO.
SOMEONE TOOK A SHOT AT HIM LAST WEEK.
WHY?
HE'S TRYING TO GET EVERYBODY FIRED. INCLUDING YOU AND ME!
YOU THINK IT WAS ANOTHER COP?
IF IT WAS, I WOULDN'T BLAME 'EM. PROTECTING THE SCUM THAT'S DESTROYING OUR CITY.
THOSE PEOPLE ARE DESTROYING WHAT OUR FOREFATHERS BUILT!
AND HE'S STOPPING US FROM STOPPING THEM! PISSES ME OFF!
AMERICA'S A MELTING POT.
AMERICA'S A **HELLHOLE!** THIS WAS A GREAT COUNTRY WHEN EVERYONE KNEW THEIR PLACE!
THAT LAST ARREST HE HEMMED US UP FOR--IF WE DIDN'T DO WHAT WE DID, THAT PERP WOULD'VE TAKEN WHAT'S OURS!
I DIDN'T DO ANYTHING! HE WAS JUST BEGGING FOR MONEY. HE SAID HE WAS JUMPED.
HE WAS A CRIMINAL! HE GETS OUR HARD-EARNED MONEY FOR DOING NOTHING!
HE CALLED US FOR HELP AND YOU BEAT HIM NEARLY TO DEATH!
NONE OF THEM DESERVE YOUR SYMPATHY. HE ***LUNGED*** AT YOU! I ***SAVED*** YOU!
RAY, THEY'RE NOT ALL THE SAME.
I'VE BEEN DOING THIS JOB A LONG TIME. I HAVEN'T SEEN A REDEEMABLE ONE YET.
DESPITE CONNORS, WE WORK WITH SOME GOOD GUYS.
THE ONES THAT TESTIFIED ABOUT OUR CHARACTER DURING THE IA INVESTIGATION? GREAT GUYS.
MAYBE YOU'RE RIGHT. MAYBE THERE ISN'T ONE WORTH SAVING.
IT'S US VERSUS THEM AND THAT'LL NEVER CHANGE.

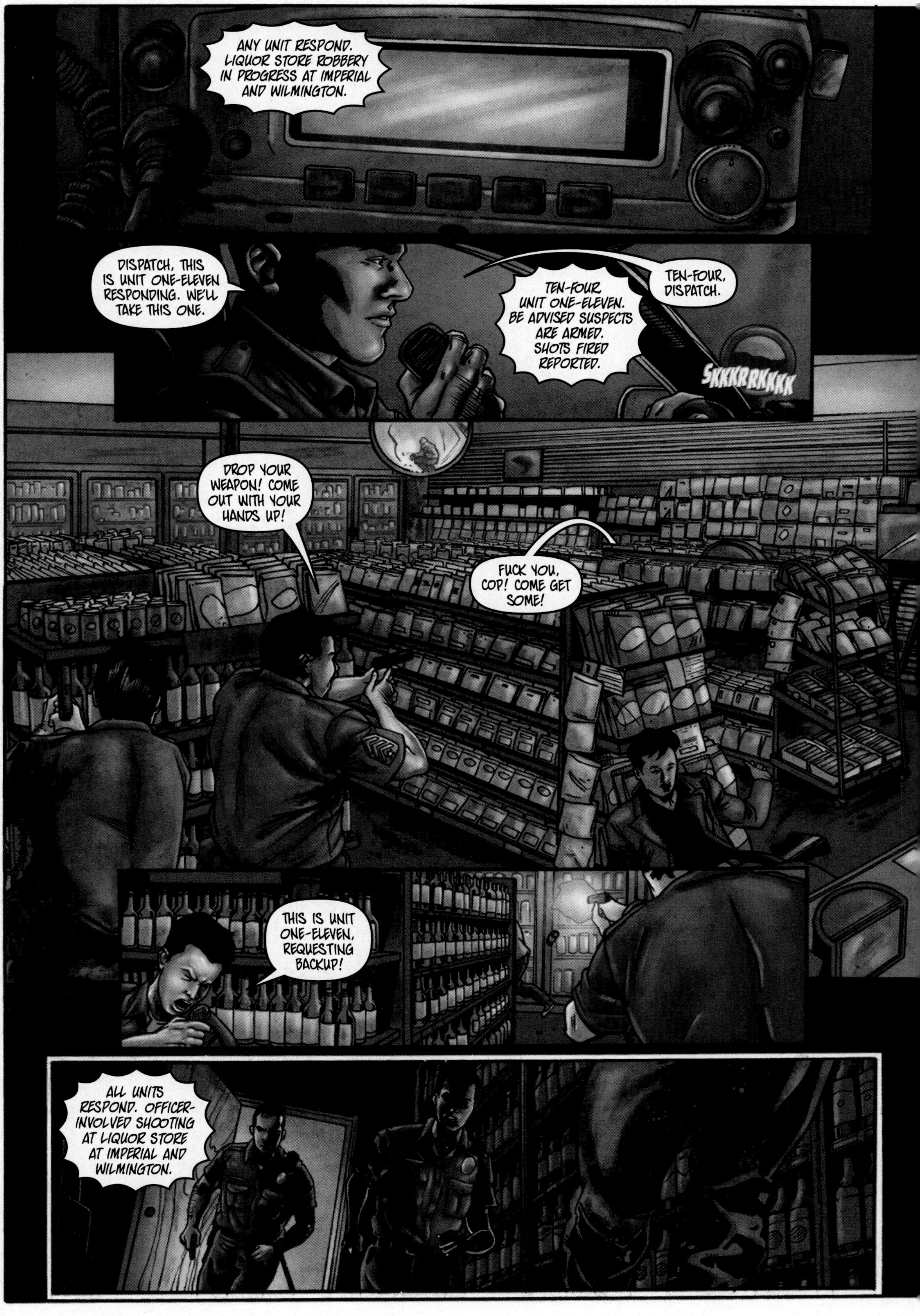
ANY UNIT RESPOND. LIQUOR STORE ROBBERY IN PROGRESS AT IMPERIAL AND WILMINGTON.
DISPATCH, THIS IS UNIT ONE-ELEVEN RESPONDING. WE'LL TAKE THIS ONE.
TEN-FOUR, UNIT ONE-ELEVEN. BE ADVISED SUSPECTS ARE ARMED. SHOTS FIRED REPORTED.
TEN-FOUR, DISPATCH.
SKKKRRKKKK
DROP YOUR WEAPON! COME OUT WITH YOUR HANDS UP!
FUCK YOU, COP! COME GET SOME!
THIS IS UNIT ONE-ELEVEN, REQUESTING BACKUP!
ALL UNITS RESPOND. OFFICER-INVOLVED SHOOTING AT LIQUOR STORE AT IMPERIAL AND WILMINGTON.

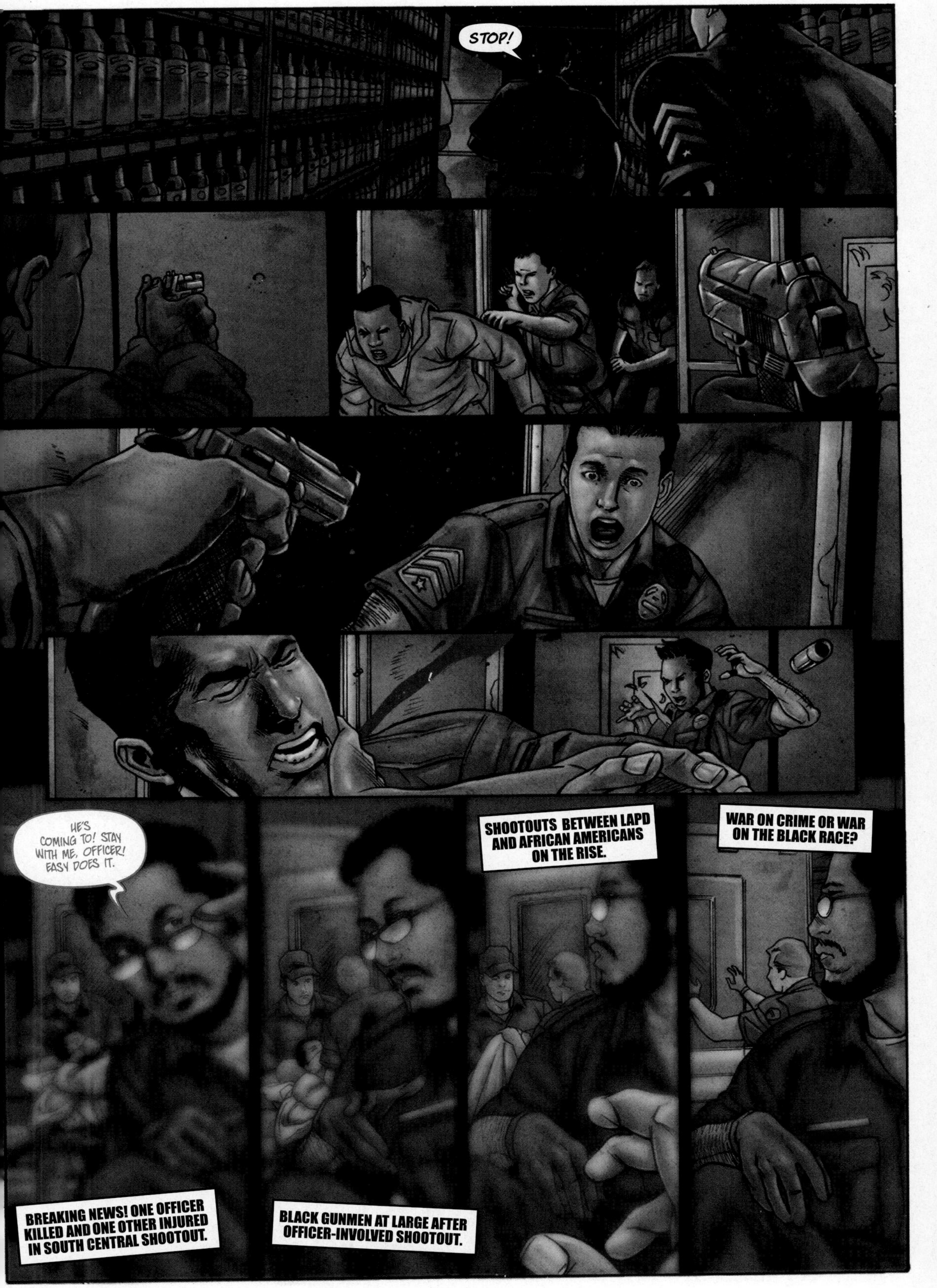
STOP!
HE'S COMING TO! STAY WITH ME, OFFICER! EASY DOES IT.
SHOOTOUTS BETWEEN LAPD AND AFRICAN AMERICANS ON THE RISE.
WAR ON CRIME OR WAR ON THE BLACK RACE?
BREAKING NEWS! ONE OFFICER KILLED AND ONE OTHER INJURED IN SOUTH CENTRAL SHOOTOUT.
BLACK GUNMEN AT LARGE AFTER OFFICER-INVOLVED SHOOTOUT.

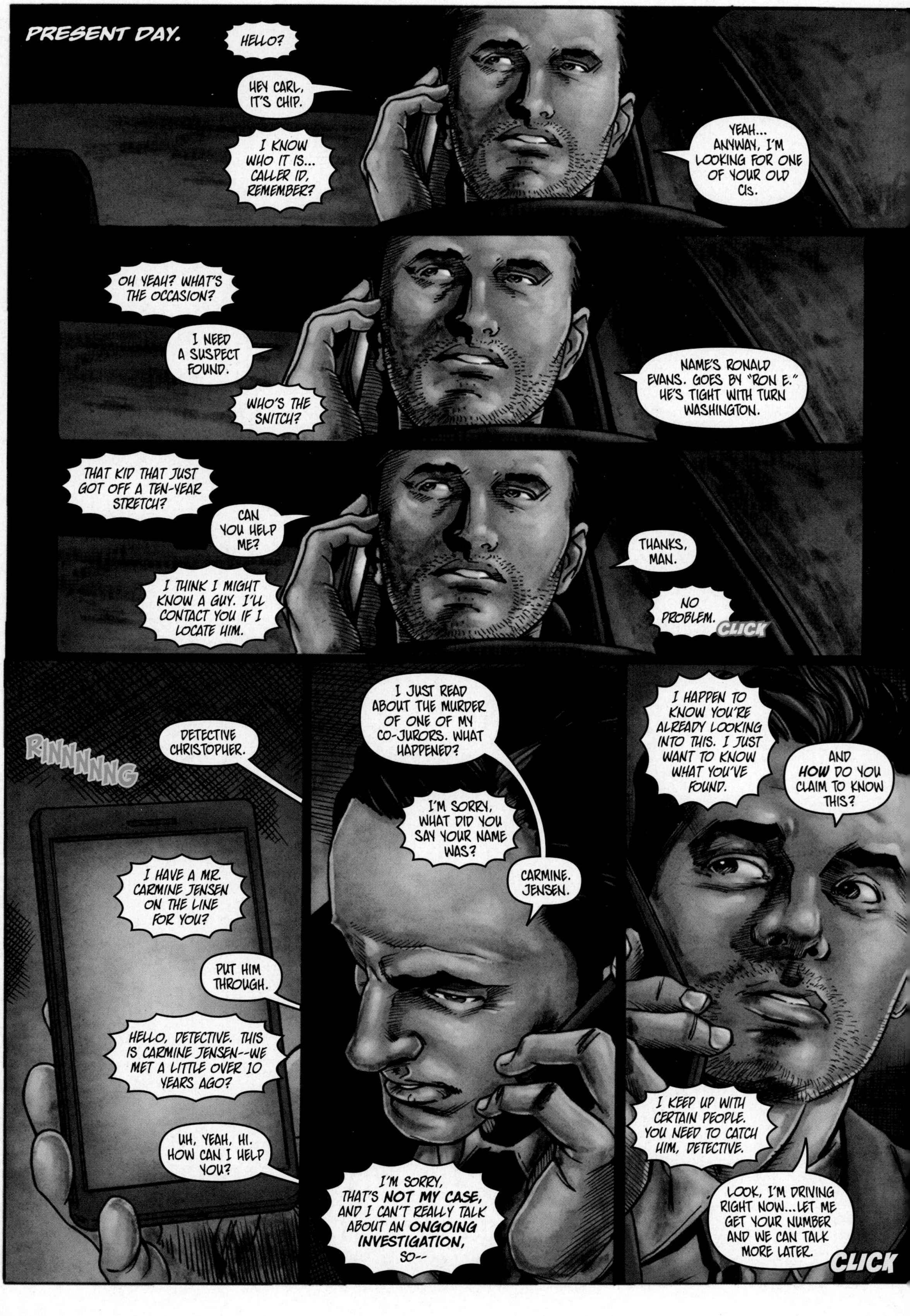
PRESENT DAY.
HELLO?
HEY CARL, IT'S CHIP.
I KNOW WHO IT IS... CALLER ID, REMEMBER?
YEAH... ANYWAY, I'M LOOKING FOR ONE OF YOUR OLD CIS.
OH YEAH? WHAT'S THE OCCASION?
I NEED A SUSPECT FOUND.
WHO'S THE SNITCH?
NAME'S RONALD EVANS. GOES BY "RON E." HE'S TIGHT WITH TURN WASHINGTON.
THAT KID THAT JUST GOT OFF A TEN-YEAR STRETCH?
CAN YOU HELP ME?
I THINK I MIGHT KNOW A GUY. I'LL CONTACT YOU IF I LOCATE HIM.
THANKS, MAN.
NO PROBLEM.
CLICK
RINNNNNG
DETECTIVE CHRISTOPHER.
I HAVE A MR. CARMINE JENSEN ON THE LINE FOR YOU?
PUT HIM THROUGH.
HELLO, DETECTIVE. THIS IS CARMINE JENSEN--WE MET A LITTLE OVER 10 YEARS AGO?
UH, YEAH, HI. HOW CAN I HELP YOU?
I JUST READ ABOUT THE MURDER OF ONE OF MY CO-JURORS. WHAT HAPPENED?
I'M SORRY, WHAT DID YOU SAY YOUR NAME WAS?
CARMINE. JENSEN.
I'M SORRY, THAT'S **NOT MY CASE**, AND I CAN'T REALLY TALK ABOUT AN **ONGOING INVESTIGATION**, SO--
I HAPPEN TO KNOW YOU'RE ALREADY LOOKING INTO THIS. I JUST WANT TO KNOW WHAT YOU'VE FOUND.
AND **HOW** DO YOU CLAIM TO KNOW THIS?
I KEEP UP WITH CERTAIN PEOPLE. YOU NEED TO CATCH HIM, DETECTIVE.
LOOK, I'M DRIVING RIGHT NOW...LET ME GET YOUR NUMBER AND WE CAN TALK MORE LATER.
CLICK

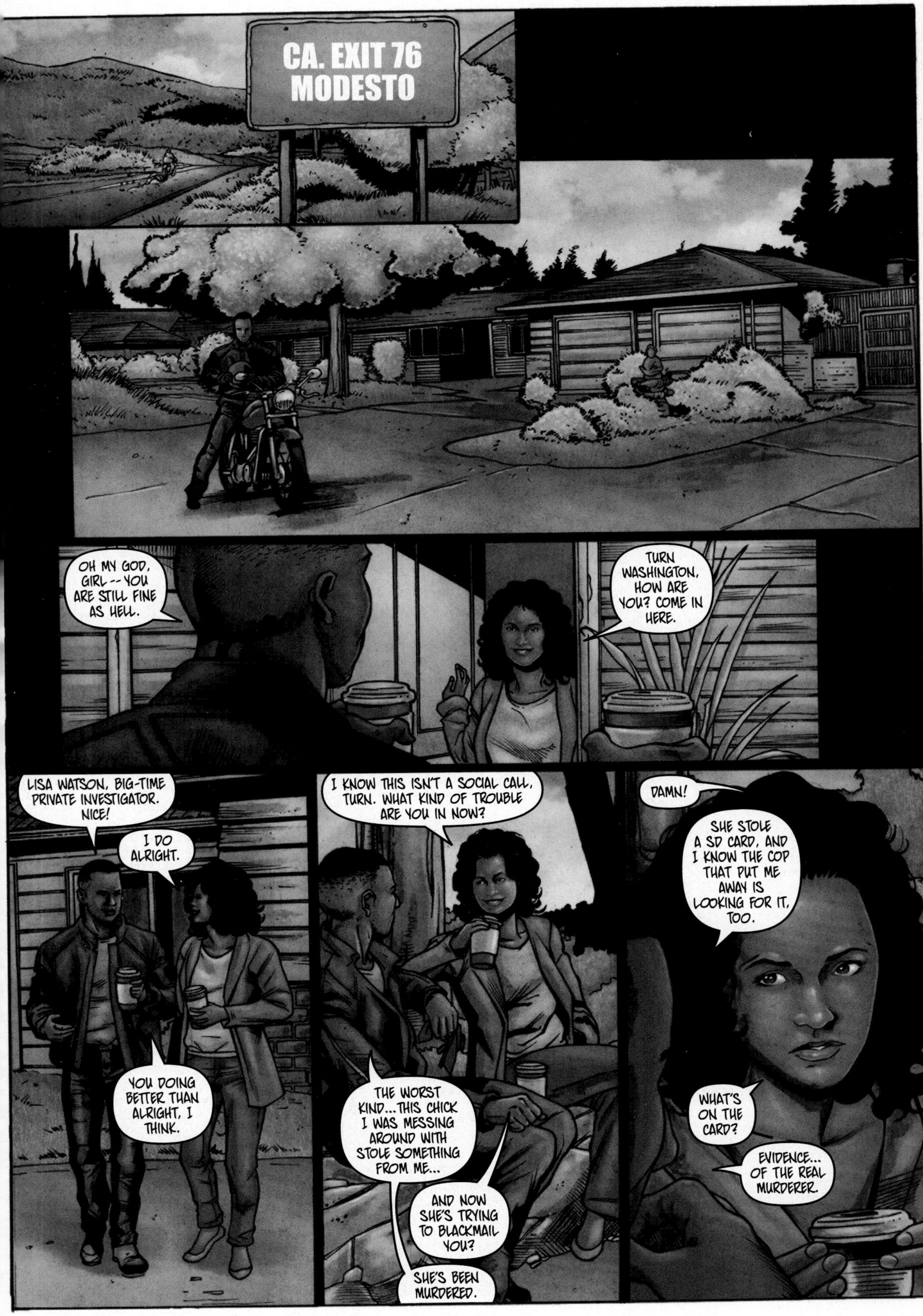
CA. EXIT 76
MODESTO
OH MY GOD, GIRL -- YOU ARE STILL FINE AS HELL.
TURN WASHINGTON, HOW ARE YOU? COME IN HERE.
LISA WATSON, BIG-TIME PRIVATE INVESTIGATOR. NICE!
I DO ALRIGHT.
YOU DOING BETTER THAN ALRIGHT, I THINK.
I KNOW THIS ISN'T A SOCIAL CALL, TURN. WHAT KIND OF TROUBLE ARE YOU IN NOW?
THE WORST KIND...THIS CHICK I WAS MESSING AROUND WITH STOLE SOMETHING FROM ME...
AND NOW SHE'S TRYING TO BLACKMAIL YOU?
SHE'S BEEN MURDERED.
DAMN!
SHE STOLE A SD CARD, AND I KNOW THE COP THAT PUT ME AWAY IS LOOKING FOR IT, TOO.
WHAT'S ON THE CARD?
EVIDENCE... OF THE REAL MURDERER.

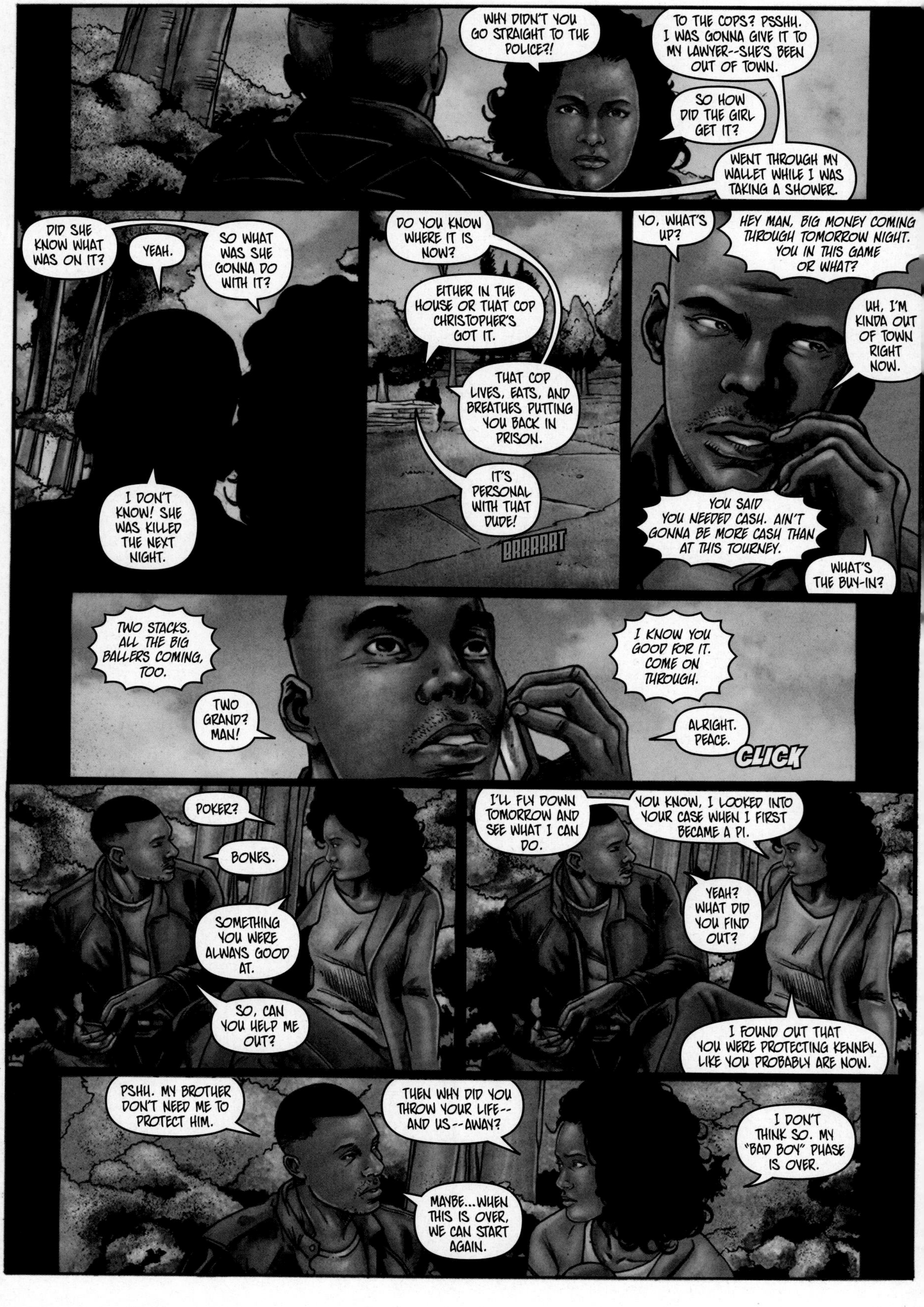
WHY DIDN'T YOU GO STRAIGHT TO THE POLICE?!
TO THE COPS? PSSHH. I WAS GONNA GIVE IT TO MY LAWYER--SHE'S BEEN OUT OF TOWN.
SO HOW DID THE GIRL GET IT?
WENT THROUGH MY WALLET WHILE I WAS TAKING A SHOWER.
DID SHE KNOW WHAT WAS ON IT?
YEAH.
SO WHAT WAS SHE GONNA DO WITH IT?
I DON'T KNOW! SHE WAS KILLED THE NEXT NIGHT.
DO YOU KNOW WHERE IT IS NOW?
EITHER IN THE HOUSE OR THAT COP CHRISTOPHER'S GOT IT.
THAT COP LIVES, EATS, AND BREATHES PUTTING YOU BACK IN PRISON.
IT'S PERSONAL WITH THAT DUDE!
BRRRRRT
YO, WHAT'S UP?
HEY MAN, BIG MONEY COMING THROUGH TOMORROW NIGHT. YOU IN THIS GAME OR WHAT?
UH, I'M KINDA OUT OF TOWN RIGHT NOW.
YOU SAID YOU NEEDED CASH. AIN'T GONNA BE MORE CASH THAN AT THIS TOURNEY.
WHAT'S THE BUY-IN?
TWO STACKS. ALL THE BIG BALLERS COMING, TOO.
TWO GRAND? MAN!
I KNOW YOU GOOD FOR IT. COME ON THROUGH.
ALRIGHT. PEACE.
CLICK
POKER?
BONES.
SOMETHING YOU WERE ALWAYS GOOD AT.
SO, CAN YOU HELP ME OUT?
I'LL FLY DOWN TOMORROW AND SEE WHAT I CAN DO.
YOU KNOW, I LOOKED INTO YOUR CASE WHEN I FIRST BECAME A PI.
YEAH? WHAT DID YOU FIND OUT?
I FOUND OUT THAT YOU WERE PROTECTING KENNEY. LIKE YOU PROBABLY ARE NOW.
PSHH. MY BROTHER DON'T NEED ME TO PROTECT HIM.
THEN WHY DID YOU THROW YOUR LIFE-- AND US--AWAY?
MAYBE...WHEN THIS IS OVER, WE CAN START AGAIN.
I DON'T THINK SO. MY "BAD BOY" PHASE IS OVER.

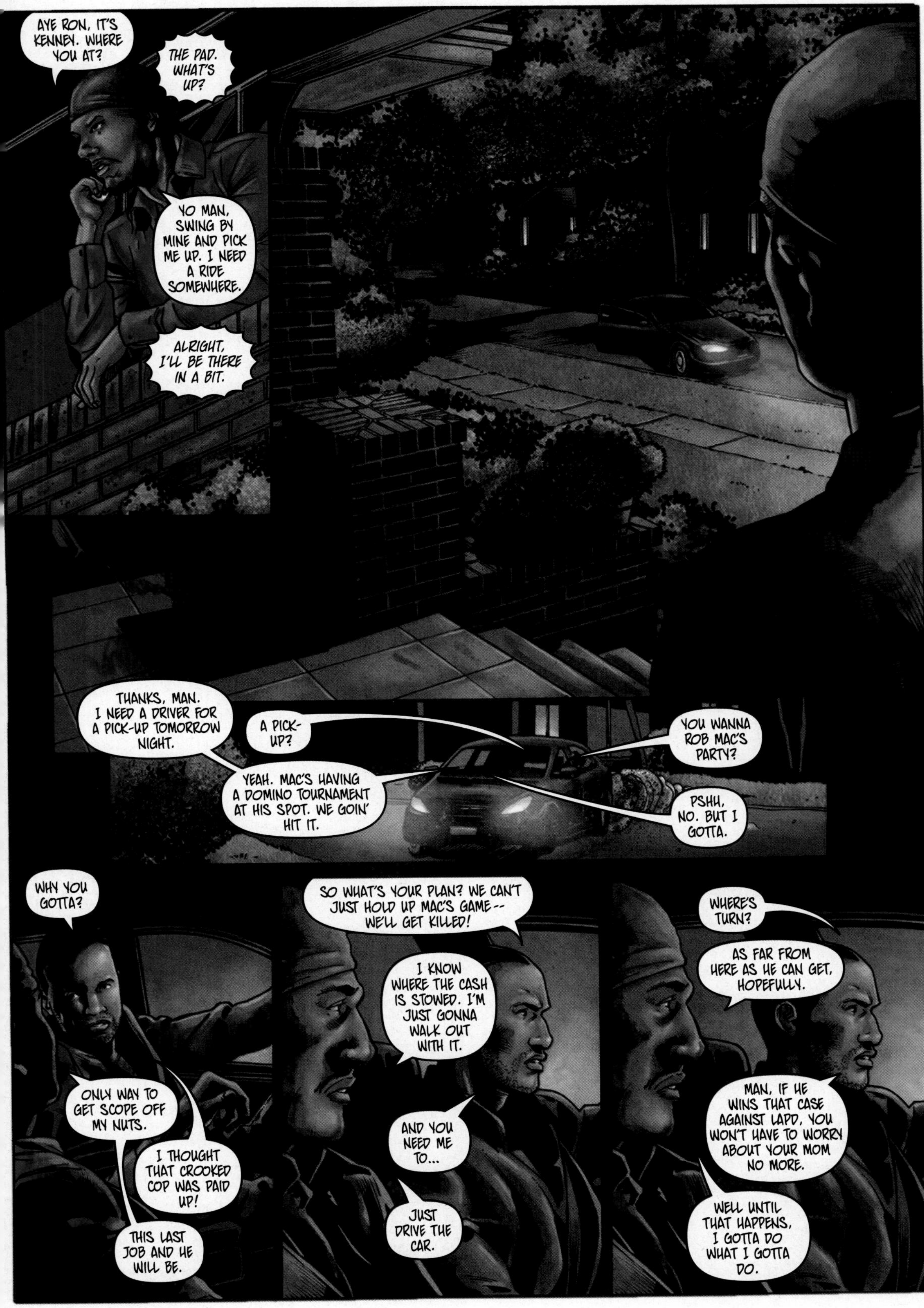
AYE RON, IT'S KENNEY. WHERE YOU AT?
THE PAD. WHAT'S UP?
YO MAN, SWING BY MINE AND PICK ME UP. I NEED A RIDE SOMEWHERE.
ALRIGHT, I'LL BE THERE IN A BIT.
THANKS, MAN. I NEED A DRIVER FOR A PICK-UP TOMORROW NIGHT.
A PICK-UP?
YEAH. MAC'S HAVING A DOMINO TOURNAMENT AT HIS SPOT. WE GOIN' HIT IT.
YOU WANNA ROB MAC'S PARTY?
PSHH, NO. BUT I GOTTA.
WHY YOU GOTTA?
ONLY WAY TO GET SCOPE OFF MY NUTS.
I THOUGHT THAT CROOKED COP WAS PAID UP!
THIS LAST JOB AND HE WILL BE.
SO WHAT'S YOUR PLAN? WE CAN'T JUST HOLD UP MAC'S GAME-- WE'LL GET KILLED!
I KNOW WHERE THE CASH IS STOWED. I'M JUST GONNA WALK OUT WITH IT.
AND YOU NEED ME TO...
JUST DRIVE THE CAR.
WHERE'S TURN?
AS FAR FROM HERE AS HE CAN GET, HOPEFULLY.
MAN, IF HE WINS THAT CASE AGAINST LAPD, YOU WON'T HAVE TO WORRY ABOUT YOUR MOM NO MORE.
WELL UNTIL THAT HAPPENS, I GOTTA DO WHAT I GOTTA DO.

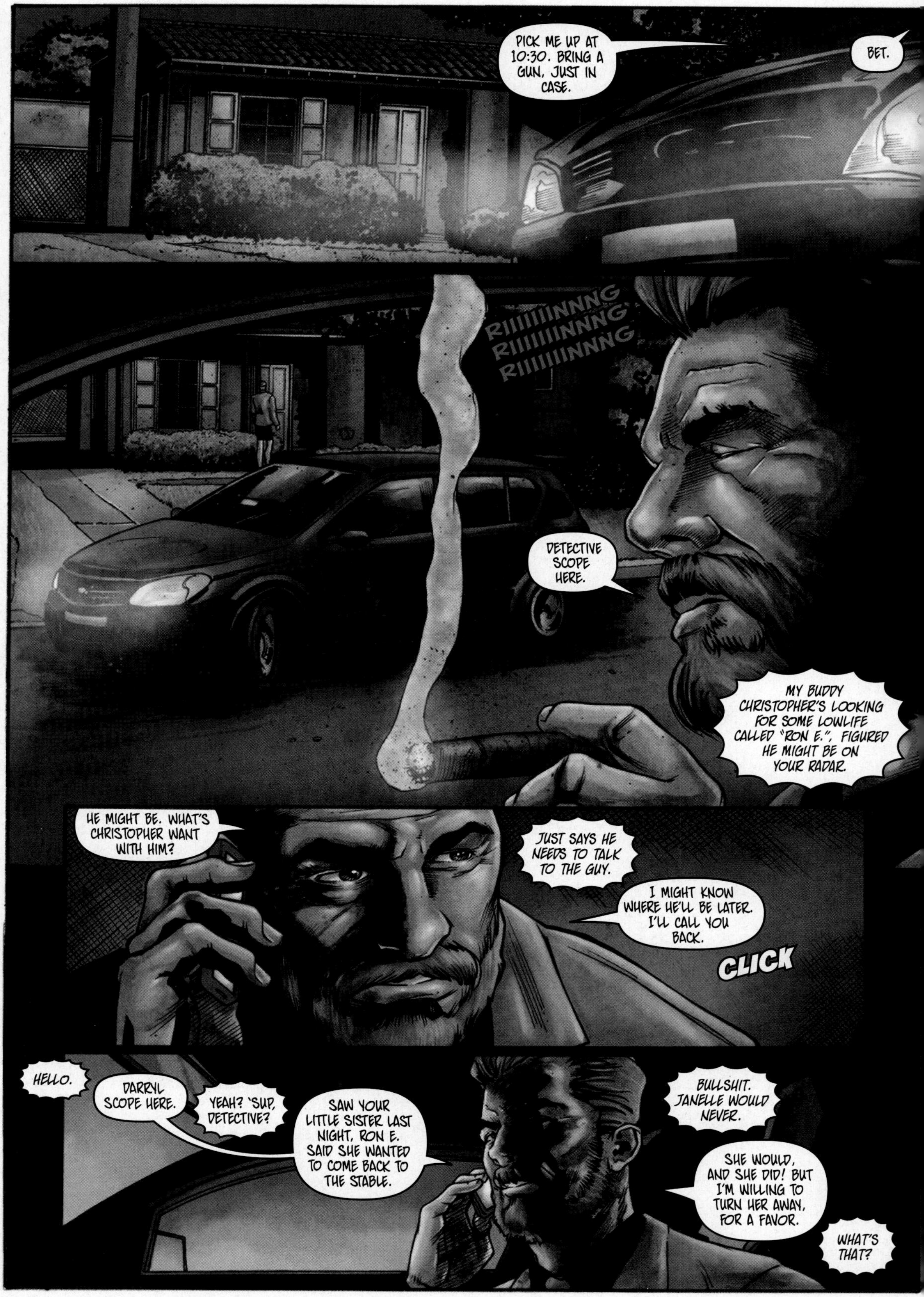
PICK ME UP AT 10:30. BRING A GUN, JUST IN CASE.
BET.
RIIIIIIINNNG RIIIIIIINNNG RIIIIIIINNNG
DETECTIVE SCOPE HERE.
MY BUDDY CHRISTOPHER'S LOOKING FOR SOME LOWLIFE CALLED "RON E.", FIGURED HE MIGHT BE ON YOUR RADAR.
HE MIGHT BE. WHAT'S CHRISTOPHER WANT WITH HIM?
JUST SAYS HE NEEDS TO TALK TO THE GUY.
I MIGHT KNOW WHERE HE'LL BE LATER. I'LL CALL YOU BACK.
CLICK
HELLO.
DARRYL SCOPE HERE.
YEAH? 'SUP, DETECTIVE?
SAW YOUR LITTLE SISTER LAST NIGHT, RON E. SAID SHE WANTED TO COME BACK TO THE STABLE.
BULLSHIT. JANELLE WOULD NEVER.
SHE WOULD, AND SHE DID! BUT I'M WILLING TO TURN HER AWAY, FOR A FAVOR.
WHAT'S THAT?

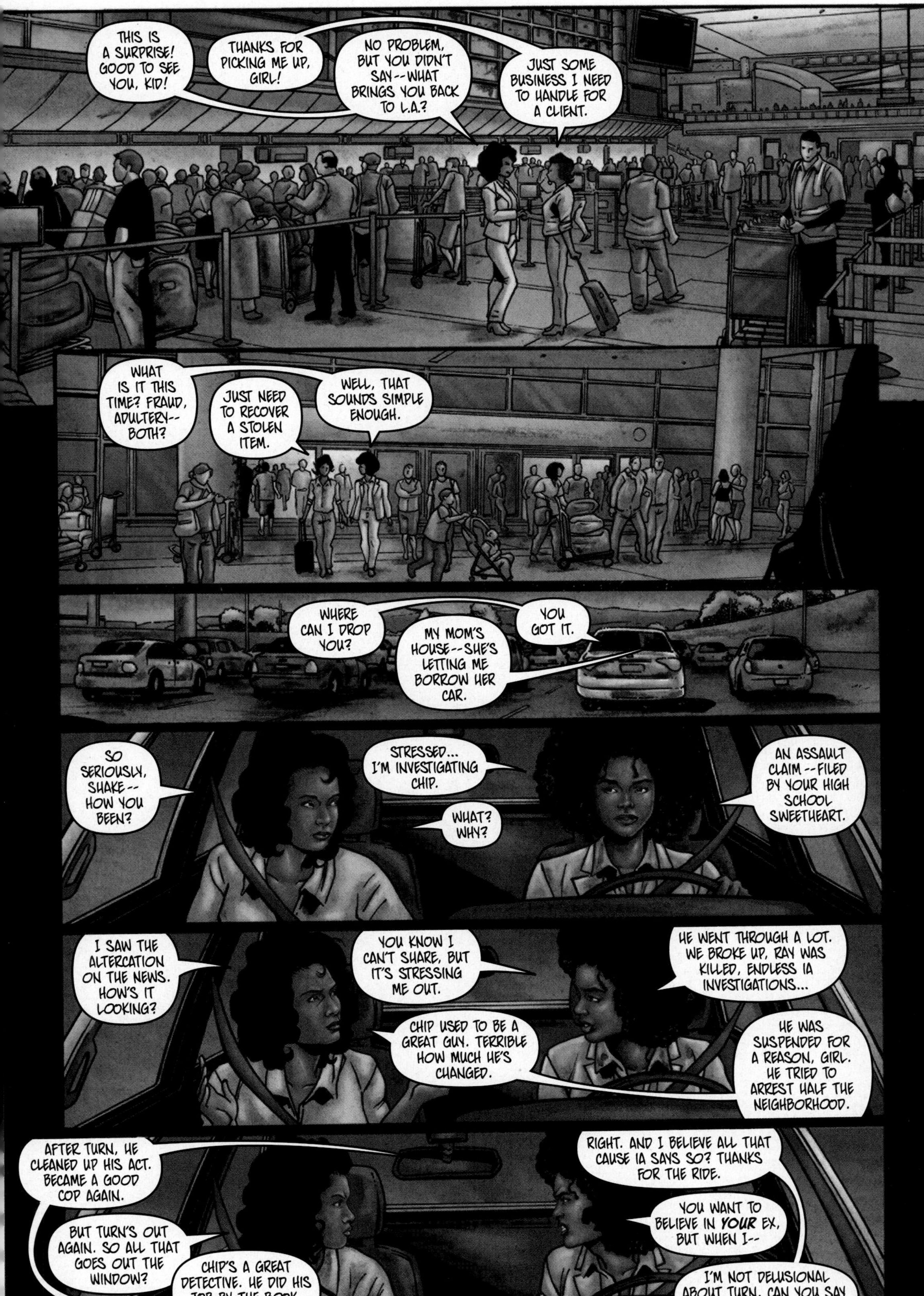
THIS IS A SURPRISE! GOOD TO SEE YOU, KID!
THANKS FOR PICKING ME UP, GIRL!
NO PROBLEM, BUT YOU DIDN'T SAY--WHAT BRINGS YOU BACK TO L.A.?
JUST SOME BUSINESS I NEED TO HANDLE FOR A CLIENT.
WHAT IS IT THIS TIME? FRAUD, ADULTERY--BOTH?
JUST NEED TO RECOVER A STOLEN ITEM.
WELL, THAT SOUNDS SIMPLE ENOUGH.
WHERE CAN I DROP YOU?
MY MOM'S HOUSE--SHE'S LETTING ME BORROW HER CAR.
YOU GOT IT.
SO SERIOUSLY, SHAKE--HOW YOU BEEN?
STRESSED... I'M INVESTIGATING CHIP.
WHAT? WHY?
AN ASSAULT CLAIM--FILED BY YOUR HIGH SCHOOL SWEETHEART.
I SAW THE ALTERCATION ON THE NEWS. HOW'S IT LOOKING?
YOU KNOW I CAN'T SHARE, BUT IT'S STRESSING ME OUT.
HE WENT THROUGH A LOT. WE BROKE UP, RAY WAS KILLED, ENDLESS IA INVESTIGATIONS...
CHIP USED TO BE A GREAT GUY. TERRIBLE HOW MUCH HE'S CHANGED.
HE WAS SUSPENDED FOR A REASON, GIRL. HE TRIED TO ARREST HALF THE NEIGHBORHOOD.
AFTER TURN, HE CLEANED UP HIS ACT. BECAME A GOOD COP AGAIN.
RIGHT. AND I BELIEVE ALL THAT CAUSE IA SAYS SO? THANKS FOR THE RIDE.
BUT TURN'S OUT AGAIN. SO ALL THAT GOES OUT THE WINDOW?
YOU WANT TO BELIEVE IN *YOUR* EX, BUT WHEN I--
CHIP'S A GREAT DETECTIVE. HE DID HIS JOB BY THE BOOK, DESPITE ALL OF IT.
I'M NOT DELUSIONAL ABOUT TURN. CAN YOU SAY THE SAME? OF CHIP?

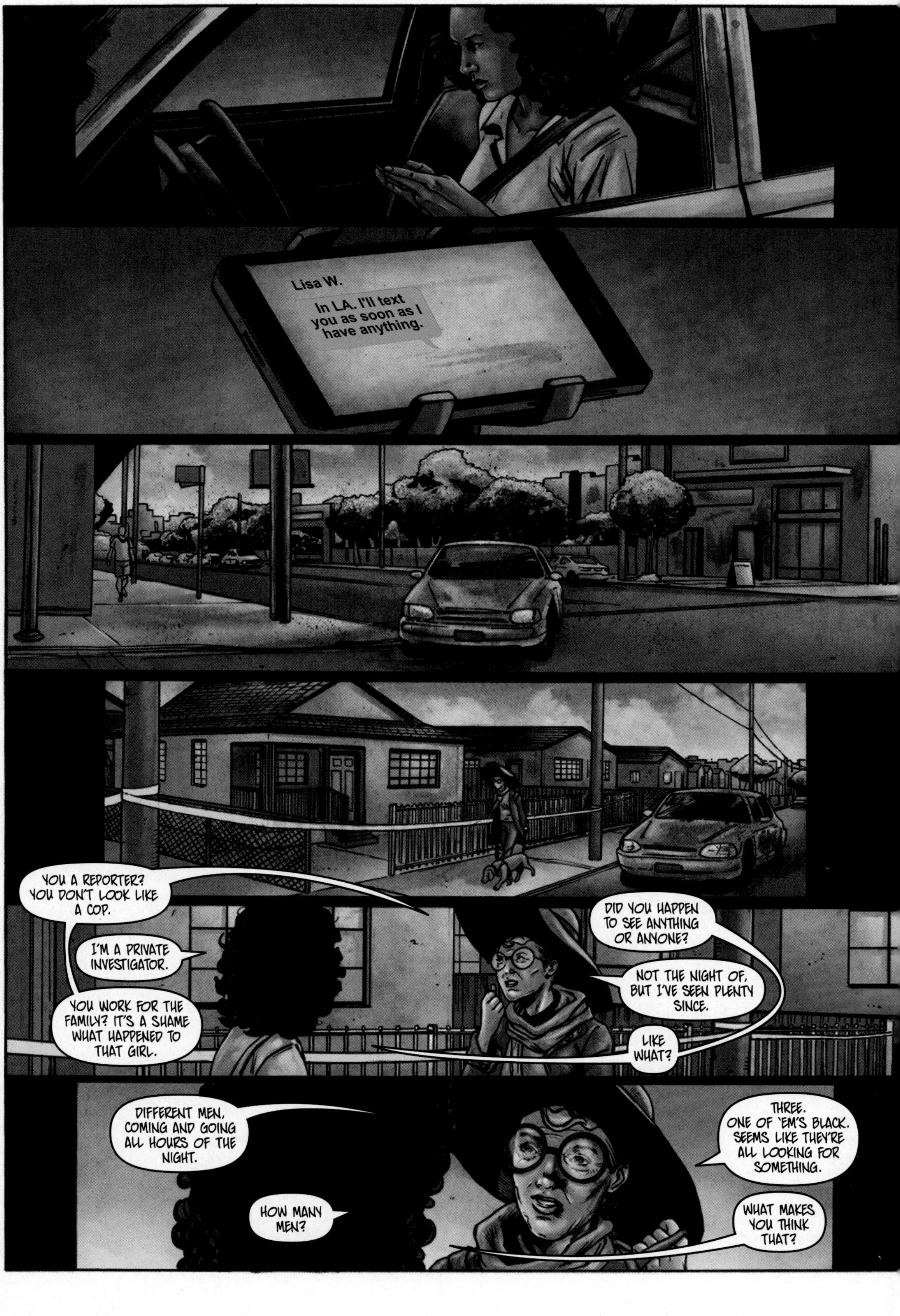
Lisa W.
In LA. I'll text you as soon as I have anything.
YOU A REPORTER? YOU DON'T LOOK LIKE A COP.
I'M A PRIVATE INVESTIGATOR.
YOU WORK FOR THE FAMILY? IT'S A SHAME WHAT HAPPENED TO THAT GIRL.
DID YOU HAPPEN TO SEE ANYTHING OR ANYONE?
NOT THE NIGHT OF, BUT I'VE SEEN PLENTY SINCE.
LIKE WHAT?
DIFFERENT MEN, COMING AND GOING ALL HOURS OF THE NIGHT.
HOW MANY MEN?
THREE. ONE OF 'EM'S BLACK. SEEMS LIKE THEY'RE ALL LOOKING FOR SOMETHING.
WHAT MAKES YOU THINK THAT?

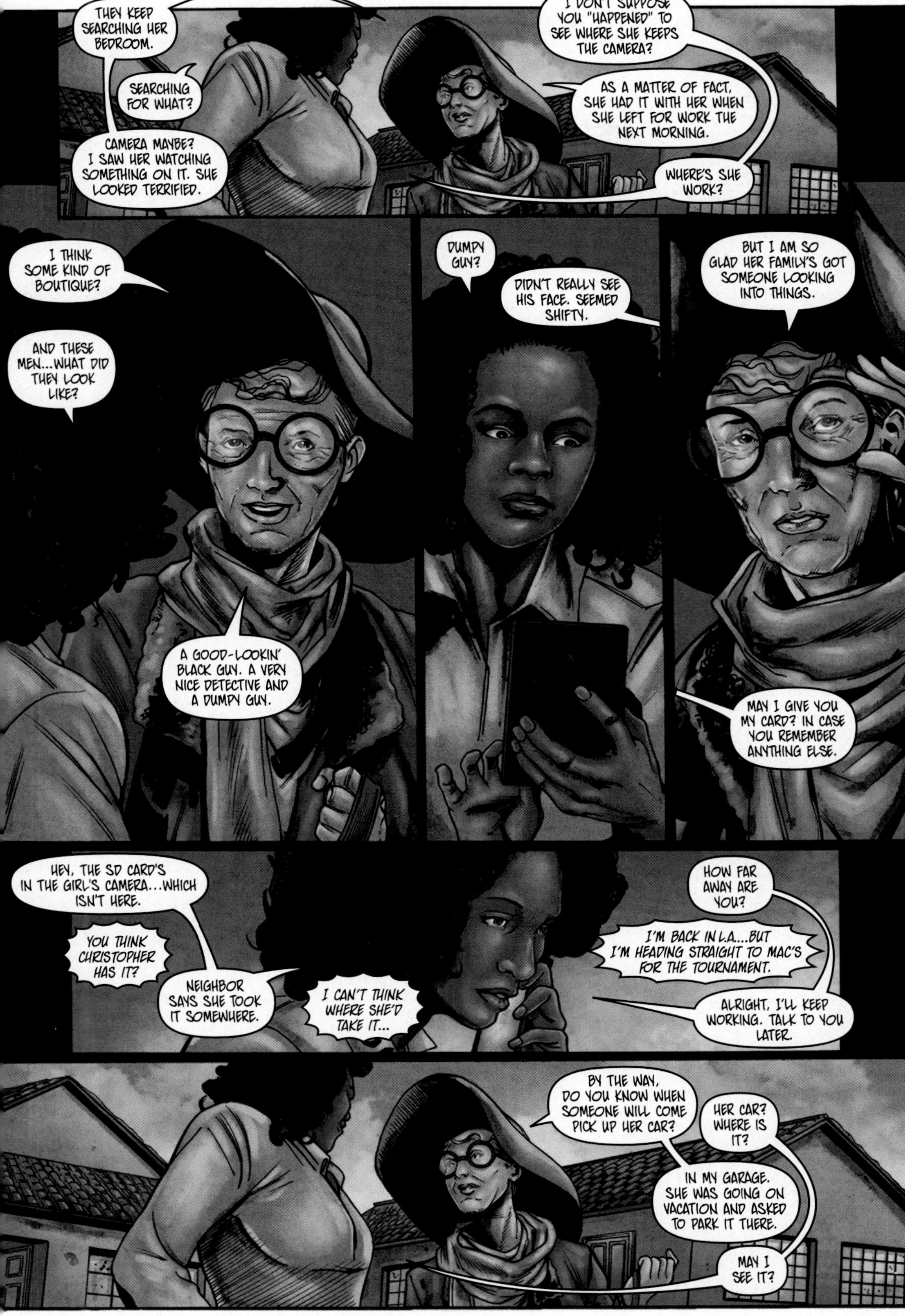
THEY KEEP SEARCHING HER BEDROOM.
I DON'T SUPPOSE YOU "HAPPENED" TO SEE WHERE SHE KEEPS THE CAMERA?
SEARCHING FOR WHAT?
CAMERA MAYBE? I SAW HER WATCHING SOMETHING ON IT. SHE LOOKED TERRIFIED.
AS A MATTER OF FACT, SHE HAD IT WITH HER WHEN SHE LEFT FOR WORK THE NEXT MORNING.
WHERE'S SHE WORK?
I THINK SOME KIND OF BOUTIQUE?
AND THESE MEN...WHAT DID THEY LOOK LIKE?
A GOOD-LOOKIN' BLACK GUY. A VERY NICE DETECTIVE AND A DUMPY GUY.
DUMPY GUY?
DIDN'T REALLY SEE HIS FACE. SEEMED SHIFTY.
BUT I AM SO GLAD HER FAMILY'S GOT SOMEONE LOOKING INTO THINGS.
MAY I GIVE YOU MY CARD? IN CASE YOU REMEMBER ANYTHING ELSE.
HEY, THE SD CARD'S IN THE GIRL'S CAMERA...WHICH ISN'T HERE.
YOU THINK CHRISTOPHER HAS IT?
NEIGHBOR SAYS SHE TOOK IT SOMEWHERE.
I CAN'T THINK WHERE SHE'D TAKE IT...
HOW FAR AWAY ARE YOU?
I'M BACK IN L.A....BUT I'M HEADING STRAIGHT TO MAC'S FOR THE TOURNAMENT.
ALRIGHT, I'LL KEEP WORKING. TALK TO YOU LATER.
BY THE WAY, DO YOU KNOW WHEN SOMEONE WILL COME PICK UP HER CAR?
HER CAR? WHERE IS IT?
IN MY GARAGE. SHE WAS GOING ON VACATION AND ASKED TO PARK IT THERE.
MAY I SEE IT?

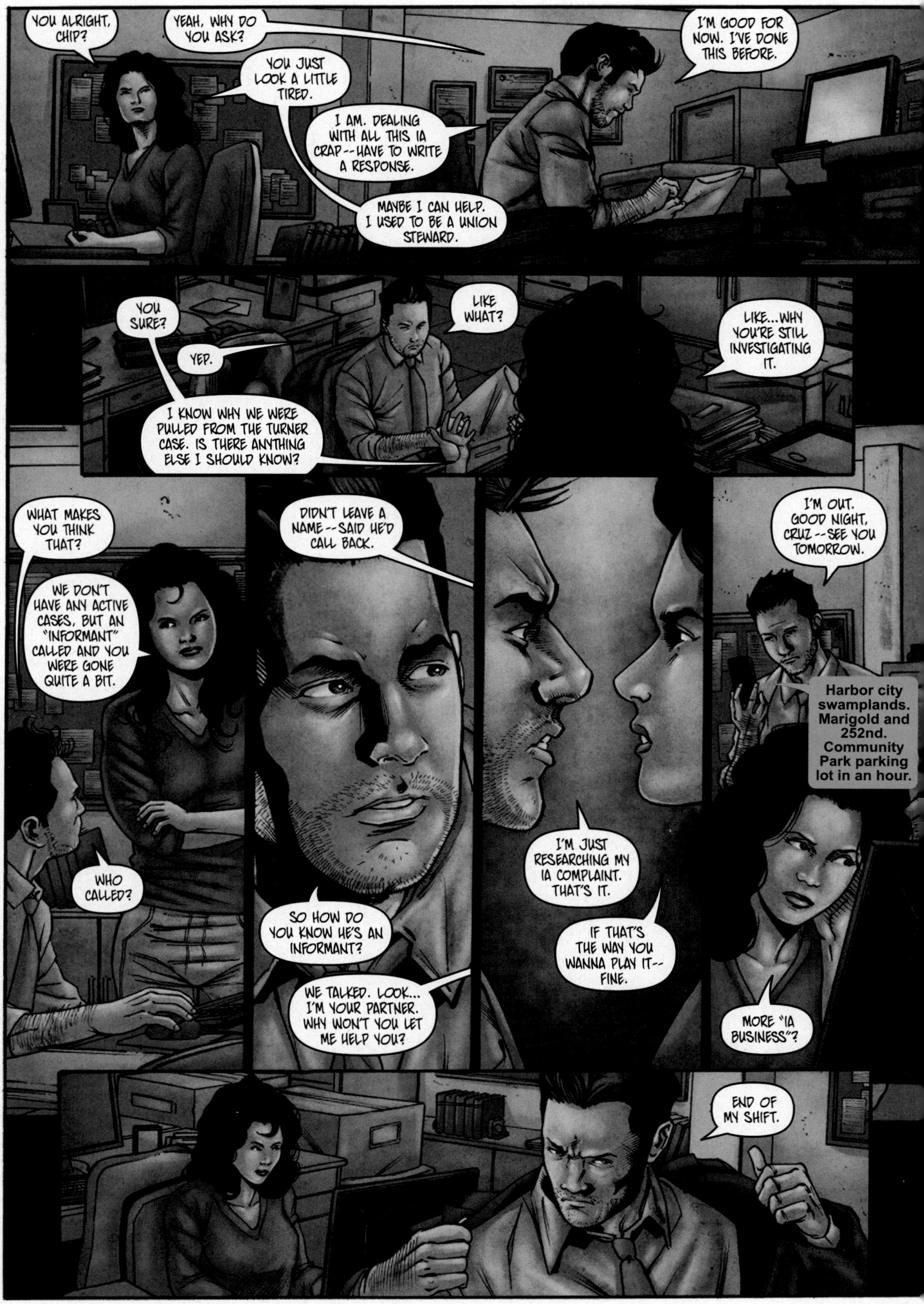

YOU ALRIGHT, CHIP?
YEAH, WHY DO YOU ASK?
YOU JUST LOOK A LITTLE TIRED.
I'M GOOD FOR NOW. I'VE DONE THIS BEFORE.
I AM. DEALING WITH ALL THIS IA CRAP--HAVE TO WRITE A RESPONSE.
MAYBE I CAN HELP. I USED TO BE A UNION STEWARD.
YOU SURE?
YEP.
I KNOW WHY WE WERE PULLED FROM THE TURNER CASE. IS THERE ANYTHING ELSE I SHOULD KNOW?
LIKE WHAT?
LIKE...WHY YOU'RE STILL INVESTIGATING IT.
WHAT MAKES YOU THINK THAT?
WE DON'T HAVE ANY ACTIVE CASES, BUT AN "INFORMANT" CALLED AND YOU WERE GONE QUITE A BIT.
WHO CALLED?
DIDN'T LEAVE A NAME--SAID HE'D CALL BACK.
SO HOW DO YOU KNOW HE'S AN INFORMANT?
WE TALKED. LOOK... I'M YOUR PARTNER. WHY WON'T YOU LET ME HELP YOU?
I'M JUST RESEARCHING MY IA COMPLAINT. THAT'S IT.
IF THAT'S THE WAY YOU WANNA PLAY IT--FINE.
I'M OUT. GOOD NIGHT, CRUZ--SEE YOU TOMORROW.
Harbor city swamplands. Marigold and 252nd. Community Park parking lot in an hour.
MORE "IA BUSINESS"?
END OF MY SHIFT.

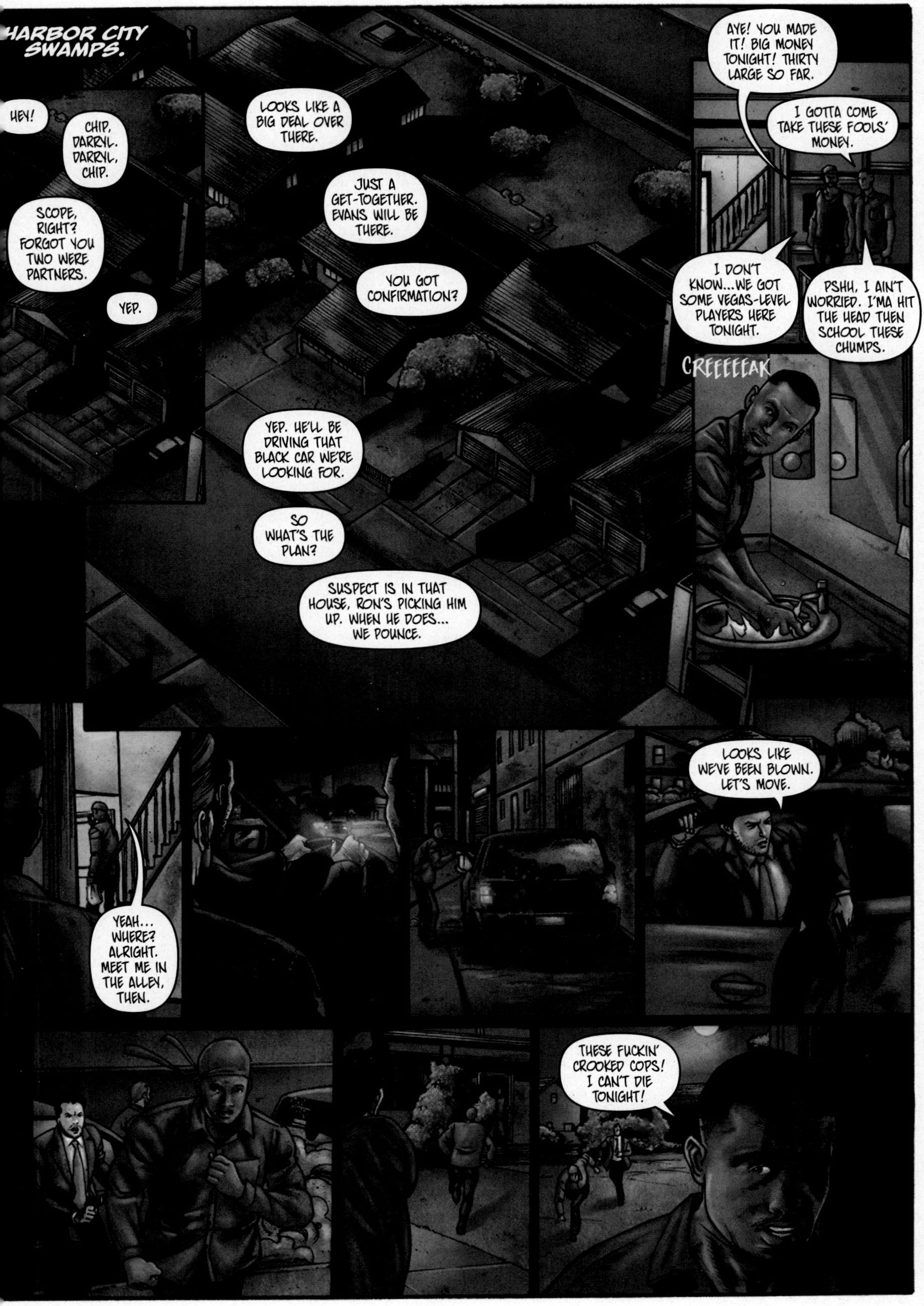
HARBOR CITY SWAMPS.
HEY!
CHIP, DARRYL. DARRYL, CHIP.
SCOPE, RIGHT? FORGOT YOU TWO WERE PARTNERS.
YEP.
LOOKS LIKE A BIG DEAL OVER THERE.
JUST A GET-TOGETHER. EVANS WILL BE THERE.
YOU GOT CONFIRMATION?
YEP. HE'LL BE DRIVING THAT BLACK CAR WE'RE LOOKING FOR.
SO WHAT'S THE PLAN?
SUSPECT IS IN THAT HOUSE, RON'S PICKING HIM UP. WHEN HE DOES... WE POUNCE.
AYE! YOU MADE IT! BIG MONEY TONIGHT! THIRTY LARGE SO FAR.
I GOTTA COME TAKE THESE FOOLS' MONEY.
I DON'T KNOW...WE GOT SOME VEGAS-LEVEL PLAYERS HERE TONIGHT.
PSHH, I AIN'T WORRIED. I'MA HIT THE HEAD THEN SCHOOL THESE CHUMPS.
CREEEEEAK
YEAH... WHERE? ALRIGHT. MEET ME IN THE ALLEY, THEN.
LOOKS LIKE WE'VE BEEN BLOWN. LET'S MOVE.
THESE FUCKIN' CROOKED COPS! I CAN'T DIE TONIGHT!

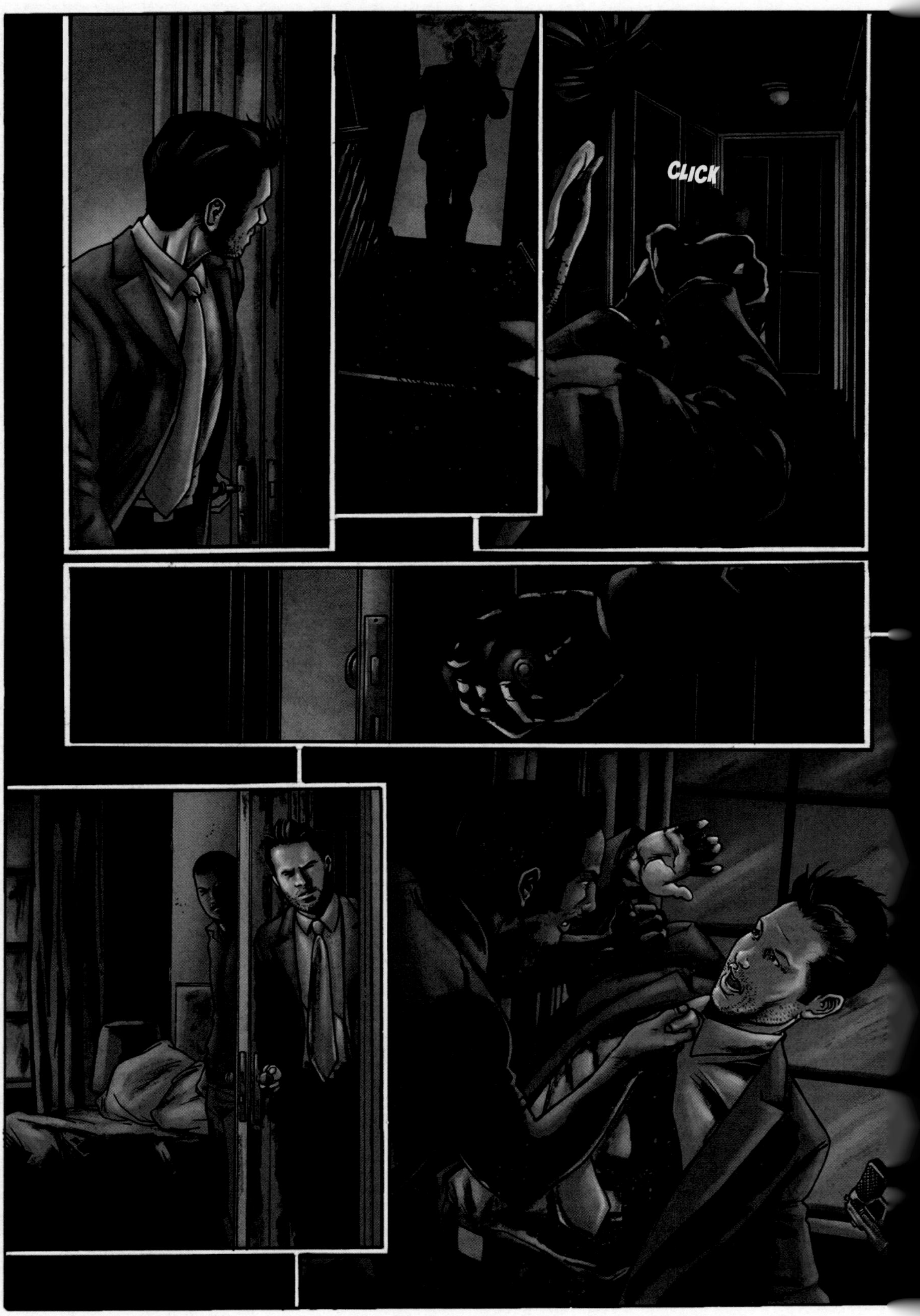
CLICK

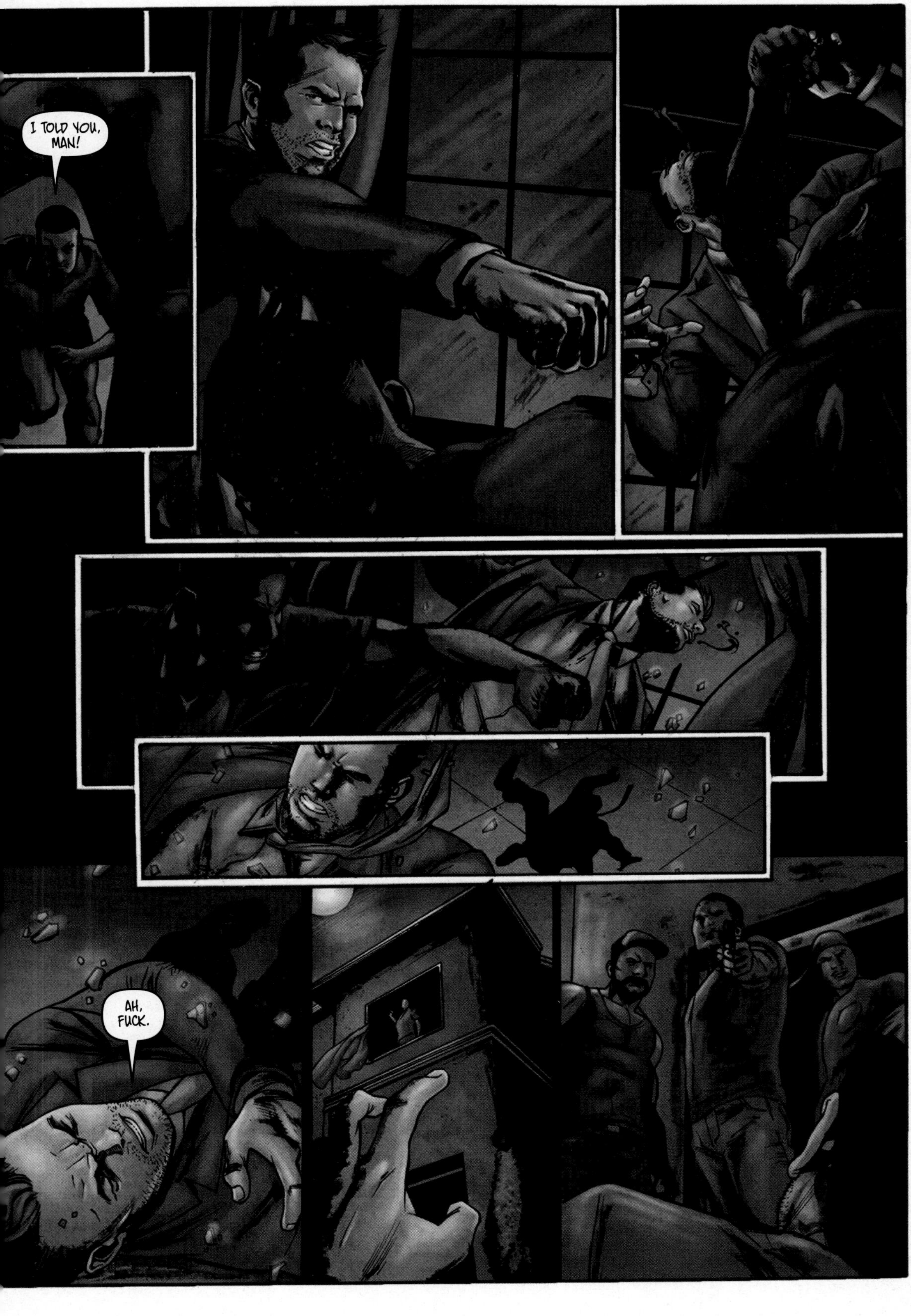
I TOLD YOU, MAN!
AH, FUCK.

CHAPTER 3

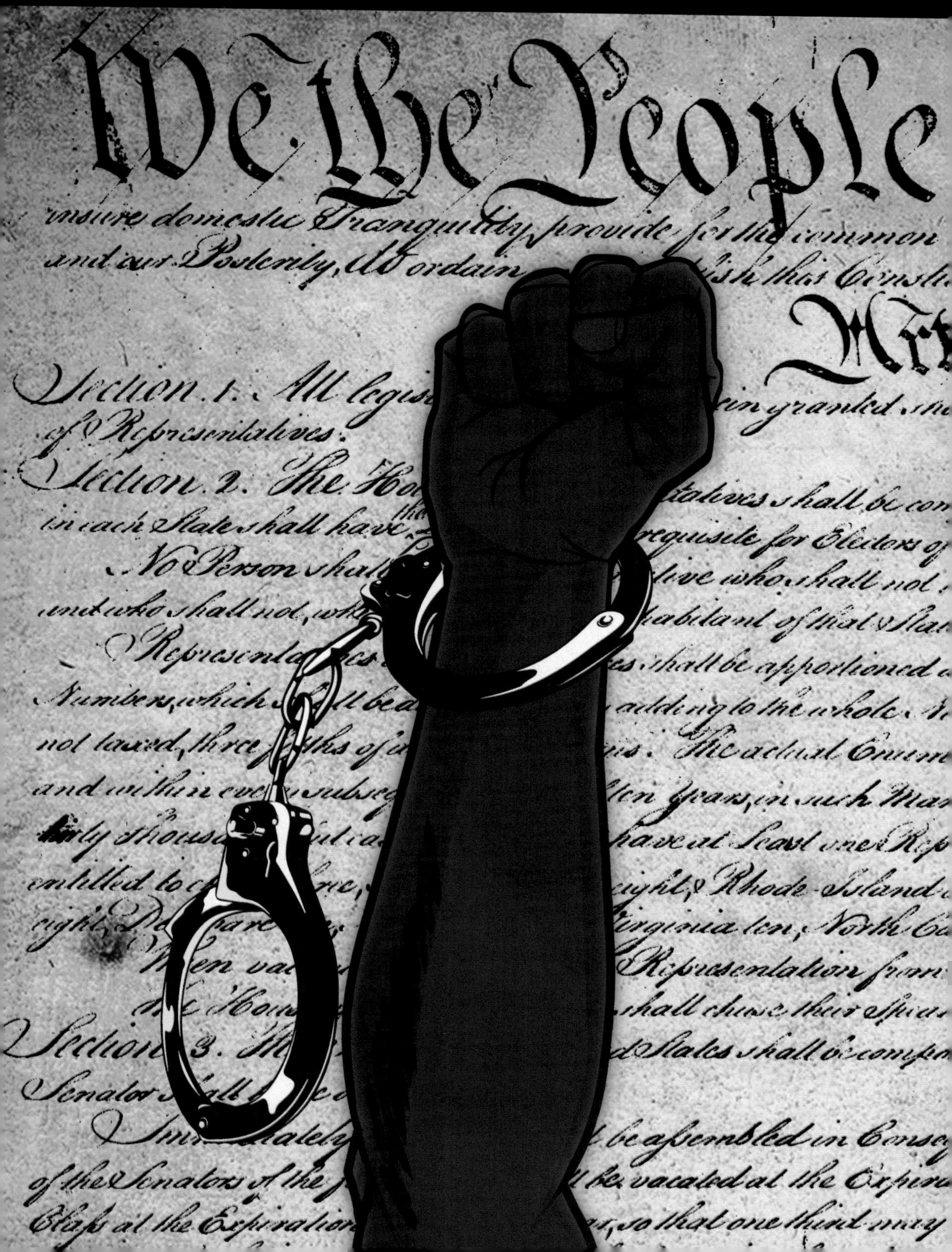
We the People

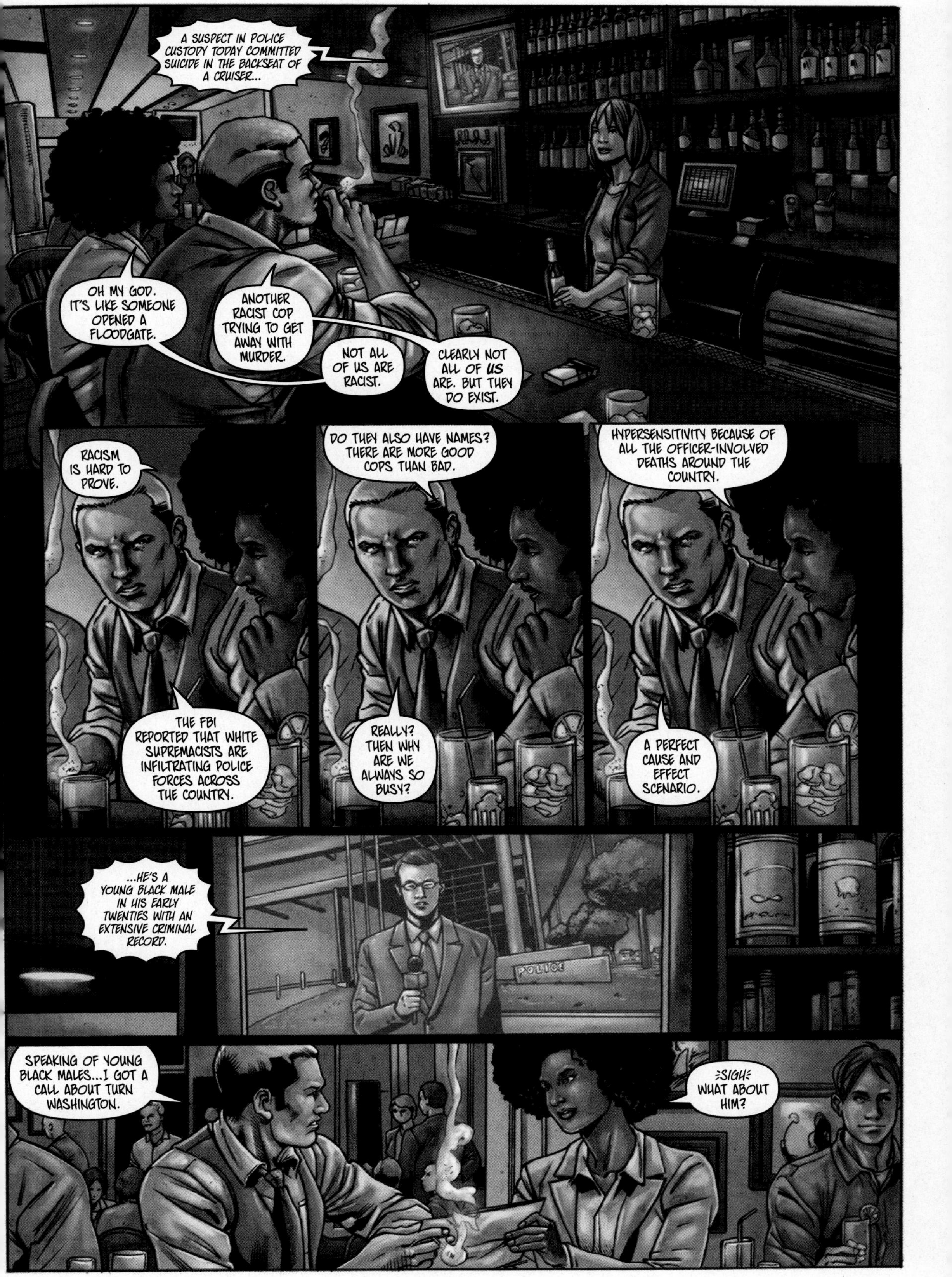
A SUSPECT IN POLICE CUSTODY TODAY COMMITTED SUICIDE IN THE BACKSEAT OF A CRUISER...
OH MY GOD. IT'S LIKE SOMEONE OPENED A FLOODGATE.
ANOTHER RACIST COP TRYING TO GET AWAY WITH MURDER.
NOT ALL OF US ARE RACIST.
CLEARLY NOT ALL OF US ARE. BUT THEY DO EXIST.
RACISM IS HARD TO PROVE.
THE FBI REPORTED THAT WHITE SUPREMACISTS ARE INFILTRATING POLICE FORCES ACROSS THE COUNTRY.
DO THEY ALSO HAVE NAMES? THERE ARE MORE GOOD COPS THAN BAD.
REALLY? THEN WHY ARE WE ALWAYS SO BUSY?
HYPERSENSITIVITY BECAUSE OF ALL THE OFFICER-INVOLVED DEATHS AROUND THE COUNTRY.
A PERFECT CAUSE AND EFFECT SCENARIO.
...HE'S A YOUNG BLACK MALE IN HIS EARLY TWENTIES WITH AN EXTENSIVE CRIMINAL RECORD.
POLICE
SPEAKING OF YOUNG BLACK MALES...I GOT A CALL ABOUT TURN WASHINGTON.
SIGH
WHAT ABOUT HIM?

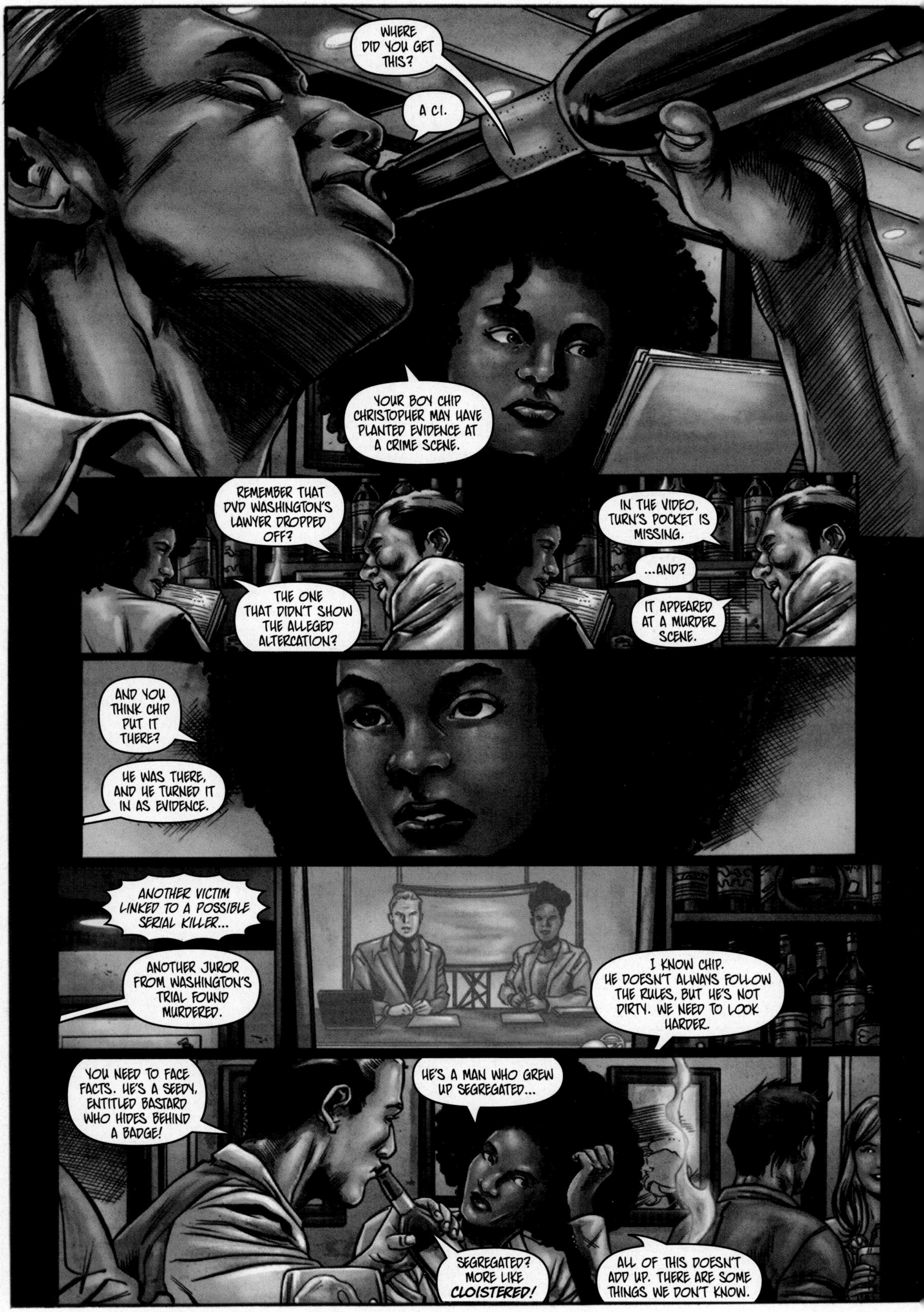
WHERE DID YOU GET THIS?
A CI.
YOUR BOY CHIP CHRISTOPHER MAY HAVE PLANTED EVIDENCE AT A CRIME SCENE.
REMEMBER THAT DVD WASHINGTON'S LAWYER DROPPED OFF?
THE ONE THAT DIDN'T SHOW THE ALLEGED ALTERCATION?
IN THE VIDEO, TURN'S POCKET IS MISSING.
...AND?
IT APPEARED AT A MURDER SCENE.
AND YOU THINK CHIP PUT IT THERE?
HE WAS THERE, AND HE TURNED IT IN AS EVIDENCE.
ANOTHER VICTIM LINKED TO A POSSIBLE SERIAL KILLER...
ANOTHER JUROR FROM WASHINGTON'S TRIAL FOUND MURDERED.
I KNOW CHIP. HE DOESN'T ALWAYS FOLLOW THE RULES, BUT HE'S NOT DIRTY. WE NEED TO LOOK HARDER.
YOU NEED TO FACE FACTS. HE'S A SEEDY, ENTITLED BASTARD WHO HIDES BEHIND A BADGE!
HE'S A MAN WHO GREW UP SEGREGATED...
SEGREGATED? MORE LIKE CLOISTERED!
ALL OF THIS DOESN'T ADD UP. THERE ARE SOME THINGS WE DON'T KNOW.

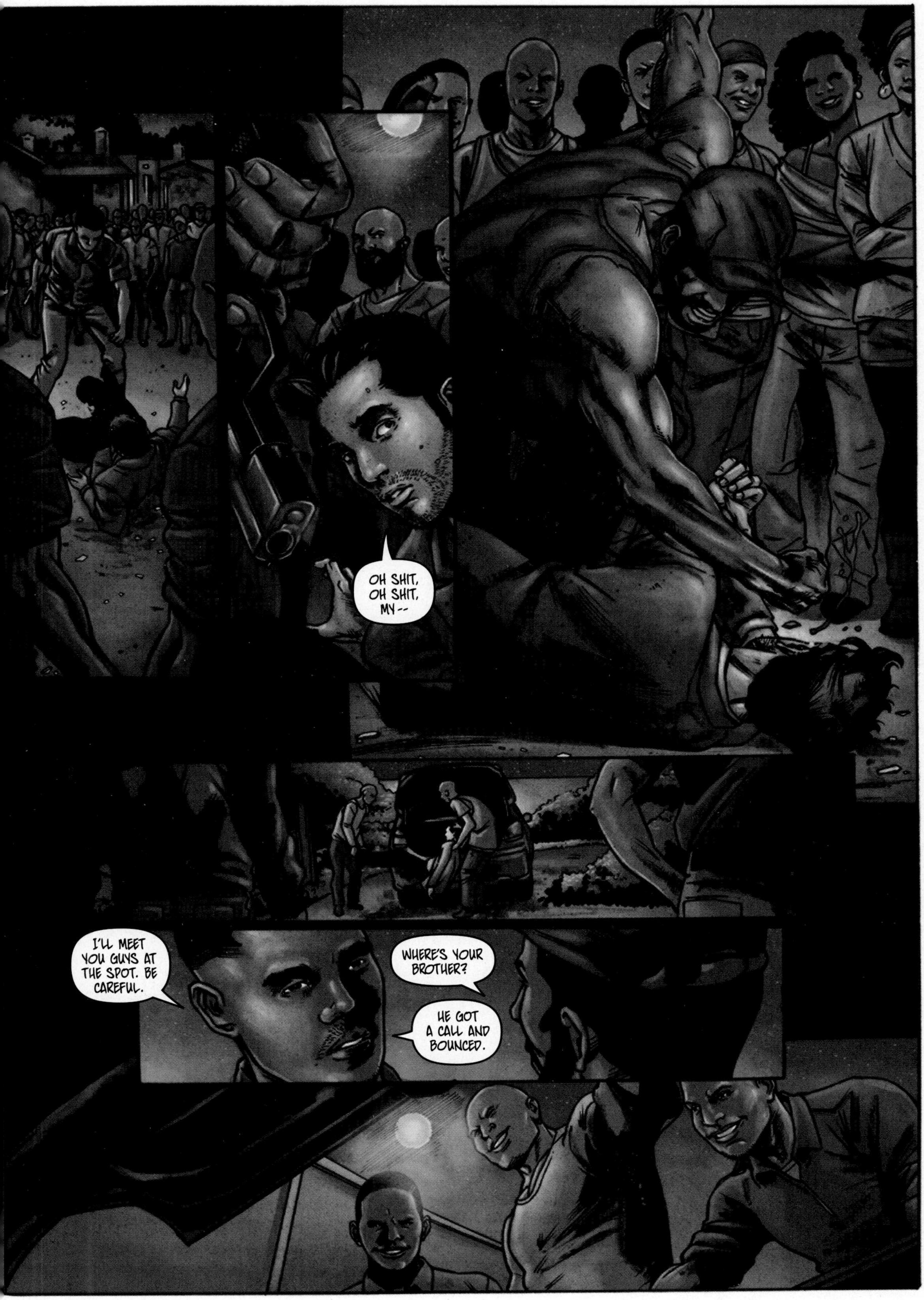
OH SHIT, OH SHIT, MY--
I'LL MEET YOU GUYS AT THE SPOT. BE CAREFUL.
WHERE'S YOUR BROTHER?
HE GOT A CALL AND BOUNCED.

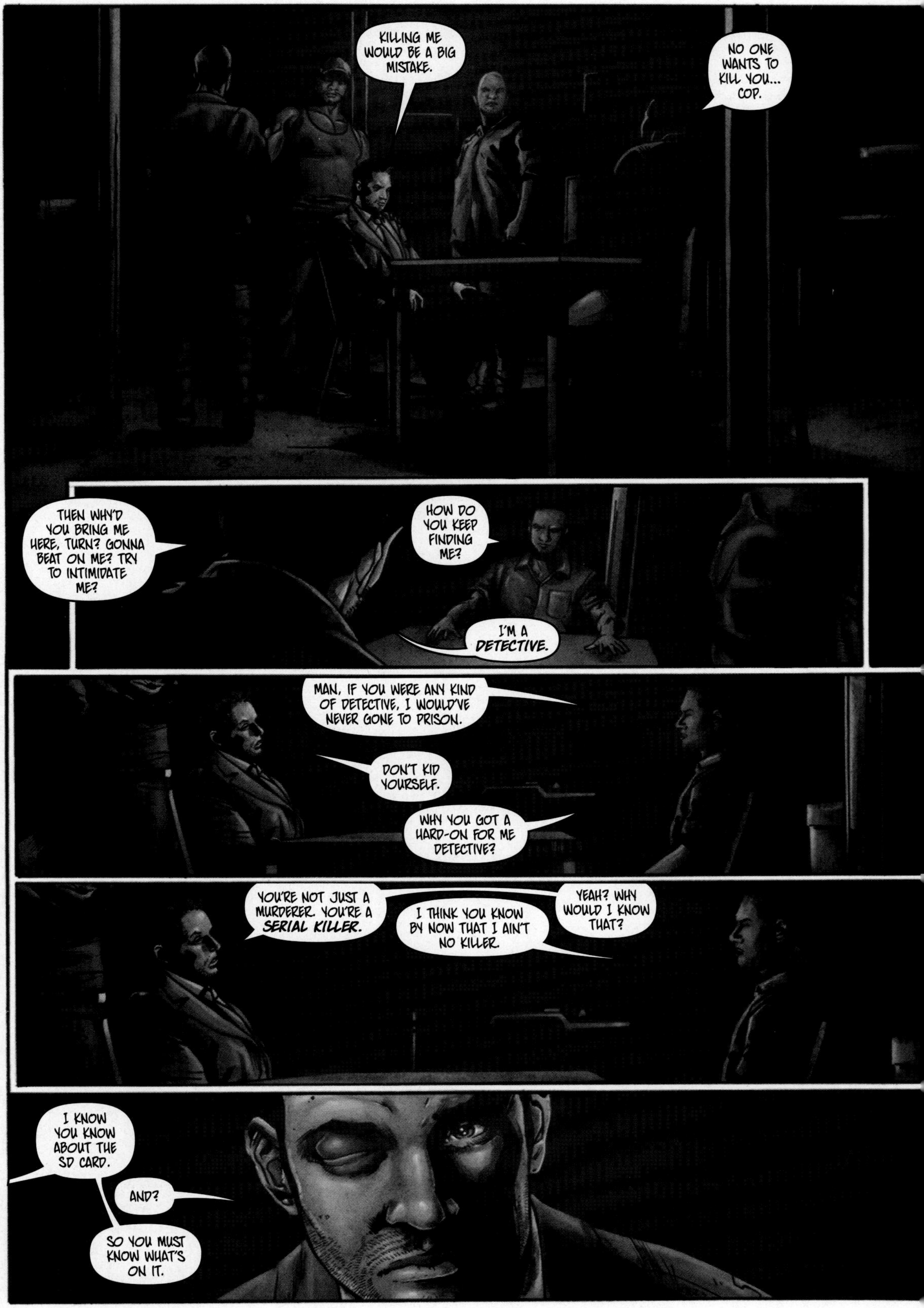
KILLING ME WOULD BE A BIG MISTAKE.
NO ONE WANTS TO KILL YOU... COP.
THEN WHY'D YOU BRING ME HERE, TURN? GONNA BEAT ON ME? TRY TO INTIMIDATE ME?
HOW DO YOU KEEP FINDING ME?
I'M A *DETECTIVE.*
MAN, IF YOU WERE ANY KIND OF DETECTIVE, I WOULD'VE NEVER GONE TO PRISON.
DON'T KID YOURSELF.
WHY YOU GOT A HARD-ON FOR ME DETECTIVE?
YOU'RE NOT JUST A MURDERER. YOU'RE A ***SERIAL KILLER.***
YEAH? WHY WOULD I KNOW THAT?
I THINK YOU KNOW BY NOW THAT I AIN'T NO KILLER.
I KNOW YOU KNOW ABOUT THE SD CARD.
AND?
SO YOU MUST KNOW WHAT'S ON IT.

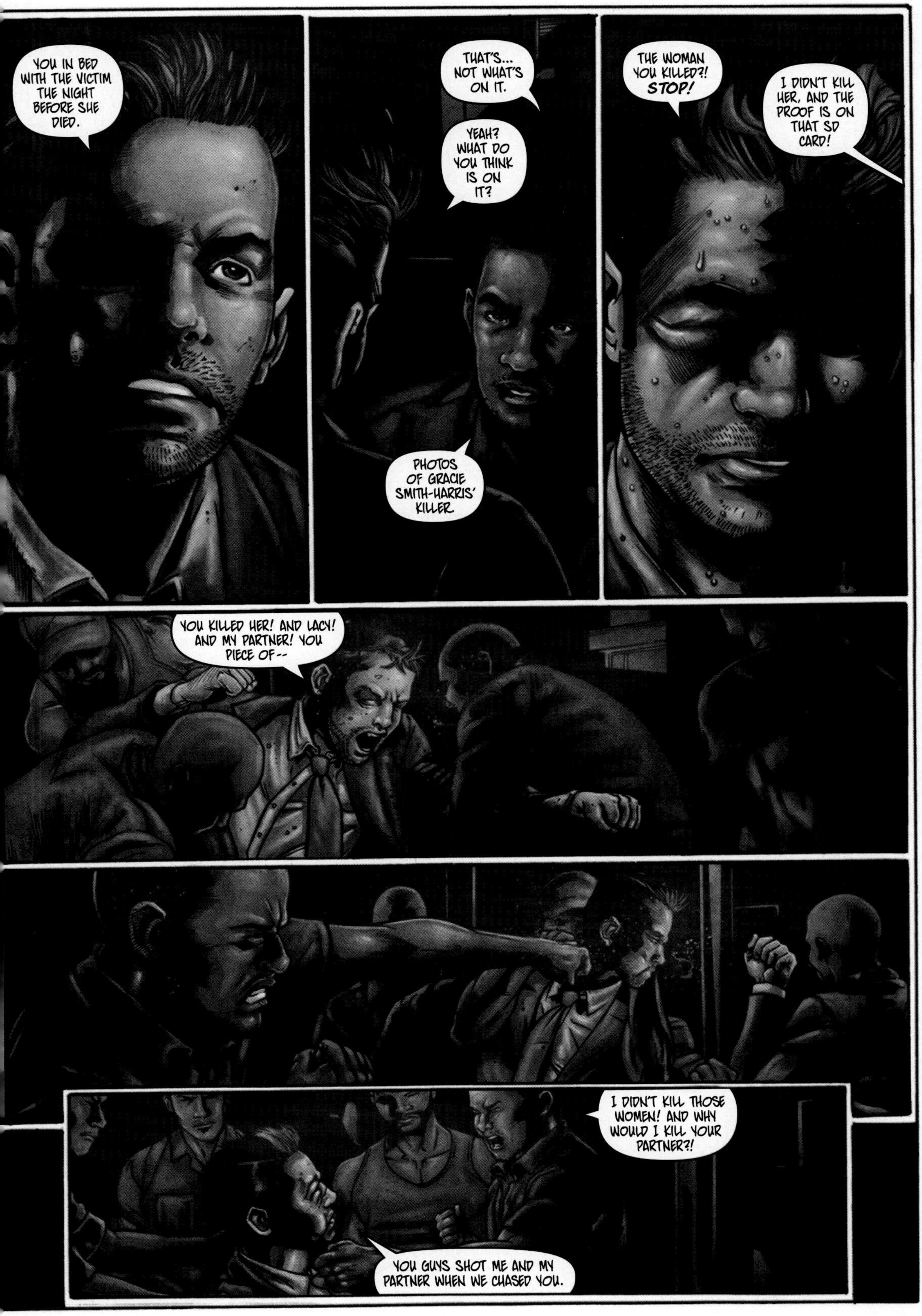
YOU IN BED WITH THE VICTIM THE NIGHT BEFORE SHE DIED.
THAT'S... NOT WHAT'S ON IT.
YEAH? WHAT DO YOU THINK IS ON IT?
PHOTOS OF GRACIE SMITH-HARRIS' KILLER.
THE WOMAN YOU KILLED?! STOP!
I DIDN'T KILL HER, AND THE PROOF IS ON THAT SD CARD!
YOU KILLED HER! AND LACY! AND MY PARTNER! YOU PIECE OF--
I DIDN'T KILL THOSE WOMEN! AND WHY WOULD I KILL YOUR PARTNER?!
YOU GUYS SHOT ME AND MY PARTNER WHEN WE CHASED YOU.

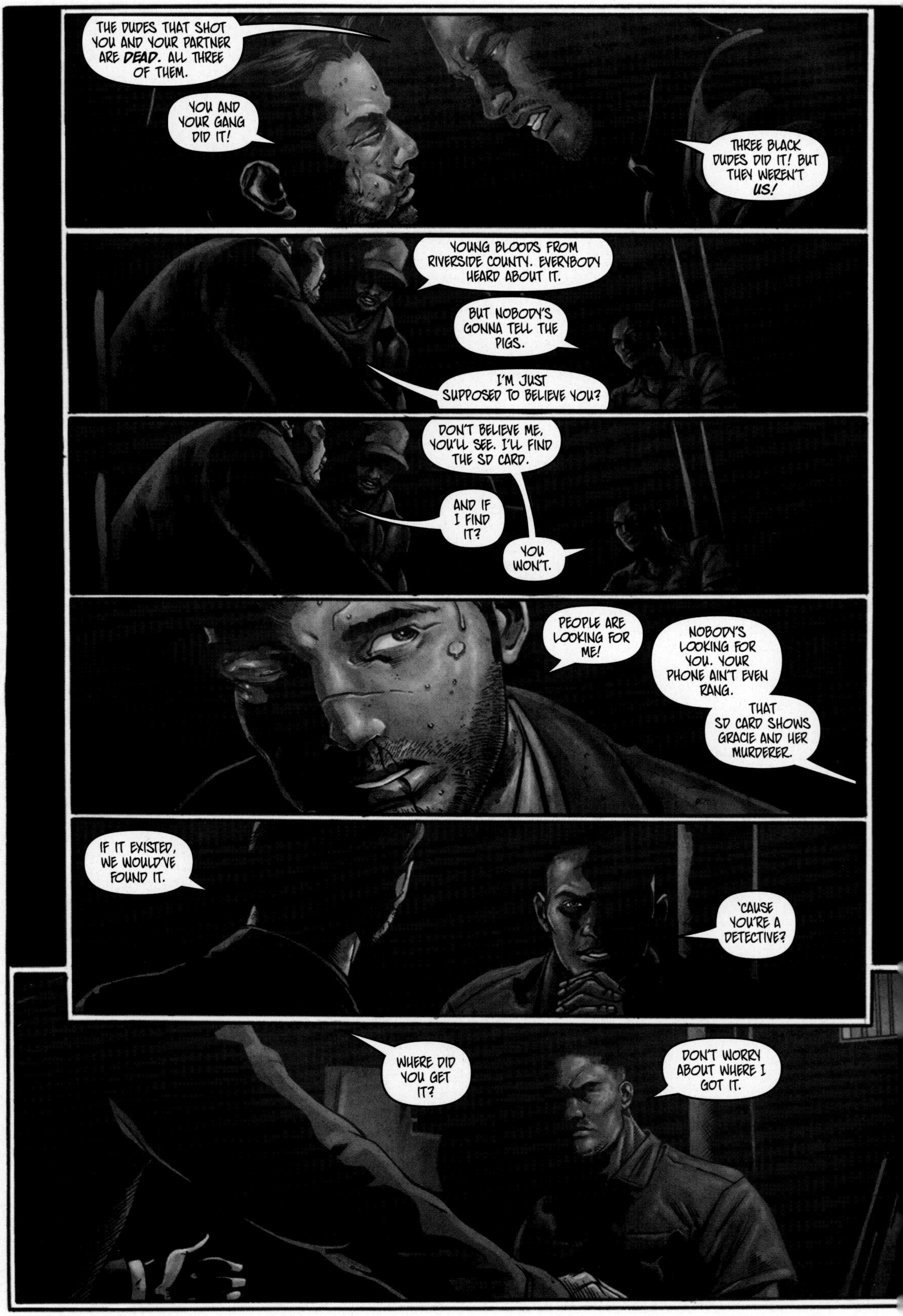
THE DUDES THAT SHOT YOU AND YOUR PARTNER ARE **DEAD**. ALL THREE OF THEM.
YOU AND YOUR GANG DID IT!
THREE BLACK DUDES DID IT! BUT THEY WEREN'T ***US!***
YOUNG BLOODS FROM RIVERSIDE COUNTY. EVERYBODY HEARD ABOUT IT.
BUT NOBODY'S GONNA TELL THE PIGS.
I'M JUST SUPPOSED TO BELIEVE YOU?
DON'T BELIEVE ME, YOU'LL SEE. I'LL FIND THE SD CARD.
AND IF I FIND IT?
YOU WON'T.
PEOPLE ARE LOOKING FOR ME!
NOBODY'S LOOKING FOR YOU. YOUR PHONE AIN'T EVEN RANG.
THAT SD CARD SHOWS GRACIE AND HER MURDERER.
IF IT EXISTED, WE WOULD'VE FOUND IT.
'CAUSE YOU'RE A DETECTIVE?
WHERE DID YOU GET IT?
DON'T WORRY ABOUT WHERE I GOT IT.

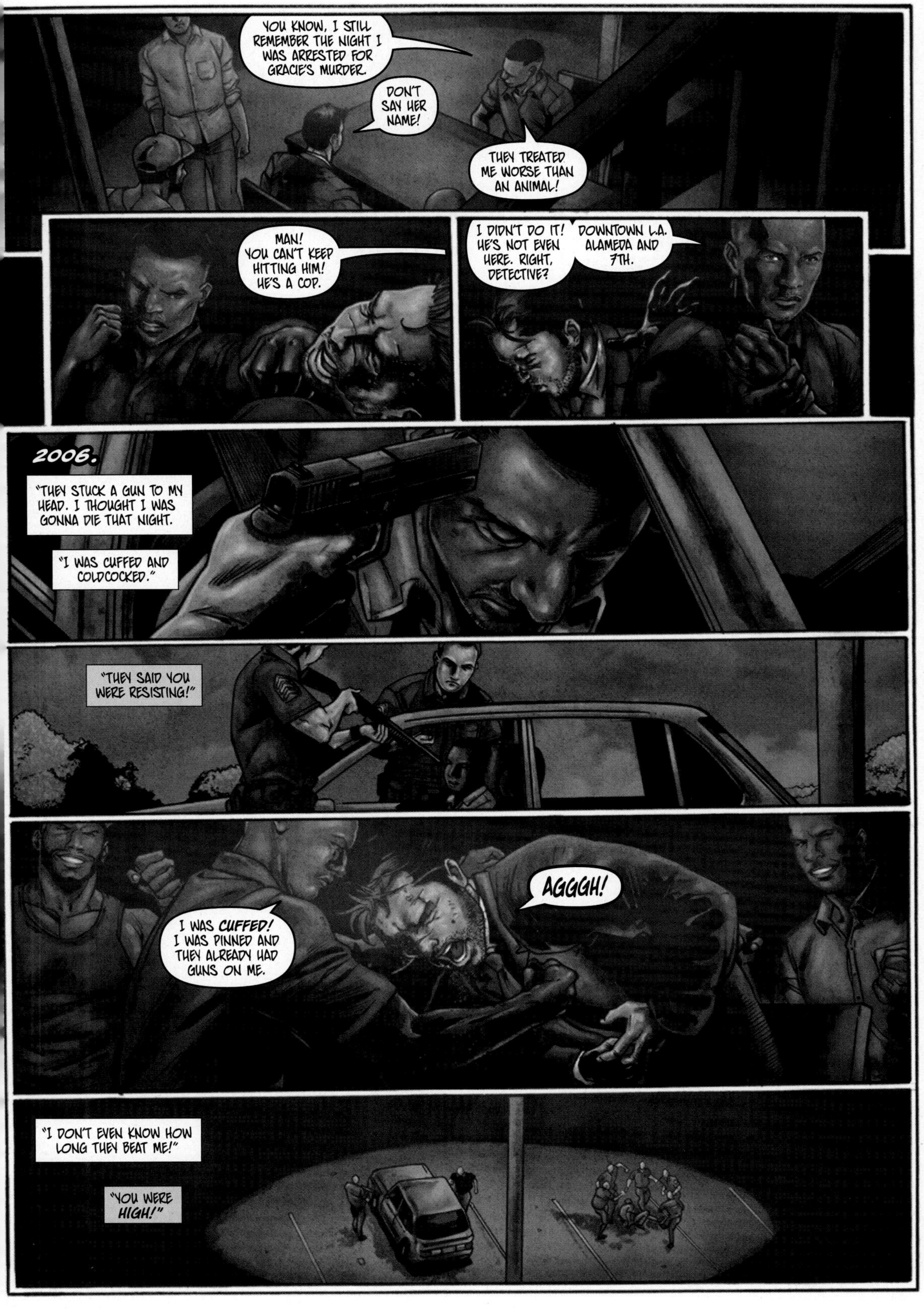

YOU KNOW, I STILL REMEMBER THE NIGHT I WAS ARRESTED FOR GRACIE'S MURDER.
DON'T SAY HER NAME!
THEY TREATED ME WORSE THAN AN ANIMAL!
MAN! YOU CAN'T KEEP HITTING HIM! HE'S A COP.
DOWNTOWN L.A. ALAMEDA AND 7TH.
I DIDN'T DO IT! HE'S NOT EVEN HERE. RIGHT, DETECTIVE?
2006.
"THEY STUCK A GUN TO MY HEAD. I THOUGHT I WAS GONNA DIE THAT NIGHT.
"I WAS CUFFED AND COLDCOCKED."
"THEY SAID YOU WERE RESISTING!"
AGGGH!
I WAS CUFFED! I WAS PINNED AND THEY ALREADY HAD GUNS ON ME.
"I DON'T EVEN KNOW HOW LONG THEY BEAT ME!"
"YOU WERE HIGH!"

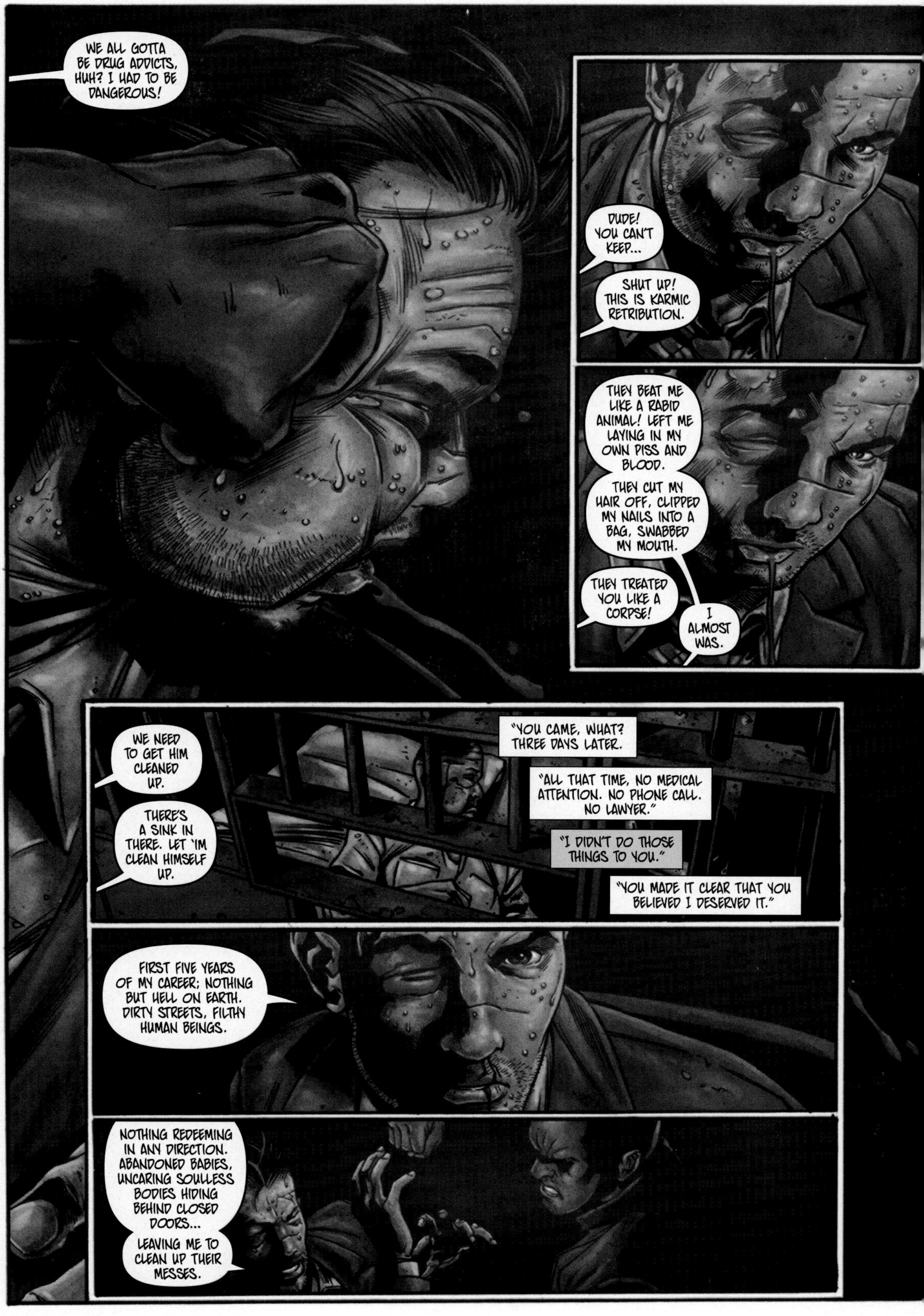
WE ALL GOTTA BE DRUG ADDICTS, HUH? I HAD TO BE DANGEROUS!
DUDE! YOU CAN'T KEEP...
SHUT UP! THIS IS KARMIC RETRIBUTION.
THEY BEAT ME LIKE A RABID ANIMAL! LEFT ME LAYING IN MY OWN PISS AND BLOOD.
THEY CUT MY HAIR OFF, CLIPPED MY NAILS INTO A BAG, SWABBED MY MOUTH.
THEY TREATED YOU LIKE A CORPSE!
I ALMOST WAS.
WE NEED TO GET HIM CLEANED UP.
THERE'S A SINK IN THERE. LET 'IM CLEAN HIMSELF UP.
"YOU CAME, WHAT? THREE DAYS LATER.
"ALL THAT TIME, NO MEDICAL ATTENTION. NO PHONE CALL. NO LAWYER."
"I DIDN'T DO THOSE THINGS TO YOU."
"YOU MADE IT CLEAR THAT YOU BELIEVED I DESERVED IT."
FIRST FIVE YEARS OF MY CAREER; NOTHING BUT HELL ON EARTH. DIRTY STREETS, FILTHY HUMAN BEINGS.
NOTHING REDEEMING IN ANY DIRECTION. ABANDONED BABIES, UNCARING SOULLESS BODIES HIDING BEHIND CLOSED DOORS...
LEAVING ME TO CLEAN UP THEIR MESSES.

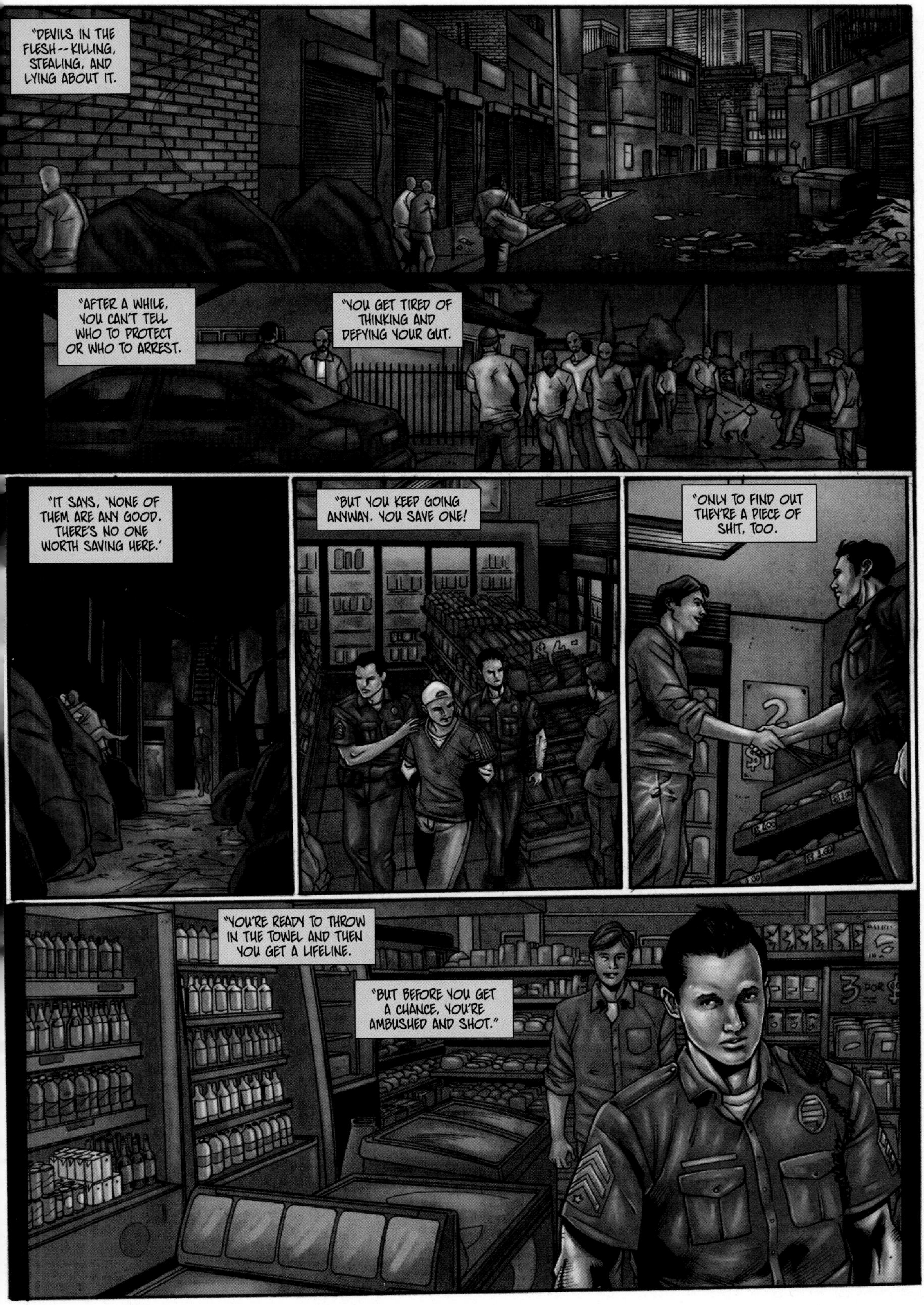
"DEVILS IN THE FLESH--KILLING, STEALING, AND LYING ABOUT IT.
"AFTER A WHILE, YOU CAN'T TELL WHO TO PROTECT OR WHO TO ARREST.
"YOU GET TIRED OF THINKING AND DEFYING YOUR GUT.
"IT SAYS, 'NONE OF THEM ARE ANY GOOD. THERE'S NO ONE WORTH SAVING HERE.'
"BUT YOU KEEP GOING ANYWAY. YOU SAVE ONE!
"ONLY TO FIND OUT THEY'RE A PIECE OF SHIT, TOO.
"YOU'RE READY TO THROW IN THE TOWEL AND THEN YOU GET A LIFELINE.
"BUT BEFORE YOU GET A CHANCE, YOU'RE AMBUSHED AND SHOT."

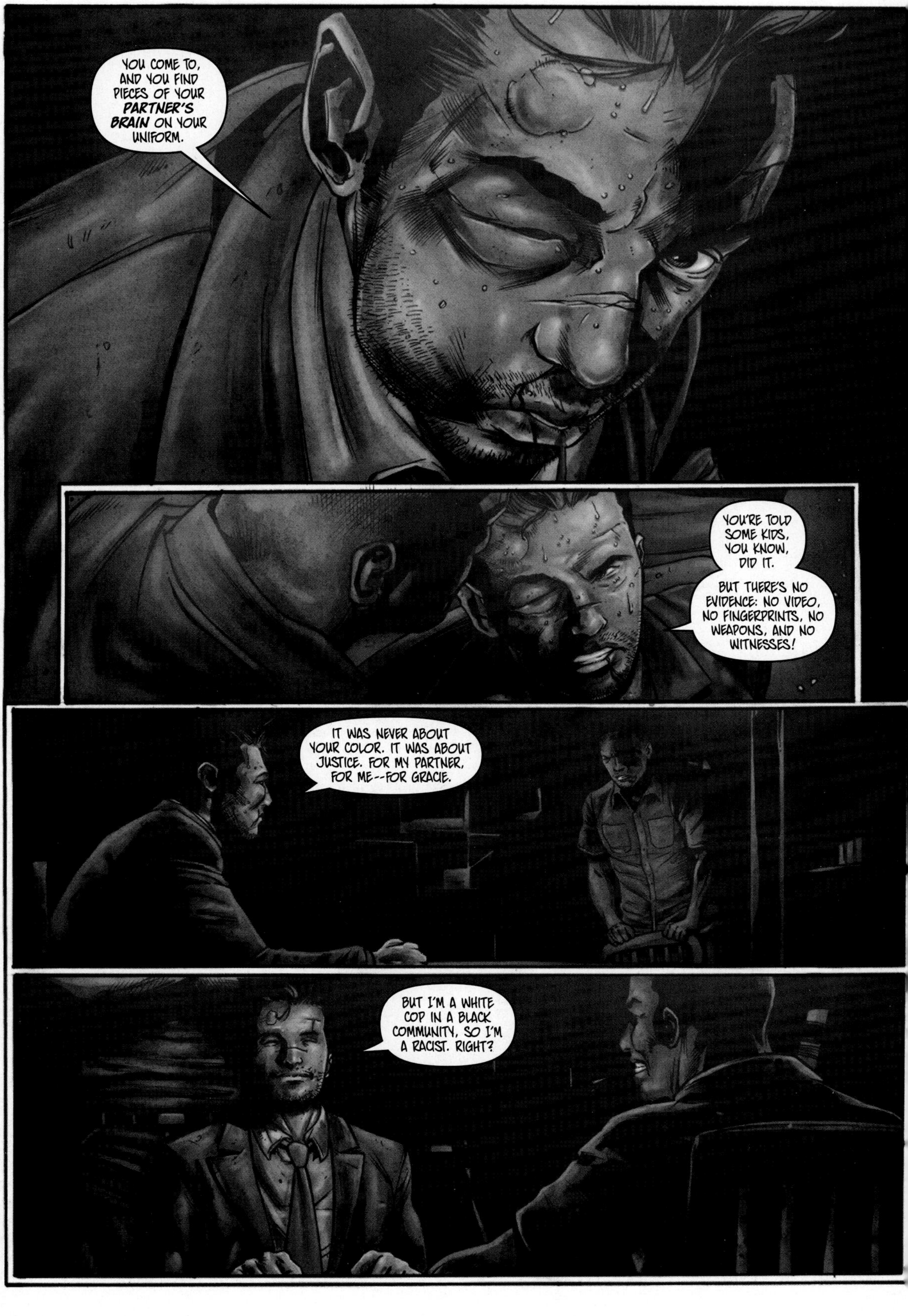
YOU COME TO, AND YOU FIND PIECES OF YOUR **PARTNER'S BRAIN** ON YOUR UNIFORM.
YOU'RE TOLD SOME KIDS, YOU KNOW, DID IT.
BUT THERE'S NO EVIDENCE: NO VIDEO, NO FINGERPRINTS, NO WEAPONS, AND NO WITNESSES!
IT WAS NEVER ABOUT YOUR COLOR. IT WAS ABOUT JUSTICE. FOR MY PARTNER, FOR ME--FOR GRACIE.
BUT I'M A WHITE COP IN A BLACK COMMUNITY, SO I'M A RACIST. RIGHT?

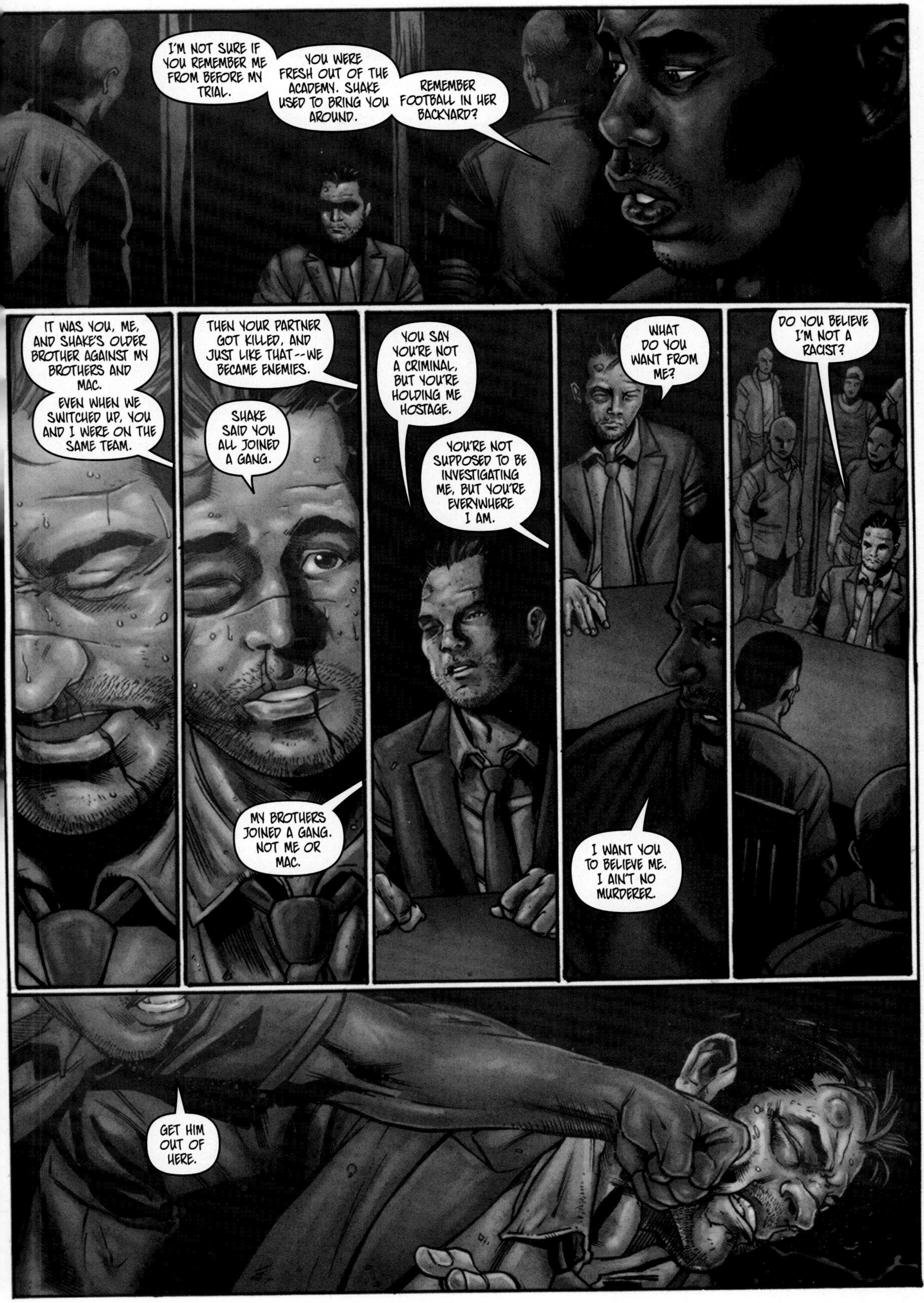
I'M NOT SURE IF YOU REMEMBER ME FROM BEFORE MY TRIAL.
YOU WERE FRESH OUT OF THE ACADEMY. SHAKE USED TO BRING YOU AROUND.
REMEMBER FOOTBALL IN HER BACKYARD?
IT WAS YOU, ME, AND SHAKE'S OLDER BROTHER AGAINST MY BROTHERS AND MAC.
EVEN WHEN WE SWITCHED UP, YOU AND I WERE ON THE SAME TEAM.
THEN YOUR PARTNER GOT KILLED, AND JUST LIKE THAT--WE BECAME ENEMIES.
SHAKE SAID YOU ALL JOINED A GANG.
MY BROTHERS JOINED A GANG. NOT ME OR MAC.
YOU SAY YOU'RE NOT A CRIMINAL, BUT YOU'RE HOLDING ME HOSTAGE.
YOU'RE NOT SUPPOSED TO BE INVESTIGATING ME, BUT YOU'RE EVERYWHERE I AM.
WHAT DO YOU WANT FROM ME?
I WANT YOU TO BELIEVE ME. I AIN'T NO MURDERER.
DO YOU BELIEVE I'M NOT A RACIST?
GET HIM OUT OF HERE.

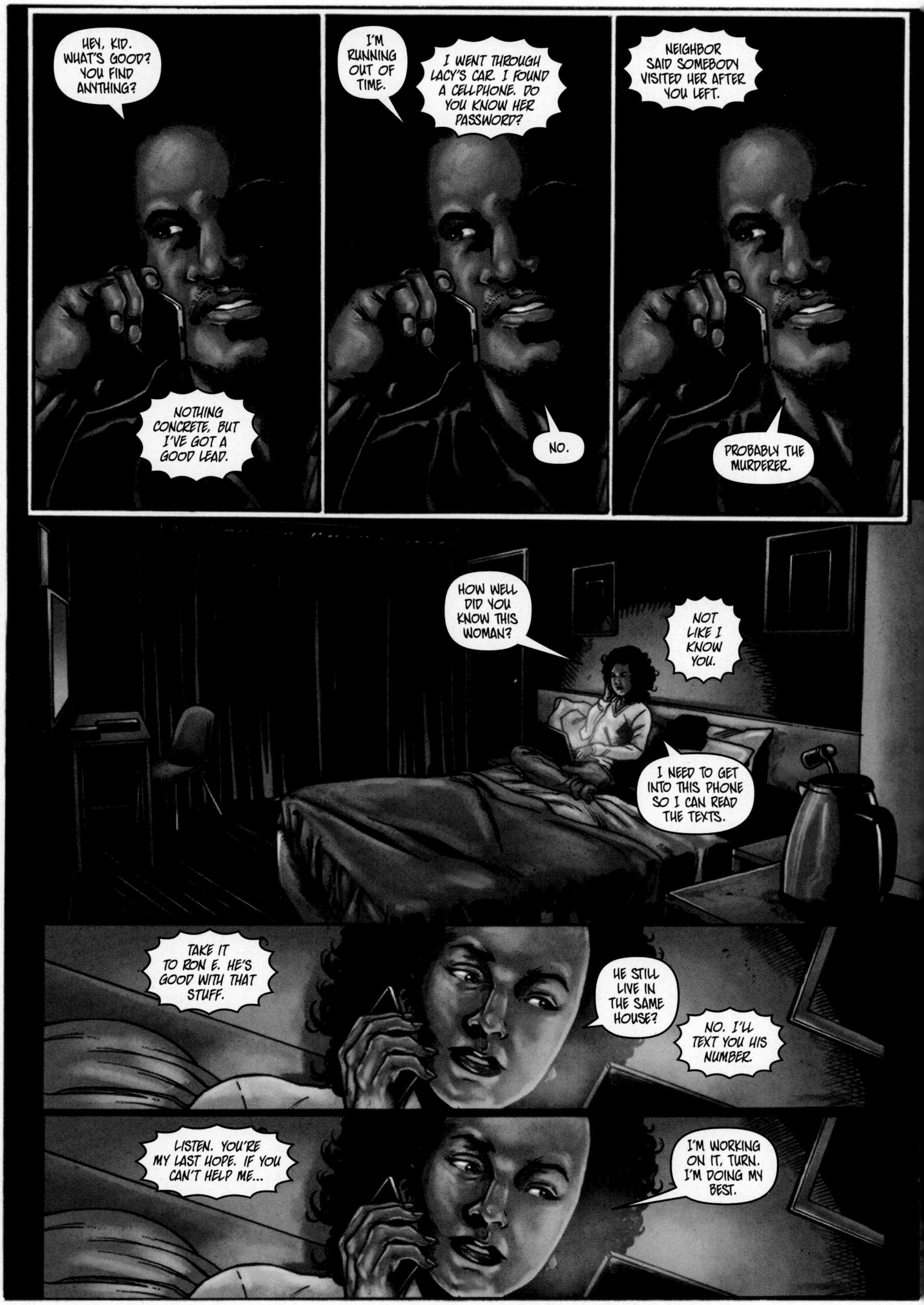
HEY, KID. WHAT'S GOOD? YOU FIND ANYTHING?
NOTHING CONCRETE, BUT I'VE GOT A GOOD LEAD.
I'M RUNNING OUT OF TIME.
I WENT THROUGH LACY'S CAR. I FOUND A CELLPHONE. DO YOU KNOW HER PASSWORD?
NO.
NEIGHBOR SAID SOMEBODY VISITED HER AFTER YOU LEFT.
PROBABLY THE MURDERER.
HOW WELL DID YOU KNOW THIS WOMAN?
NOT LIKE I KNOW YOU.
I NEED TO GET INTO THIS PHONE SO I CAN READ THE TEXTS.
TAKE IT TO RON E. HE'S GOOD WITH THAT STUFF.
HE STILL LIVE IN THE SAME HOUSE?
NO. I'LL TEXT YOU HIS NUMBER.
LISTEN. YOU'RE MY LAST HOPE. IF YOU CAN'T HELP ME...
I'M WORKING ON IT, TURN. I'M DOING MY BEST.

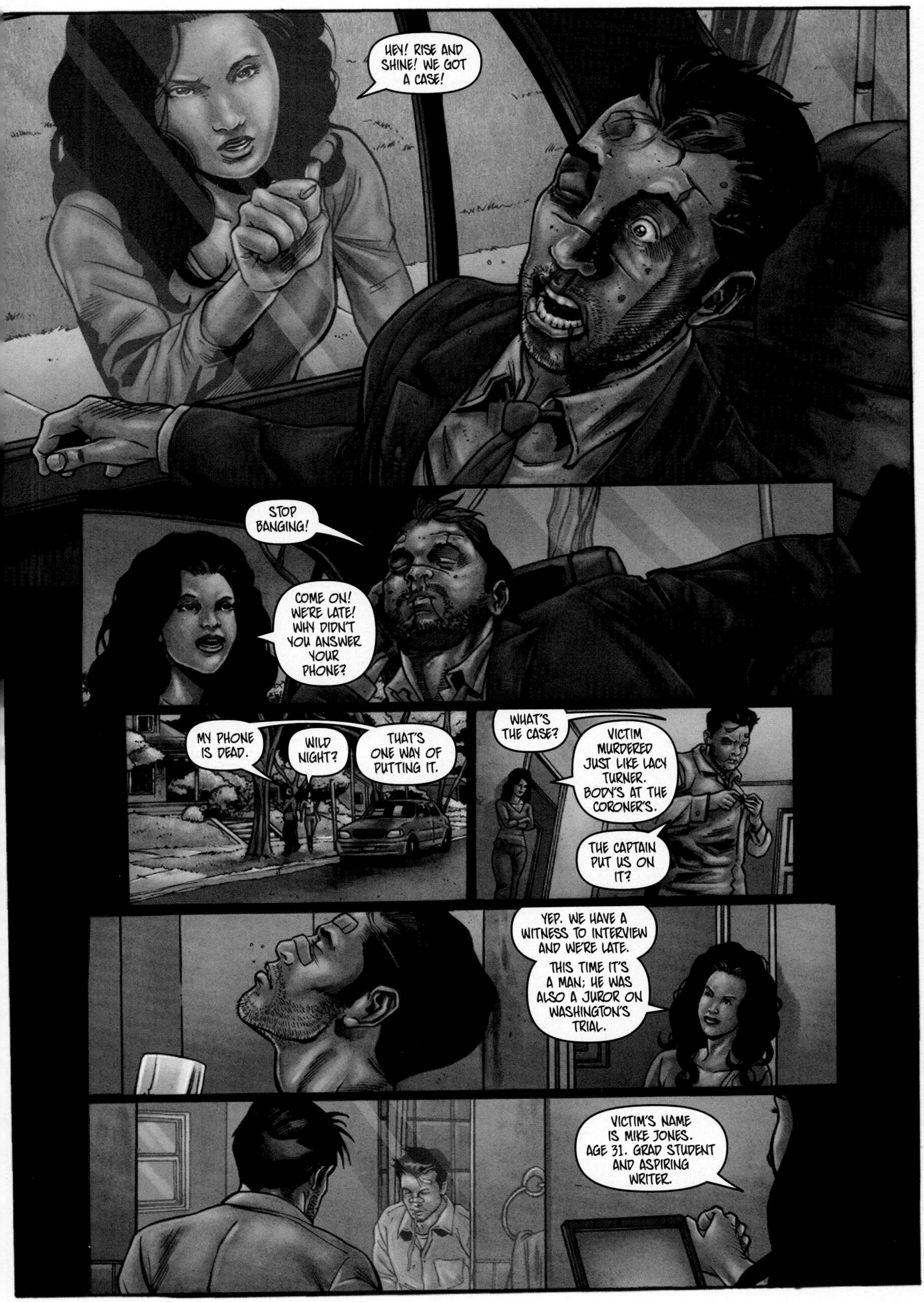
HEY! RISE AND SHINE! WE GOT A CASE!
STOP BANGING!
COME ON! WE'RE LATE! WHY DIDN'T YOU ANSWER YOUR PHONE?
MY PHONE IS DEAD.
WILD NIGHT?
THAT'S ONE WAY OF PUTTING IT.
WHAT'S THE CASE?
VICTIM MURDERED JUST LIKE LACY TURNER. BODY'S AT THE CORONER'S.
THE CAPTAIN PUT US ON IT?
YEP. WE HAVE A WITNESS TO INTERVIEW AND WE'RE LATE.
THIS TIME IT'S A MAN; HE WAS ALSO A JUROR ON WASHINGTON'S TRIAL.
VICTIM'S NAME IS MIKE JONES. AGE 31. GRAD STUDENT AND ASPIRING WRITER.

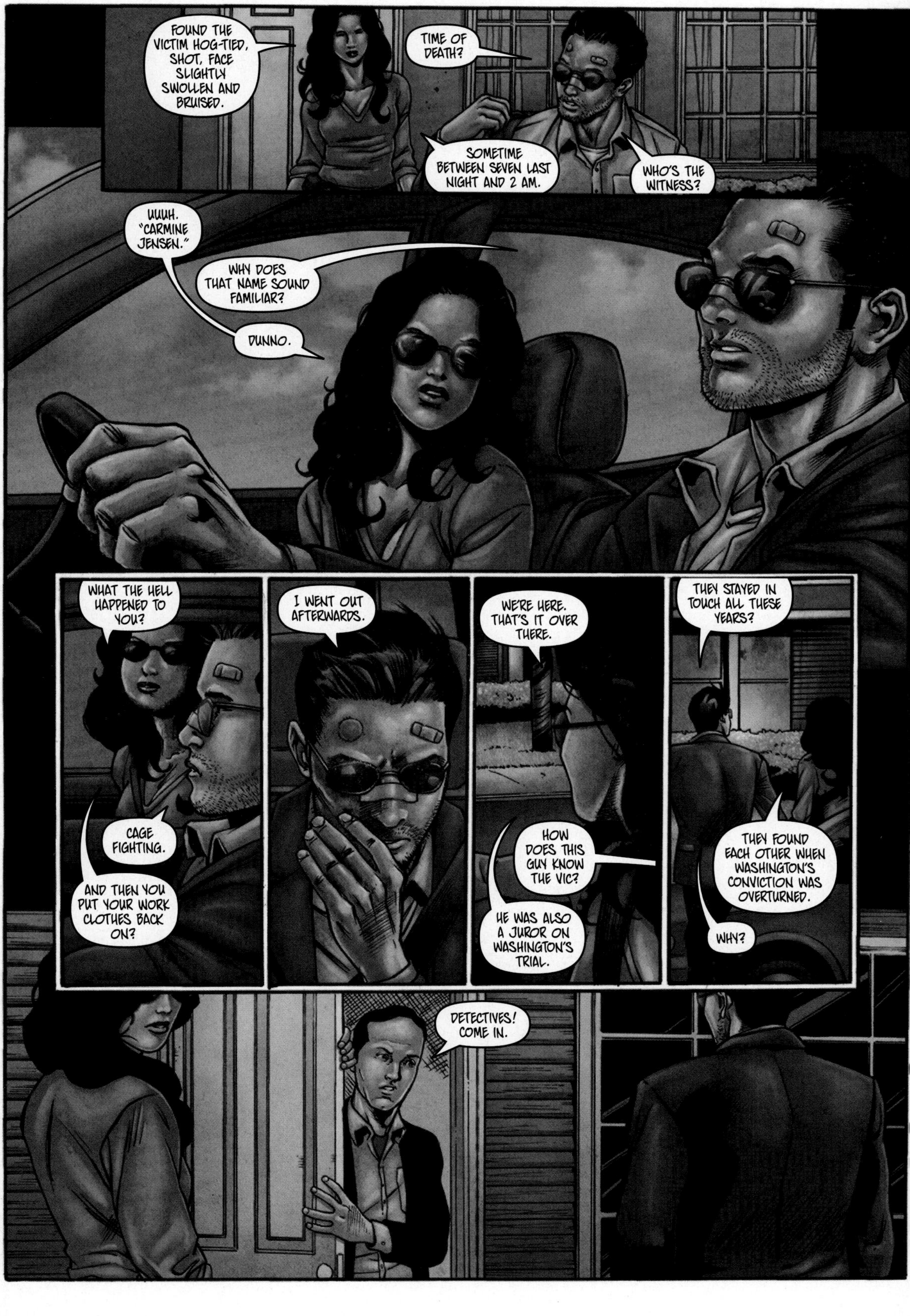
FOUND THE VICTIM HOG-TIED, SHOT, FACE SLIGHTLY SWOLLEN AND BRUISED.
TIME OF DEATH?
SOMETIME BETWEEN SEVEN LAST NIGHT AND 2 AM.
WHO'S THE WITNESS?
UUUH. "CARMINE JENSEN."
WHY DOES THAT NAME SOUND FAMILIAR?
DUNNO.
WHAT THE HELL HAPPENED TO YOU?
CAGE FIGHTING.
AND THEN YOU PUT YOUR WORK CLOTHES BACK ON?
I WENT OUT AFTERWARDS.
WE'RE HERE. THAT'S IT OVER THERE.
HOW DOES THIS GUY KNOW THE VIC?
HE WAS ALSO A JUROR ON WASHINGTON'S TRIAL.
THEY STAYED IN TOUCH ALL THESE YEARS?
THEY FOUND EACH OTHER WHEN WASHINGTON'S CONVICTION WAS OVERTURNED.
WHY?
DETECTIVES! COME IN.

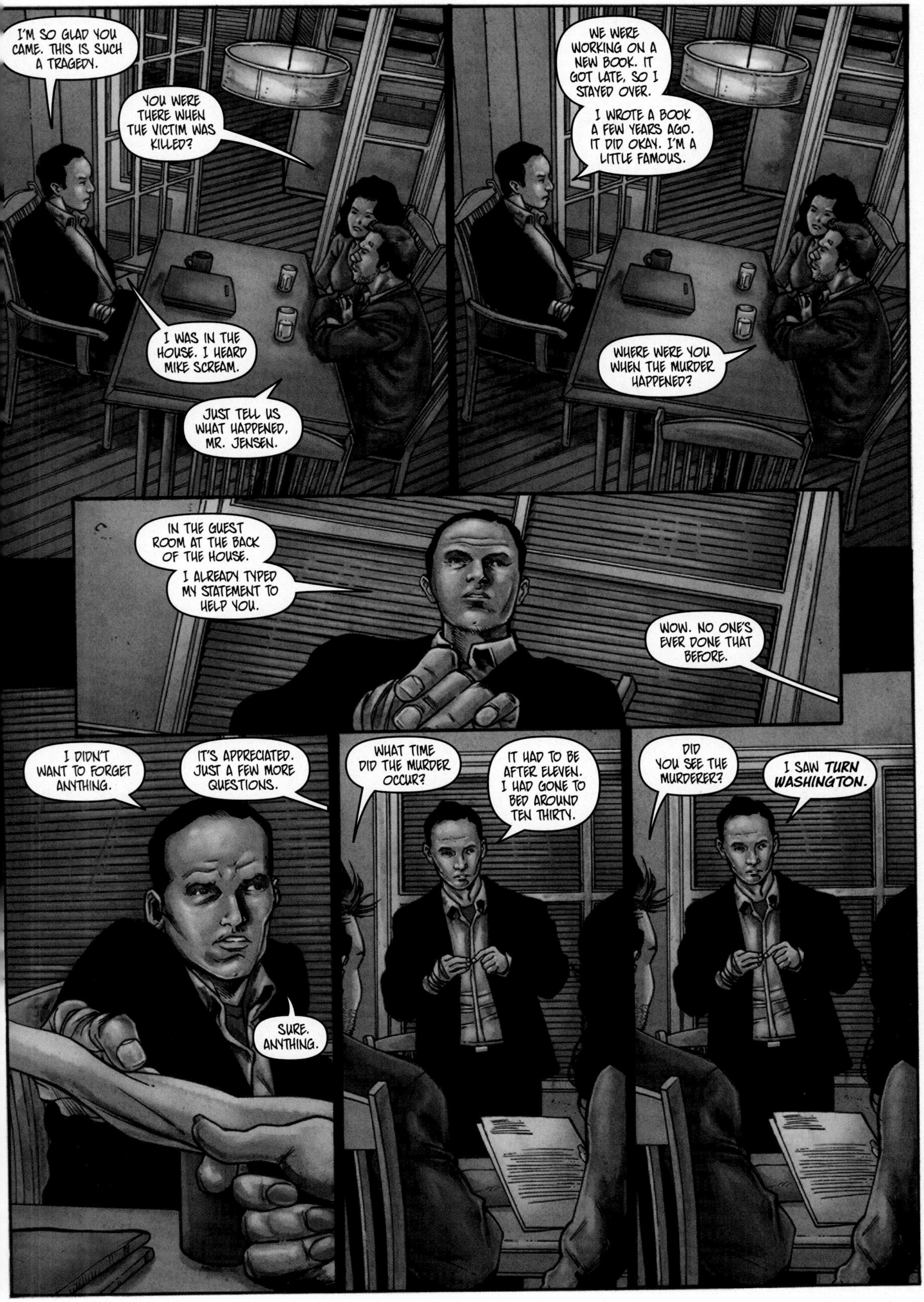
I'M SO GLAD YOU CAME. THIS IS SUCH A TRAGEDY.
YOU WERE THERE WHEN THE VICTIM WAS KILLED?
I WAS IN THE HOUSE. I HEARD MIKE SCREAM.
JUST TELL US WHAT HAPPENED, MR. JENSEN.
WE WERE WORKING ON A NEW BOOK. IT GOT LATE, SO I STAYED OVER.
I WROTE A BOOK A FEW YEARS AGO. IT DID OKAY. I'M A LITTLE FAMOUS.
WHERE WERE YOU WHEN THE MURDER HAPPENED?
IN THE GUEST ROOM AT THE BACK OF THE HOUSE.
I ALREADY TYPED MY STATEMENT TO HELP YOU.
WOW. NO ONE'S EVER DONE THAT BEFORE.
I DIDN'T WANT TO FORGET ANYTHING.
IT'S APPRECIATED. JUST A FEW MORE QUESTIONS.
SURE. ANYTHING.
WHAT TIME DID THE MURDER OCCUR?
IT HAD TO BE AFTER ELEVEN. I HAD GONE TO BED AROUND TEN THIRTY.
DID YOU SEE THE MURDERER?
I SAW **TURN WASHINGTON.**

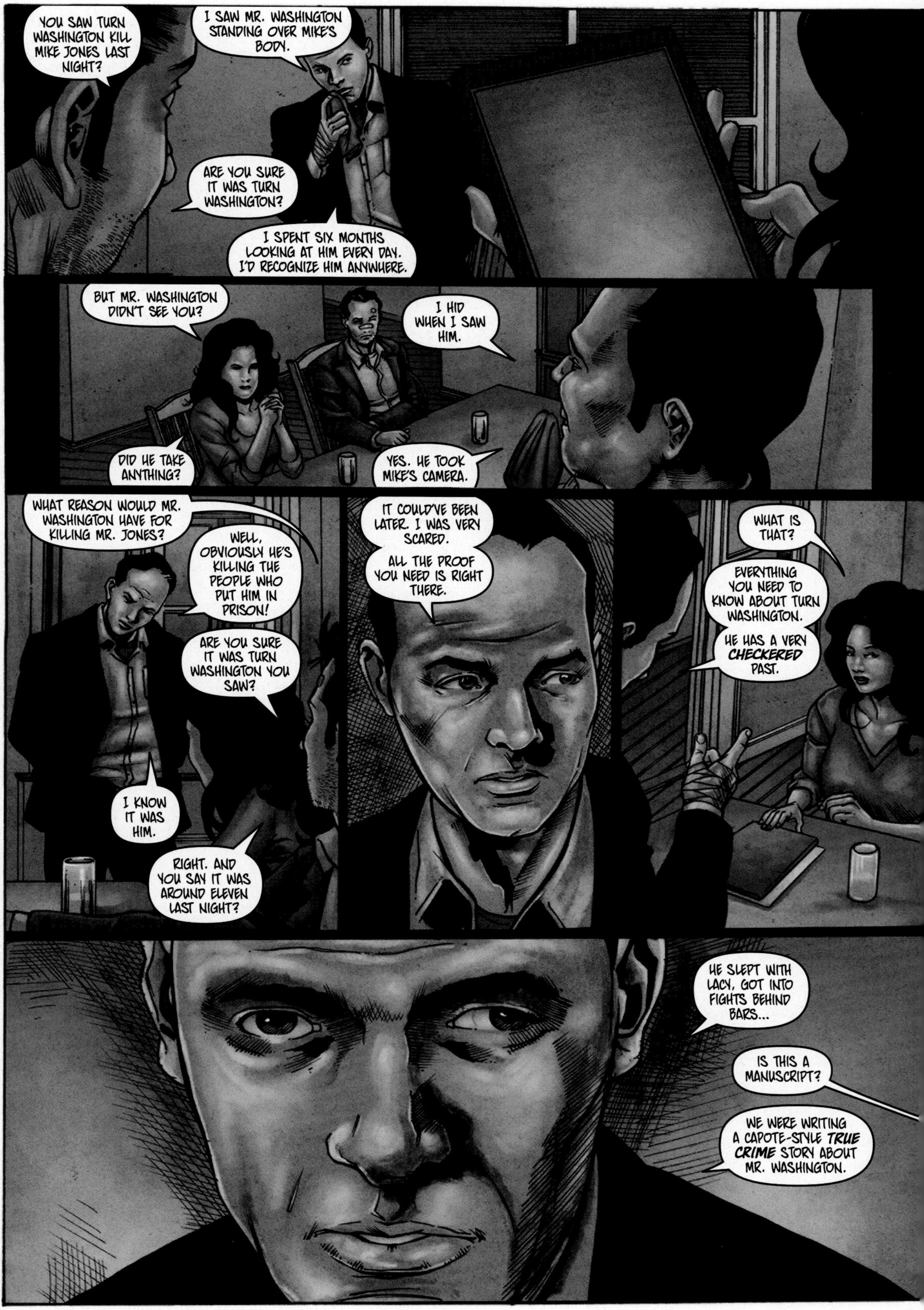
YOU SAW TURN WASHINGTON KILL MIKE JONES LAST NIGHT?
I SAW MR. WASHINGTON STANDING OVER MIKE'S BODY.
ARE YOU SURE IT WAS TURN WASHINGTON?
I SPENT SIX MONTHS LOOKING AT HIM EVERY DAY. I'D RECOGNIZE HIM ANYWHERE.
BUT MR. WASHINGTON DIDN'T SEE YOU?
I HID WHEN I SAW HIM.
DID HE TAKE ANYTHING?
YES. HE TOOK MIKE'S CAMERA.
WHAT REASON WOULD MR. WASHINGTON HAVE FOR KILLING MR. JONES?
WELL, OBVIOUSLY HE'S KILLING THE PEOPLE WHO PUT HIM IN PRISON!
ARE YOU SURE IT WAS TURN WASHINGTON YOU SAW?
I KNOW IT WAS HIM.
RIGHT. AND YOU SAY IT WAS AROUND ELEVEN LAST NIGHT?
IT COULD'VE BEEN LATER. I WAS VERY SCARED.
ALL THE PROOF YOU NEED IS RIGHT THERE.
WHAT IS THAT?
EVERYTHING YOU NEED TO KNOW ABOUT TURN WASHINGTON.
HE HAS A VERY ***CHECKERED*** PAST.
HE SLEPT WITH LACY, GOT INTO FIGHTS BEHIND BARS...
IS THIS A MANUSCRIPT?
WE WERE WRITING A CAPOTE-STYLE ***TRUE CRIME*** STORY ABOUT MR. WASHINGTON.

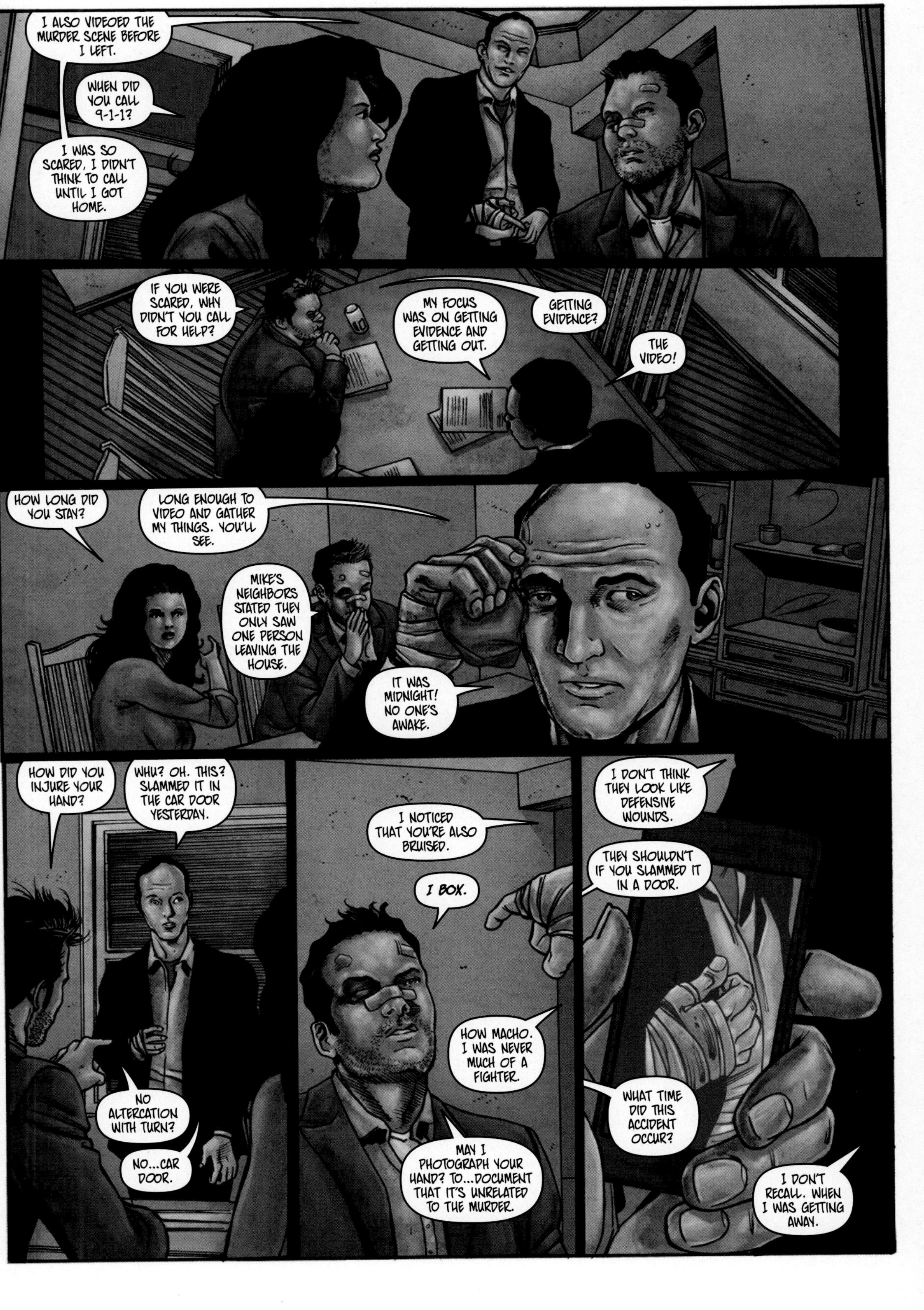
I ALSO VIDEOED THE MURDER SCENE BEFORE I LEFT.
WHEN DID YOU CALL 9-1-1?
I WAS SO SCARED, I DIDN'T THINK TO CALL UNTIL I GOT HOME.
IF YOU WERE SCARED, WHY DIDN'T YOU CALL FOR HELP?
MY FOCUS WAS ON GETTING EVIDENCE AND GETTING OUT.
GETTING EVIDENCE?
THE VIDEO!
HOW LONG DID YOU STAY?
LONG ENOUGH TO VIDEO AND GATHER MY THINGS. YOU'LL SEE.
MIKE'S NEIGHBORS STATED THEY ONLY SAW ONE PERSON LEAVING THE HOUSE.
IT WAS MIDNIGHT! NO ONE'S AWAKE.
HOW DID YOU INJURE YOUR HAND?
WHU? OH. THIS? SLAMMED IT IN THE CAR DOOR YESTERDAY.
NO ALTERCATION WITH TURN?
NO...CAR DOOR.
I NOTICED THAT YOU'RE ALSO BRUISED.
I BOX.
HOW MACHO. I WAS NEVER MUCH OF A FIGHTER.
MAY I PHOTOGRAPH YOUR HAND? TO...DOCUMENT THAT IT'S UNRELATED TO THE MURDER.
I DON'T THINK THEY LOOK LIKE DEFENSIVE WOUNDS.
THEY SHOULDN'T IF YOU SLAMMED IT IN A DOOR.
WHAT TIME DID THIS ACCIDENT OCCUR?
I DON'T RECALL. WHEN I WAS GETTING AWAY.

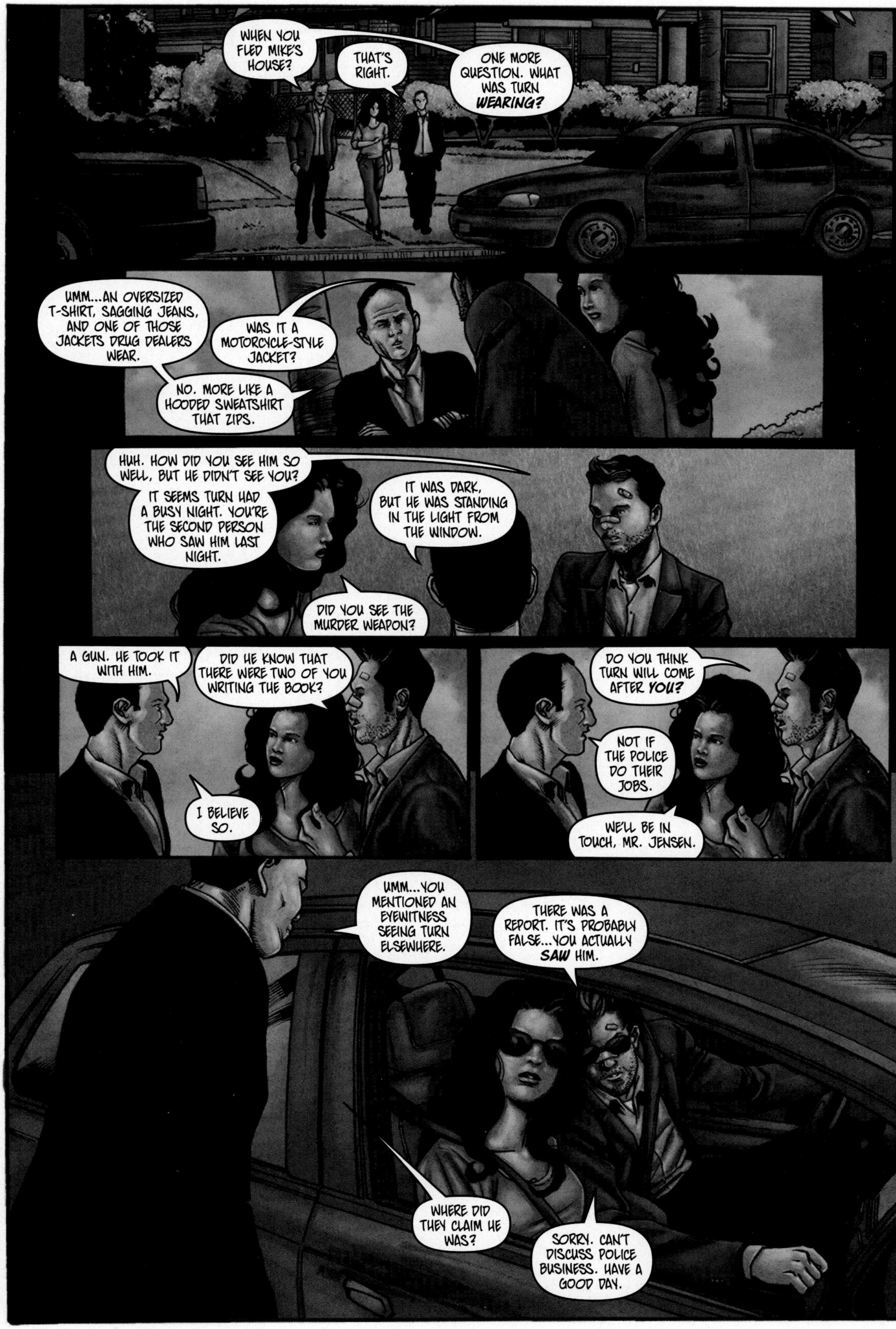
WHEN YOU FLED MIKE'S HOUSE?
THAT'S RIGHT.
ONE MORE QUESTION. WHAT WAS TURN *WEARING?*
UMM...AN OVERSIZED T-SHIRT, SAGGING JEANS, AND ONE OF THOSE JACKETS DRUG DEALERS WEAR.
WAS IT A MOTORCYCLE-STYLE JACKET?
NO. MORE LIKE A HOODED SWEATSHIRT THAT ZIPS.
HUH. HOW DID YOU SEE HIM SO WELL, BUT HE DIDN'T SEE YOU?
IT WAS DARK, BUT HE WAS STANDING IN THE LIGHT FROM THE WINDOW.
IT SEEMS TURN HAD A BUSY NIGHT. YOU'RE THE SECOND PERSON WHO SAW HIM LAST NIGHT.
DID YOU SEE THE MURDER WEAPON?
A GUN. HE TOOK IT WITH HIM.
DID HE KNOW THAT THERE WERE TWO OF YOU WRITING THE BOOK?
I BELIEVE SO.
DO YOU THINK TURN WILL COME AFTER *YOU?*
NOT IF THE POLICE DO THEIR JOBS.
WE'LL BE IN TOUCH, MR. JENSEN.
UMM...YOU MENTIONED AN EYEWITNESS SEEING TURN ELSEWHERE.
THERE WAS A REPORT. IT'S PROBABLY FALSE...YOU ACTUALLY *SAW* HIM.
WHERE DID THEY CLAIM HE WAS?
SORRY. CAN'T DISCUSS POLICE BUSINESS. HAVE A GOOD DAY.

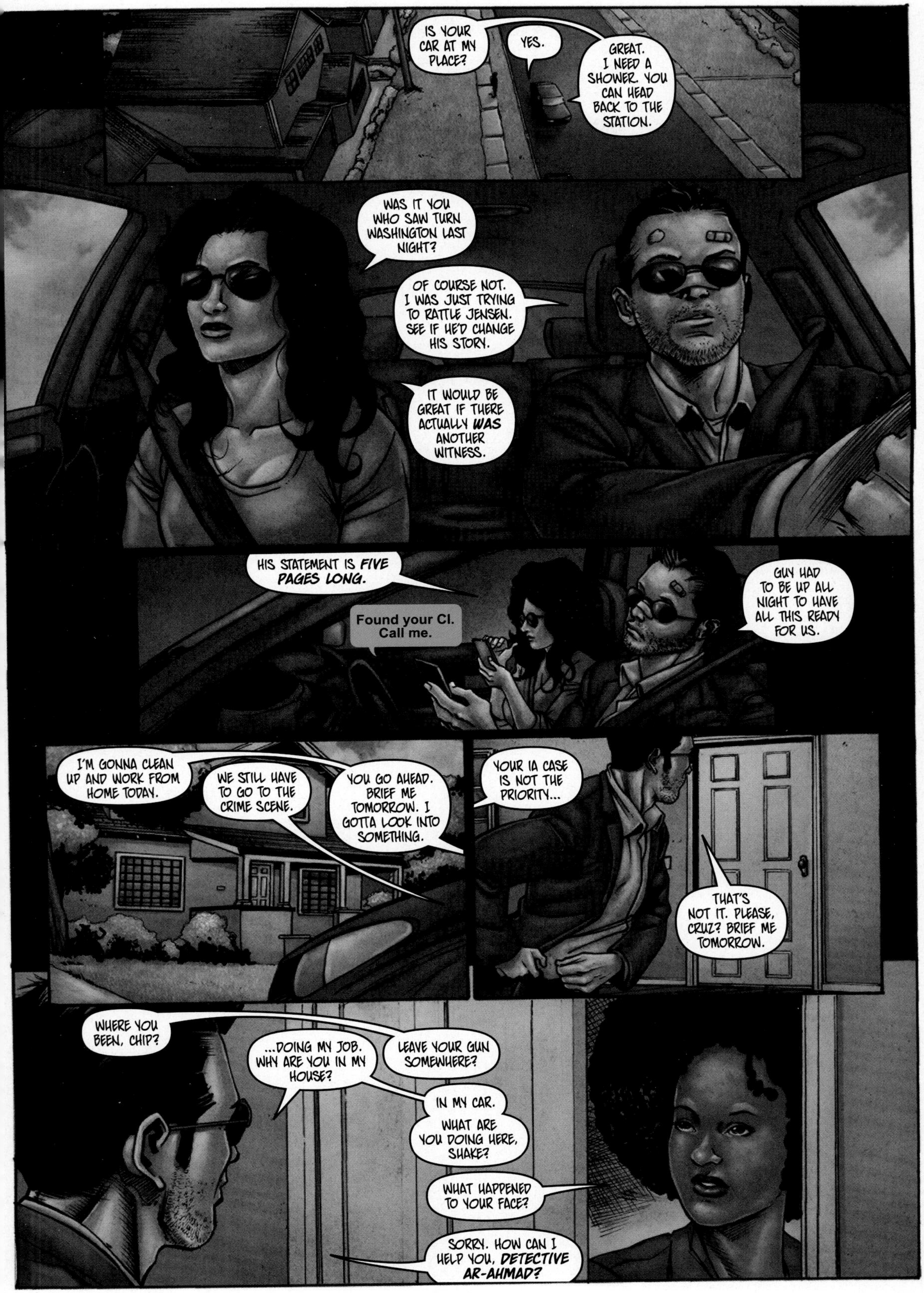
IS YOUR CAR AT MY PLACE?
YES.
GREAT. I NEED A SHOWER. YOU CAN HEAD BACK TO THE STATION.
WAS IT YOU WHO SAW TURN WASHINGTON LAST NIGHT?
OF COURSE NOT. I WAS JUST TRYING TO RATTLE JENSEN. SEE IF HE'D CHANGE HIS STORY.
IT WOULD BE GREAT IF THERE ACTUALLY WAS ANOTHER WITNESS.
HIS STATEMENT IS FIVE PAGES LONG.
GUY HAD TO BE UP ALL NIGHT TO HAVE ALL THIS READY FOR US.
Found your CI. Call me.
I'M GONNA CLEAN UP AND WORK FROM HOME TODAY.
WE STILL HAVE TO GO TO THE CRIME SCENE.
YOU GO AHEAD. BRIEF ME TOMORROW. I GOTTA LOOK INTO SOMETHING.
YOUR IA CASE IS NOT THE PRIORITY...
THAT'S NOT IT. PLEASE, CRUZ? BRIEF ME TOMORROW.
WHERE YOU BEEN, CHIP?
LEAVE YOUR GUN SOMEWHERE?
...DOING MY JOB. WHY ARE YOU IN MY HOUSE?
IN MY CAR.
WHAT ARE YOU DOING HERE, SHAKE?
WHAT HAPPENED TO YOUR FACE?
SORRY. HOW CAN I HELP YOU, DETECTIVE AR-AHMAD?

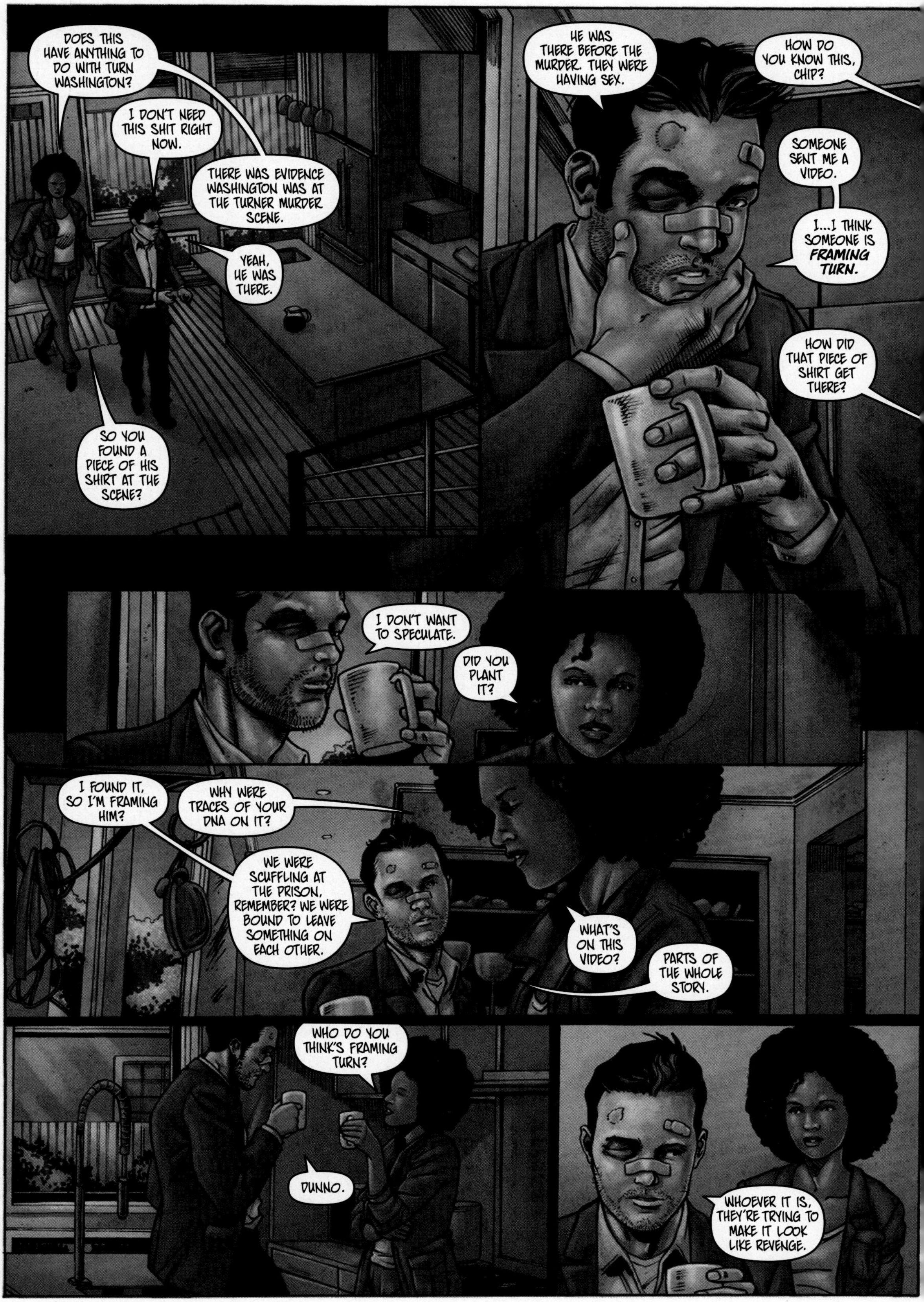
DOES THIS HAVE ANYTHING TO DO WITH TURN WASHINGTON?
I DON'T NEED THIS SHIT RIGHT NOW.
THERE WAS EVIDENCE WASHINGTON WAS AT THE TURNER MURDER SCENE.
YEAH, HE WAS THERE.
SO YOU FOUND A PIECE OF HIS SHIRT AT THE SCENE?
HE WAS THERE BEFORE THE MURDER. THEY WERE HAVING SEX.
HOW DO YOU KNOW THIS, CHIP?
SOMEONE SENT ME A VIDEO.
I...I THINK SOMEONE IS *FRAMING TURN.*
HOW DID THAT PIECE OF SHIRT GET THERE?
I DON'T WANT TO SPECULATE.
DID YOU PLANT IT?
I FOUND IT, SO I'M FRAMING HIM?
WHY WERE TRACES OF YOUR DNA ON IT?
WE WERE SCUFFLING AT THE PRISON, REMEMBER? WE WERE BOUND TO LEAVE SOMETHING ON EACH OTHER.
WHAT'S ON THIS VIDEO?
PARTS OF THE WHOLE STORY.
WHO DO YOU THINK'S FRAMING TURN?
DUNNO.
WHOEVER IT IS, THEY'RE TRYING TO MAKE IT LOOK LIKE REVENGE.

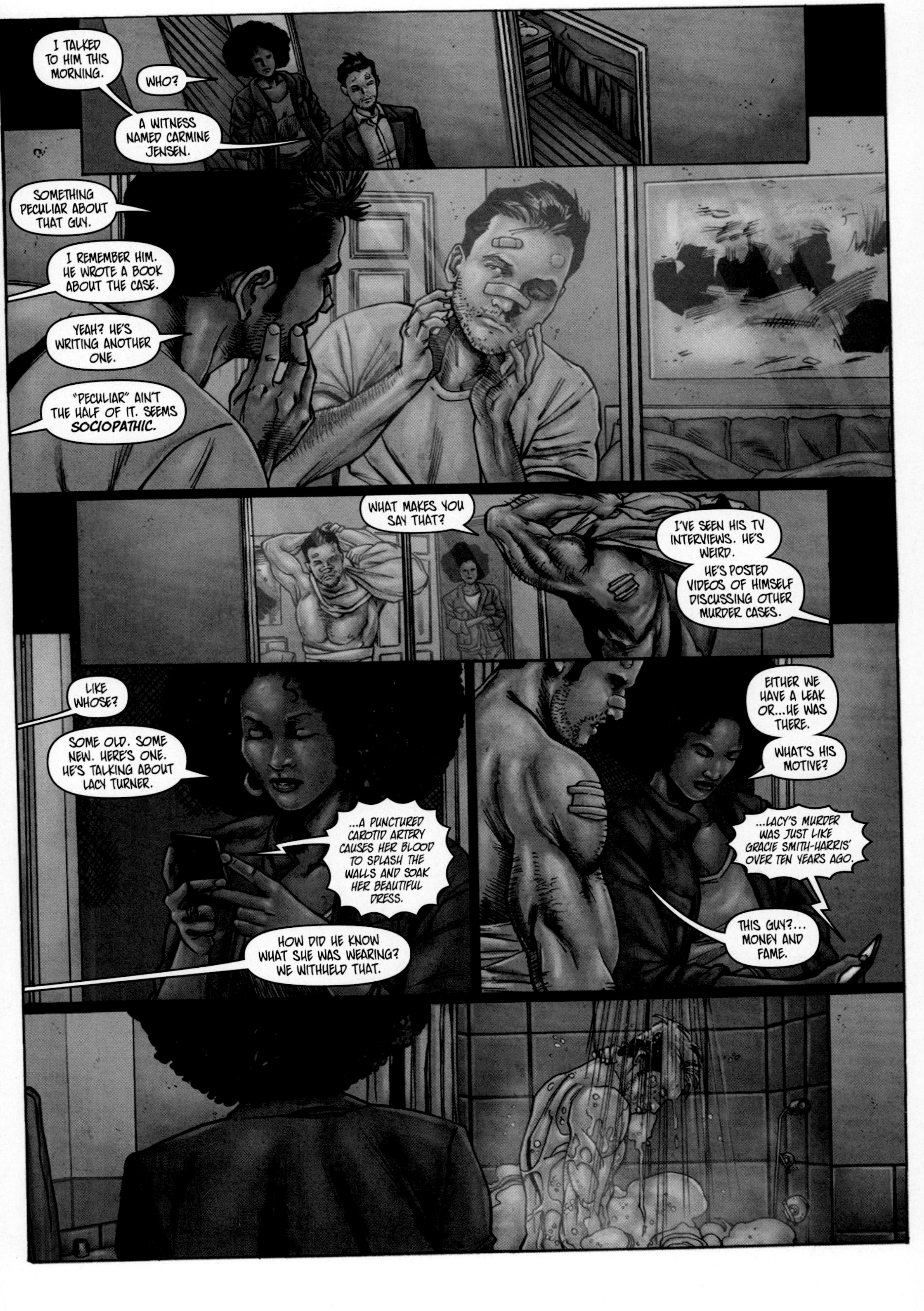
I TALKED TO HIM THIS MORNING.
WHO?
A WITNESS NAMED CARMINE JENSEN.
SOMETHING PECULIAR ABOUT THAT GUY.
I REMEMBER HIM. HE WROTE A BOOK ABOUT THE CASE.
YEAH? HE'S WRITING ANOTHER ONE.
"PECULIAR" AIN'T THE HALF OF IT. SEEMS SOCIOPATHIC.
WHAT MAKES YOU SAY THAT?
I'VE SEEN HIS TV INTERVIEWS. HE'S WEIRD.
HE'S POSTED VIDEOS OF HIMSELF DISCUSSING OTHER MURDER CASES.
LIKE WHOSE?
SOME OLD. SOME NEW. HERE'S ONE. HE'S TALKING ABOUT LACY TURNER.
...A PUNCTURED CAROTID ARTERY CAUSES HER BLOOD TO SPLASH THE WALLS AND SOAK HER BEAUTIFUL DRESS.
HOW DID HE KNOW WHAT SHE WAS WEARING? WE WITHHELD THAT.
EITHER WE HAVE A LEAK OR...HE WAS THERE.
WHAT'S HIS MOTIVE?
...LACY'S MURDER WAS JUST LIKE GRACIE SMITH-HARRIS' OVER TEN YEARS AGO.
THIS GUY?... MONEY AND FAME.

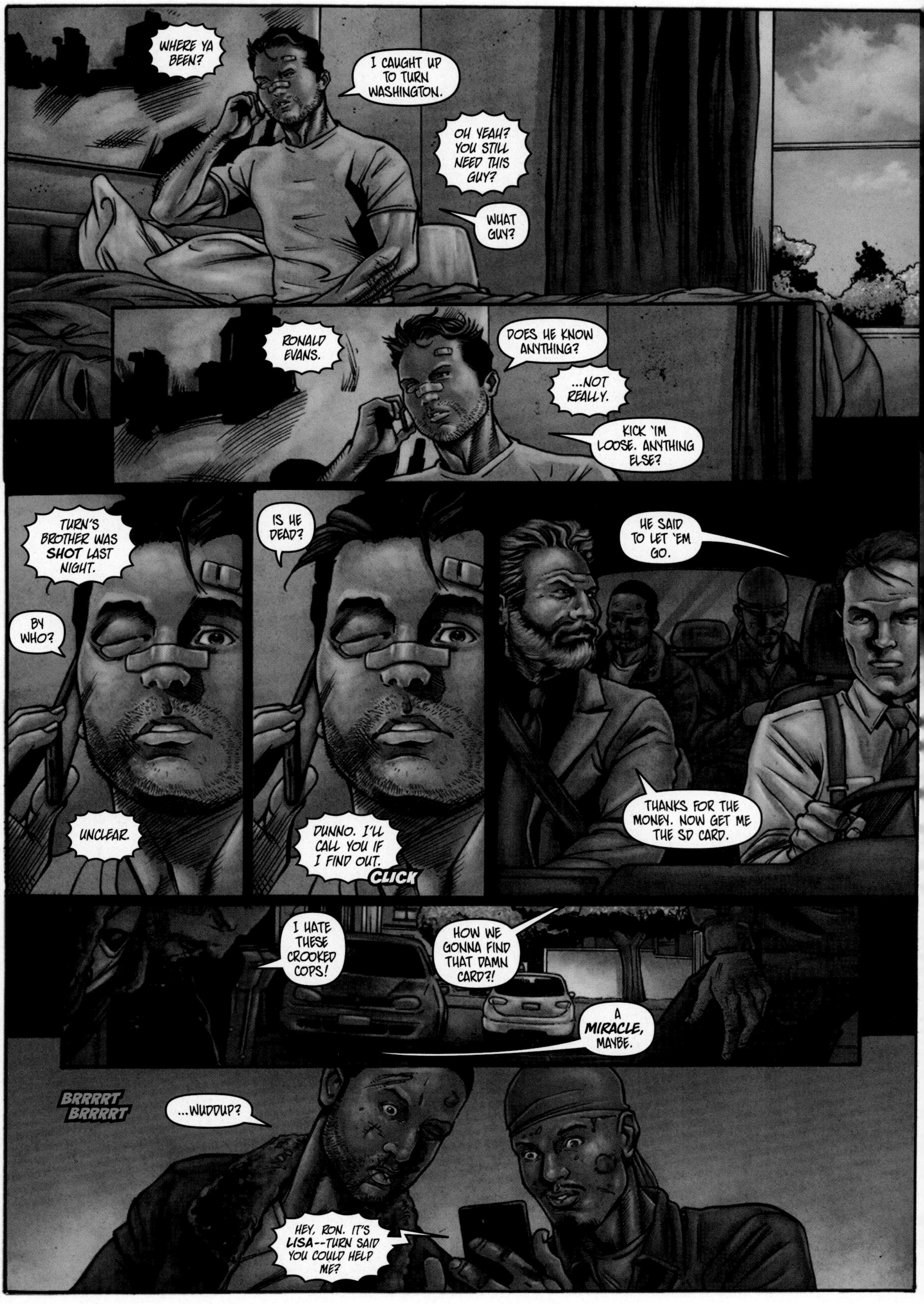

WHERE YA BEEN?
I CAUGHT UP TO TURN WASHINGTON.
OH YEAH? YOU STILL NEED THIS GUY?
WHAT GUY?
RONALD EVANS.
DOES HE KNOW ANYTHING?
...NOT REALLY.
KICK 'IM LOOSE. ANYTHING ELSE?
TURN'S BROTHER WAS SHOT LAST NIGHT.
BY WHO?
UNCLEAR.
IS HE DEAD?
DUNNO. I'LL CALL YOU IF I FIND OUT.
CLICK
HE SAID TO LET 'EM GO.
THANKS FOR THE MONEY. NOW GET ME THE SD CARD.
I HATE THESE CROOKED COPS!
HOW WE GONNA FIND THAT DAMN CARD?!
A MIRACLE, MAYBE.
BRRRRT BRRRRT
...WUDDUP?
HEY, RON. IT'S LISA--TURN SAID YOU COULD HELP ME?

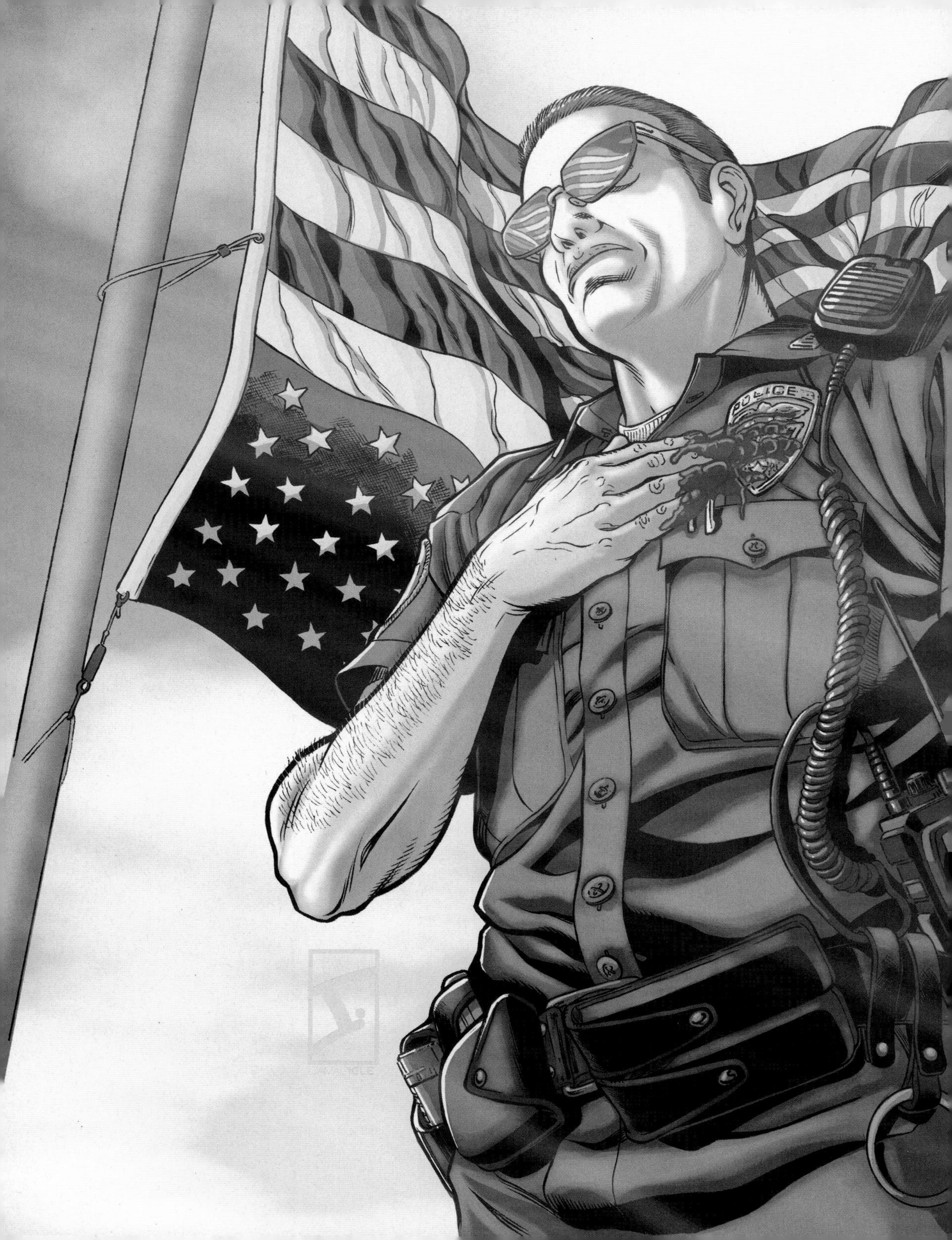
POLICE

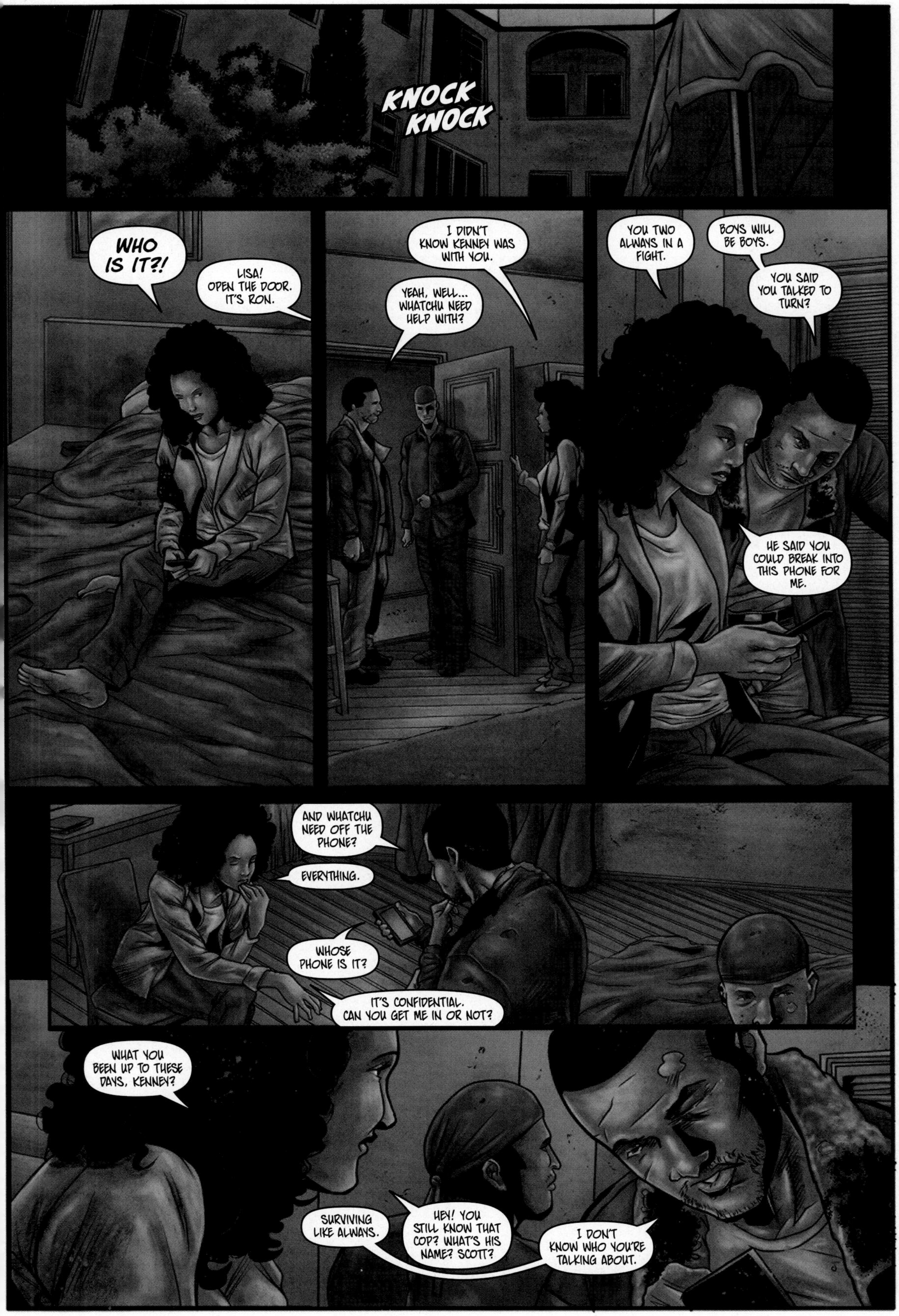
KNOCK
KNOCK
WHO IS IT?!
LISA! OPEN THE DOOR. IT'S RON.
I DIDN'T KNOW KENNEY WAS WITH YOU.
YEAH, WELL... WHATCHU NEED HELP WITH?
YOU TWO ALWAYS IN A FIGHT.
BOYS WILL BE BOYS.
YOU SAID YOU TALKED TO TURN?
HE SAID YOU COULD BREAK INTO THIS PHONE FOR ME.
AND WHATCHU NEED OFF THE PHONE?
EVERYTHING.
WHOSE PHONE IS IT?
IT'S CONFIDENTIAL. CAN YOU GET ME IN OR NOT?
WHAT YOU BEEN UP TO THESE DAYS, KENNEY?
SURVIVING LIKE ALWAYS.
HEY! YOU STILL KNOW THAT COP? WHAT'S HIS NAME? SCOTT?
I DON'T KNOW WHO YOU'RE TALKING ABOUT.

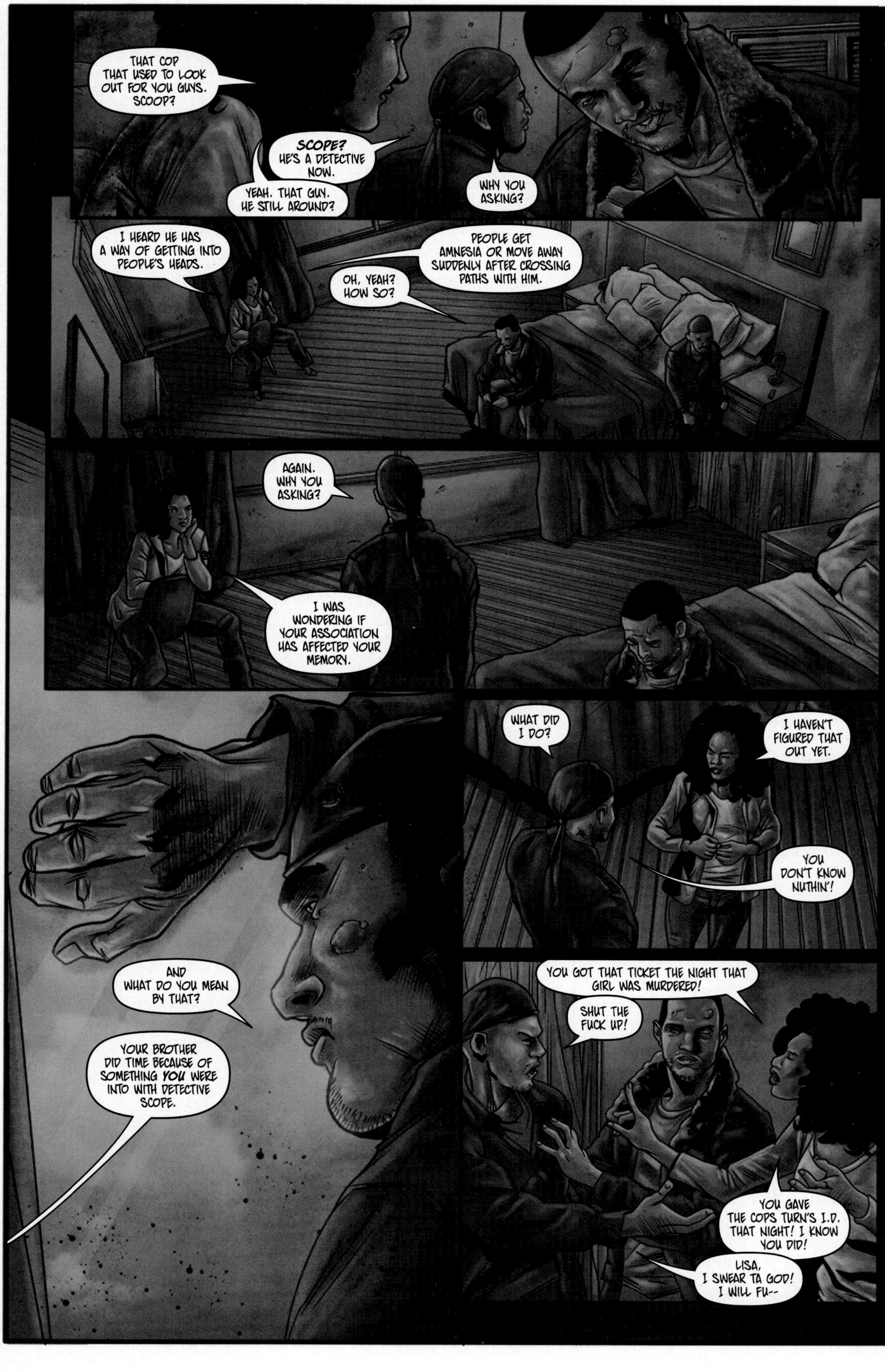
THAT COP THAT USED TO LOOK OUT FOR YOU GUYS. SCOOP?
SCOPE? HE'S A DETECTIVE NOW.
YEAH. THAT GUY. HE STILL AROUND?
WHY YOU ASKING?
I HEARD HE HAS A WAY OF GETTING INTO PEOPLE'S HEADS.
OH, YEAH? HOW SO?
PEOPLE GET AMNESIA OR MOVE AWAY SUDDENLY AFTER CROSSING PATHS WITH HIM.
AGAIN. WHY YOU ASKING?
I WAS WONDERING IF YOUR ASSOCIATION HAS AFFECTED YOUR MEMORY.
AND WHAT DO YOU MEAN BY THAT?
YOUR BROTHER DID TIME BECAUSE OF SOMETHING YOU WERE INTO WITH DETECTIVE SCOPE.
WHAT DID I DO?
I HAVEN'T FIGURED THAT OUT YET.
YOU DON'T KNOW NUTHIN'!
YOU GOT THAT TICKET THE NIGHT THAT GIRL WAS MURDERED!
SHUT THE FUCK UP!
YOU GAVE THE COPS TURN'S I.D. THAT NIGHT! I KNOW YOU DID!
LISA, I SWEAR TA GOD! I WILL FU--

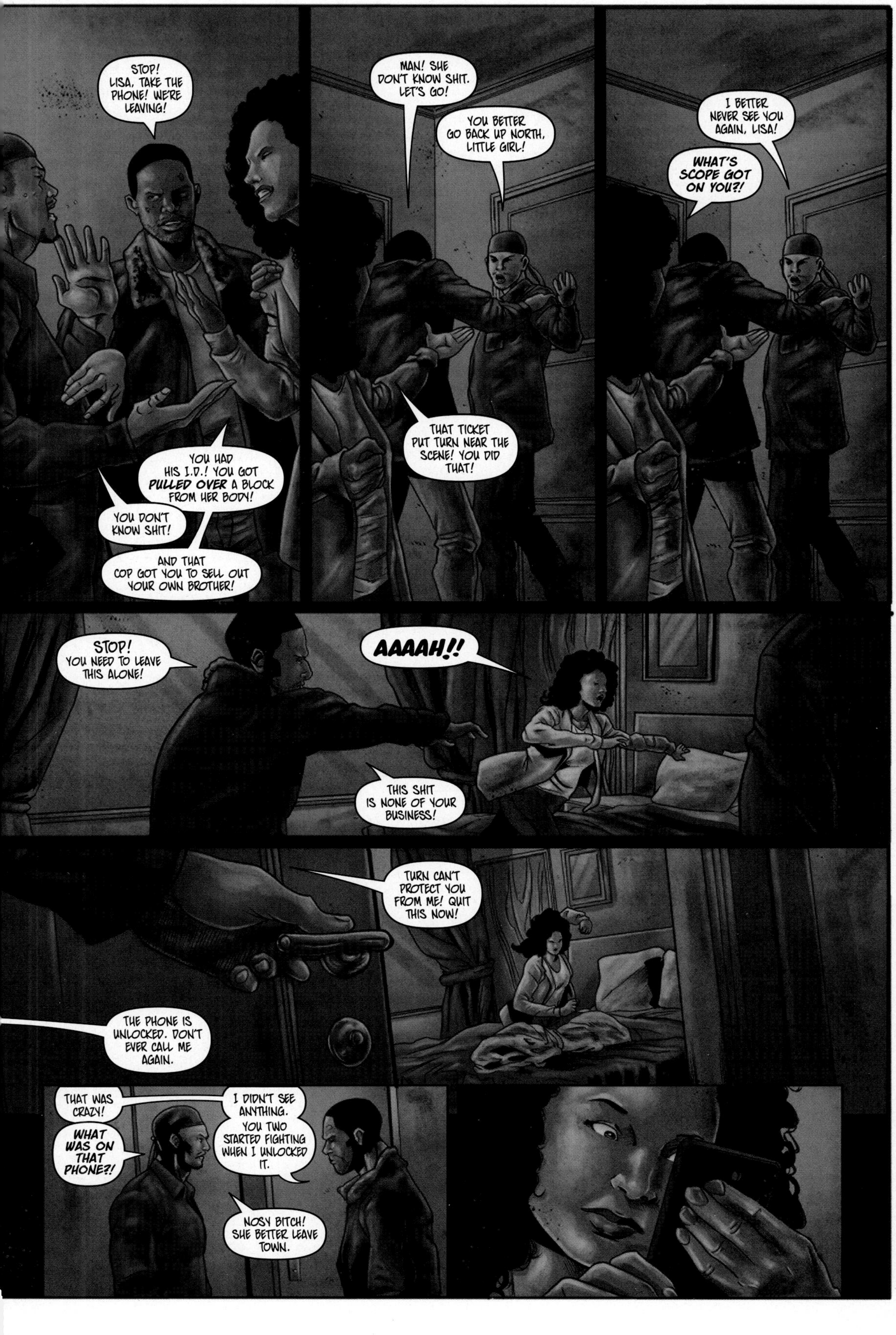
STOP! LISA, TAKE THE PHONE! WE'RE LEAVING!
YOU HAD HIS I.D.! YOU GOT PULLED OVER A BLOCK FROM HER BODY!
YOU DON'T KNOW SHIT!
AND THAT COP GOT YOU TO SELL OUT YOUR OWN BROTHER!
MAN! SHE DON'T KNOW SHIT. LET'S GO!
YOU BETTER GO BACK UP NORTH, LITTLE GIRL!
THAT TICKET PUT TURN NEAR THE SCENE! YOU DID THAT!
I BETTER NEVER SEE YOU AGAIN, LISA!
WHAT'S SCOPE GOT ON YOU?!
STOP! YOU NEED TO LEAVE THIS ALONE!
AAAAH!!
THIS SHIT IS NONE OF YOUR BUSINESS!
TURN CAN'T PROTECT YOU FROM ME! QUIT THIS NOW!
THE PHONE IS UNLOCKED. DON'T EVER CALL ME AGAIN.
THAT WAS CRAZY!
WHAT WAS ON THAT PHONE?!
I DIDN'T SEE ANYTHING. YOU TWO STARTED FIGHTING WHEN I UNLOCKED IT.
NOSY BITCH! SHE BETTER LEAVE TOWN.

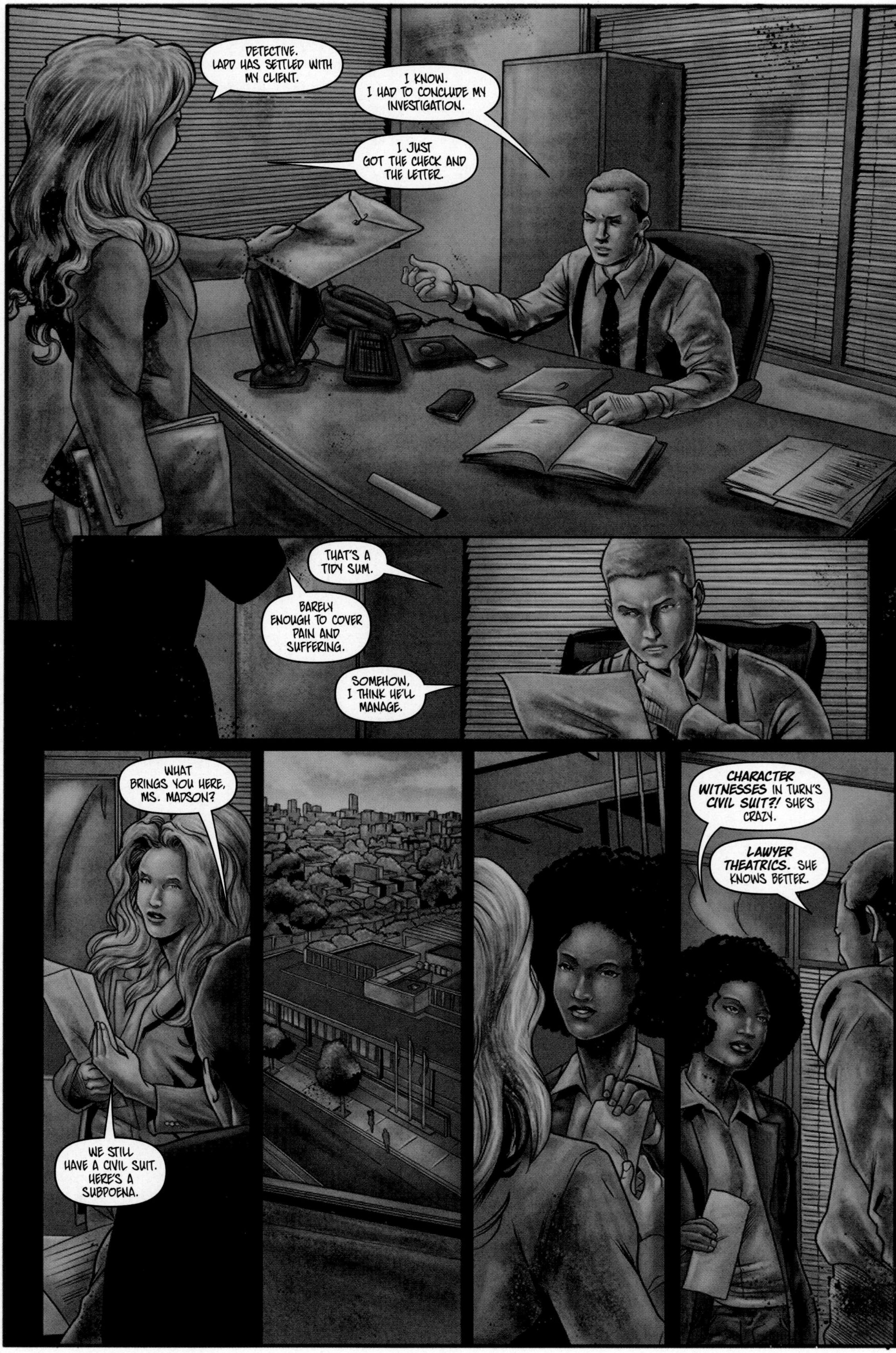
DETECTIVE. LAPD HAS SETTLED WITH MY CLIENT.
I KNOW. I HAD TO CONCLUDE MY INVESTIGATION.
I JUST GOT THE CHECK AND THE LETTER.
THAT'S A TIDY SUM.
BARELY ENOUGH TO COVER PAIN AND SUFFERING.
SOMEHOW, I THINK HE'LL MANAGE.
WHAT BRINGS YOU HERE, MS. MADSON?
WE STILL HAVE A CIVIL SUIT. HERE'S A SUBPOENA.
CHARACTER WITNESSES IN TURN'S CIVIL SUIT?! SHE'S CRAZY.
LAWYER THEATRICS. SHE KNOWS BETTER.

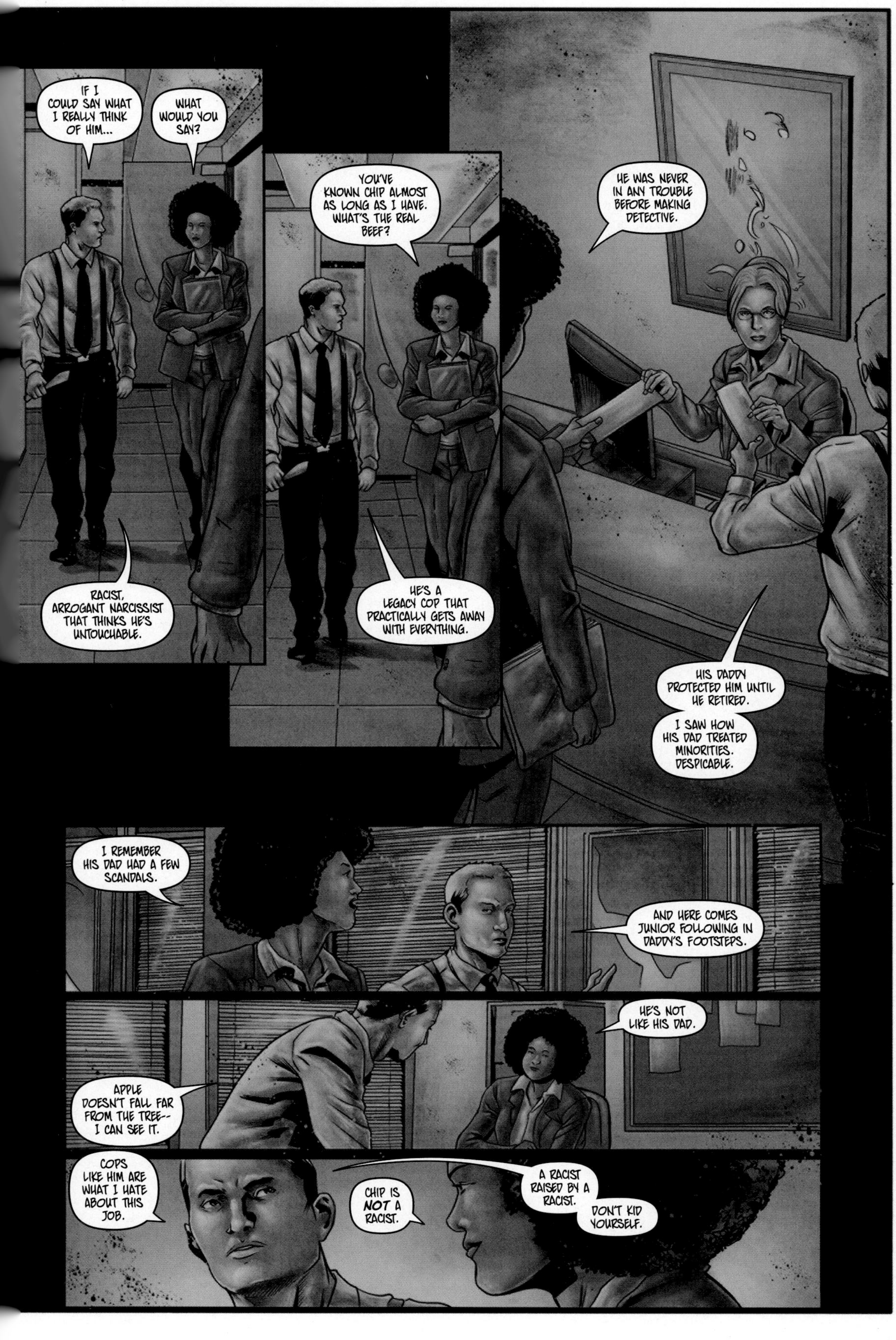
IF I COULD SAY WHAT I REALLY THINK OF HIM...
WHAT WOULD YOU SAY?
RACIST, ARROGANT NARCISSIST THAT THINKS HE'S UNTOUCHABLE.
YOU'VE KNOWN CHIP ALMOST AS LONG AS I HAVE. WHAT'S THE REAL BEEF?
HE'S A LEGACY COP THAT PRACTICALLY GETS AWAY WITH EVERYTHING.
HE WAS NEVER IN ANY TROUBLE BEFORE MAKING DETECTIVE.
HIS DADDY PROTECTED HIM UNTIL HE RETIRED.
I SAW HOW HIS DAD TREATED MINORITIES. DESPICABLE.
I REMEMBER HIS DAD HAD A FEW SCANDALS.
AND HERE COMES JUNIOR FOLLOWING IN DADDY'S FOOTSTEPS.
HE'S NOT LIKE HIS DAD.
APPLE DOESN'T FALL FAR FROM THE TREE-- I CAN SEE IT.
COPS LIKE HIM ARE WHAT I HATE ABOUT THIS JOB.
CHIP IS NOT A RACIST.
A RACIST RAISED BY A RACIST.
DON'T KID YOURSELF.

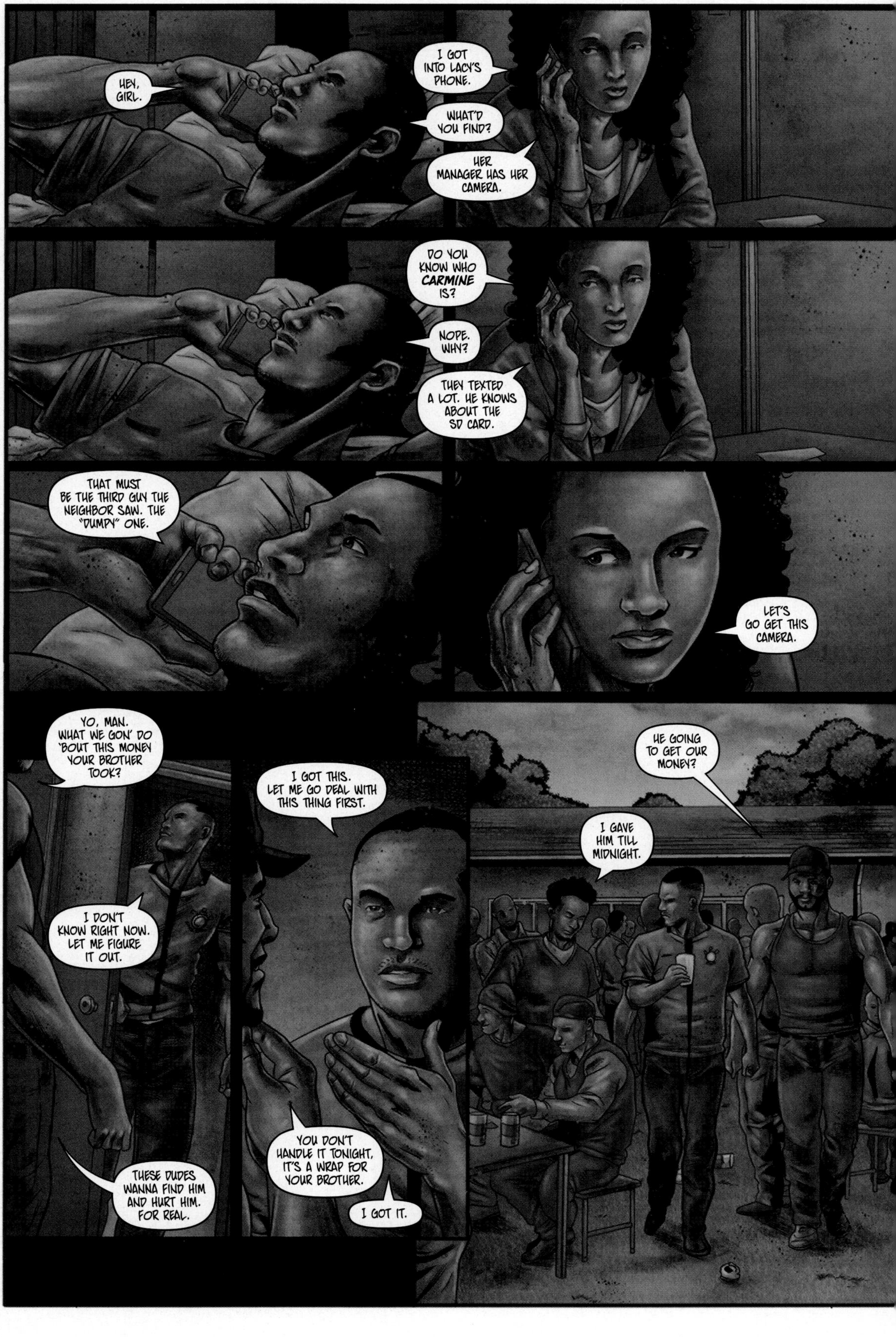
HEY, GIRL.
I GOT INTO LACY'S PHONE.
WHAT'D YOU FIND?
HER MANAGER HAS HER CAMERA.
DO YOU KNOW WHO **CARMINE** IS?
NOPE. WHY?
THEY TEXTED A LOT. HE KNOWS ABOUT THE SD CARD.
THAT MUST BE THE THIRD GUY THE NEIGHBOR SAW. THE "DUMPY" ONE.
LET'S GO GET THIS CAMERA.
YO, MAN. WHAT WE GON' DO 'BOUT THIS MONEY YOUR BROTHER TOOK?
I DON'T KNOW RIGHT NOW. LET ME FIGURE IT OUT.
THESE DUDES WANNA FIND HIM AND HURT HIM. FOR REAL.
I GOT THIS. LET ME GO DEAL WITH THIS THING FIRST.
YOU DON'T HANDLE IT TONIGHT, IT'S A WRAP FOR YOUR BROTHER.
I GOT IT.
HE GOING TO GET OUR MONEY?
I GAVE HIM TILL MIDNIGHT.

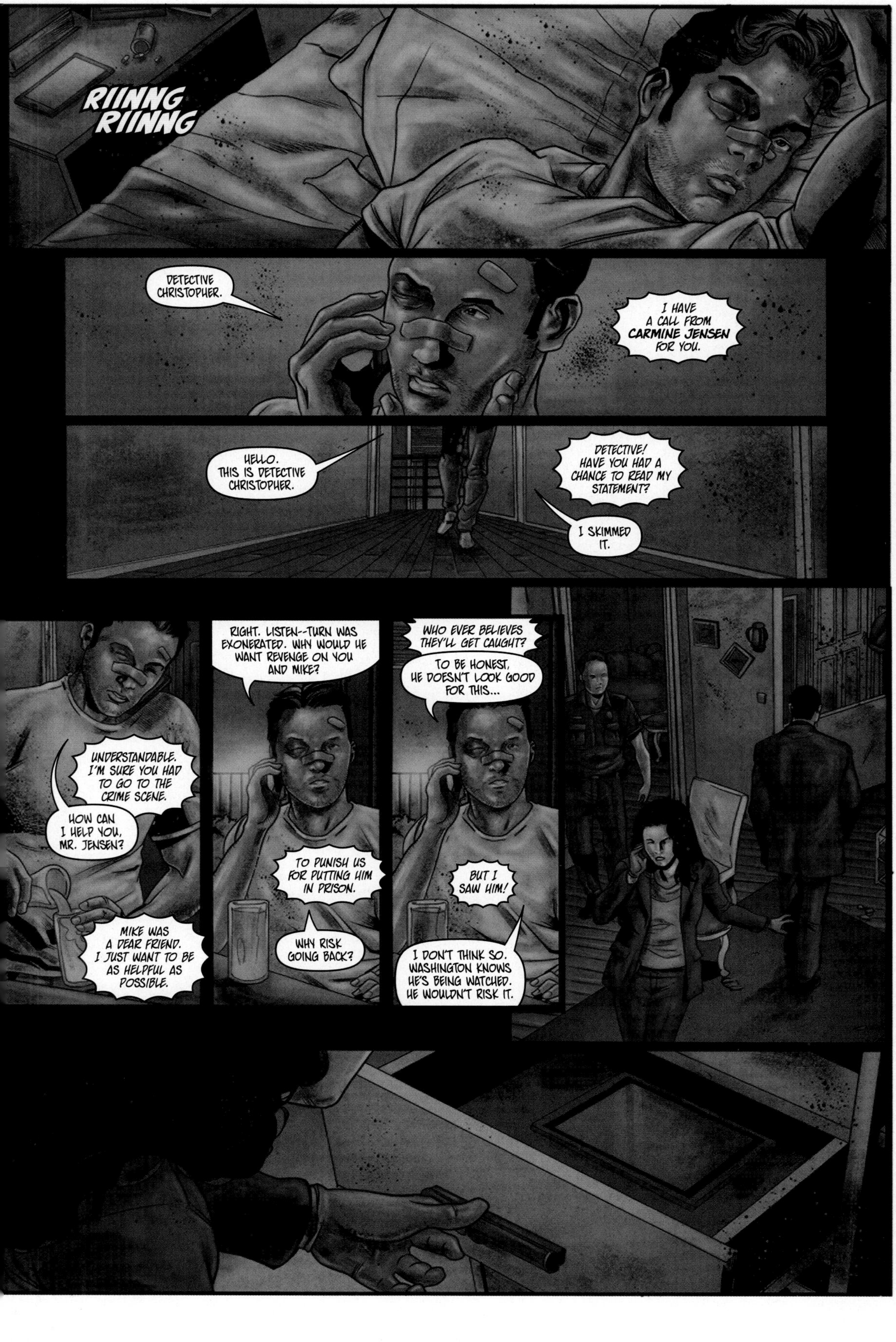
RIINNG RIINNG
DETECTIVE CHRISTOPHER.
I HAVE A CALL FROM CARMINE JENSEN FOR YOU.
HELLO. THIS IS DETECTIVE CHRISTOPHER.
DETECTIVE! HAVE YOU HAD A CHANCE TO READ MY STATEMENT?
I SKIMMED IT.
UNDERSTANDABLE. I'M SURE YOU HAD TO GO TO THE CRIME SCENE.
HOW CAN I HELP YOU, MR. JENSEN?
MIKE WAS A DEAR FRIEND. I JUST WANT TO BE AS HELPFUL AS POSSIBLE.
RIGHT. LISTEN--TURN WAS EXONERATED. WHY WOULD HE WANT REVENGE ON YOU AND MIKE?
TO PUNISH US FOR PUTTING HIM IN PRISON.
WHY RISK GOING BACK?
WHO EVER BELIEVES THEY'LL GET CAUGHT?
TO BE HONEST, HE DOESN'T LOOK GOOD FOR THIS...
BUT I SAW HIM!
I DON'T THINK SO. WASHINGTON KNOWS HE'S BEING WATCHED. HE WOULDN'T RISK IT.

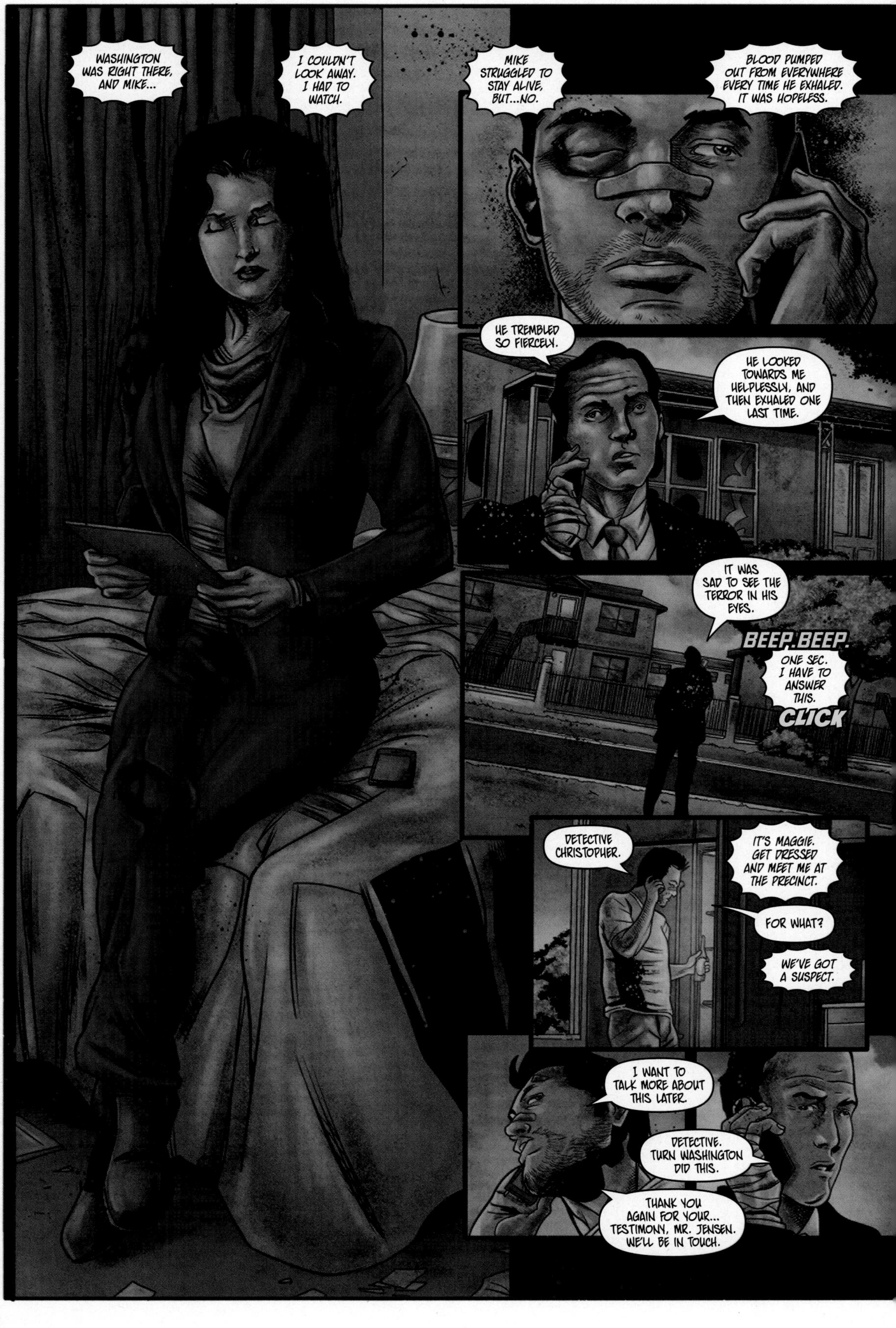
WASHINGTON WAS RIGHT THERE, AND MIKE...
I COULDN'T LOOK AWAY. I HAD TO WATCH.
MIKE STRUGGLED TO STAY ALIVE, BUT...NO.
BLOOD PUMPED OUT FROM EVERYWHERE EVERY TIME HE EXHALED. IT WAS HOPELESS.
HE TREMBLED SO FIERCELY.
HE LOOKED TOWARDS ME HELPLESSLY, AND THEN EXHALED ONE LAST TIME.
IT WAS SAD TO SEE THE TERROR IN HIS EYES.
BEEP. BEEP.
ONE SEC. I HAVE TO ANSWER THIS.
CLICK
DETECTIVE CHRISTOPHER.
IT'S MAGGIE. GET DRESSED AND MEET ME AT THE PRECINCT.
FOR WHAT?
WE'VE GOT A SUSPECT.
I WANT TO TALK MORE ABOUT THIS LATER.
DETECTIVE. TURN WASHINGTON DID THIS.
THANK YOU AGAIN FOR YOUR... TESTIMONY, MR. JENSEN. WE'LL BE IN TOUCH.

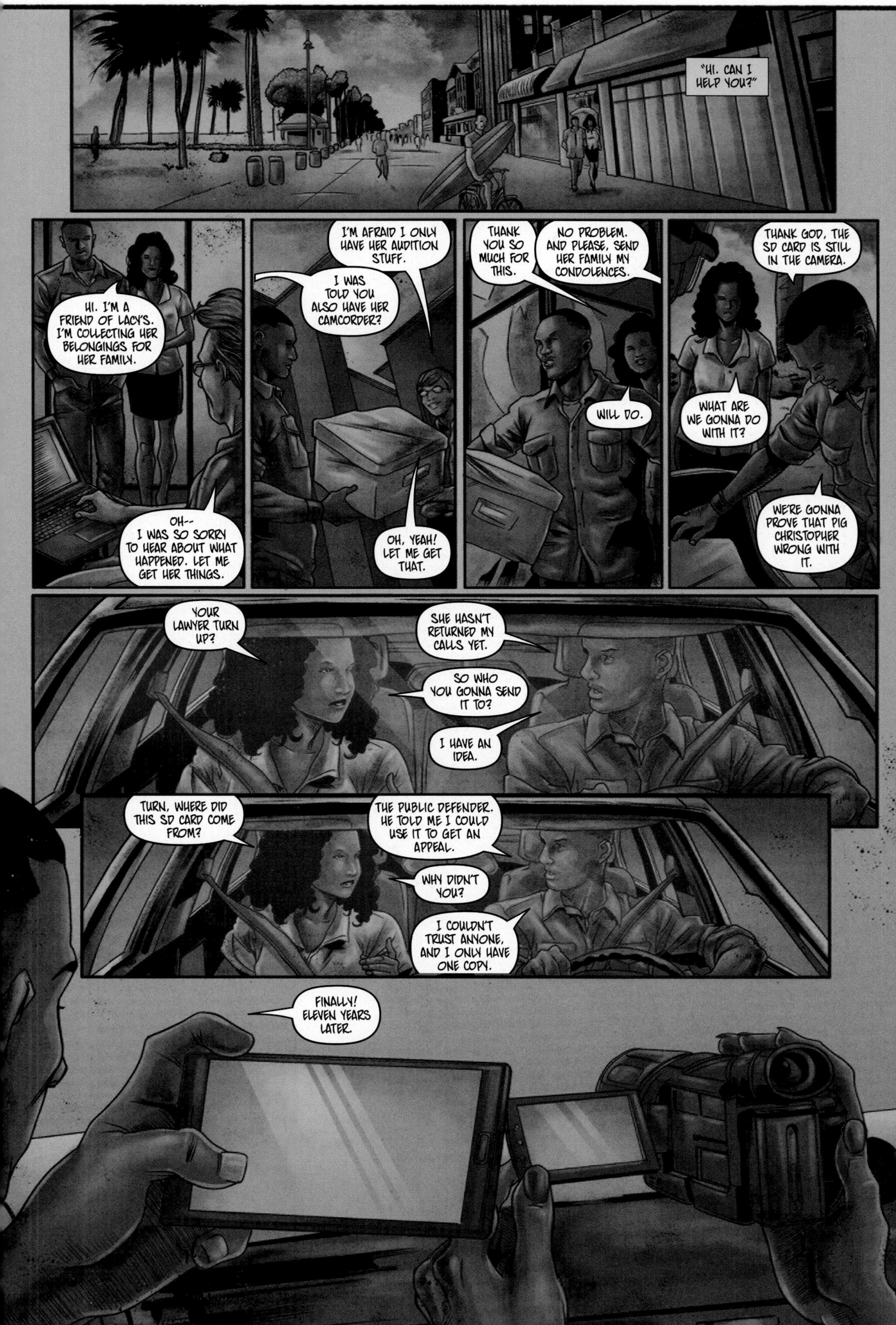
"HI. CAN I HELP YOU?"
HI. I'M A FRIEND OF LACY'S. I'M COLLECTING HER BELONGINGS FOR HER FAMILY.
OH-- I WAS SO SORRY TO HEAR ABOUT WHAT HAPPENED. LET ME GET HER THINGS.
I'M AFRAID I ONLY HAVE HER AUDITION STUFF.
I WAS TOLD YOU ALSO HAVE HER CAMCORDER?
OH, YEAH! LET ME GET THAT.
THANK YOU SO MUCH FOR THIS.
NO PROBLEM. AND PLEASE, SEND HER FAMILY MY CONDOLENCES.
WILL DO.
THANK GOD, THE SD CARD IS STILL IN THE CAMERA.
WHAT ARE WE GONNA DO WITH IT?
WE'RE GONNA PROVE THAT PIG CHRISTOPHER WRONG WITH IT.
YOUR LAWYER TURN UP?
SHE HASN'T RETURNED MY CALLS YET.
SO WHO YOU GONNA SEND IT TO?
I HAVE AN IDEA.
TURN, WHERE DID THIS SD CARD COME FROM?
THE PUBLIC DEFENDER. HE TOLD ME I COULD USE IT TO GET AN APPEAL.
WHY DIDN'T YOU?
I COULDN'T TRUST ANYONE, AND I ONLY HAVE ONE COPY.
FINALLY! ELEVEN YEARS LATER.

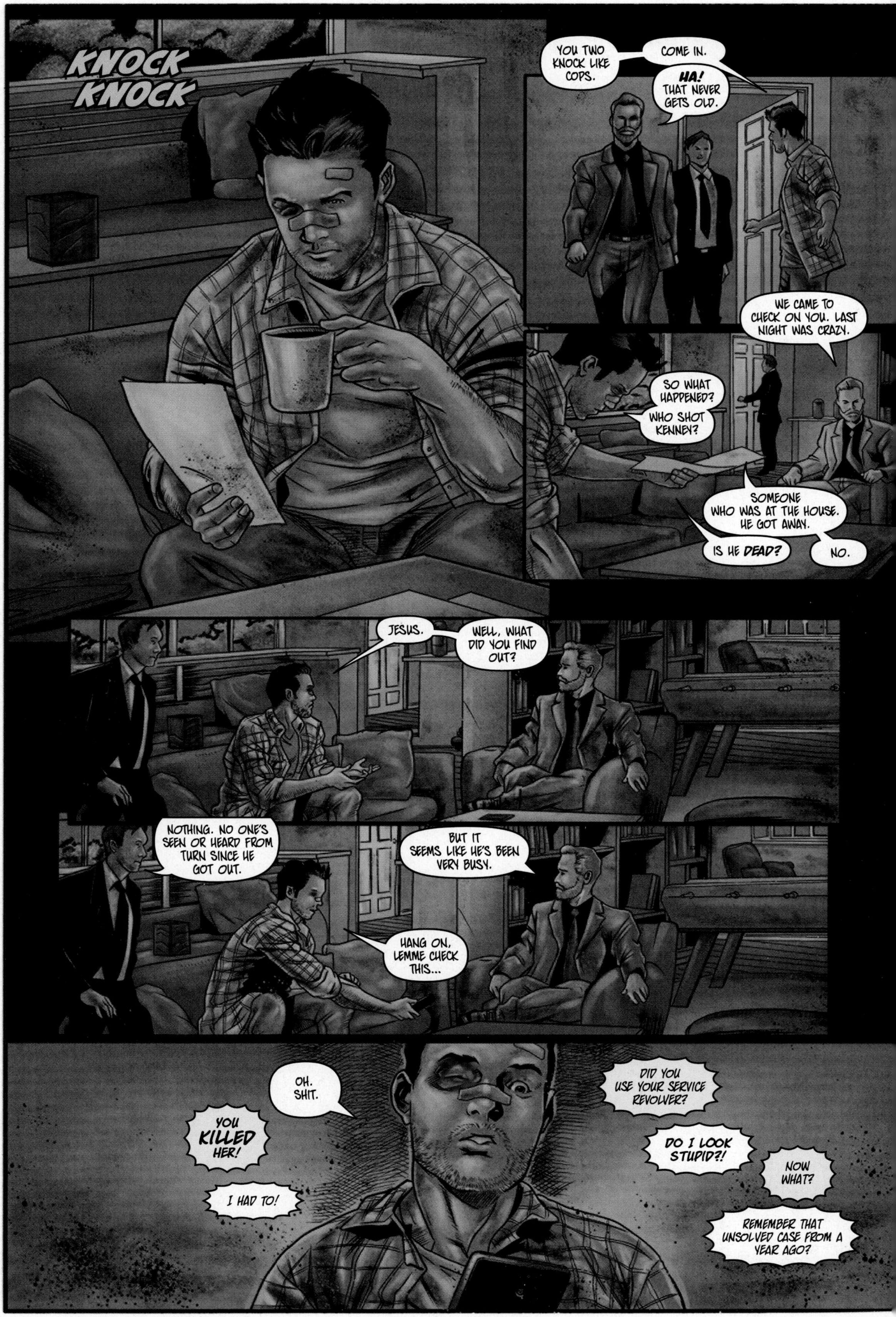
KNOCK KNOCK
YOU TWO KNOCK LIKE COPS.
COME IN.
HA! THAT NEVER GETS OLD.
WE CAME TO CHECK ON YOU. LAST NIGHT WAS CRAZY.
SO WHAT HAPPENED?
WHO SHOT KENNEY?
SOMEONE WHO WAS AT THE HOUSE. HE GOT AWAY.
IS HE DEAD?
NO.
JESUS.
WELL, WHAT DID YOU FIND OUT?
NOTHING. NO ONE'S SEEN OR HEARD FROM TURN SINCE HE GOT OUT.
BUT IT SEEMS LIKE HE'S BEEN VERY BUSY.
HANG ON, LEMME CHECK THIS...
OH. SHIT.
YOU KILLED HER!
I HAD TO!
DID YOU USE YOUR SERVICE REVOLVER?
DO I LOOK STUPID?!
NOW WHAT?
REMEMBER THAT UNSOLVED CASE FROM A YEAR AGO?

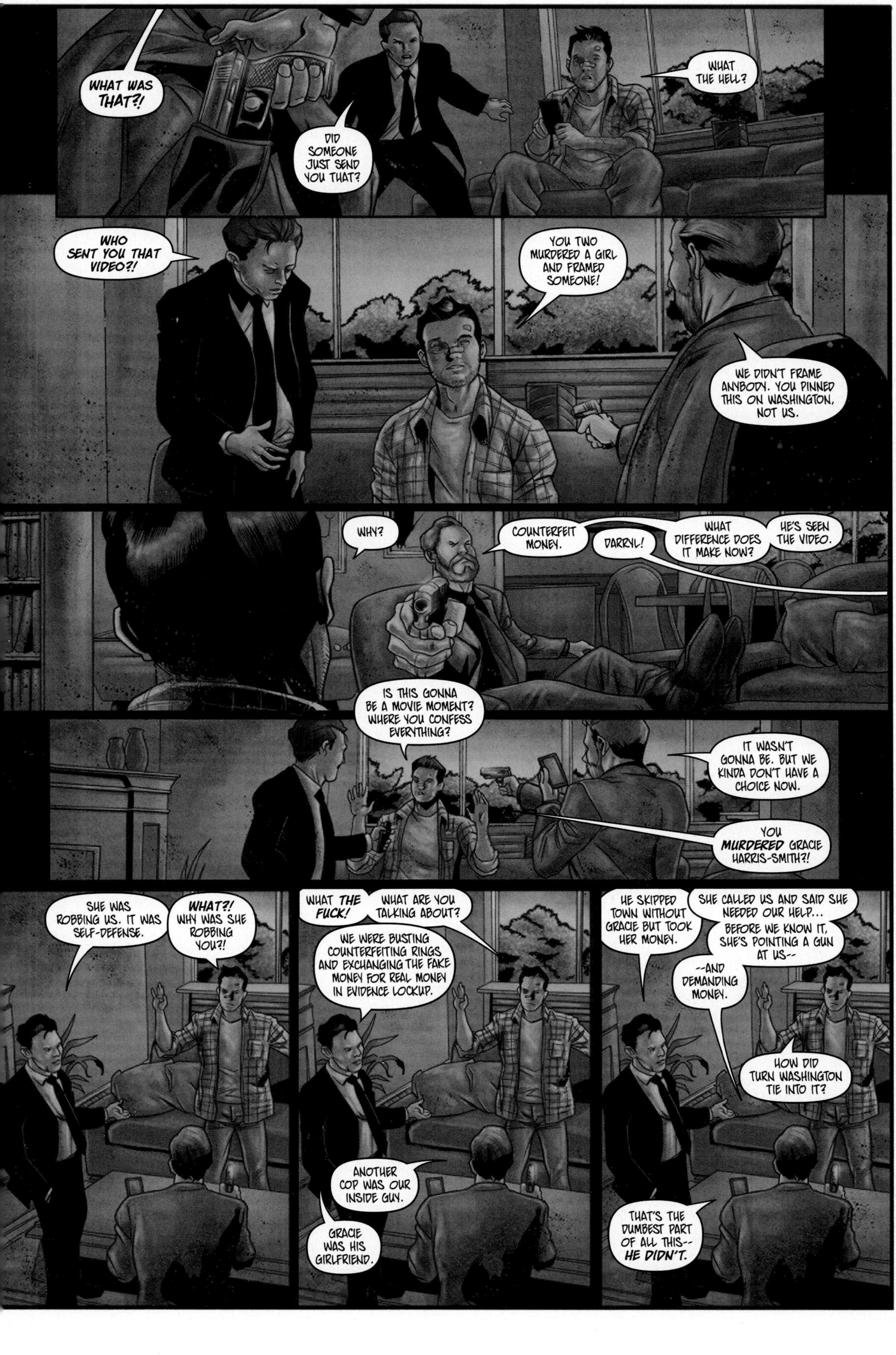
WHAT WAS THAT?!
DID SOMEONE JUST SEND YOU THAT?
WHAT THE HELL?
WHO SENT YOU THAT VIDEO?!
YOU TWO MURDERED A GIRL AND FRAMED SOMEONE!
WE DIDN'T FRAME ANYBODY. YOU PINNED THIS ON WASHINGTON, NOT US.
WHY?
COUNTERFEIT MONEY.
DARRYL!
WHAT DIFFERENCE DOES IT MAKE NOW?
HE'S SEEN THE VIDEO.
IS THIS GONNA BE A MOVIE MOMENT? WHERE YOU CONFESS EVERYTHING?
IT WASN'T GONNA BE. BUT WE KINDA DON'T HAVE A CHOICE NOW.
YOU MURDERED GRACIE HARRIS-SMITH?!
SHE WAS ROBBING US. IT WAS SELF-DEFENSE.
WHAT?! WHY WAS SHE ROBBING YOU?!
WHAT THE FUCK!
WHAT ARE YOU TALKING ABOUT?
WE WERE BUSTING COUNTERFEITING RINGS AND EXCHANGING THE FAKE MONEY FOR REAL MONEY IN EVIDENCE LOCKUP.
ANOTHER COP WAS OUR INSIDE GUY.
GRACIE WAS HIS GIRLFRIEND.
HE SKIPPED TOWN WITHOUT GRACIE BUT TOOK HER MONEY.
SHE CALLED US AND SAID SHE NEEDED OUR HELP...
BEFORE WE KNOW IT, SHE'S POINTING A GUN AT US--
--AND DEMANDING MONEY.
HOW DID TURN WASHINGTON TIE INTO IT?
THAT'S THE DUMBEST PART OF ALL THIS--
HE DIDN'T.

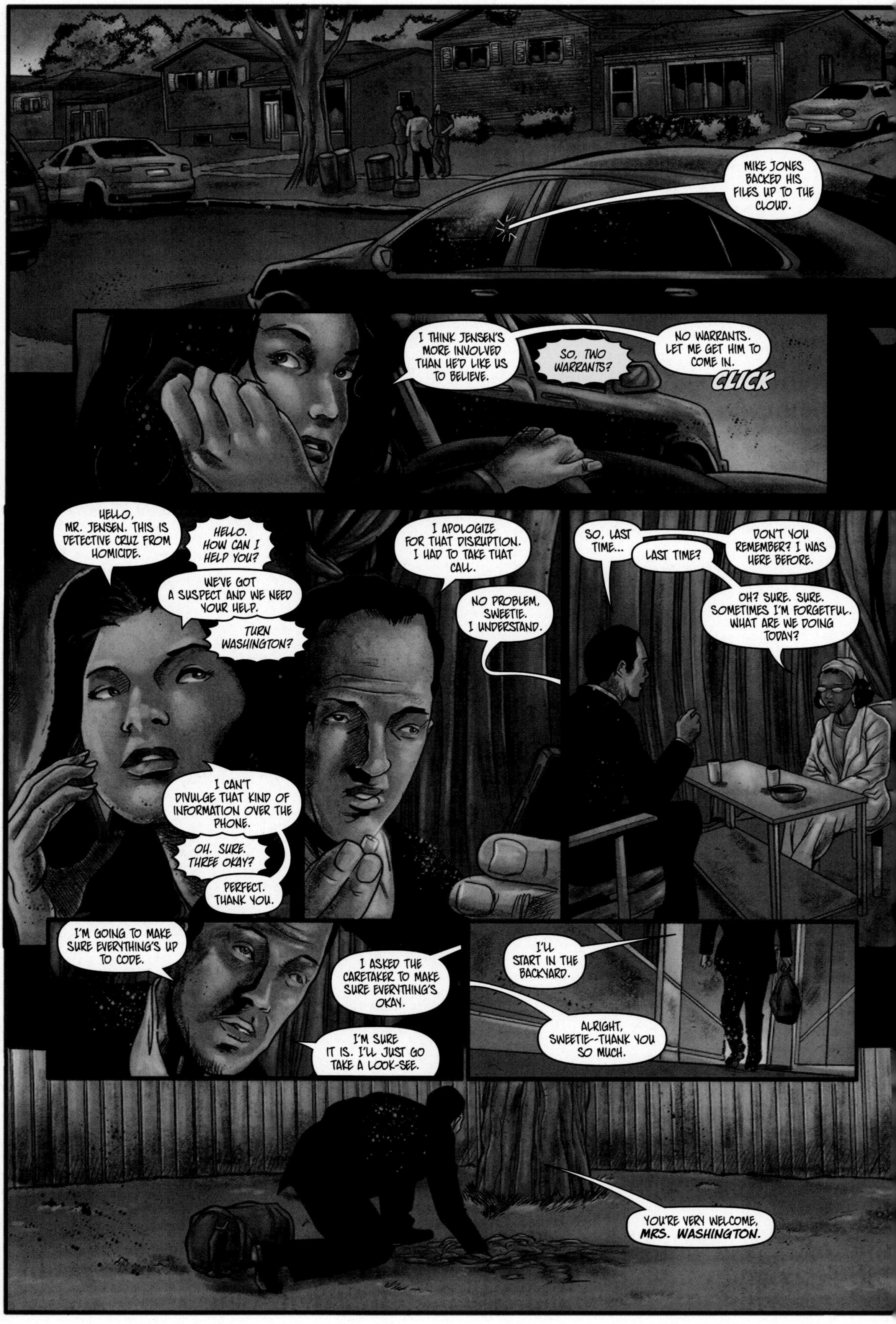
MIKE JONES BACKED HIS FILES UP TO THE CLOUD.
I THINK JENSEN'S MORE INVOLVED THAN HE'D LIKE US TO BELIEVE.
SO, TWO WARRANTS?
NO WARRANTS. LET ME GET HIM TO COME IN.
CLICK
HELLO, MR. JENSEN. THIS IS DETECTIVE CRUZ FROM HOMICIDE.
HELLO. HOW CAN I HELP YOU?
WE'VE GOT A SUSPECT AND WE NEED YOUR HELP.
TURN WASHINGTON?
I CAN'T DIVULGE THAT KIND OF INFORMATION OVER THE PHONE.
OH. SURE. THREE OKAY?
PERFECT. THANK YOU.
I APOLOGIZE FOR THAT DISRUPTION. I HAD TO TAKE THAT CALL.
NO PROBLEM, SWEETIE. I UNDERSTAND.
SO, LAST TIME...
LAST TIME?
DON'T YOU REMEMBER? I WAS HERE BEFORE.
OH? SURE. SURE. SOMETIMES I'M FORGETFUL. WHAT ARE WE DOING TODAY?
I'M GOING TO MAKE SURE EVERYTHING'S UP TO CODE.
I ASKED THE CARETAKER TO MAKE SURE EVERYTHING'S OKAY.
I'M SURE IT IS. I'LL JUST GO TAKE A LOOK-SEE.
I'LL START IN THE BACKYARD.
ALRIGHT, SWEETIE--THANK YOU SO MUCH.
YOU'RE VERY WELCOME, MRS. WASHINGTON.

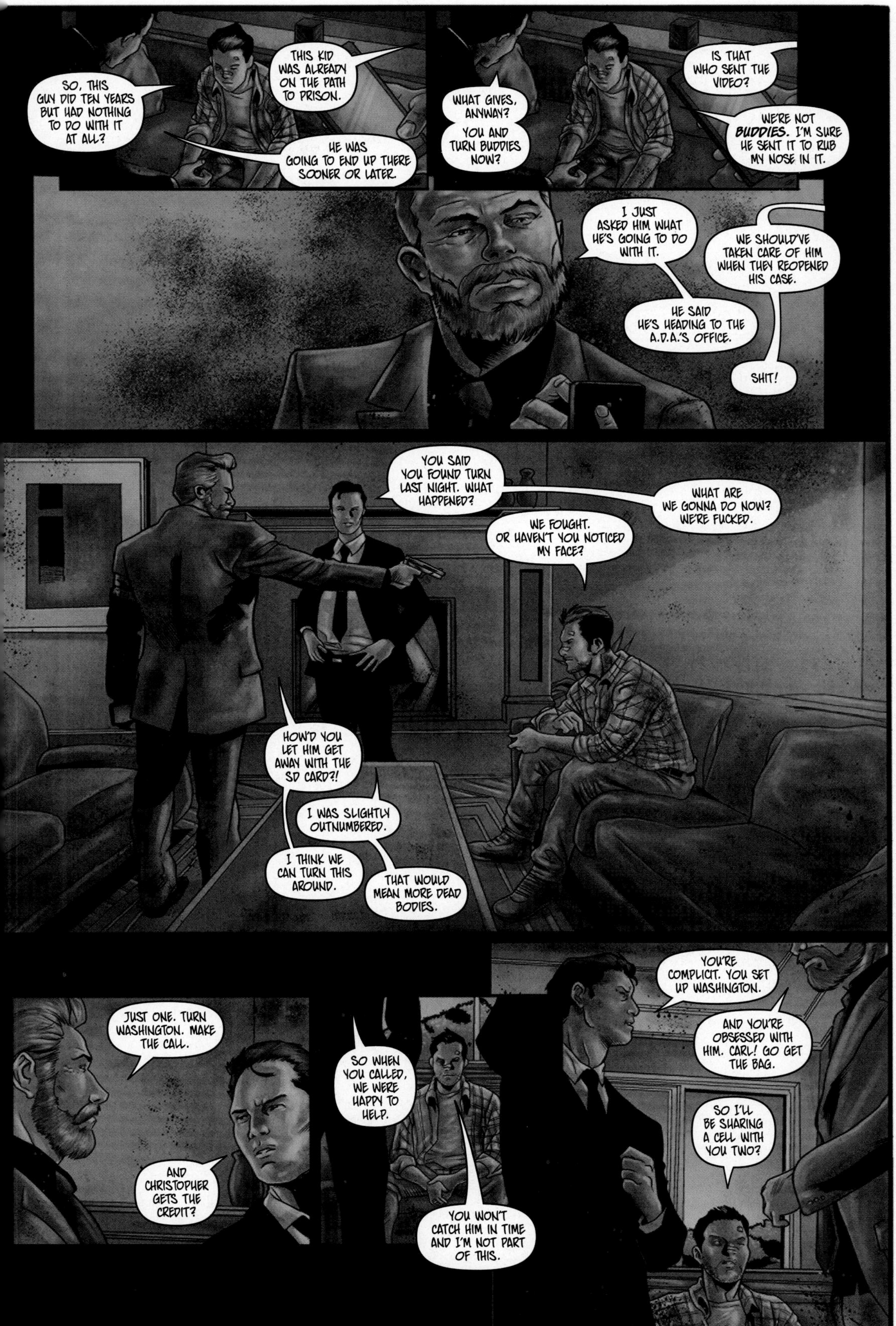

SO, THIS GUY DID TEN YEARS BUT HAD NOTHING TO DO WITH IT AT ALL?
THIS KID WAS ALREADY ON THE PATH TO PRISON.
HE WAS GOING TO END UP THERE SOONER OR LATER.
WHAT GIVES, ANYWAY?
YOU AND TURN BUDDIES NOW?
IS THAT WHO SENT THE VIDEO?
WE'RE NOT BUDDIES. I'M SURE HE SENT IT TO RUB MY NOSE IN IT.
I JUST ASKED HIM WHAT HE'S GOING TO DO WITH IT.
WE SHOULD'VE TAKEN CARE OF HIM WHEN THEY REOPENED HIS CASE.
HE SAID HE'S HEADING TO THE A.D.A.'S OFFICE.
SHIT!
YOU SAID YOU FOUND TURN LAST NIGHT. WHAT HAPPENED?
WHAT ARE WE GONNA DO NOW? WE'RE FUCKED.
WE FOUGHT. OR HAVEN'T YOU NOTICED MY FACE?
HOW'D YOU LET HIM GET AWAY WITH THE SD CARD?!
I WAS SLIGHTLY OUTNUMBERED.
I THINK WE CAN TURN THIS AROUND.
THAT WOULD MEAN MORE DEAD BODIES.
JUST ONE. TURN WASHINGTON. MAKE THE CALL.
AND CHRISTOPHER GETS THE CREDIT?
SO WHEN YOU CALLED, WE WERE HAPPY TO HELP.
YOU WON'T CATCH HIM IN TIME AND I'M NOT PART OF THIS.
YOU'RE COMPLICIT. YOU SET UP WASHINGTON.
AND YOU'RE OBSESSED WITH HIM. CARL! GO GET THE BAG.
SO I'LL BE SHARING A CELL WITH YOU TWO?

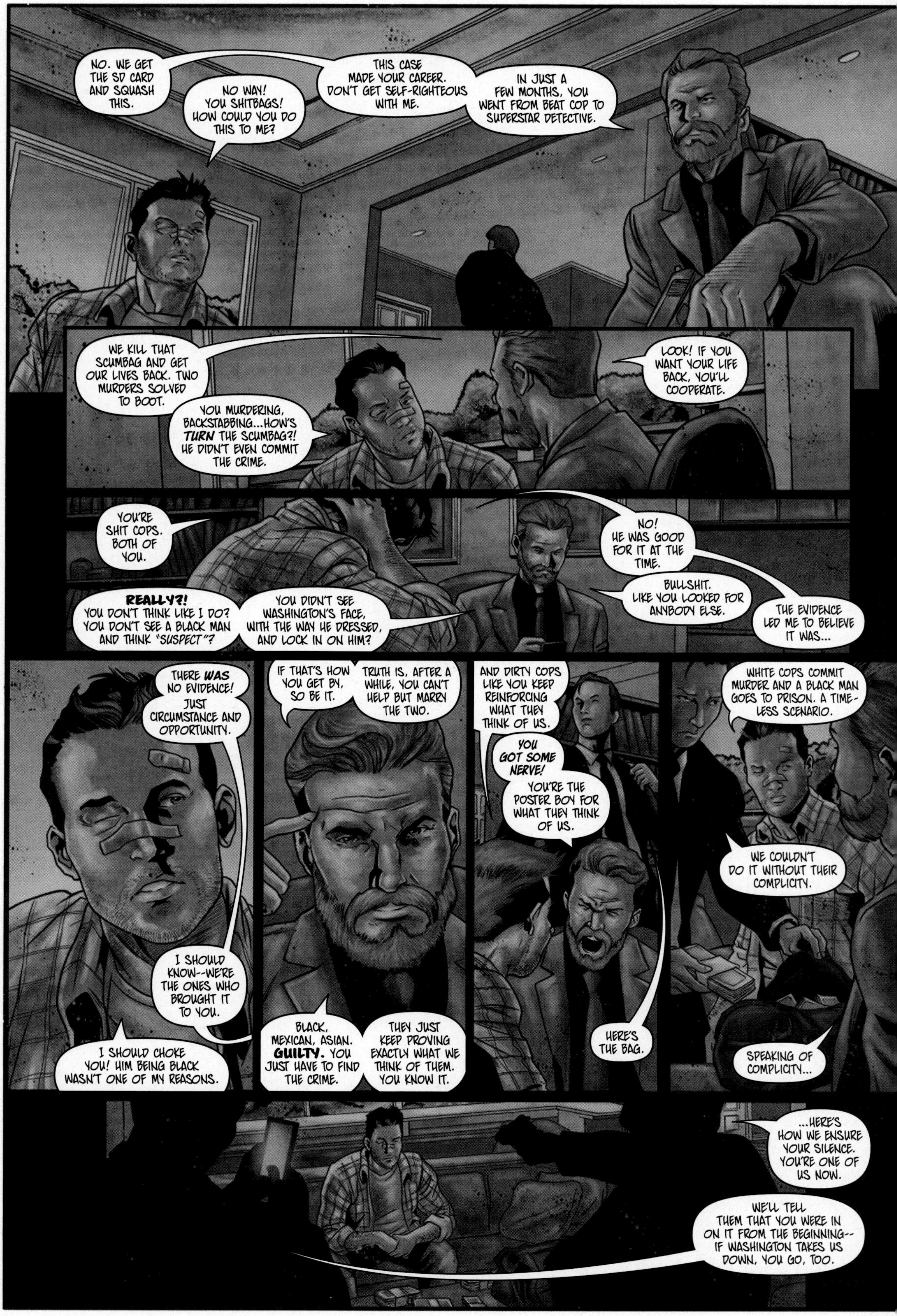
NO. WE GET THE SD CARD AND SQUASH THIS.
NO WAY! YOU SHITBAGS! HOW COULD YOU DO THIS TO ME?
THIS CASE MADE YOUR CAREER. DON'T GET SELF-RIGHTEOUS WITH ME.
IN JUST A FEW MONTHS, YOU WENT FROM BEAT COP TO SUPERSTAR DETECTIVE.
WE KILL THAT SCUMBAG AND GET OUR LIVES BACK. TWO MURDERS SOLVED TO BOOT.
YOU MURDERING, BACKSTABBING...HOW'S *TURN* THE SCUMBAG?! HE DIDN'T EVEN COMMIT THE CRIME.
LOOK! IF YOU WANT YOUR LIFE BACK, YOU'LL COOPERATE.
YOU'RE SHIT COPS. BOTH OF YOU.
NO! HE WAS GOOD FOR IT AT THE TIME.
BULLSHIT. LIKE YOU LOOKED FOR ANYBODY ELSE.
THE EVIDENCE LED ME TO BELIEVE IT WAS...
REALLY?! YOU DON'T THINK LIKE I DO? YOU DON'T SEE A BLACK MAN AND THINK "*SUSPECT*"?
YOU DIDN'T SEE WASHINGTON'S FACE, WITH THE WAY HE DRESSED, AND LOCK IN ON HIM?
THERE **WAS** NO EVIDENCE! JUST CIRCUMSTANCE AND OPPORTUNITY.
I SHOULD KNOW--WE'RE THE ONES WHO BROUGHT IT TO YOU.
I SHOULD CHOKE YOU! HIM BEING BLACK WASN'T ONE OF MY REASONS.
IF THAT'S HOW YOU GET BY, SO BE IT.
TRUTH IS, AFTER A WHILE, YOU CAN'T HELP BUT MARRY THE TWO.
BLACK, MEXICAN, ASIAN. **GUILTY.** YOU JUST HAVE TO FIND THE CRIME.
THEY JUST KEEP PROVING EXACTLY WHAT WE THINK OF THEM. YOU KNOW IT.
AND DIRTY COPS LIKE YOU KEEP REINFORCING WHAT THEY THINK OF US.
YOU GOT SOME NERVE!
YOU'RE THE POSTER BOY FOR WHAT THEY THINK OF US.
HERE'S THE BAG.
WHITE COPS COMMIT MURDER AND A BLACK MAN GOES TO PRISON. A TIMELESS SCENARIO.
WE COULDN'T DO IT WITHOUT THEIR COMPLICITY.
SPEAKING OF COMPLICITY...
...HERE'S HOW WE ENSURE YOUR SILENCE. YOU'RE ONE OF US NOW.
WE'LL TELL THEM THAT YOU WERE IN ON IT FROM THE BEGINNING--IF WASHINGTON TAKES US DOWN, YOU GO, TOO.

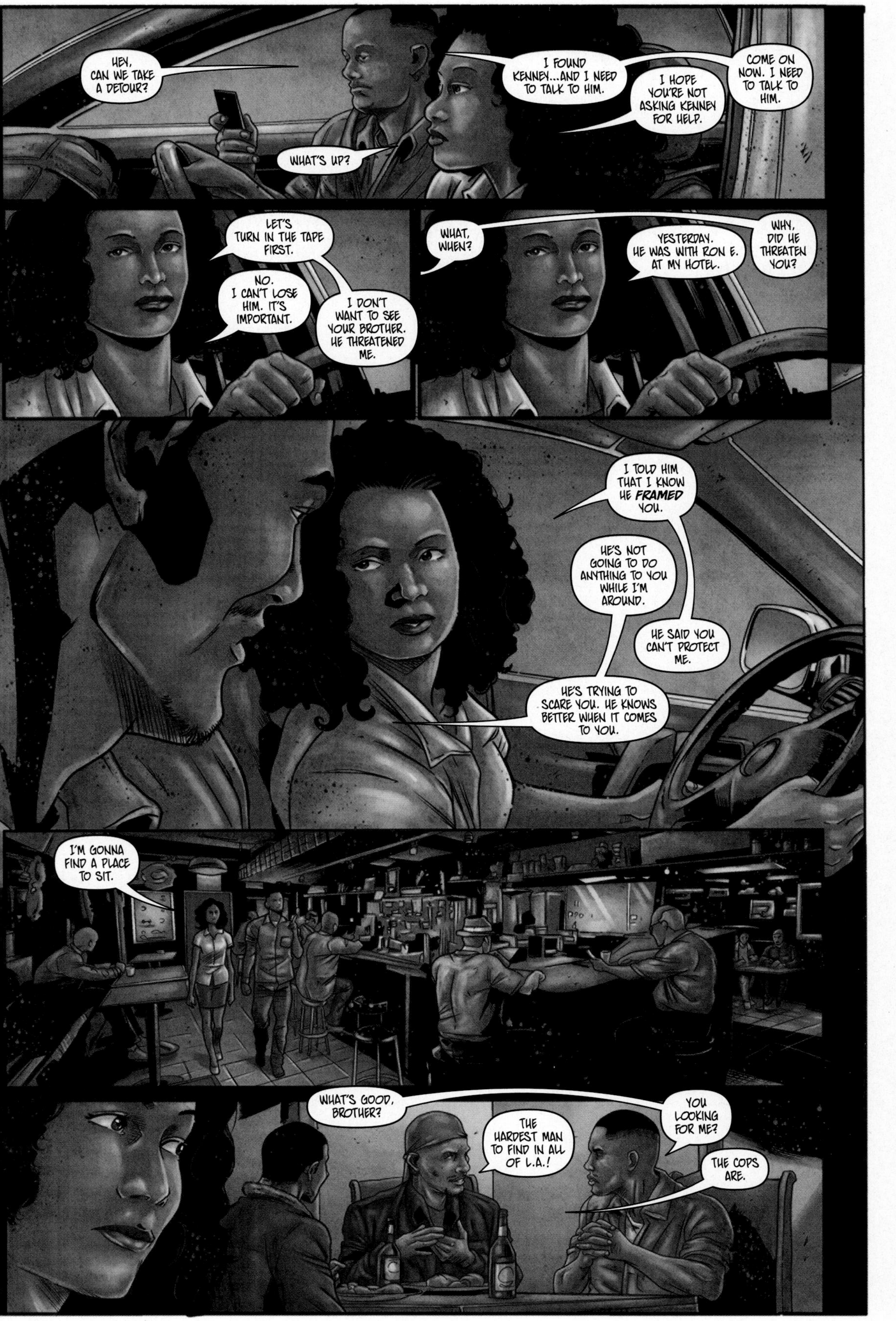
HEY, CAN WE TAKE A DETOUR?
WHAT'S UP?
I FOUND KENNEY...AND I NEED TO TALK TO HIM.
I HOPE YOU'RE NOT ASKING KENNEY FOR HELP.
COME ON NOW. I NEED TO TALK TO HIM.
LET'S TURN IN THE TAPE FIRST.
NO. I CAN'T LOSE HIM. IT'S IMPORTANT.
I DON'T WANT TO SEE YOUR BROTHER. HE THREATENED ME.
WHAT, WHEN?
YESTERDAY. HE WAS WITH RON E. AT MY HOTEL.
WHY, DID HE THREATEN YOU?
I TOLD HIM THAT I KNOW HE FRAMED YOU.
HE SAID YOU CAN'T PROTECT ME.
HE'S NOT GOING TO DO ANYTHING TO YOU WHILE I'M AROUND.
HE'S TRYING TO SCARE YOU. HE KNOWS BETTER WHEN IT COMES TO YOU.
I'M GONNA FIND A PLACE TO SIT.
WHAT'S GOOD, BROTHER?
THE HARDEST MAN TO FIND IN ALL OF L.A.!
YOU LOOKING FOR ME?
THE COPS ARE.

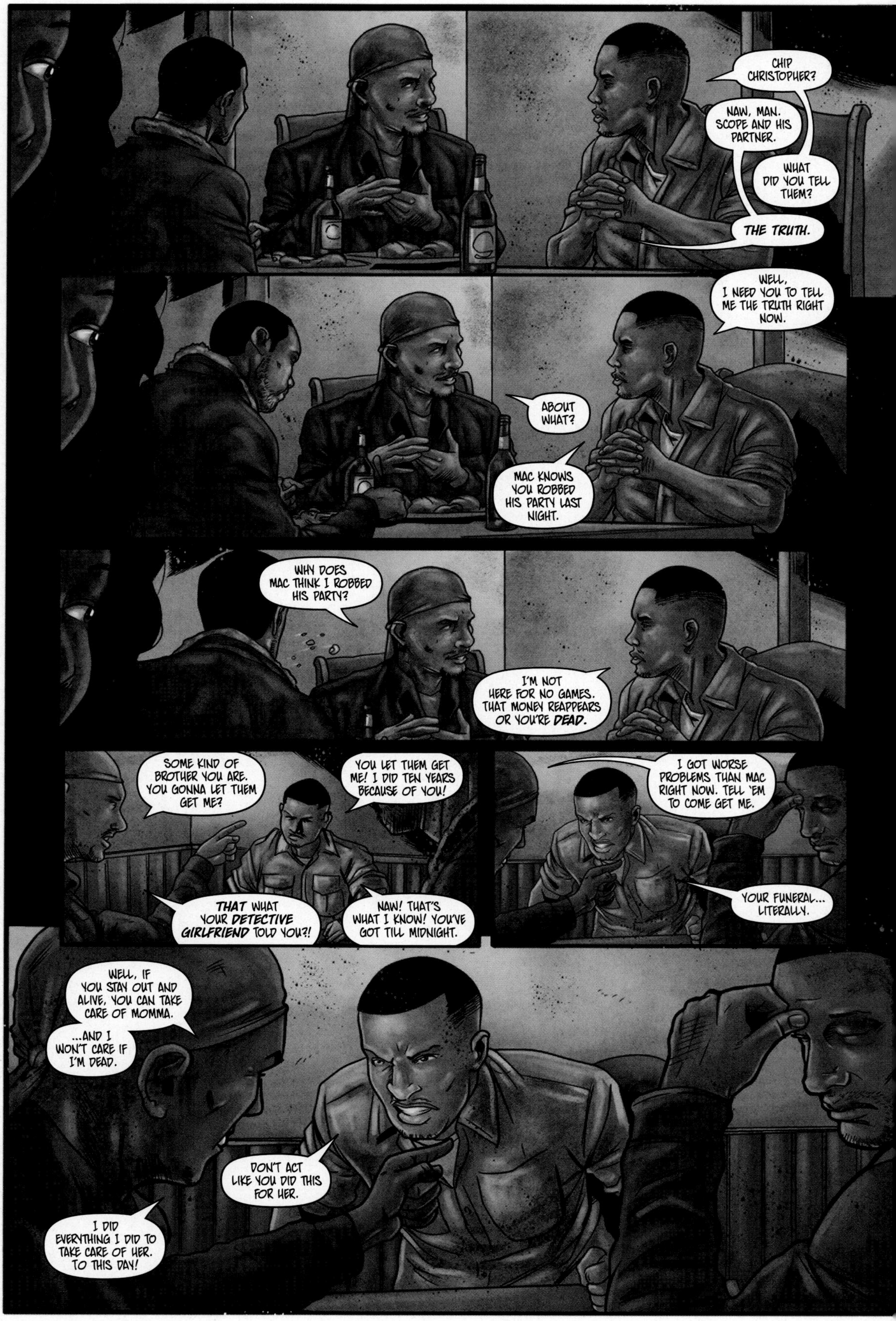
CHIP CHRISTOPHER?
NAW, MAN. SCOPE AND HIS PARTNER.
WHAT DID YOU TELL THEM?
THE TRUTH.
WELL, I NEED YOU TO TELL ME THE TRUTH RIGHT NOW.
ABOUT WHAT?
MAC KNOWS YOU ROBBED HIS PARTY LAST NIGHT.
WHY DOES MAC THINK I ROBBED HIS PARTY?
I'M NOT HERE FOR NO GAMES. THAT MONEY REAPPEARS OR YOU'RE DEAD.
SOME KIND OF BROTHER YOU ARE. YOU GONNA LET THEM GET ME?
YOU LET THEM GET ME! I DID TEN YEARS BECAUSE OF YOU!
THAT WHAT YOUR DETECTIVE GIRLFRIEND TOLD YOU?!
NAW! THAT'S WHAT I KNOW! YOU'VE GOT TILL MIDNIGHT.
I GOT WORSE PROBLEMS THAN MAC RIGHT NOW. TELL 'EM TO COME GET ME.
YOUR FUNERAL... LITERALLY.
WELL, IF YOU STAY OUT AND ALIVE, YOU CAN TAKE CARE OF MOMMA.
...AND I WON'T CARE IF I'M DEAD.
DON'T ACT LIKE YOU DID THIS FOR HER.
I DID EVERYTHING I DID TO TAKE CARE OF HER. TO THIS DAY!

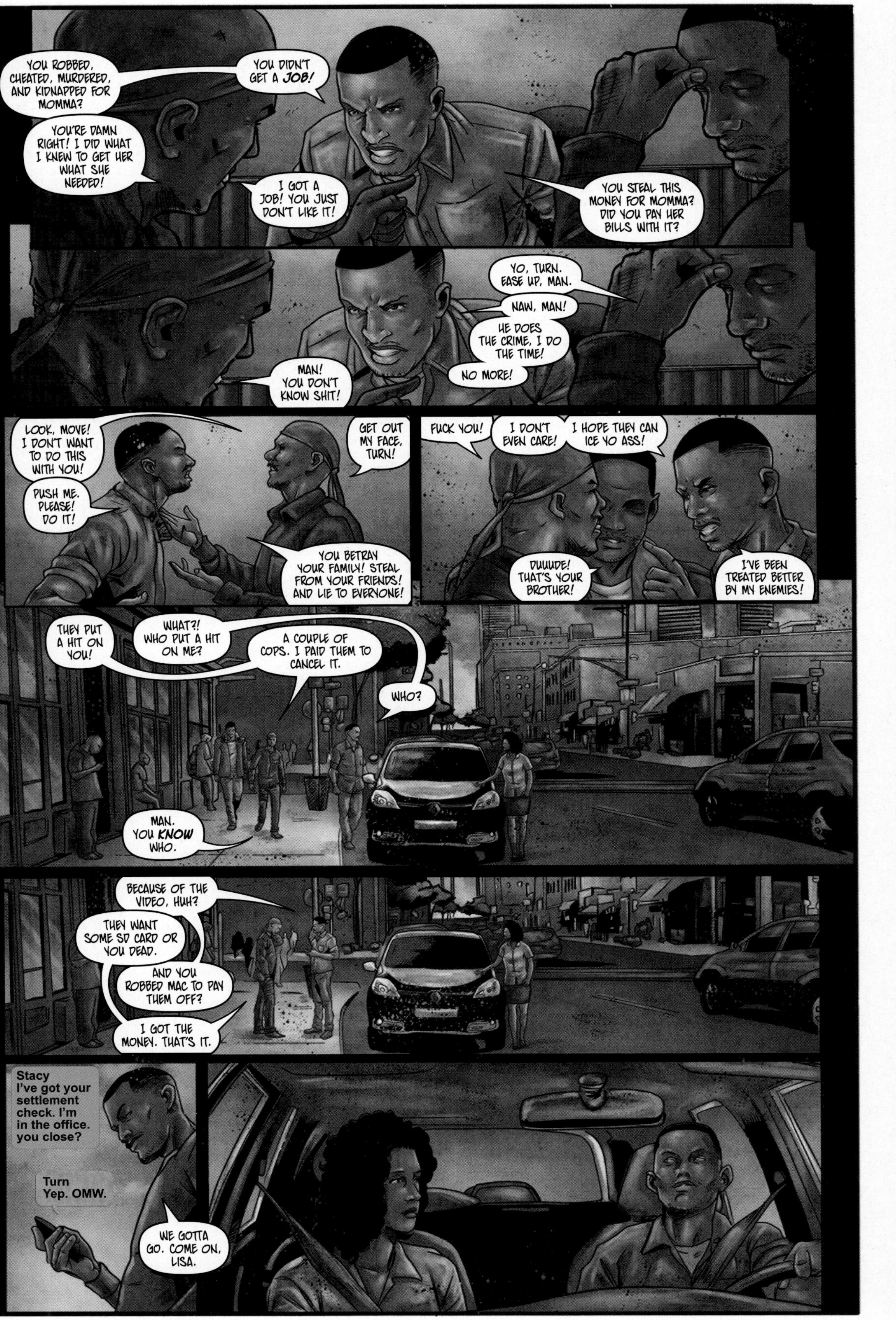
YOU ROBBED, CHEATED, MURDERED, AND KIDNAPPED FOR MOMMA?
YOU DIDN'T GET A JOB!
YOU'RE DAMN RIGHT! I DID WHAT I KNEW TO GET HER WHAT SHE NEEDED!
I GOT A JOB! YOU JUST DON'T LIKE IT!
YOU STEAL THIS MONEY FOR MOMMA? DID YOU PAY HER BILLS WITH IT?
YO, TURN. EASE UP, MAN.
NAW, MAN!
HE DOES THE CRIME, I DO THE TIME!
NO MORE!
MAN! YOU DON'T KNOW SHIT!
LOOK, MOVE! I DON'T WANT TO DO THIS WITH YOU!
GET OUT MY FACE, TURN!
PUSH ME. PLEASE! DO IT!
YOU BETRAY YOUR FAMILY! STEAL FROM YOUR FRIENDS! AND LIE TO EVERYONE!
FUCK YOU!
I DON'T EVEN CARE!
I HOPE THEY CAN ICE YO ASS!
DUUUDE! THAT'S YOUR BROTHER!
I'VE BEEN TREATED BETTER BY MY ENEMIES!
THEY PUT A HIT ON YOU!
WHAT?! WHO PUT A HIT ON ME?
A COUPLE OF COPS. I PAID THEM TO CANCEL IT.
WHO?
MAN. YOU KNOW WHO.
BECAUSE OF THE VIDEO, HUH?
THEY WANT SOME SD CARD OR YOU DEAD.
AND YOU ROBBED MAC TO PAY THEM OFF?
I GOT THE MONEY. THAT'S IT.
Stacy
I've got your settlement check. I'm in the office. you close?
Turn
Yep. OMW.
WE GOTTA GO. COME ON, LISA.

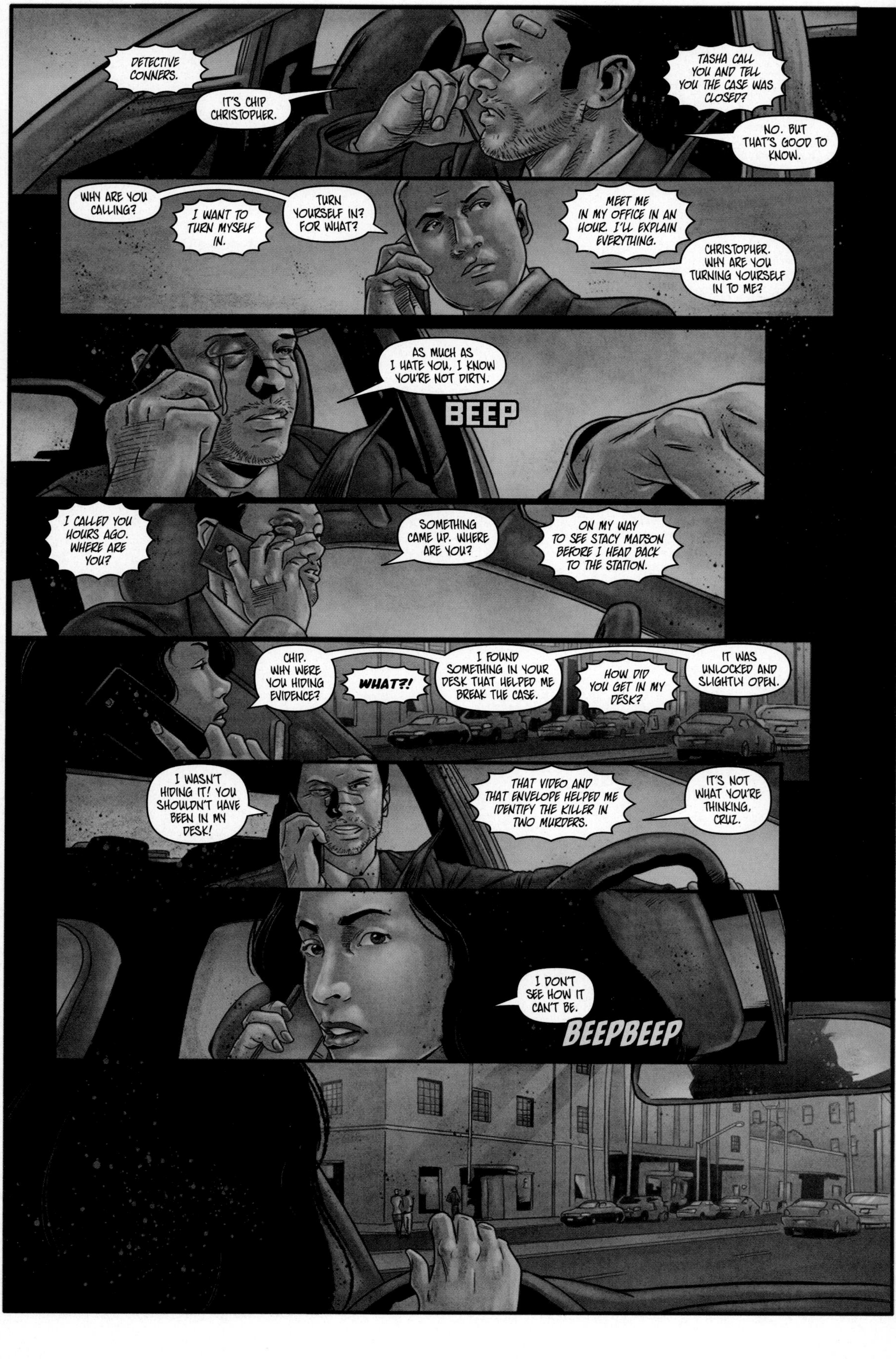
DETECTIVE CONNERS.
IT'S CHIP CHRISTOPHER.
TASHA CALL YOU AND TELL YOU THE CASE WAS CLOSED?
NO. BUT THAT'S GOOD TO KNOW.
WHY ARE YOU CALLING?
I WANT TO TURN MYSELF IN.
TURN YOURSELF IN? FOR WHAT?
MEET ME IN MY OFFICE IN AN HOUR. I'LL EXPLAIN EVERYTHING.
CHRISTOPHER. WHY ARE YOU TURNING YOURSELF IN TO ME?
AS MUCH AS I HATE YOU, I KNOW YOU'RE NOT DIRTY.
BEEP
I CALLED YOU HOURS AGO. WHERE ARE YOU?
SOMETHING CAME UP. WHERE ARE YOU?
ON MY WAY TO SEE STACY MADSON BEFORE I HEAD BACK TO THE STATION.
CHIP. WHY WERE YOU HIDING EVIDENCE?
WHAT?!
I FOUND SOMETHING IN YOUR DESK THAT HELPED ME BREAK THE CASE.
HOW DID YOU GET IN MY DESK?
IT WAS UNLOCKED AND SLIGHTLY OPEN.
I WASN'T HIDING IT! YOU SHOULDN'T HAVE BEEN IN MY DESK!
THAT VIDEO AND THAT ENVELOPE HELPED ME IDENTIFY THE KILLER IN TWO MURDERS.
IT'S NOT WHAT YOU'RE THINKING, CRUZ.
I DON'T SEE HOW IT CAN'T BE.
BEEPBEEP

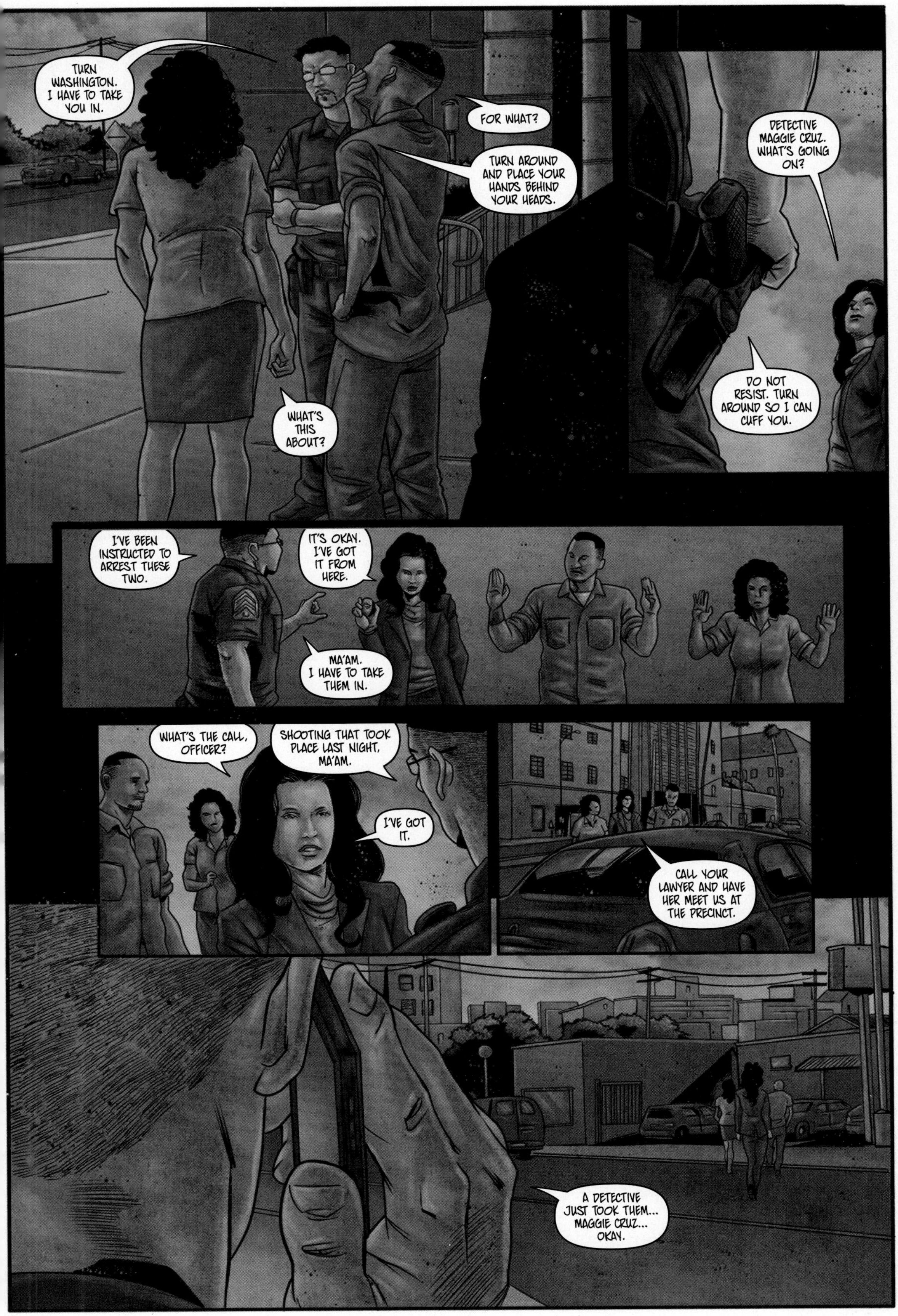
TURN WASHINGTON. I HAVE TO TAKE YOU IN.
FOR WHAT?
TURN AROUND AND PLACE YOUR HANDS BEHIND YOUR HEADS.
WHAT'S THIS ABOUT?
DETECTIVE MAGGIE CRUZ. WHAT'S GOING ON?
DO NOT RESIST. TURN AROUND SO I CAN CUFF YOU.
I'VE BEEN INSTRUCTED TO ARREST THESE TWO.
IT'S OKAY. I'VE GOT IT FROM HERE.
MA'AM. I HAVE TO TAKE THEM IN.
WHAT'S THE CALL, OFFICER?
SHOOTING THAT TOOK PLACE LAST NIGHT, MA'AM.
I'VE GOT IT.
CALL YOUR LAWYER AND HAVE HER MEET US AT THE PRECINCT.
A DETECTIVE JUST TOOK THEM... MAGGIE CRUZ... OKAY.

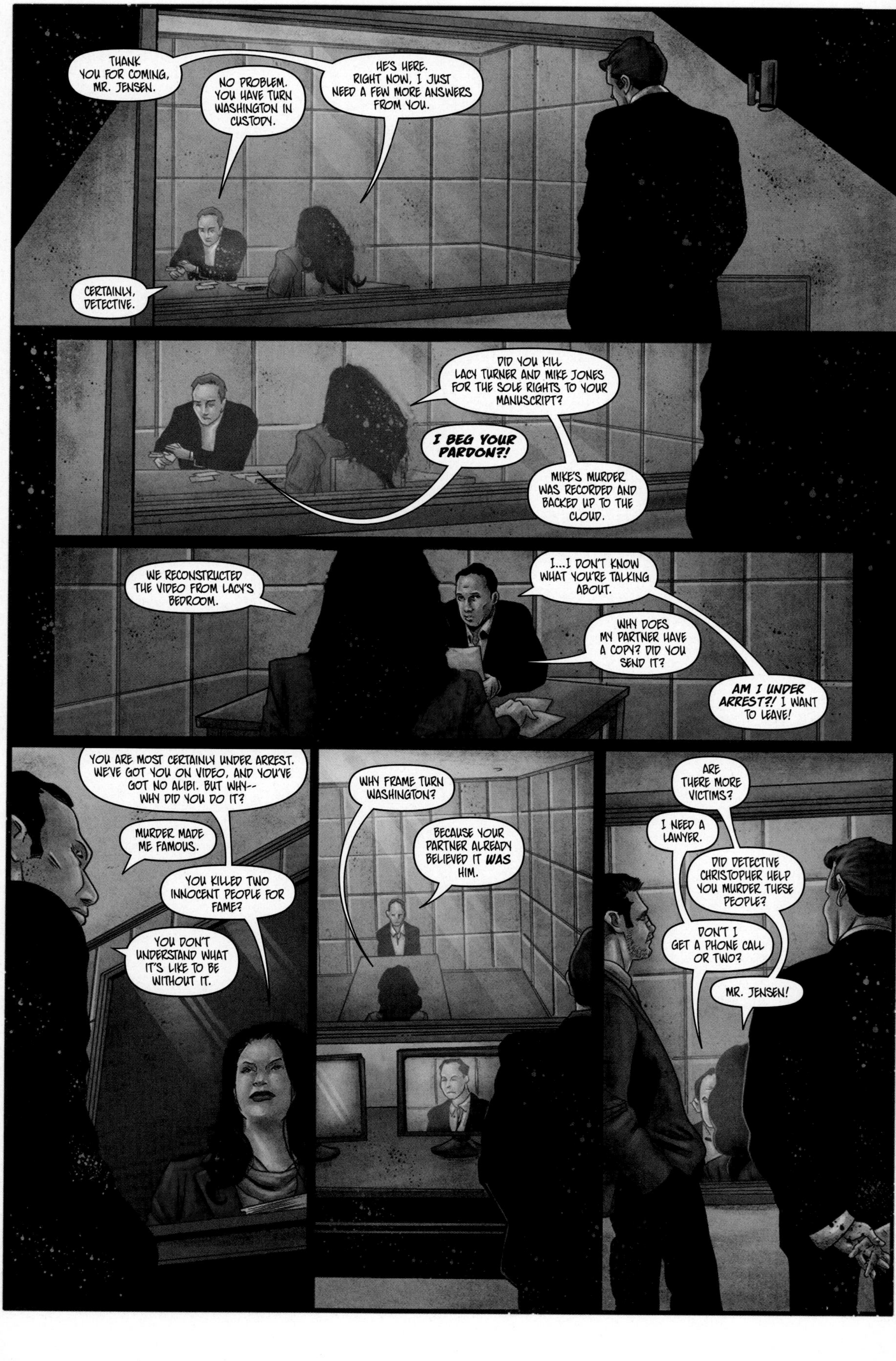

THANK YOU FOR COMING, MR. JENSEN.
NO PROBLEM. YOU HAVE TURN WASHINGTON IN CUSTODY.
HE'S HERE. RIGHT NOW, I JUST NEED A FEW MORE ANSWERS FROM YOU.
CERTAINLY, DETECTIVE.
DID YOU KILL LACY TURNER AND MIKE JONES FOR THE SOLE RIGHTS TO YOUR MANUSCRIPT?
I BEG YOUR PARDON?!
MIKE'S MURDER WAS RECORDED AND BACKED UP TO THE CLOUD.
WE RECONSTRUCTED THE VIDEO FROM LACY'S BEDROOM.
I...I DON'T KNOW WHAT YOU'RE TALKING ABOUT.
WHY DOES MY PARTNER HAVE A COPY? DID YOU SEND IT?
AM I UNDER ARREST?! I WANT TO LEAVE!
YOU ARE MOST CERTAINLY UNDER ARREST. WE'VE GOT YOU ON VIDEO, AND YOU'VE GOT NO ALIBI. BUT WHY-- WHY DID YOU DO IT?
MURDER MADE ME FAMOUS.
YOU KILLED TWO INNOCENT PEOPLE FOR FAME?
YOU DON'T UNDERSTAND WHAT IT'S LIKE TO BE WITHOUT IT.
WHY FRAME TURN WASHINGTON?
BECAUSE YOUR PARTNER ALREADY BELIEVED IT WAS HIM.
ARE THERE MORE VICTIMS?
I NEED A LAWYER.
DID DETECTIVE CHRISTOPHER HELP YOU MURDER THESE PEOPLE?
DON'T I GET A PHONE CALL OR TWO?
MR. JENSEN!

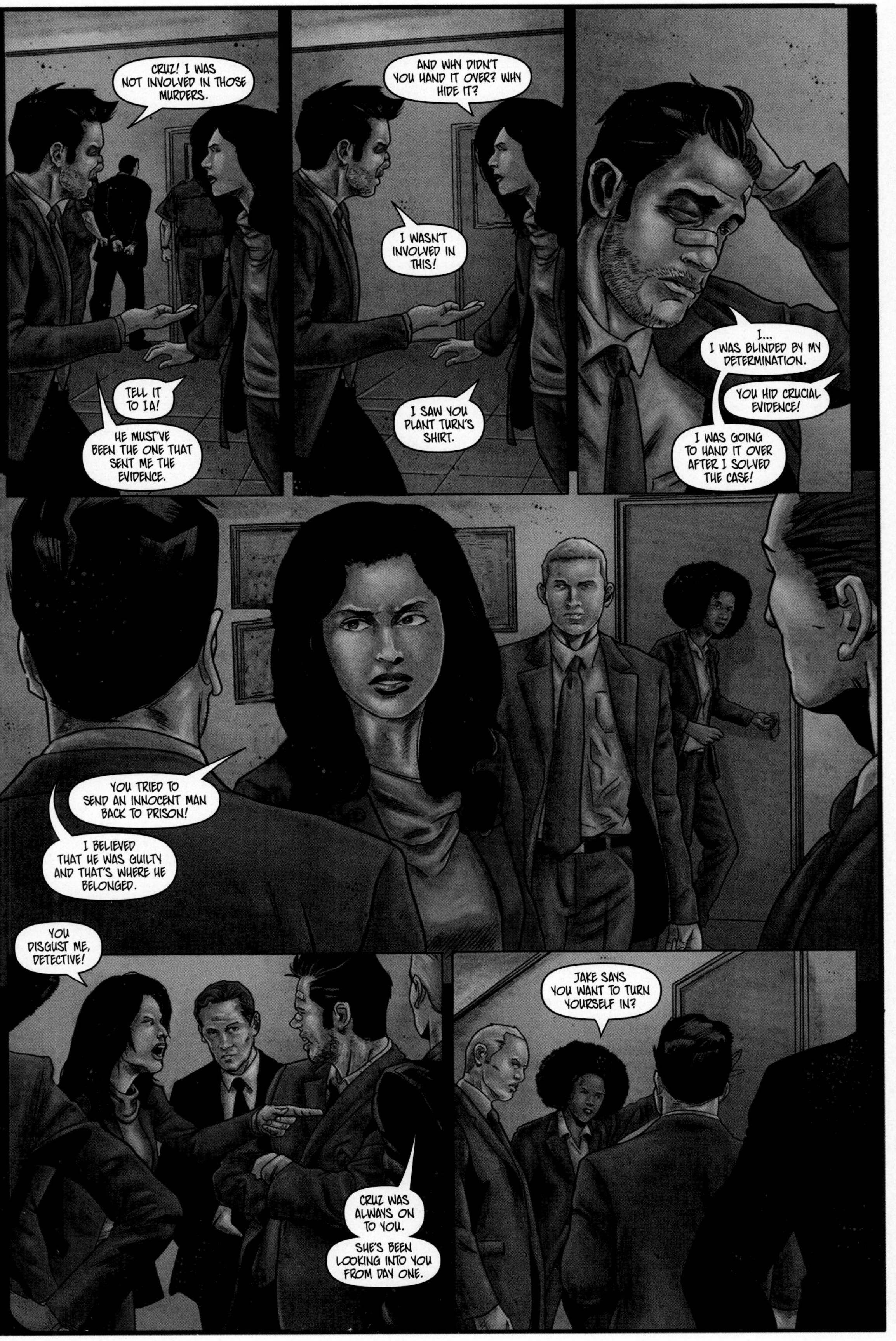
CRUZ! I WAS NOT INVOLVED IN THOSE MURDERS.
TELL IT TO IA!
HE MUST'VE BEEN THE ONE THAT SENT ME THE EVIDENCE.
AND WHY DIDN'T YOU HAND IT OVER? WHY HIDE IT?
I WASN'T INVOLVED IN THIS!
I SAW YOU PLANT TURN'S SHIRT.
I... I WAS BLINDED BY MY DETERMINATION.
YOU HID CRUCIAL EVIDENCE!
I WAS GOING TO HAND IT OVER AFTER I SOLVED THE CASE!
YOU TRIED TO SEND AN INNOCENT MAN BACK TO PRISON!
I BELIEVED THAT HE WAS GUILTY AND THAT'S WHERE HE BELONGED.
YOU DISGUST ME, DETECTIVE!
CRUZ WAS ALWAYS ON TO YOU.
SHE'S BEEN LOOKING INTO YOU FROM DAY ONE.
JAKE SAYS YOU WANT TO TURN YOURSELF IN?

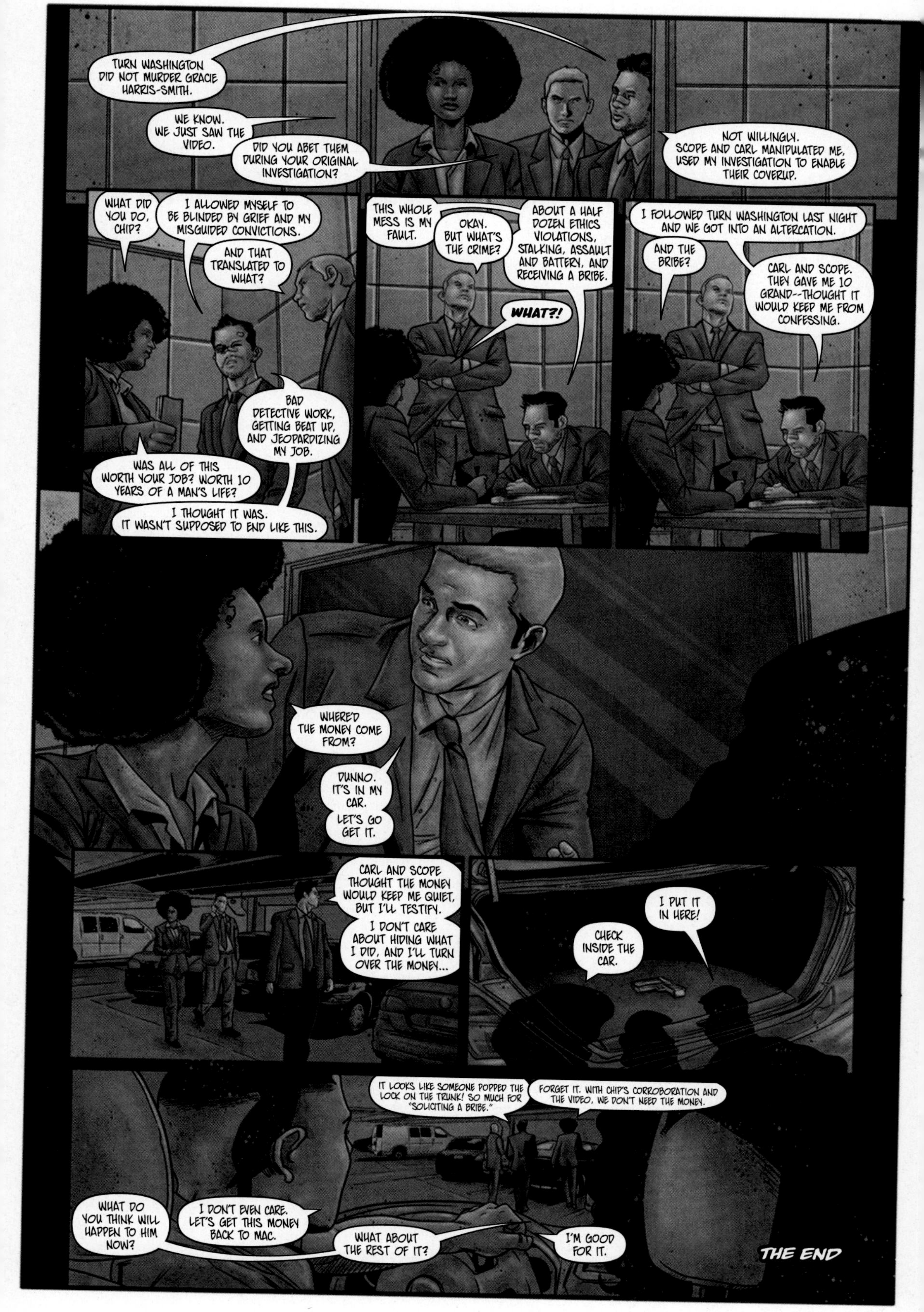
TURN WASHINGTON DID NOT MURDER GRACIE HARRIS-SMITH.
WE KNOW. WE JUST SAW THE VIDEO.
DID YOU ABET THEM DURING YOUR ORIGINAL INVESTIGATION?
NOT WILLINGLY. SCOPE AND CARL MANIPULATED ME, USED MY INVESTIGATION TO ENABLE THEIR COVERUP.
WHAT DID YOU DO, CHIP?
I ALLOWED MYSELF TO BE BLINDED BY GRIEF AND MY MISGUIDED CONVICTIONS.
AND THAT TRANSLATED TO WHAT?
BAD DETECTIVE WORK, GETTING BEAT UP, AND JEOPARDIZING MY JOB.
WAS ALL OF THIS WORTH YOUR JOB? WORTH 10 YEARS OF A MAN'S LIFE?
I THOUGHT IT WAS. IT WASN'T SUPPOSED TO END LIKE THIS.
THIS WHOLE MESS IS MY FAULT.
OKAY. BUT WHAT'S THE CRIME?
ABOUT A HALF DOZEN ETHICS VIOLATIONS, STALKING, ASSAULT AND BATTERY, AND RECEIVING A BRIBE.
WHAT?!
I FOLLOWED TURN WASHINGTON LAST NIGHT AND WE GOT INTO AN ALTERCATION.
AND THE BRIBE?
CARL AND SCOPE. THEY GAVE ME 10 GRAND--THOUGHT IT WOULD KEEP ME FROM CONFESSING.
WHERE'D THE MONEY COME FROM?
DUNNO. IT'S IN MY CAR.
LET'S GO GET IT.
CARL AND SCOPE THOUGHT THE MONEY WOULD KEEP ME QUIET, BUT I'LL TESTIFY.
I DON'T CARE ABOUT HIDING WHAT I DID, AND I'LL TURN OVER THE MONEY...
I PUT IT IN HERE!
CHECK INSIDE THE CAR.
IT LOOKS LIKE SOMEONE POPPED THE LOCK ON THE TRUNK! SO MUCH FOR "SOLICITING A BRIBE."
FORGET IT. WITH CHIP'S CORROBORATION AND THE VIDEO, WE DON'T NEED THE MONEY.
WHAT DO YOU THINK WILL HAPPEN TO HIM NOW?
I DON'T EVEN CARE. LET'S GET THIS MONEY BACK TO MAC.
WHAT ABOUT THE REST OF IT?
I'M GOOD FOR IT.
THE END

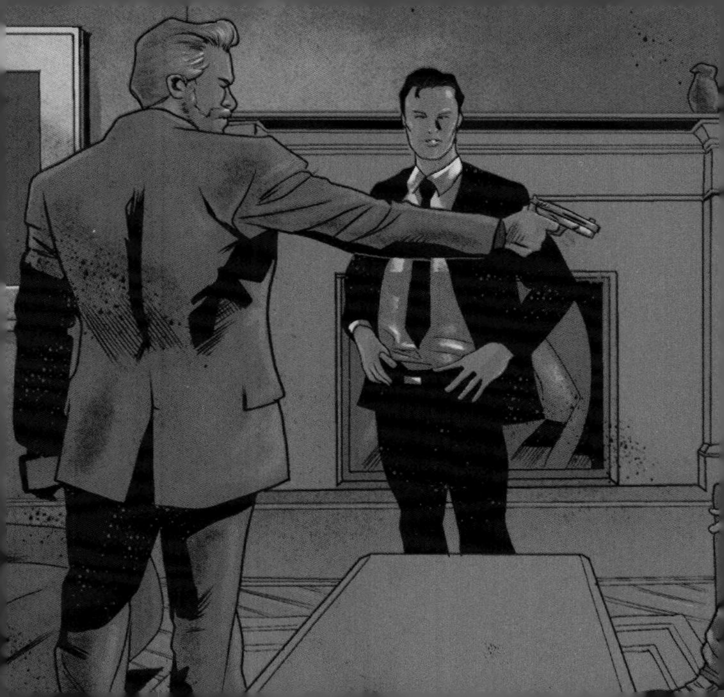

COVER GALLERY

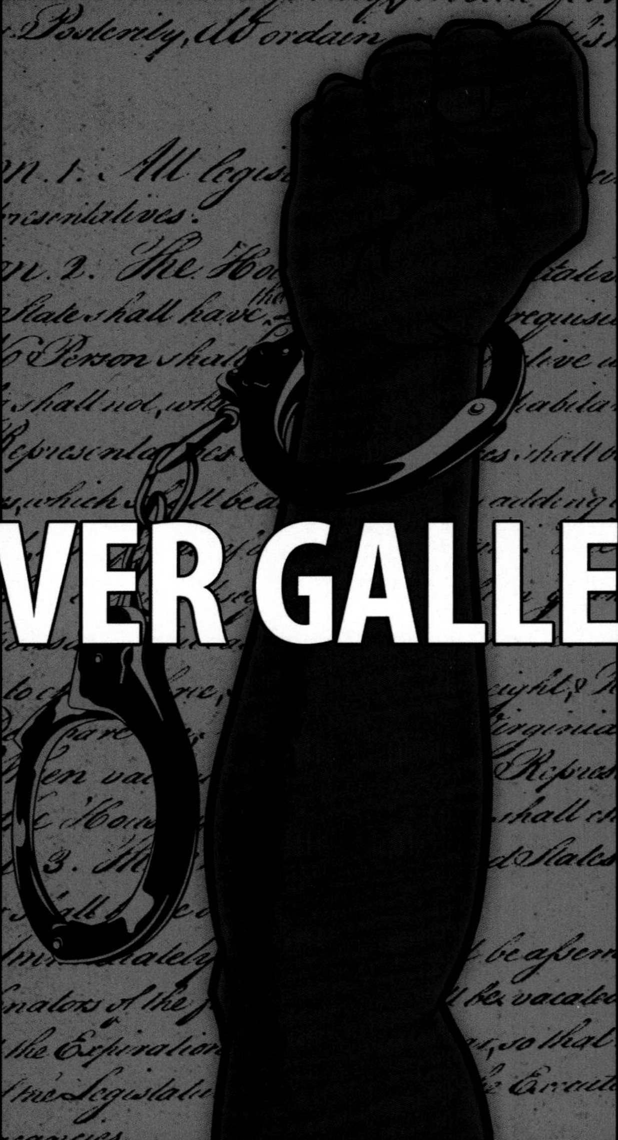

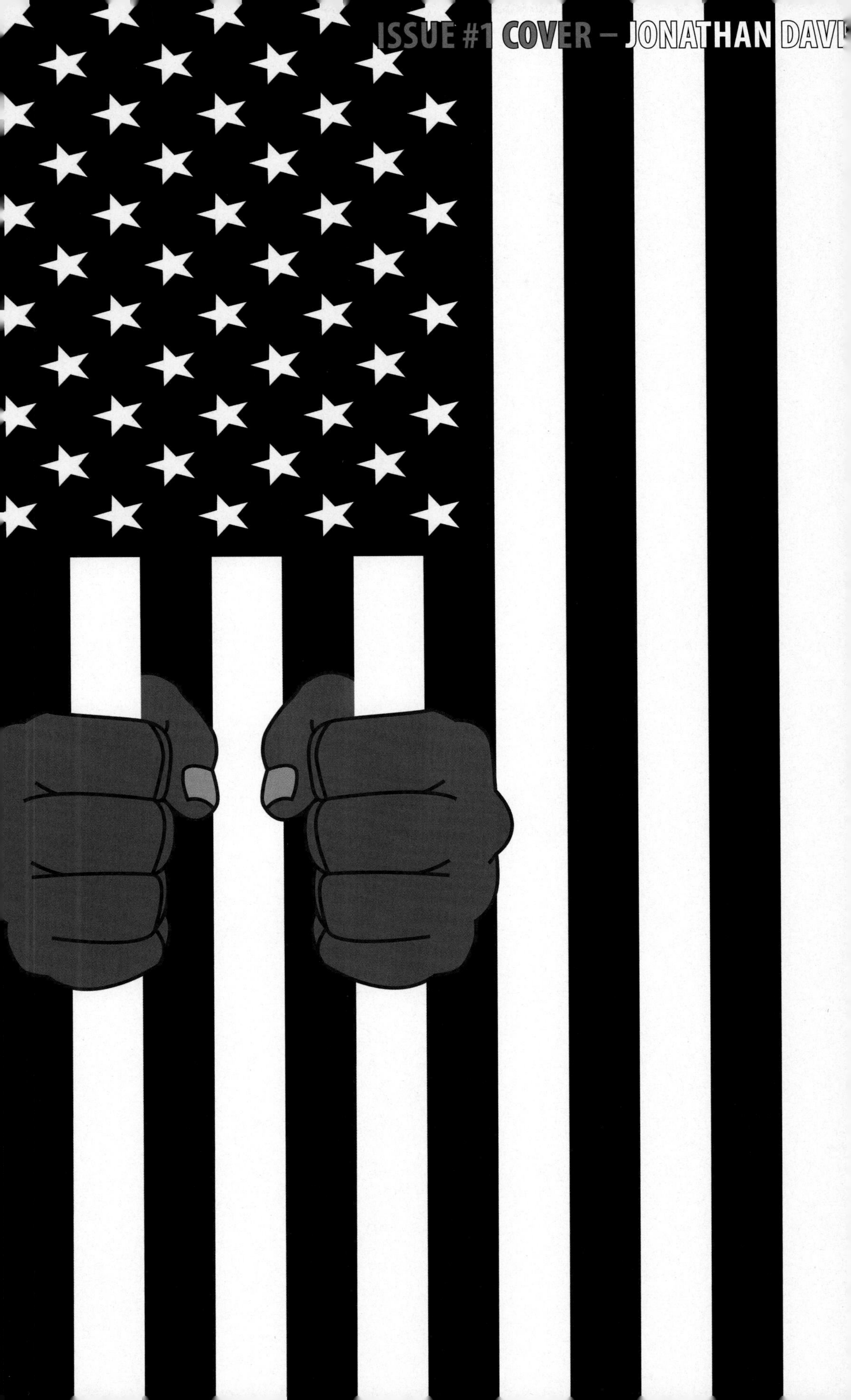

ISSUE #1 COVER – JONATHAN DAVI

ISSUE #2 COVER — LINDA SEJIC

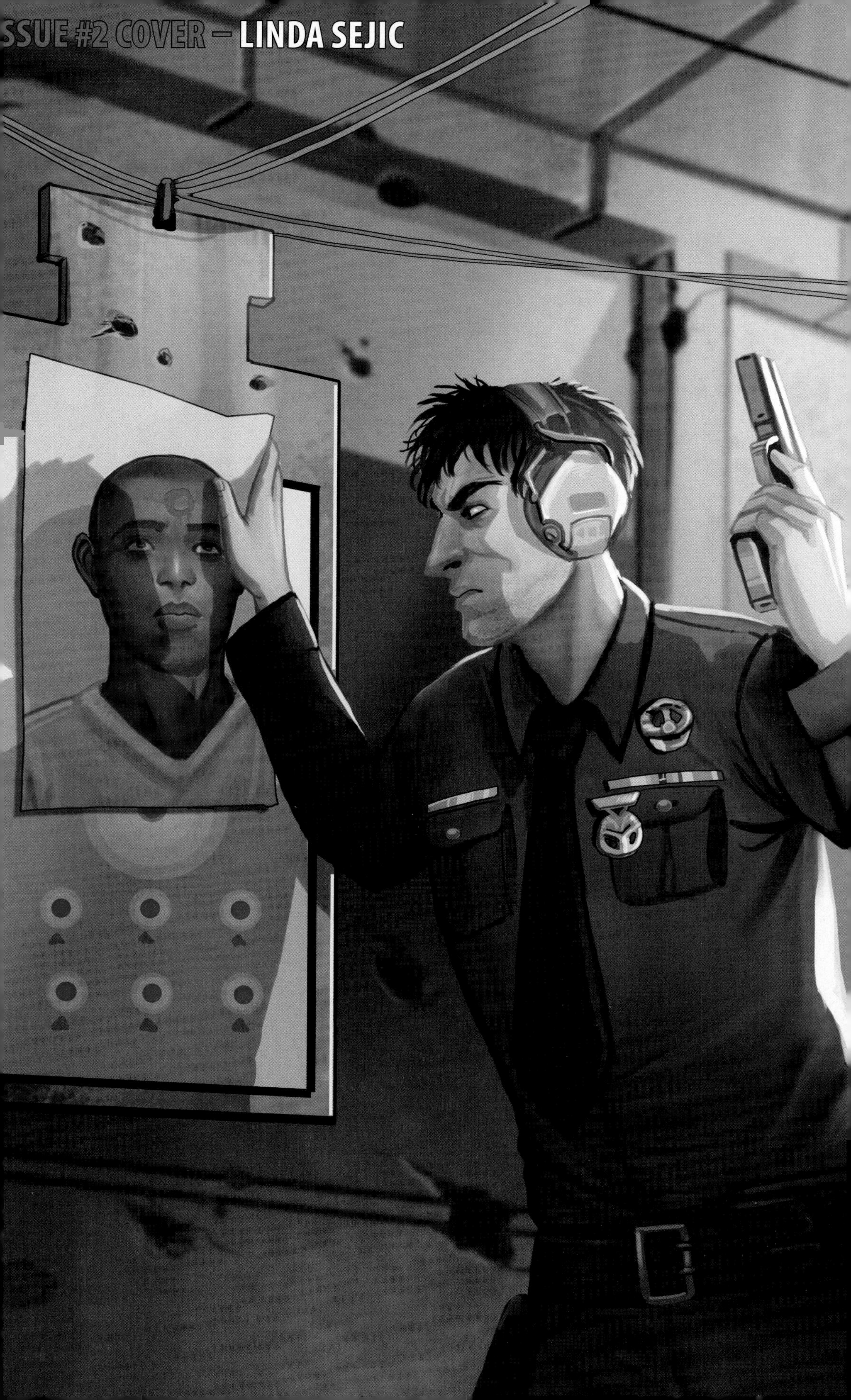

ISSUE #3 COVER – RASTA ESCOTT EL

ISSUE #4 COVER – JAMAL IGLE

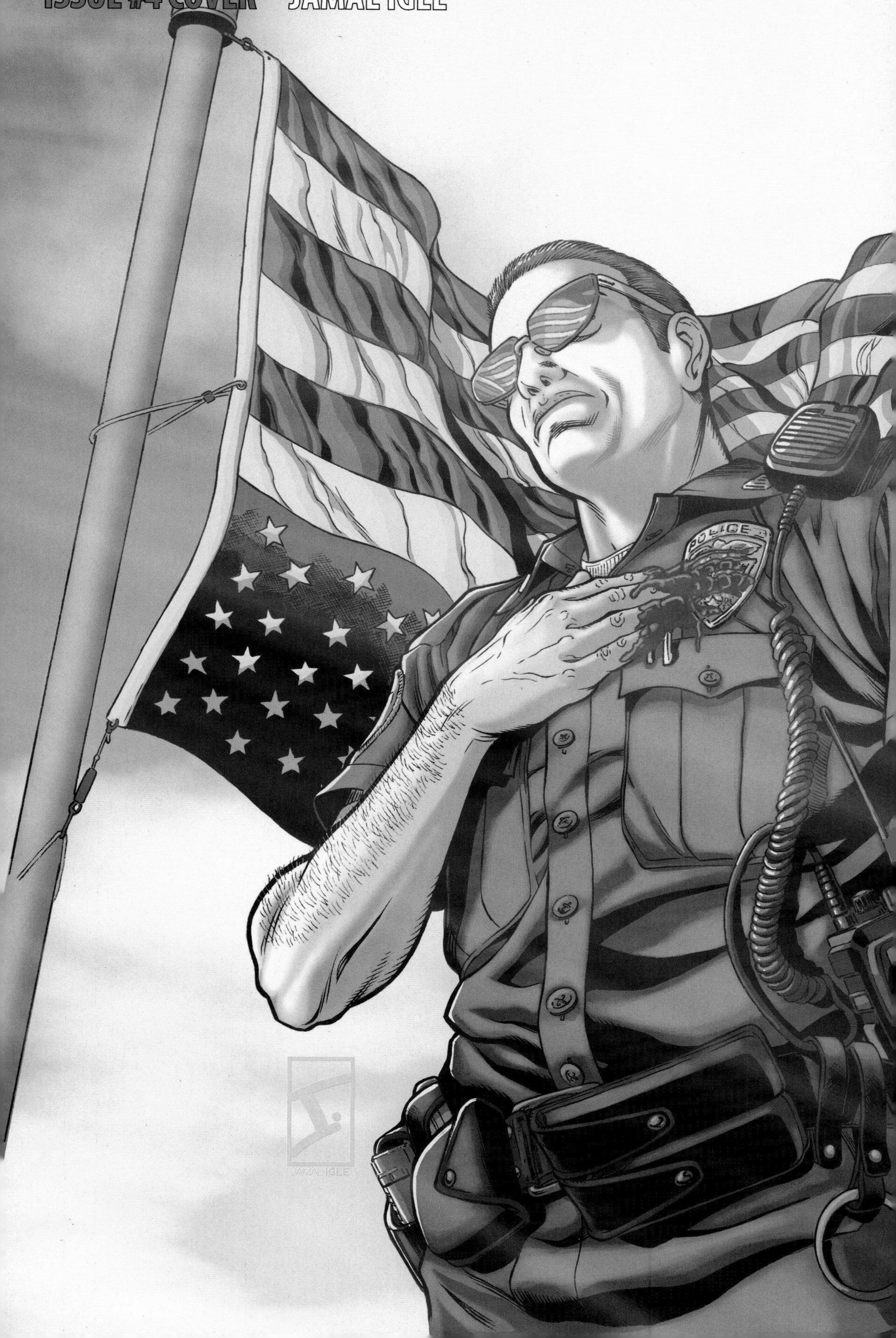
POLICE
JAMAL IGLE

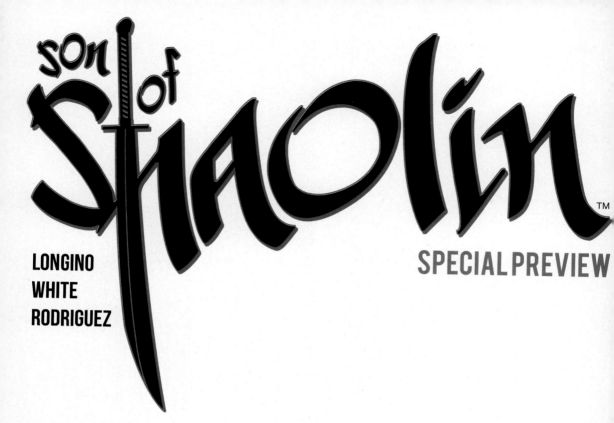

SON OF SHAOLIN™

LONGINO
WHITE
RODRIGUEZ

SPECIAL PREVIEW

FOLLOW #IMAGECOMICS #TOPCOW

IMAGECOMICS.COM • TOPCOW.COM

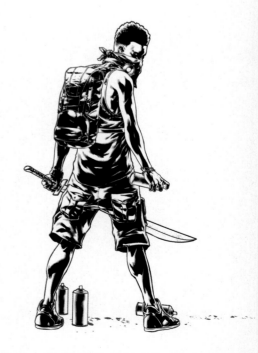

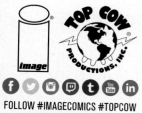

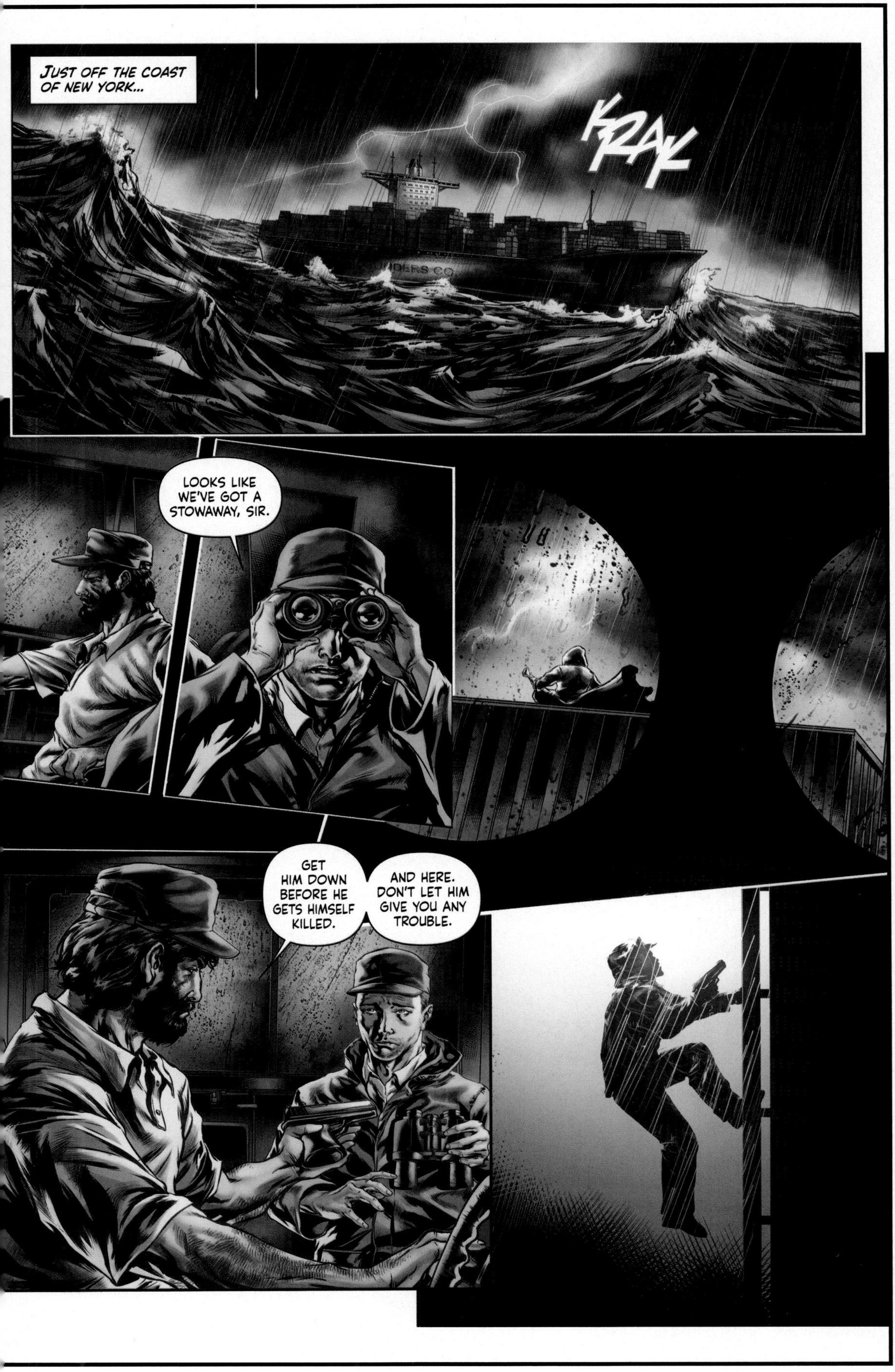
JUST OFF THE COAST OF NEW YORK...
KRAK
LOOKS LIKE WE'VE GOT A STOWAWAY, SIR.
GET HIM DOWN BEFORE HE GETS HIMSELF KILLED.
AND HERE. DON'T LET HIM GIVE YOU ANY TROUBLE.

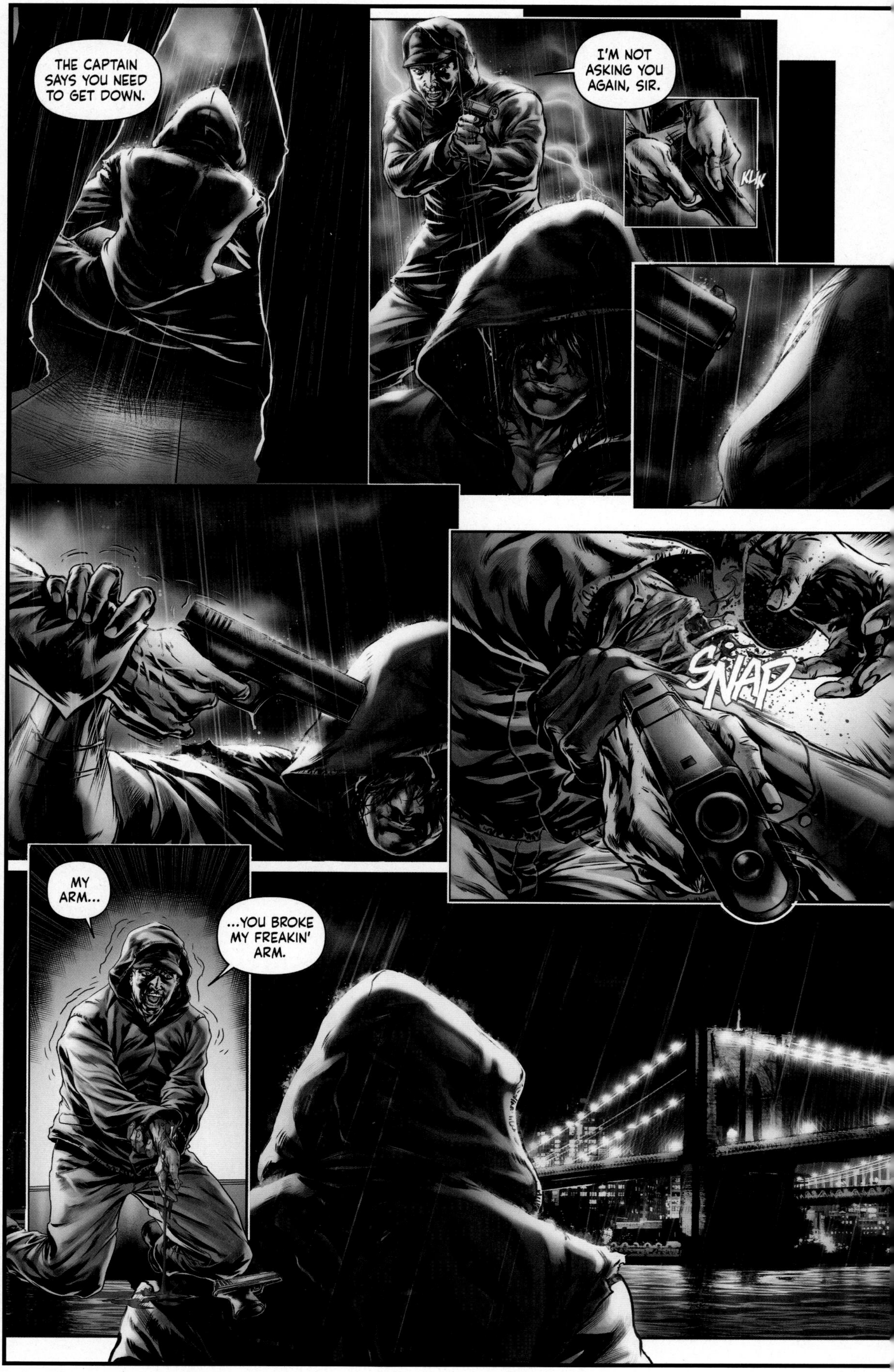
THE CAPTAIN SAYS YOU NEED TO GET DOWN.
I'M NOT ASKING YOU AGAIN, SIR.
KLIK
SNAP
MY ARM...
...YOU BROKE MY FREAKIN' ARM.

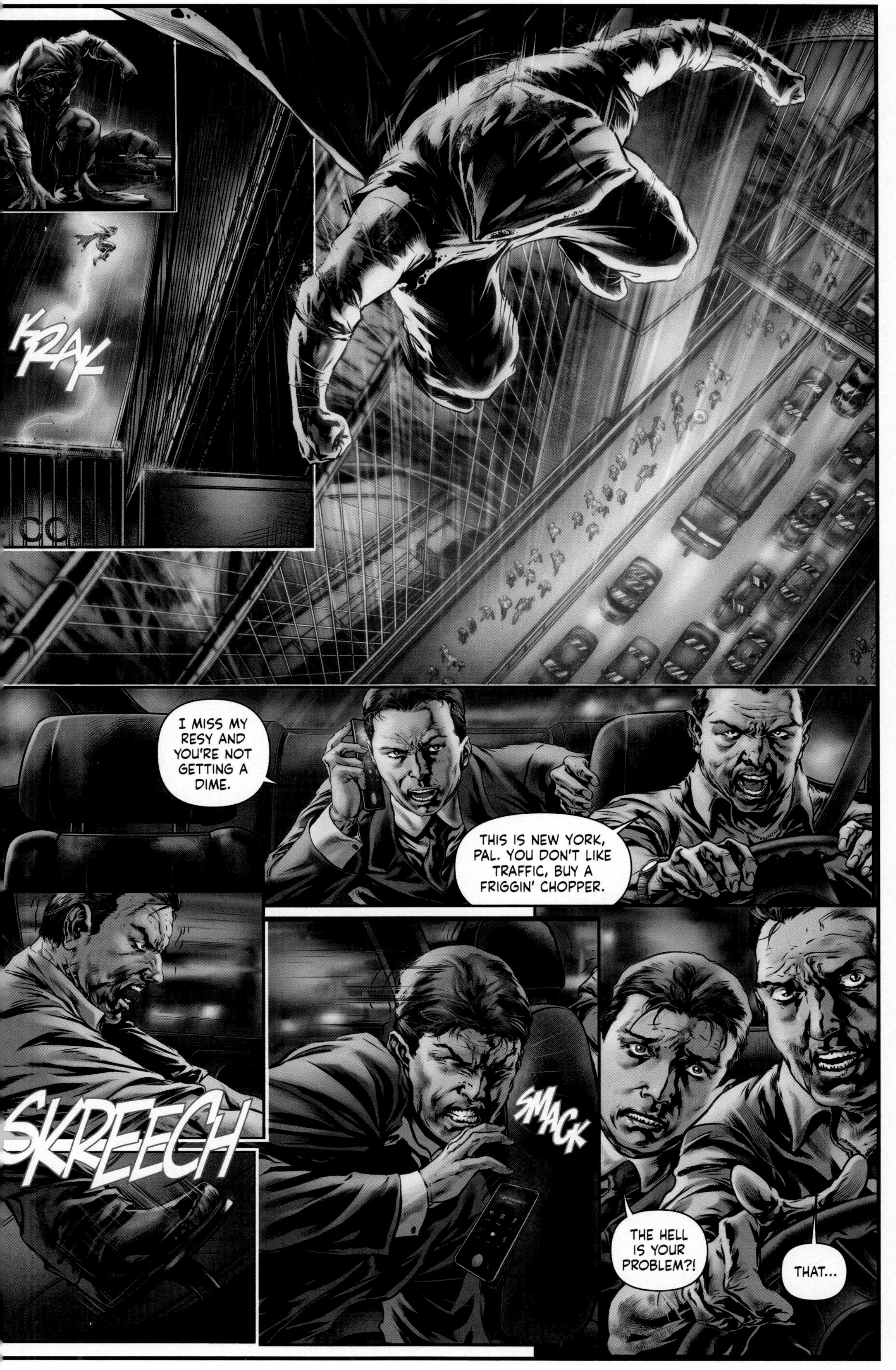
KRAK
I MISS MY RESY AND YOU'RE NOT GETTING A DIME.
THIS IS NEW YORK, PAL. YOU DON'T LIKE TRAFFIC, BUY A FRIGGIN' CHOPPER.
SKREECH
SMACK
THE HELL IS YOUR PROBLEM?!
THAT...

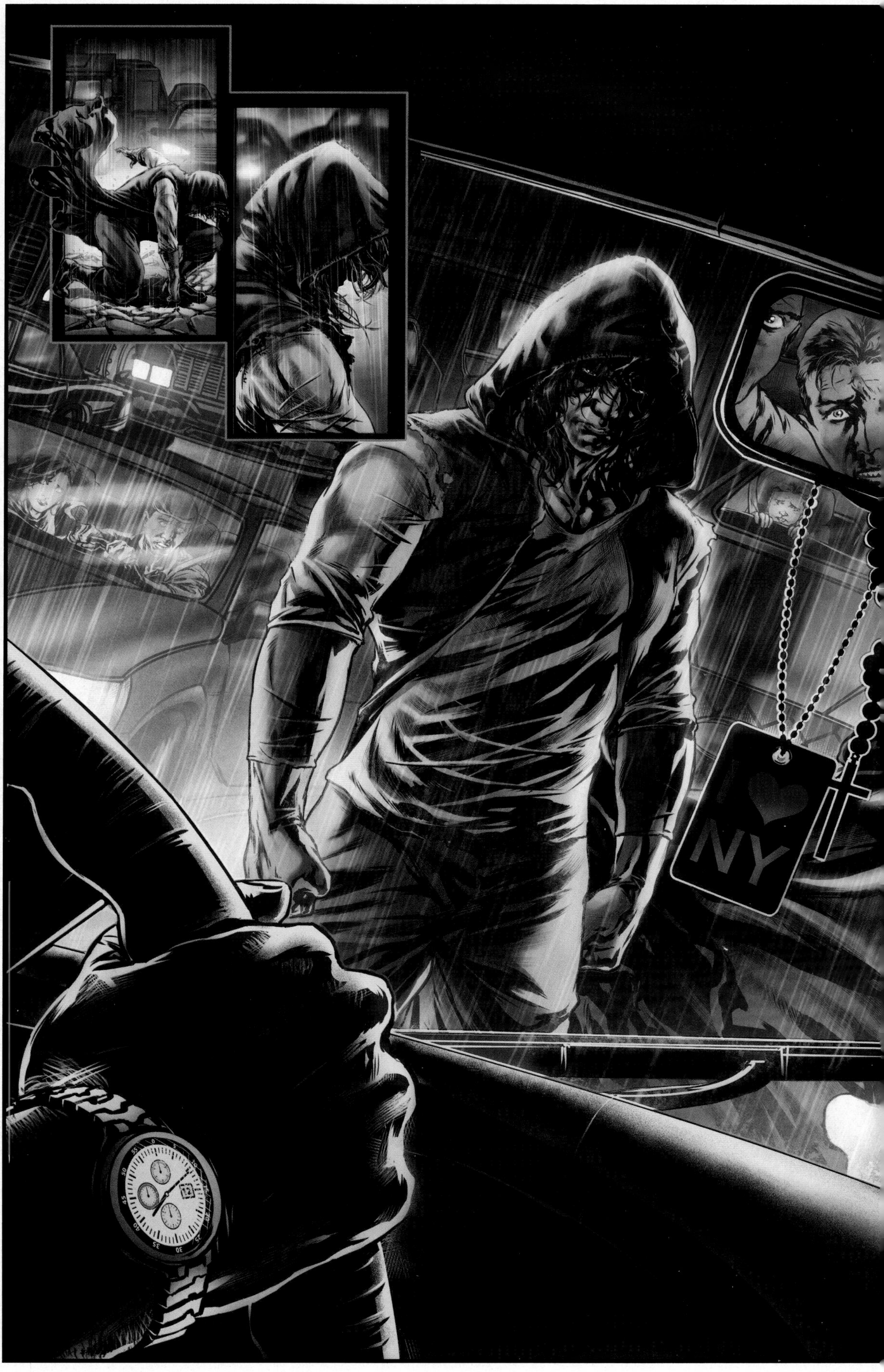
NY

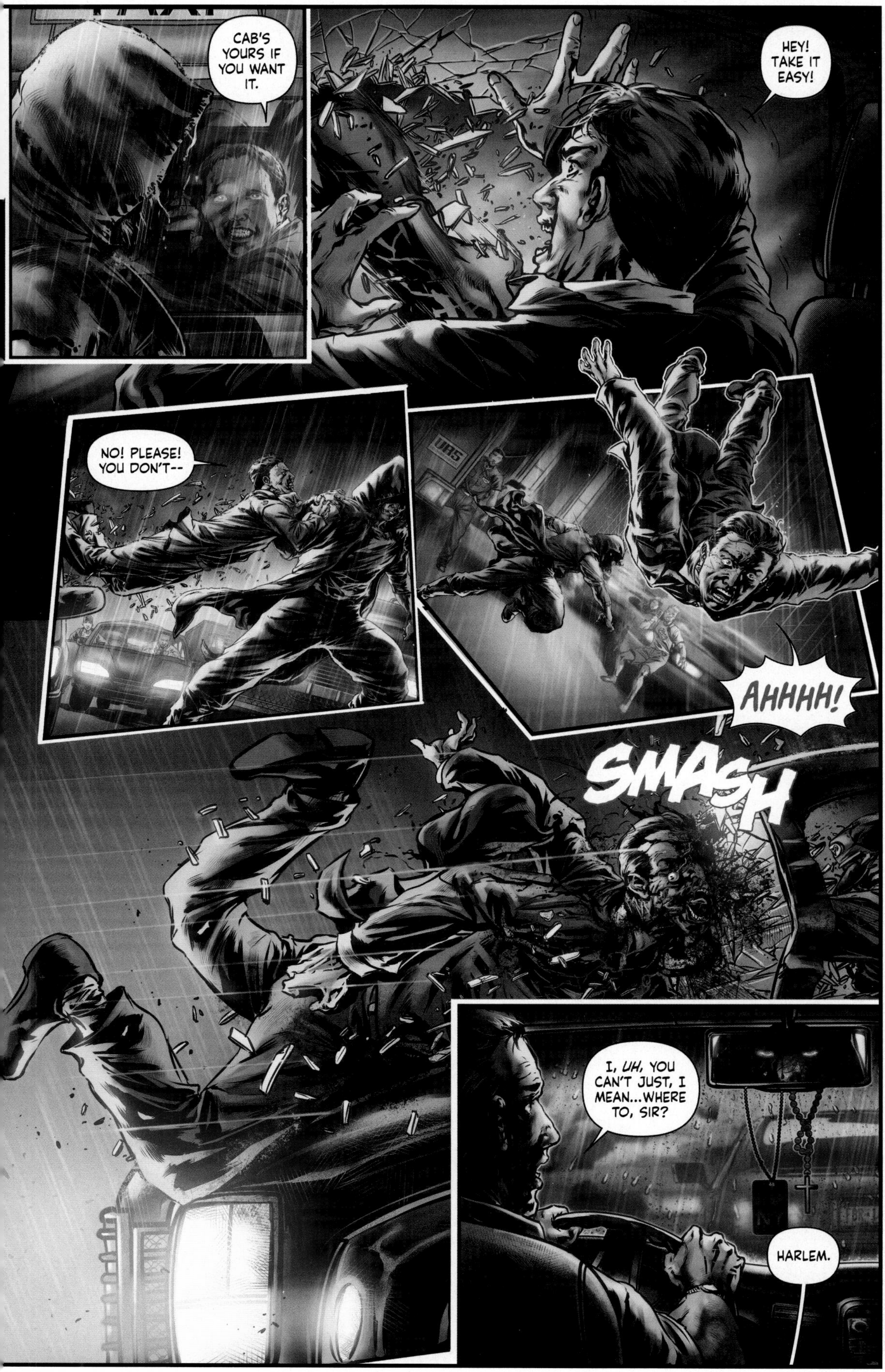
CAB'S YOURS IF YOU WANT IT.
HEY! TAKE IT EASY!
NO! PLEASE! YOU DON'T--
AHHHH!
SMASH
I, UH, YOU CAN'T JUST, I MEAN...WHERE TO, SIR?
HARLEM.

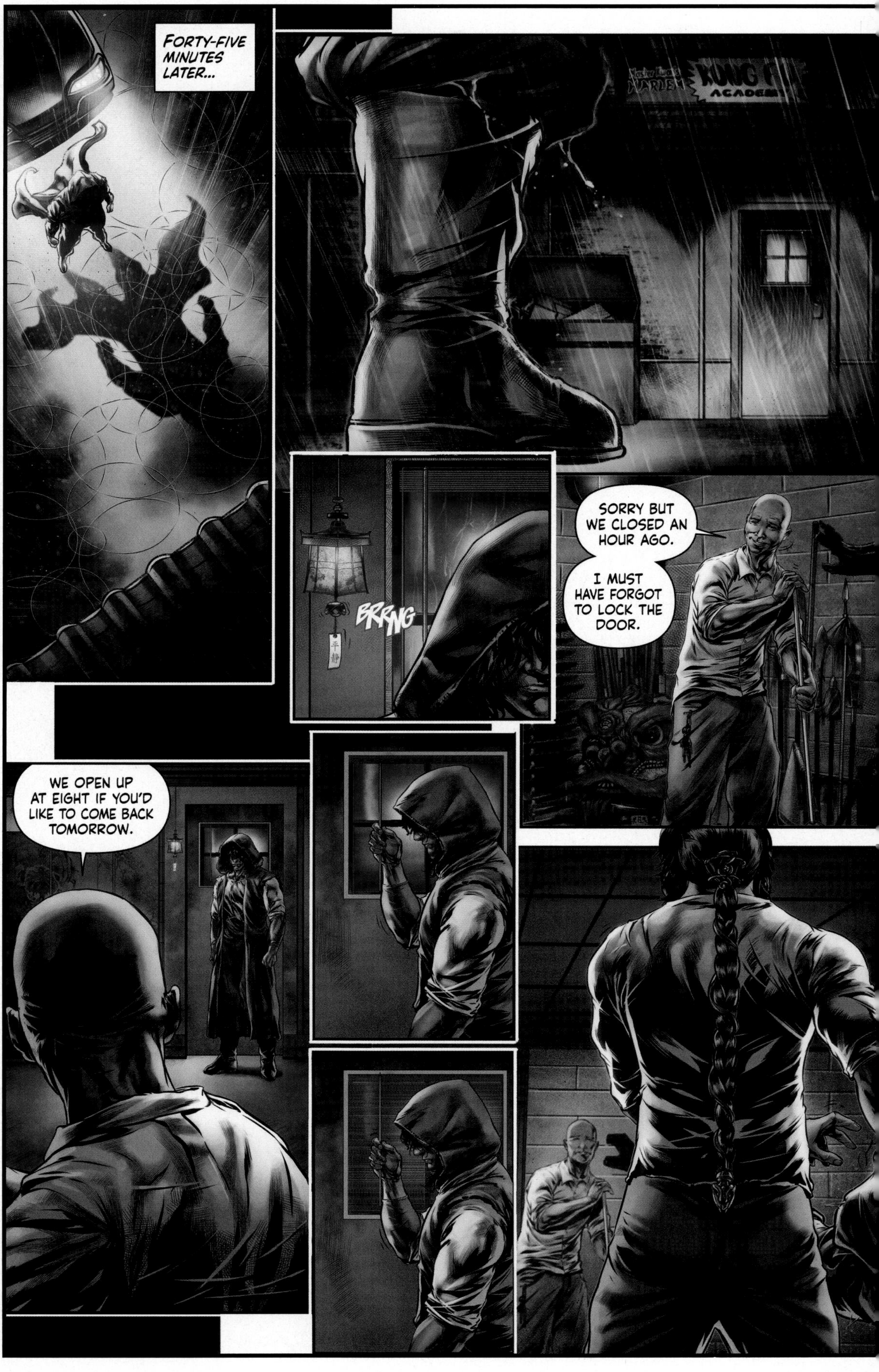
FORTY-FIVE MINUTES LATER...
BRRNG
SORRY BUT WE CLOSED AN HOUR AGO.
I MUST HAVE FORGOT TO LOCK THE DOOR.
WE OPEN UP AT EIGHT IF YOU'D LIKE TO COME BACK TOMORROW.

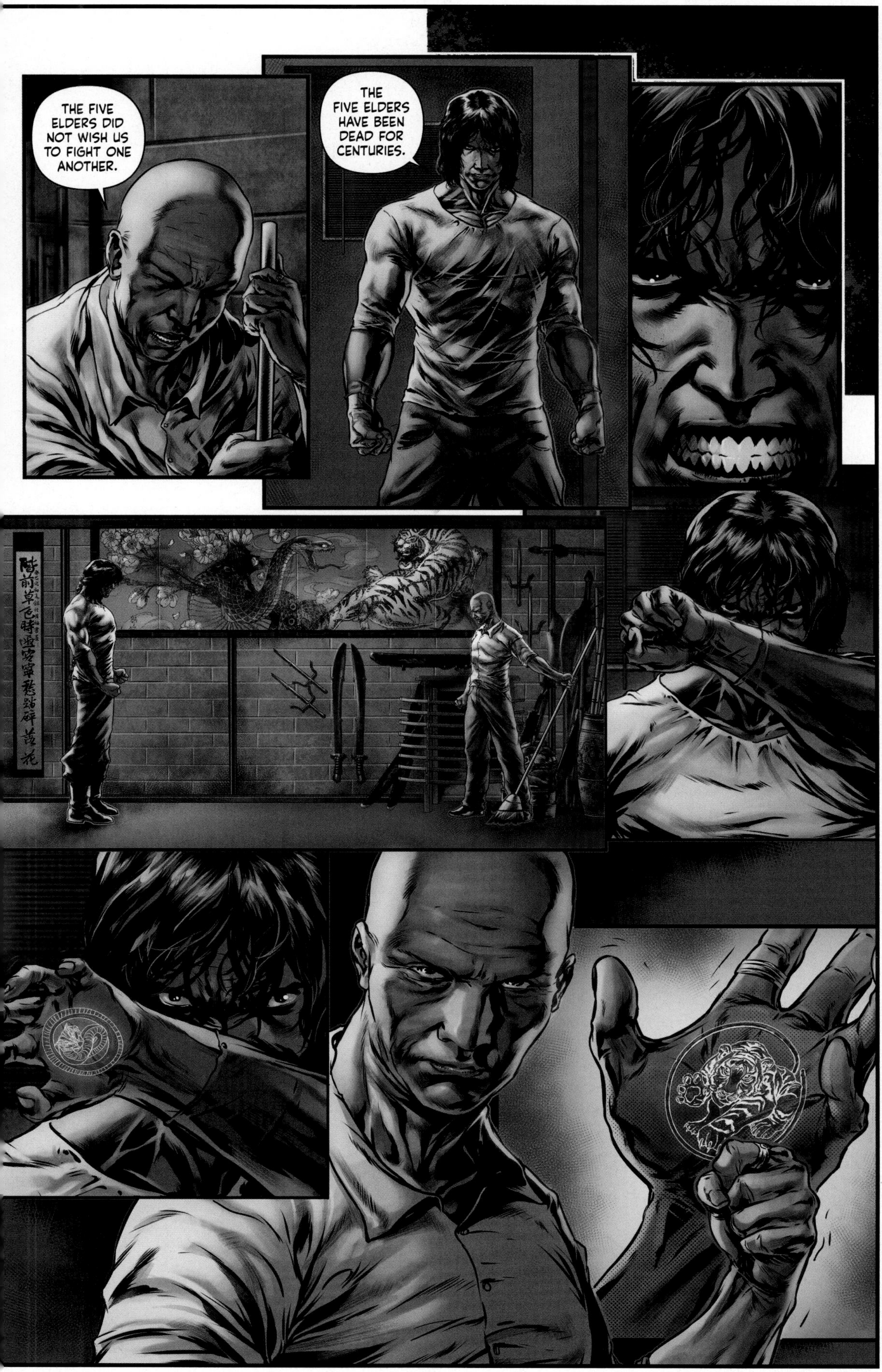
THE FIVE ELDERS DID NOT WISH US TO FIGHT ONE ANOTHER.
THE FIVE ELDERS HAVE BEEN DEAD FOR CENTURIES.

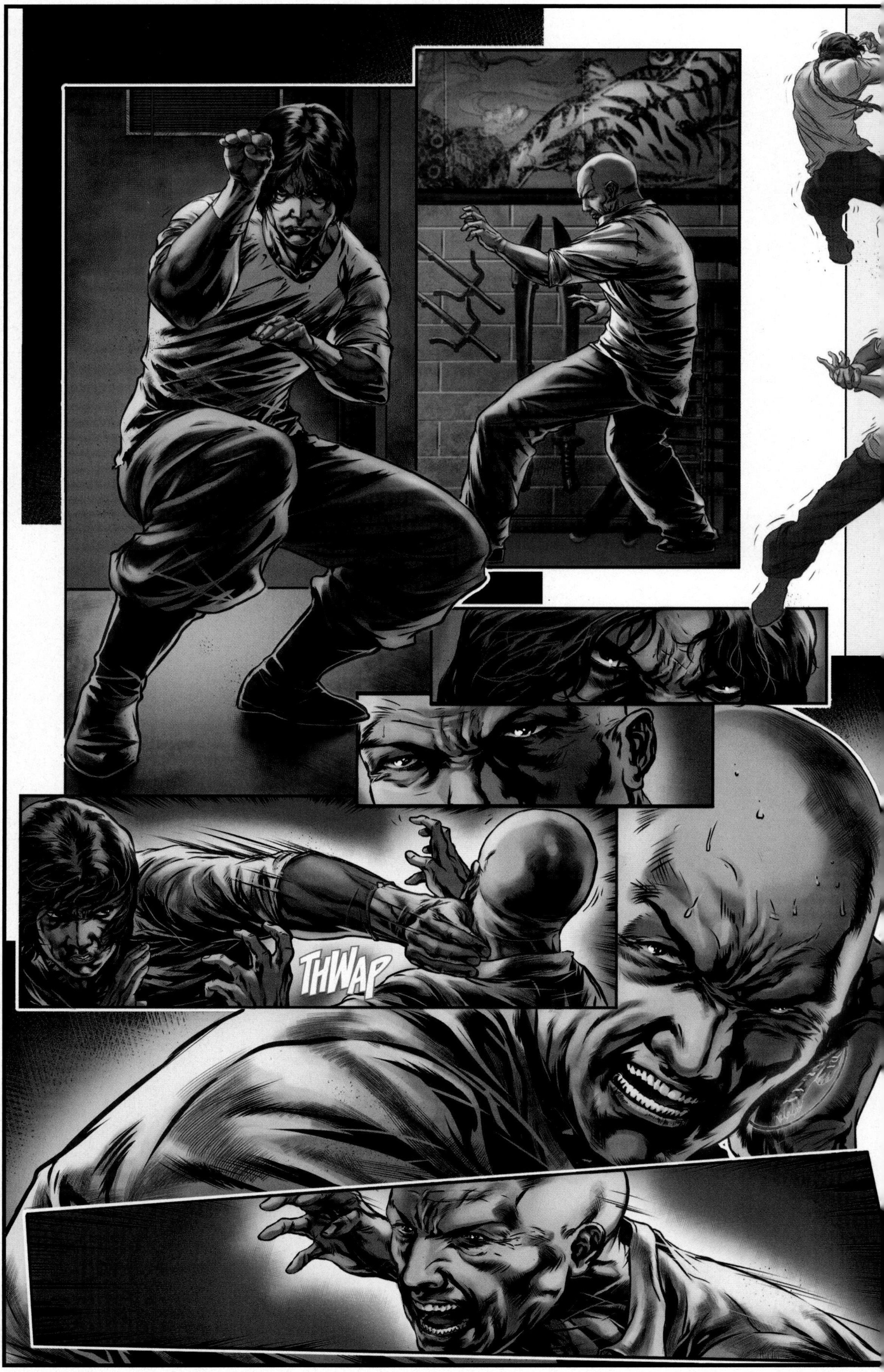
THWAP

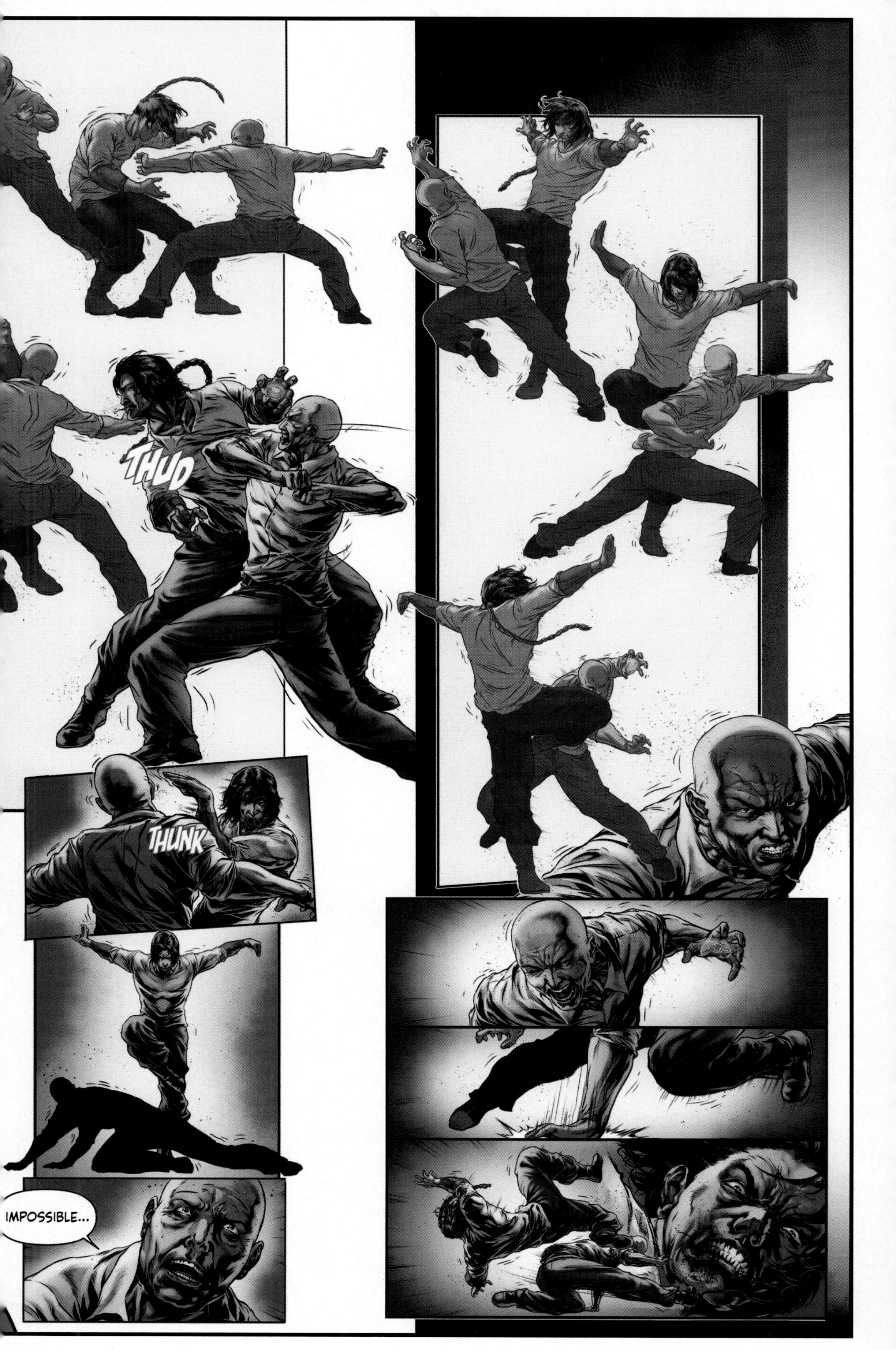
THUD
THUNK
IMPOSSIBLE...

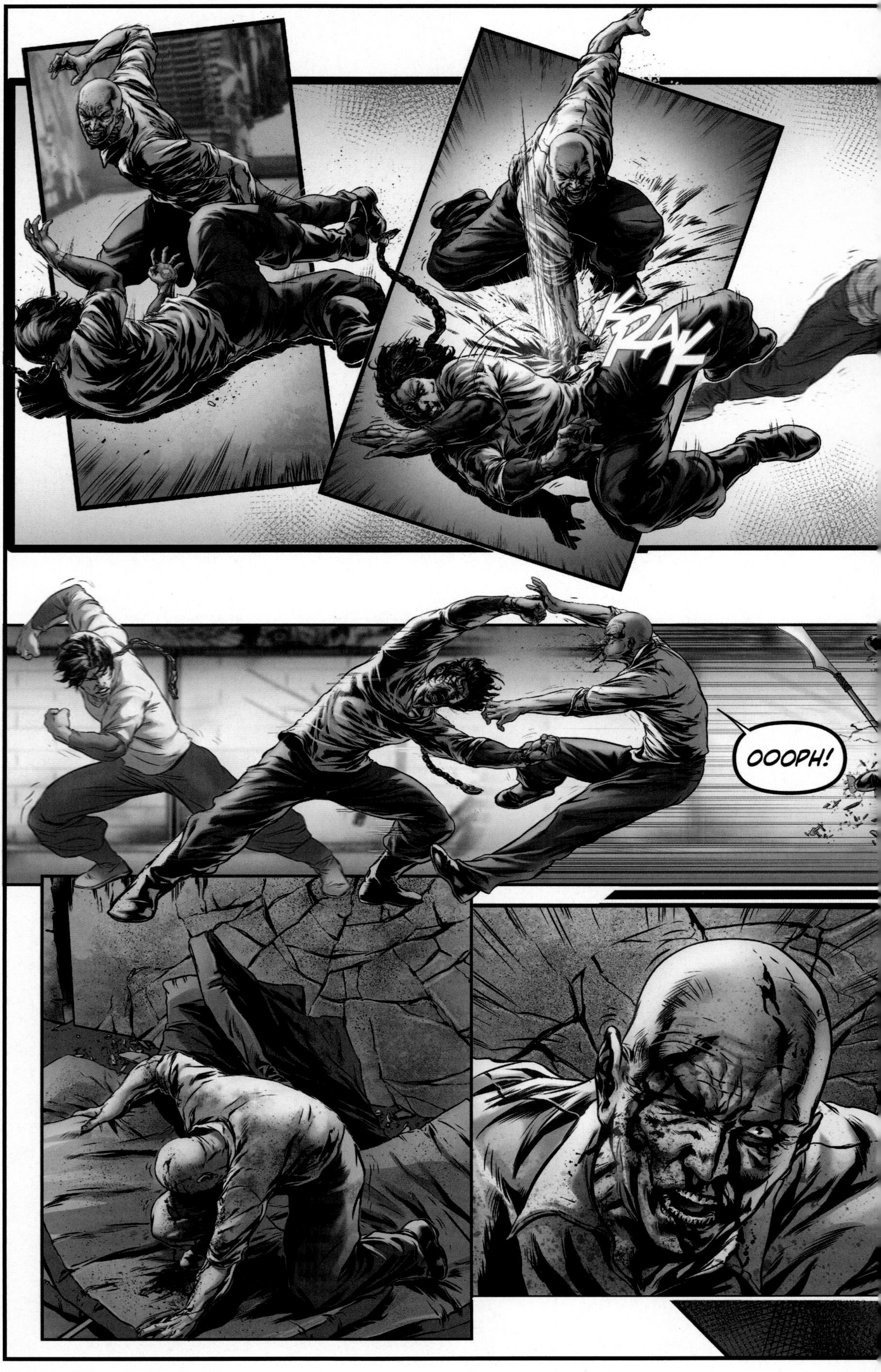
KRAK
OOOPH!

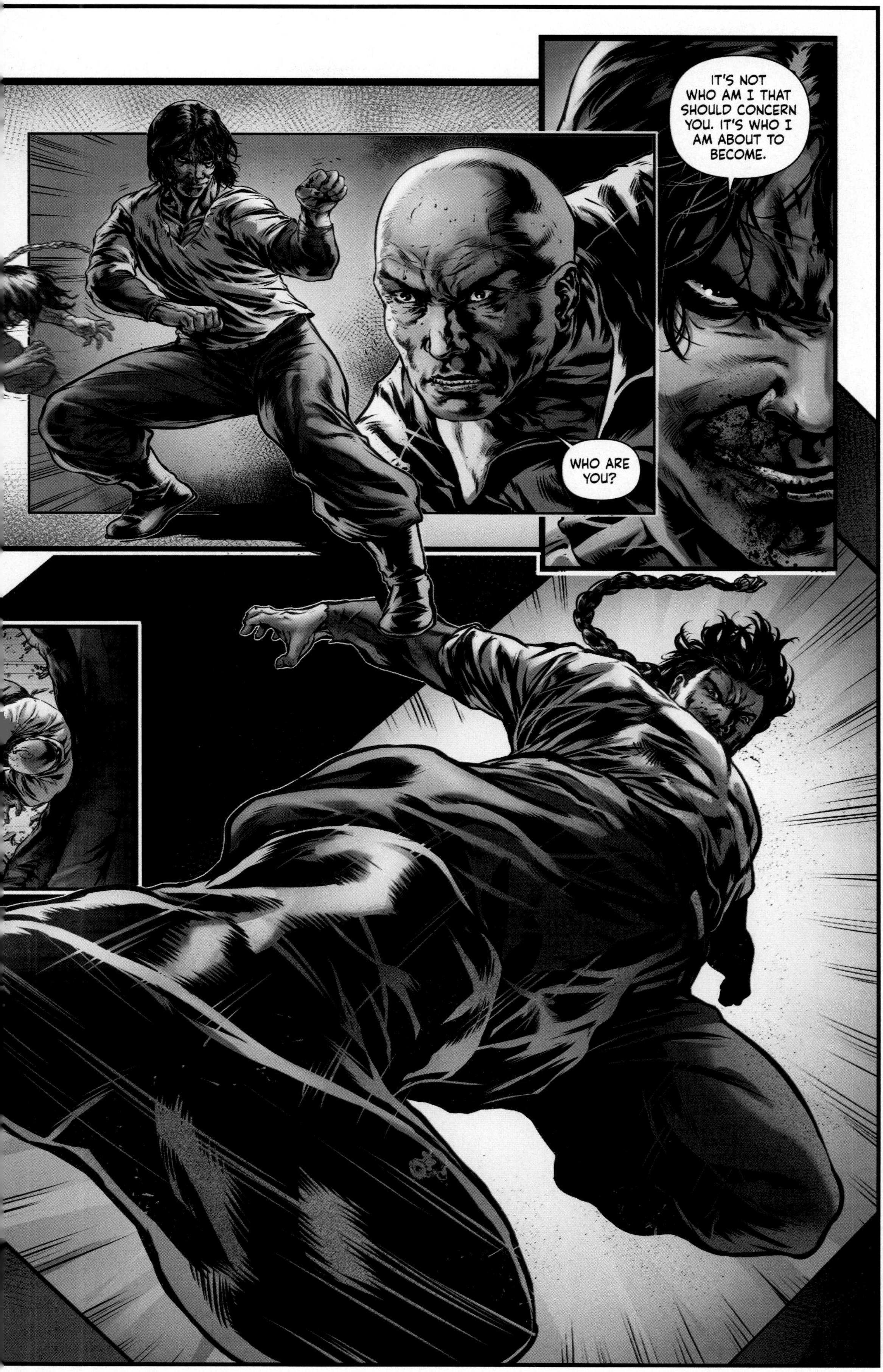
WHO ARE YOU?
IT'S NOT WHO AM I THAT SHOULD CONCERN YOU. IT'S WHO I AM ABOUT TO BECOME.

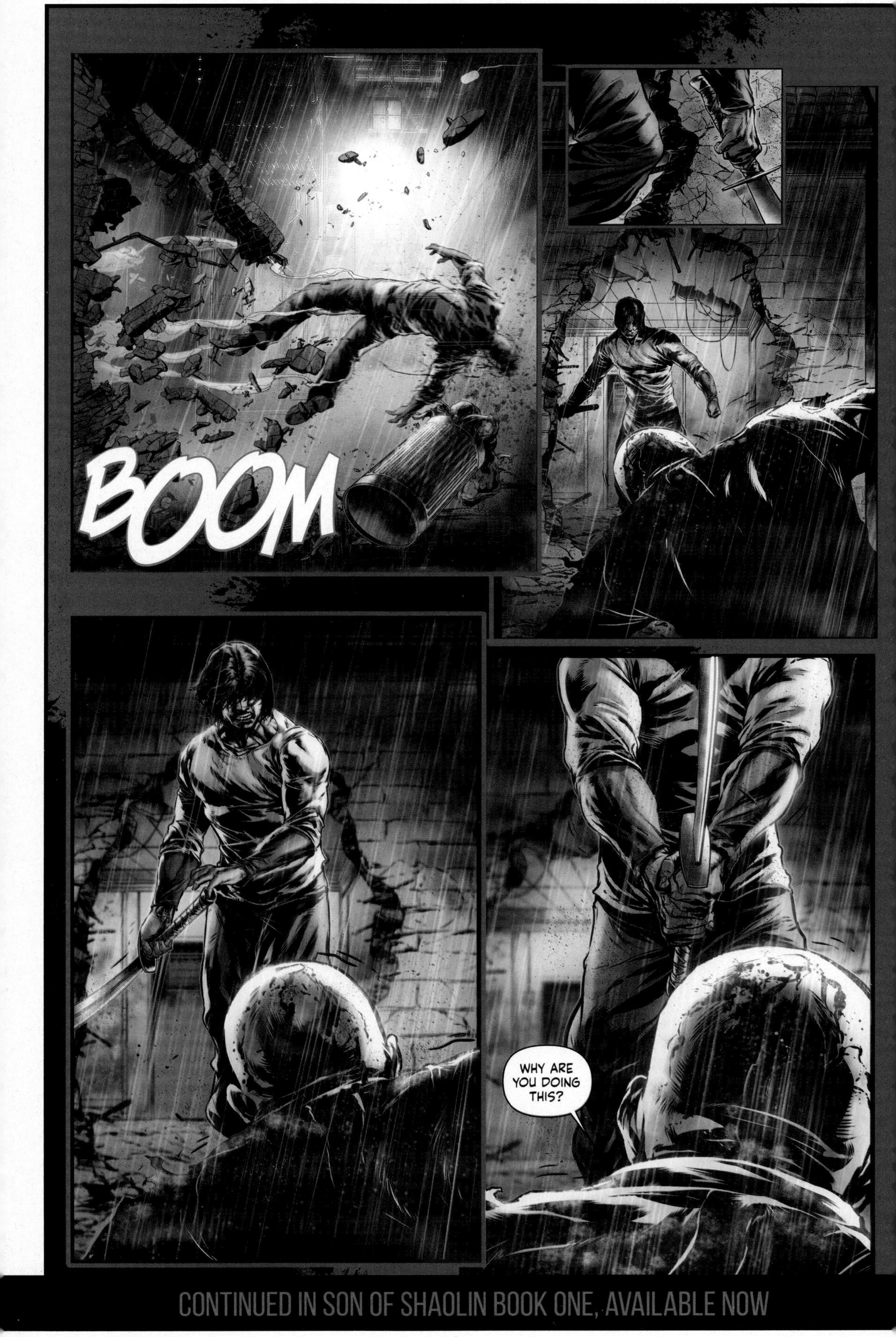
BOOM
WHY ARE YOU DOING THIS?

CONTINUED IN SON OF SHAOLIN BOOK ONE, AVAILABLE NOW